SO-AYQ-963

**Selected praise for Caitlin Brennan's
White Magic series**
The Mountain's Call
Song of Unmaking
Shattered Dance [coming October 2006]

"Definitely a don't-put-this-down page-turner!"
—*New York Times* bestselling author Mercedes Lackey
on *The Mountain's Call*

"Animal lovers and romantic fantasy aficionados alike
will appreciate this…coming-of-age story and an
exhilarating romantic adventure."
—*Romantic Times BOOKclub*

"A riveting plot, complex characters, beautiful
descriptions, and heaps of magic."
—*Romance Reviews Today* on *The Mountain's Call*

"Caitlin Brennan has created a masterpiece
of legend and lore with her first novel. Hauntingly
beautiful and extremely powerful… Take Tolkien and
Lackey and mix them together and you get this new
magic that is Caitlin's own. You will stay enthralled
with each page turned."
—*The Best Reviews* on *The Mountain's Call*

"This…second book in this magnificent romantic
fantasy series…is full of more action, romance and
drama than its prequel…. The battle scenes are
magnificent, the characters are realistic and the
storyline is pure magic; readers will eagerly await
the next book in this tantalizing series."
—*The Best Reviews* on *Song of Unmaking*

CAITLIN BRENNAN

THE MOUNTAIN'S CALL

LUNA™

www.LUNA-Books.com

If you purchased this book without a cover you should be aware that this book is stolen property. It was reported as "unsold and destroyed" to the publisher, and neither the author nor the publisher has received any payment for this "stripped book."

THE MOUNTAIN'S CALL

ISBN-13: 978-0-373-80256-2
ISBN-10:   0-373-80256-0

Copyright © 2004 by Judith Tarr

First mass market printing: September 2006

First trade printing: September 2004

Author Photo by Lynn Glazer

All rights reserved. Except for use in any review, the reproduction or utilization of this work in whole or in part in any form by any electronic, mechanical or other means, now known or hereafter invented, including xerography, photocopying and recording, or in any information storage or retrieval system, is forbidden without the written permission of the editorial office, Worldwide Library, 233 Broadway, New York, NY 10279 U.S.A.

All characters in this book have no existence outside the imagination of the author and have no relation whatsoever to anyone bearing the same name or names. They are not even distantly inspired by any individual known or unknown to the author, and all incidents are pure invention.

This edition published by arrangement with Harlequin Books S.A.

® and TM are trademarks of Harlequin Books S.A., used under license. Trademarks indicated with ® are registered in the United States Patent and Trademark Office, the Canadian Trade Marks Office and in other countries.

www.LUNA-Books.com

Printed in U.S.A.

For the Ladies

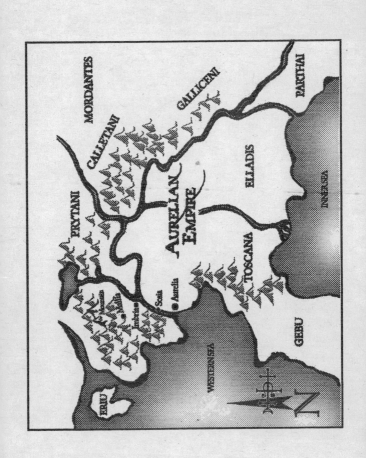

Chapter One

The Mountain floated over the long roll of field and forest. Even in summer its peak was white with snow. In early spring, when the grass had begun to grow green in the valleys, its summit was locked in winter.

There was a fire of magic in its heart, welling up from the deep roots of the earth. It bubbled like a spring from the white fang of the peak, and rippled in waves through the vault of heaven. The tides of time began to swirl and shift.

In the citadel on the Mountain's knees, the master of the Schools of Peace and War woke from a stranger dream than most. He stumbled from bed, flung open the shutters and peered up at the glow of dawn on the snowbound slopes.

Every spring the power rose; every spring the Mountain's Call went out, summoning young men to the testing. Every spring and summer they came, straggling in from the far reaches of Aurelia's empire, coming to claim the magic that they hoped was theirs. White magic, stallion magic. Magic of time and the gods.

This year's Call was different. How it was different, or what it portended, the master could not tell. The gods in their pastures, cropping the new green grass, would not answer when he asked. The Ladies in the high valleys, greater than gods, chose not to acknowledge him at all.

This was a mystery, that silence said. Even the master of the school must wait and see, and hope that when the answer came, it would be one that he could accept.

Valeria had been walking in a fog for days. Sometimes she wondered if she was ill. Other times, she was sure that she was losing her mind.

There was a voice in her head. It called to her with the sound of wind through pines. It whispered in the hollows of her skull. *Come. Come to me.*

She staggered on the path to the widow Rufo's house. Her mother's hand gripped her wrist and wrenched her upright.

The pain helped Valeria to focus. It was harder every day. Sometimes now she could barely see. She had to struggle to hear what people said to her. She thought she might be losing her mind altogether, except that there was a deep sense of rightness to it. She was meant to hear this call. She was meant to go—

"Valeria!" Her mother's voice cut through the fog of confusion. She blinked half-wittedly. She was standing in the widow Rufo's cottage. Her head just missed brushing the roofbeam.

"Valeria," Morag said. "Start brewing the tea."

Valeria's hands knew what to do even when her wits were drifting away toward gods knew where. She dipped water from the barrel by the door and poured it into the kettle, then set it to boil on the hearth. The fire had burned too low. She whispered a Word. The banked logs burst into flame.

The widow Rufo's breath rattled. Morag spread a paste of pungent herbs over the bony chest and covered it with soft cloths. Herbs just as pungent steeped in the boiling water, brewing into tea. When it was strong enough, Morag coaxed it into her sip by sip.

Valeria squatted by the fire. It was full of visions. White mountains. White clouds. The toss of a white mane, and a noble head on a proud arched neck, turning to fix her with an eye as dark as deep water. The depths of it were full of stars. *Come*, said the white god. *Come to me.*

"She's getting worse."

Valeria lay in the wide bed with her three younger sisters. She was the innermost, with Caia's warmth on one side and the chill of the wall on the other. Her sisters were snoring on three different notes. They almost drowned out the murmur of their mother's voice on the other side of the wall.

"She can barely keep her mind on her work," Morag went on. "She started to say a birthing spell over Edwy's burned hand this morning—thanks to Sun and Moon I caught her in time, or he'd have sprouted a crop of new fingers."

Her father's laughter rumbled through the wall. Morag slapped him. He grunted. "There now," he said in his deep voice, roughened from years of bellowing orders on battlefields. "What was that for?"

"You know perfectly well what for," Morag said sharply. "Our daughter is losing her mind."

"If she were a boy," Titus said, "I'd be thinking it was the Call. I saw it a time or two when I was in the legion. One of the youngest recruits would get up one fine spring morning with his eyes all strange, pick up his kit and walk out of the barracks, and no one with any sense would try to stop him. Our girl's just about the same age as they were, and gods know she has a way with animals. Horses follow her like puppies. The way she taught the goat to dance—"

"She is not a boy," said Morag. "This is a spring sickness. There's magic in it, she stinks of it, but it is not—"

"What if it is?"

"It can't be," Morag said flatly. "Women aren't Called. She has a good deal more magic than she knows what to do with, and it's laid her open to some contagion off the mountains."

Titus grunted the way he did when he was not minded to argue with his wife, but neither was he inclined to agree with her. "You'd better cure her, then, if she's as sick as that."

"I'll cure her," said Morag. Her tone was grim. "You go in the morning, husband, and talk to Aengus. She likes that son of his well enough. There's time to make it a double wedding."

"I'm not sure—" said Titus.

"Do it," Morag said with a snap like a door shutting.

That was all they said that night. Valeria lay very still, trying not to touch either Caia or the wall. Caia would not be pleased at all, not after she had bragged to everyone about being the first of all four sisters to marry. She was a year younger than Valeria and the beauty of the family. Their father had not had to go begging for a husband for that one. Wellin Smith had asked for her.

Aengus' son Donn was unlikely to refuse Titus' eldest daughter. He had been trailing after Valeria since they were both in short tunics. He had an attractive face and decent conversation, and a little magic, which was useful in his father's mill. He could offer his wife a good inheritance and a comfortable living, even a maid if she wanted one.

It was a good match. Valeria should be happy. Her

mother would cure her of these dreams and fancies. She would marry a man she rather liked, give him children and continue with her education in herb-healing and earth magic. When the time came, she would inherit her mother's place in the village, and be a wisewoman.

That was the life she was born to. It was better than most young women could hope for.

She was ill, that was all, as her mother had said. Because it was spring and she was coming to her six-teenth summer, and because she had listened hungrily all her life to stories of the Call and the white gods and the school on the Mountain, she had deluded herself into thinking that this bout of brain fever was some-thing more. That was why she was dreaming in broad daylight and stumbling over her own feet, and feeling ever more strongly that she should take whatever she could carry and run away. She could not possibly be hearing the Call that had never come to a woman in all the years that it had been ringing through the planes of the aether.

Valeria slid from doubt and darkness into a dream of white horses galloping in a field under the white teeth of mountains. They were all mares with heavy bellies, and foals running beside them. The young ones were dark, black or brown, with the white of adulthood shining through.

They ran in wide sweeps across the green field.

The swoops and curves made her think of a flock of birds in flight. Augurs could read omens in the passage of birds, but these white horses could shape the future. They could make it happen. They were the moon, and time was the tide.

A voice was speaking. She could not see who spoke, or tell if it was a man's voice or a woman's. It came up out of the earth and down from the air. "Look," it said. "See. Understand. There is a prophecy—remember it. One will come of the pure line, true child of First Stallion and Queen Mare. That one will seal the bond of soul and spirit with a child of man. Together they shall be both the salvation and destruction of the people."

Words welled up, a flood of questions, but there was no one to ask. She could only watch in silence.

The mares and foals circled the field in a graceful arc and leaped into the sky, spinning away like a swirl of snow. Down on the field, a single pale shape stood motionless. The solid quarters and the heavy crest marked him a stallion, even before he turned and she recognized him. She had dreamed him once already.

He was young, dappled with silver like the moon. As massive as he was, he was somewhat soft around the edges. He was beautiful and perfect but still, somehow, unfinished. *Come,* he said as he had before. *Come to me.*

She woke in the dark before dawn, with the dream slipping away before she could grasp it. She was standing in the open air. The sky was heavy with rain, but it had not yet begun to fall. She was dressed in her brothers' hand-me-downs. They were faded and much mended, but they were warm. There was a weight on her back.

She remembered as if it had been part of her dream how she had slipped out of bed without disturbing her sisters. She had found the old legionary pack that her eldest brother Rodry had brought home on his last leave, and filled it with food and clothing, enough for a week and more. When she woke, she was filling a water bottle in the stream that ran underneath the dairy house.

Her face was turned toward the Mountain. It was too far away to see, but she could feel it. When she turned in the wrong direction, her skin itched and quivered.

The bottle was full. She thrust the stopper in and hung it from her belt. The sky was lightening just a little. She set off down the path from her father's farm to the northward road.

Her mother was waiting where the path joined the road. Valeria's feet would have carried her on past, but Morag stood in the way. When Valeria sidestepped, Morag was there. "No," said her mother. "You will not."

"I have to," Valeria said.

"You will not," said Morag. She gripped Valeria's wrists and spoke a Word.

The cords of the binding spell were invisible, but

they were strong. Valeria could not move her numbed lips to speak the counterspell. Spellbound and helpless, she staggered behind her mother. Every step she took away from the Mountain was a nightmare of discomfort, but she could do nothing about it. Her mother's magic was too strong.

The root cellar smelled of earth and damp and the strings of garlic that hung from the beams. Barrels of turnips and beets and potatoes lined the walls. There was one window high up, barely big enough for a cat to climb through. The trapdoor in the ceiling was securely bolted on the other side.

It was not terribly uncomfortable, for a prison. Valeria had a feather bed to lie on. She had a firepot and a rack of lamps with more than enough oil to keep them burning. Morag had left her with the herbal and the book of earth spells, but a binding kept her from working any spell that might help her escape.

"I'll let you out on your wedding day," Morag had said when she shut Valeria in the cellar. "Between now and then, you will do your lessons and ponder your future, and I will see that you get over this sickness."

"It's not a sickness," Valeria said through clenched teeth. "You know what it is."

"I know what you think it is. You know it's impossible. You are the only one of my daughters who was born with magic. You will have ample opportunity to develop and use it—but you will do it here in Imbria where you belong."

"I don't belong here," Valeria said. "I belong on the Mountain."

"You do not," said Morag. "No woman does. And so they will tell you if you keep on trying to answer their Call. They'll break your heart. They'll laugh in your face and send you away. I'm sparing you that, daughter. Someday, Sun and Moon willing, you'll learn to forgive me."

That would never happen. Valeria had come out of her dream-ridden fog into a trammeled fury. She was awake now, and her mind was as clear as it could be.

She remembered when she had first heard the story, as vivid as if it had happened this morning. She could see the market in the bright sunlight, with its booths of vegetables and fruit, heaped greens and sides of mutton and beef and strings of fish.

A stranger lounged on the bench outside Lemmer's wineshop. "Oh, aye," he said in an odd rolling accent. "The horse magicians send out a Call every spring, just before the passes open in the mountains. It's meant for boys who are almost men, or men who are still mostly boys. Fourteen, fifteen, sixteen summers old. Never younger. Only rarely older. It binds them and compels them to go to the Mountain."

Valeria was much younger then, not yet in skirts. Strangers took her for a boy, as lanky and gawky as she was. "Only boys?" she asked this stranger. "No girls?"

wove together earth and water and air, and made it all one single shining thing.

She tried to ride the pony as she rode in her dreams. He did not see the point in it, and bucked her off more often than not. The big slow plow horses were more accommodating, but they were earthbound. They had no element of fire. The goats, who loved to dance, were too small for even a child to sit on.

None of them was as perfect as the white dream-horses. None of them would make her a rider. Only the white gods could do that, and only their riders could teach her.

Now, against all hope, she was Called. She was summoned to the testing. The magic was in her, even though she was a woman.

Morag's binding rattled Valeria's skull. Her lesser magics were all suppressed. Even the greater one, the one Morag would not acknowledge, was weakened and slow. She had to wait until night, when the sun's singing was stilled, and humans were asleep in the quiet harmony of the stars. Then if she listened, she could hear the overlapping voices of the world. She resisted the urge to find the patterns in them, and once she had found them, to make sense of them. There was no time for that, only for the Call.

The horses were locked in the stable. The dogs were loose in the yard as they were every night. They were not as intelligent as the horses, but they were more subservient, and for her purposes more useful. They thought it a great game to tug and pull at the bolt that secured the trapdoor, until after a white-knuckled while it slid free.

She was up among them in no time at all. They fell over one another in delight, tongues flapping, tails wagging frantically. She rubbed each big shaggy head and pulled each pair of ears and thanked them from the bottom of her heart. Then she sent them back to guard duty.

Her brother's pack was back on its hook in the toolshed. The waterskin was beside it. This time Valeria made sure she was not followed. The rats in the walls and the pigeons in the rafters assured her that her mother was asleep beside her father. Morag had committed a cardinal error of warfare, as Titus would be sure to remind her when they woke and found their daughter gone. She had underestimated the enemy.

Anger was still strong in Valeria. It ate the twinge of guilt and the impulse to stop and say goodbye to her brothers and sisters. What if she never saw them again?

What a soldier did not know, he could not betray. That was another of Titus' maxims. Valeria left them all sleeping the sleep of the happily ignorant.

No one was waiting for her this time. The road was empty under the chilly starlight. She paused where the path turned onto the road. The warding rune on the post there was meant to keep intruders out but not—

she drew a breath of relief—to keep the family in. She did not look back. In her mind's eye she saw her father's farmstead in its fold of the hills, with its thatched roofs and its wooden palisade and its border of trees.

She said farewell in her heart, but her eyes were fixed on the shadow on shadow that was the wall of mountains. Her feet were itching to begin the journey. The first step was the hardest, but each one after that was easier, until she was striding headlong, almost running, into the north.

Chapter Two

The horse followed Valeria for a day before she gave in to his importuning and let him carry her. He was clean and well fed and his hooves had been trimmed recently, but he refused to acknowledge that he belonged to anyone. He insisted that he had come for her. He was neither white nor a stallion, but Valeria did not care about that. His back was comfortable and his gaits were smooth. She could have paid gold and done worse.

She had defied her mother and abandoned her family, all of whom, in spite of her anger, she missed terribly. She was a fugitive, living off what she could forage and trying to stretch her few provisions for as long as she could. She barely knew where she was going or how long it would take to get there. And yet she was happy, even when the last snow of winter caught her on the road and forced her into an empty barn for a day and a night.

The bindings on her magic had slipped loose after she'd passed the runepost at the border of the farm. She could call fire to warm her and the horse. There was hay in the deserted barn, cut last year but still dry and clean. The horse ate a good deal of it, and she slept on the rest. A few half-wild hens roosted in a corner of the barn. Their eggs were small, but there were a decent number of them. With the last of the bread and dried apples from home, Valeria had a feast while the storm howled outside.

When she rode out through melting snow, the second morning after she came to the barn, she had cut her long hair short. It was practical, and she thought it might also be safer if she was out riding the roads alone, to be taken for a boy. Her head felt odd and light, and her ears were cold.

The horse pranced, glad to be free again. Valeria's rump was not so happy. It was just beginning to recover from the effects of too much riding after too little practice.

She would need better discipline than that if she was to be a rider. She gritted her teeth and suffered through it.

Before the storm came, she had met few people on the road. Most of those were farmers going to market.

She had seen an imperial courier once, galloping flat out on his spotted horse.

A troop of legionaries tramped past not long after she left the barn. She resisted the urge to hide from them. She was not a fugitive. She was Called. Her horse, bridleless and saddleless and obeying her without question, would tell anyone that. So would the road she was on, which led north to the Mountain and the white gods.

In the stories she had heard, the Called could ask for food and lodging at the imperial way stations. The day after the last of her provisions ran out, she tested it. It was that or resort to stealing.

The man in charge of the station had the same toughened-leather look as her father, and the same accent, too. Wherever a legionary came from, after twenty years in the emperor's service he came out talking that way, usually with a voice gone raw from bellowing orders in all weathers above all manner of uproar.

He did not ask her who she was or what she was doing. As she had hoped, it was obvious. He gave her a seat at the table in the mess hall and a bed in the barracks, and showed her where she could stable the horse. When the horse was bedded down with a manger full of good hay and a pan of barley, she went to claim her own dinner.

There were only a handful of other people in the station tonight. They were all imperial couriers either resting between runs or waiting for the relay to reach them. Most of them, like the stationmaster, asked no questions. One or two watched her without being blatant about it. They all seemed to know each other. She was the only stranger.

She finished her dinner as quickly as she could, trying not to choke. She barely tasted the stew and bread and beer. She escaped before anyone could strike up a conversation.

She left before the sun came up. The cook was just taking the first loaves out of the oven when she came down from the room. He gave her a loaf so hot and fresh she could barely hold it, with a wedge of cheese thrust into a slit in the crust. The cheese had melted into the bread. She ate it in a state of bliss, and belched her appreciation.

"Gods give you good luck," the cook said, "and a safe journey. May the testing favor you."

She hoped she did not look too startled. "Thank— thank you," she said.

The cook smiled and touched her forehead. "For luck," he said. "Never had anyone Called from your village before, did you?"

She shook her head. "I've heard all the stories. But—"

"You give luck," the cook said, "and take it, too. Stop at the stations. Don't try to go it on your own. Most people respect the Call, but a few might try to steal the luck."

"How do they—"

The cook slashed his hand across his throat. "It's in the blood, they say. I don't believe it— I think it's in the soul, and killing you unmakes it. Those on the Mountain, they know for sure, but they're not telling the likes of us."

"I don't know anything about it," Valeria said.

"You'll learn," said the cook. "Best be on your way now. It's a long way to the Mountain, and time's not standing still."

"How long—"

"Three days for a courier," the cook said. "Ten, maybe, at ordinary pace, and allowing for weather and delays. Ask at the stations if there's a caravan heading the way you need to go. That's safest. You might even meet others of the Called."

A shiver ran down her spine. In her dreams she had always been alone. She had not thought about what the Call would mean. She went to a place where everyone had the same kind of magic as she did. She would not be alone any longer.

If and when they found out she was not a boy—

She would deal with that when it happened. For now she had to go to the Mountain. That was all she could think about, and all she needed to think about.

When she fetched the horse from the stable, having discovered that she could commandeer a saddle and bridle for him, she was struck with a sudden attack of cowardice. She turned him south-ward, back the way she had come.

The Call snapped like a noose around her neck. She almost lost her breakfast. She turned northward and saved it, but the message was clear. She was bound to this road. She had to ride it to the end.

The hunt passed her not long after the sun came up. The hounds came first, then the huntsmen. The hunt itself was a little distance behind. She had seen few nobles in her life, but these were obviously wellborn. Their horses' caparisons were elaborate, with ornately tooled saddles and chased silver bits and stirrups. The long manes were braided with ribbons in colors that matched the riders' coats. The riders wore enough gold to dazzle her.

They looked down their noses at the lone traveler on the side of the road. She felt grubby and common in her patched coat. Her boots were walking boots—one of the lordlings remarked on them as he rode elegantly by. The horse was still in winter coat. Even a good grooming could not make him look less shaggy.

Valeria lifted her chin and looked the riders in the eye. She was Called. And what were they?

As soon as she did it, she knew she had made a mistake. One of them, big and uncommonly fair-haired for this part of the world, raked her with a glance that sharpened suddenly. She had seen that look in the leader of a dog pack that had been going casually about its business until it caught wind of a newborn lamb. This was the same sudden gleam in the eye, the same flash of fang.

He was not hunting to eat. He was hunting for pleasure. It mattered little to him whether his prey was animal or human.

Valeria kept the horse, and herself, perfectly still. It might be too little too late, but she called up what magic she could in her rattled state, and did her best to seem as dull and unworthy as possible. Above all, she took care not to give him any further indication that she was one of the Called. If anyone would kill her for luck, this man would.

It seemed to work. The nobleman let his eyes slide away from her. The rest of them rode past without stopping or pausing, with only brief glances if they troubled with her at all.

Valeria nearly collapsed in relief. She was safe, she thought. Even so, she stayed where she was for long enough to see how, just before the road bent around a hill, they turned off into the trees. Then she waited a while longer, until she was sure she no longer heard them.

When she rode on, she stayed well away from the path through the trees, keeping to the open road. It curved again, then again, weaving through a range of wooded hills.

Gradually the hills closed in. The trees were taller, their branches laced overhead. The bright sunlight dimmed, filtering through needles of spruce and pine.

There was still snow here. It had a deep cold smell under the sharp sweetness of evergreen.

The horse arched his neck and tensed his back. When a bird started out of cover, he almost went skyward with it.

Valeria soothed him with a purring trill, stroking his neck over and over. It softened a little. He went forward on tiptoe. Every now and then he expressed himself with an explosive snort.

The hunt found Valeria just where the road opened again and started to descend into a deep river valley. In the distance she saw the roofs of a town. It was a substantial place, with a wall around it and the tower of a temple rising out of it.

She heard the hounds singing. Whatever they were chasing, it was coming this way.

Best be out of its way when the hunt came through, she thought. She was not afraid—yet. She let the horse pick up a trot and then a canter, aiming toward the town.

By the time she came out on the level, the hounds were in full cry behind her. The horse had forsaken any pretense of civilization. He felt himself a hunted thing. He knew nothing but speed.

His panic was sucking her down. She fought it. The hounds were closing in. She could not see or hear the huntsmen, or the nobles on their pretty horses. They must be far behind. Or—

Just as she turned from looking back at the hounds, their masters rode out of the trees ahead. They were laughing. Their leader laughed loudest of all, mocking her stupidity. This was an ambush, and she had ridden blindly into it.

The horse had the bit in his teeth. She let the reins fall on his neck as he veered wildly away from the on-rushing horsemen, and sang to the hounds.

They had the taste of blood from a doe that they had caught and torn apart under the trees. The horse was larger and sweeter. She sang away the sweetness and the temptation. She sang them to sleep.

They dropped where they ran, tumbling over one another. It happened none too soon. The horse was flagging. He was a sturdy beast, but he was not built to race.

The hunters on their slender-legged beauties were gaining fast. Her horse's twists and evasions barely gave them pause. They ran right over the hounds.

There were too many horses to master all at once, and Valeria was tired. Her own horse stumbled just as she scraped together the strength to try another working. His legs tangled, and he somersaulted. They parted in midair.

She lay winded, wheezing for breath. Her head was spinning. Huge shapes swirled around her. Gold flashed in her eyes. Hands wrenched at her, tearing at her clothes.

She fought blindly, still struggling to breathe. The

magic was beaten out of her. She kicked and clawed. Her coat was gone. Her shirt shredded in their hands.

Her breasts gave them pause, but that was all too brief. They yowled with glee. It would not have mattered if she had been a boy. A girl was much, much better.

Two of them pinned her arms. Two more pried her legs apart. The fifth, whose face she already knew too well, stood above her, tugging at his belt.

She arched and twisted. She was completely empty of rational thought. Magic—she had magic somewhere. If she could only—

The earth shrugged. The hot, hard thing that had been thrusting at her dropped away. Her wrists and ankles throbbed so badly that for a long while she was not even sure that they were free.

Someone bent over her. She surged up in pure, blind rage.

He rocked back a step, but then he braced against her. He caught her hands and held her at arm's length.

All too slowly she understood that he was not one of the hunters. He wore no gold. His coat was plain leather. The hunters had been big men, brown-haired, with broad red faces. She would never forget any of those faces. This one was slim and dark and not much taller than she. His eyes were an odd pale color, almost silver. With his thin arched nose and long mouth, they made him look stern and cold.

She looked around dazedly. Her attackers lay like

the wreck of a storm, heaped one on top of the other. Their horses stood beyond them in a neat line.

A small wind began to blow, stinging her many scratches. She turned her wrists in her rescuer's grip. He let her go. She started to cover herself, but it was a little too late for that.

Mutely he took off his coat and held it out. She took it just as wordlessly. As plain as it was, it was beautifully made, of leather as soft as butter. The shirt he wore under it was fine linen, and clean. She caught herself admiring the width of his shoulders.

Her stomach turned over. She barely had time to toss the coat out of the way before she doubled up, retching into the grass.

She was beyond empty when she could finally stand straight again. Her head felt light, dizzy. She started to reach for the coat and staggered.

The dark man caught her before she fell. Her skin flinched at his touch, but she made it stop. His lips tightened. "Sit here," he said, pointing to his coat where it lay on the ground.

He had a deeper voice than she had expected, speaking imperial Aurelian with an accent so pure it sounded stilted. He must be from the heart of the empire, from Aurelia itself.

She did not consciously decide to do as he told her. He let go of her, and her knees would not hold her up. She crumpled in a heap.

He turned his back on her and walked away. She

stared after him in disbelief. Anger drove out a storm of tears. How could he—what did he think—

She was shaking uncontrollably. Her stomach had nothing more to cast up. If she could find the horse, she would get to him and mount somehow and escape before her rescuer came back.

The horse was dead. Maybe she had felt him die. She did not remember. He lay not far from her with his neck at an unnatural angle. Flies were already buzzing around him.

The other horses were still in their line as if tied. She supposed she should wonder at that, just as she should grieve for the horse who had served her so well. She would, later. She was in shock. She knew that dispassionately, from the training her mother had bullied into her. She needed warmth, quiet and a dose of tonic.

The sun was not too cold. It was quiet where she lay. None of her attackers had moved, but they were breathing. She could hear them. They must be asleep or unconscious.

The dark man swam into view above her as he had before. This time she simply stared at him. He carried a bundle that unfolded into a shirt as fine as his own, a pair of soft trousers, and a pair of boots. The boots were for riding.

He dressed her as if she was a child. These clothes were better than the best she had had at home. They fit much better than her brothers' hand-me-downs.

When she was dressed, with his coat over the shirt, he filled a wooden cup from a wineskin and made her drink. She swallowed in spite of herself, and choked. The wine was so strong it made her dizzy. There was something in it. Valerian—hellebore—

She pushed the cup away. "Are you trying to poison me?"

"So," he said. "You can talk. No, it's not poison. It's something to calm you."

"Not for shock," she said. "That makes it worse. Plain water is better. And rest. If there's an herbalist in the town—"

"I'm sure there is," he said. "Can you ride?"

"I can ride anything."

That was the wine making her giddy. He arched a brow but refrained from comment. "I meant, can you ride now?"

"Anything," she said. "Any time."

"If you say so," he said. He turned toward the line of horses. One of them shook its head as if he had freed it from a spell, and walked docilely toward him. It was a handsome thing as they all were, coal-black with a star. Its trappings were crimson and green.

He smoothed the mane on its neck, grimacing at the ribbons, and said to Valeria, "We'll get you something less gaudy in Mallia."

"You've been very kind," she said. "You saved my life and more, and I'm very grateful. But now I think—"

"Don't worry," he said. "You won't be charged with stealing the horse. It's due you as compensation—and not only for rape. This is one pack of hellions that won't be terrorizing these parts again."

She stared at him. "Again? This isn't the first—"

"They're notorious," the dark man said. "And, unfortunately, too well born to be brought to account. The emperor's justice is not as well administered here as one might hope."

"But that means—you—I—"

"Their hunting days are over," the dark man said. His voice was as soft as ever, but something in it made her shiver.

Valeria's sight was blurring again. She had meant to say something more, but what it was, she could not remember.

While she groped for words, he lifted her and deposited her lightly in the saddle. He was a great deal stronger than he looked. She was almost as big as he was, and he had not shown any sign of strain.

She clung to the high ornate saddle and tried to stop her head from whirling. The horse was quiet under her. It found her weight negligible after the well-fed lordling it had been carrying, and her balance even in this state was better than his.

Her rescuer made no move to claim any of the horses for himself. He walked through the field of the fallen. Most he left where they lay, but he paused beside one. When he turned the man onto his back,

Valeria recognized the face. It had hung above her just before the earth shook and flung them all down.

The man's breeches were tangled around his ankles. His thick red organ flapped limply. Her rescuer bent over him. There was a knife in his hand.

Valeria's throat closed. She knew the penalty for rape. Except that this man had not quite—

She meant to say so. The words would not come. She watched without a sound as the dark man made two quick, merciless cuts. It was just like gelding a colt. He flung the offal with a gesture of such perfectly controlled fury that her jaw dropped. Before the bloody bundle could strike the ground, a crow appeared out of nowhere and caught it and carried it away.

When the man turned back toward her, his eyes were so pale they seemed to have no color at all. He lifted a shoulder just visibly.

The horse on the end of the line left the others and trotted toward him. Now that she saw it apart from the rest, she realized that it was different. Its saddle and bridle were as plain but as excellently made as the rider's clothes. The horse was very like them in quality, a sturdy grey cob with an arched nose and an intelligent eye. It was neither as tall nor by any means as elegant as the others, but Valeria would have laid wagers that it would still be going when they had dropped with exhaustion.

The dark man mounted without touching the stirrup. With no perceptible instruction, the grey horse turned toward the town. The black followed of its own accord.

The movement of a horse under her did as much to bring Valeria back to herself as anything she could have done. Her stomach was a tight and painful knot, but she had mastered it.

She would have to decide how she felt about the dark man's rough justice. The civilized part of her deplored it. The sane part was wondering what price he would pay for it, if the lordling's family really was as powerful as he had said. The rest of her was dancing with bloodthirsty glee.

She fixed her eyes on him to steady herself. He had a beautiful seat on his blocky little horse. He sat upright but not at all stiff, with a deep, soft leg and a supple hip. He moved as the horse moved, as if he were a part of it.

She had never seen anyone ride like that, except in dreams. If the riders on the Mountain could teach her to ride even a fraction as well, she would call herself happy.

She tried to imitate him, a little. The effort reminded her forcefully that she had been tumbling on rocky ground and fighting off rape not long before. She persisted until the memory faded. Then there was only the horse under her and the rider in front of her and the town of Mallia drawing steadily closer.

Chapter Three

The hostages joined the caravan in Mallia. They had been riding at a punishing pace, thanks to their escort. The emperor's guard had no love to spare for the sons of barbarian chieftains who had made war against the empire. Even if the emperor had seen fit to take them as hostages for their fathers' good behavior, the emperor's soldiers saw no reason to treat them as anything but enemies.

Euan Rohe had a tougher rump than most. But after far too many days on imperial remounts, with a change at every station and a bare pause to eat or piss, he was hobbling as badly as the others. He groaned in relief when he heard that they were to stop for a whole night in this little pimple of a town.

For a town this small and this close to the heart of

the empire, it had a sizable garrison. There was a legion quartered here under an elderly but able commander. He inspected his temporary charges with a singular lack of expression and said to his orderly, "Clear out the west barracks. Tell the veterans to keep their opinions to themselves, or they'll be answering to me."

Euan felt his brows go up. There had been no need for the man to say that in the hostages' hearing. It was a challenge of sorts, and a warning.

They had had a good number of those as they rode from the frontier. He knew better than to take them for granted. A hostage survived by staying on guard.

The west barracks made a decent prison. Its windows were high and barred, and the guards took station near the doors. It seemed excessive for half a dozen hostages, but that was the empire of Aurelia. It did everything to excess.

The hostages were determined not to cause trouble. There would be enough of that later, the One God willing. They ate what they were fed and went directly to sleep.

It was still dark when they were rousted out. The caravan was just starting to assemble. It was a merchant caravan for the most part, but some of it was even more heavily guarded than the hostages. That was the treasure transport, carrying coin and tribute to the school on the Mountain.

Euan was in no way eager to climb into the saddle.

He delayed as long as he could, which was a fair while with a caravan of this size.

As he busied himself with the sixth or seventh readjustment of a bridle strap, the commander came out of the legionaries' barracks with a pair of his countrymen. They were both much younger than he. One was a hawk-faced man who walked like a warrior, light and dangerous. The other was a boy. Or…

Euan peered. Boys could be beautiful in Aurelia, with their smooth olive skin and black curly hair. He had mistaken a few for girls in his time, and been royally embarrassed by it, too. This must be a boy. Girls in this country wore skirts and did not cut their hair. And yet…

This was interesting. He busied himself with his horse's girth and watched under his brows. The commander and the hawk-faced man took the boy, if boy it was, to the caravan master. Euan could not hear every word they said, but it was clear the young person was being entrusted to the caravan for transport north.

The boy did not say anything while they made arrangements for him. His eyes were wide, taking in the caravan. They widened even further as he caught sight of the hostages in their ring of guards. From the look of him, he had never seen princes of the Caletanni before.

Euan rather thought the boy liked what he saw. He would probably die before he admitted it. Gavin favored him with a broad and mocking grin. The boy looked away hastily.

The negotiations were short and amicable. Whoever the hawk-faced man was, he won a degree of respect from the caravan master that even the legionary commander could not match. The boy must be a relative, from the way the caravan master treated him.

The boy broke his silence when the horses were brought out. His horse was a pretty black of a much lighter and more elegant breed than Euan's big dray horse. He seemed to be looking for another, and not seeing it. "Aren't you coming?" he asked the hawk-faced man.

His voice was as ambiguous as his face. If it was a boy's, it was on the light side, but it was deep for a girl's.

"I have other business here," the man said. "You'll be safe with Master Rowan. He'll look after you as if you were his own, and take you where you want to go."

The boy set his lips together. Euan could see how unhappy he was, but he did not whine or beg. He turned his back and mounted the black horse, then waited for the rest of them with an air of cold disdain.

The man shook his head slightly, but did not press the issue. They were either brothers or lovers, Euan thought. No one else would wage war over matters so small.

At long last the caravan began to move. Its pace was slow, dictated by the mules and the oxen. They would be on the road for days longer than strictly necessary, but none of the hostages minded overmuch. They needed time to rest and steady their minds before they reached their destination.

Their guards' vigilance was less strict in the caravan than it had been on the way from the border. They were allowed to move somewhat among the men of the caravan, and to carry on conversations. They used the opportunity to practice their Aurelian as well as the horsemanship they had been practicing, forcibly, since the day they were sent on this journey.

The boy from Mallia had his own small tent, which was pitched every night beside the caravan master's. One of the master's servants saw to his needs. He ate his meals with the master or his guards. He was kept as close as a virgin daughter.

Euan loved a challenge. He scouted the ground and laid his plan. By the second day he was ready to make his move.

The night before, they had stayed in one of the imperial caravanserais. Tonight they were too far from the nearest town to cover the distance before dark. They camped along the road instead, setting up a guarded camp with earthen walls in the legionary style.

While most of the guards were busy with the earthwork, Euan saw his opening. The boy insisted on taking care of his own horse, against some opposition. Euan chose to station his horse in the line not far from the black, and to practice his newly acquired horse-tending skills.

The boy was much better at it than he was. He hardly needed to pretend to be inept. As he had hoped, his fumbling brought the boy over to lend a hand.

This was not a boy. Euan was sure of that as they worked side by side to rub the horse down and feed him his nose bag of barley. It was like a fragrance so faint he was barely aware of it. This was a young woman.

Once Euan had assured himself of that, he could not see her as a man. Her hands were too slender and her throat too smooth. Her face was too fine to be male, even young imperial male.

He kept his thoughts to himself and stood with her while the horse ate his barley, watching the last of the earthwork go up around them. "You build a city in an hour," he said. "Then in the morning, in much less than an hour, the wall will be gone and the camp with it. It's a very imperial thing. Even for a night you raise up a fortress."

She slanted a glance at him. Her eyes were a fascinating color, not exactly brown, not exactly green, with flecks of gold like sunlight in a forest pool. "You speak Aurelian well," she said.

"I work at it."

"The way you work at your riding?"

He snorted. "We're not born on a horse's back and suckled on mares' milk the way you people are." He paused. "Am I really that bad?"

"The others are worse."

"Probably not by much."

The corner of her mouth turned up. "You could almost learn to ride."

"I hope so," he said. "That's what we're doing. We're going to the Mountain, to the School of War. We're supposed to learn to be cavalrymen."

"I suppose if anyone can teach you, the masters there can."

"So everyone hopes," Euan said. He paused before he cast the dice. "My name is Euan. And yours?"

"Valens," she said.

That was a man's name. Euan was careful not to comment on it. "I take it you're for the Mountain, too. School of War?"

"I'm Called," she said.

She spoke as if he must know what she was talking about. It took him a while to understand, then to realize what, in this case, it meant. He almost said, "But surely women aren't—"

He caught himself just in time. This was beyond interesting. It was a gift from the One God.

He would have to play it very, very carefully. He bent his head in respect, as he had heard one should, and let her see a little of his fascination. "You're the first I've seen," he said. "No wonder they're transporting you with the treasure."

Her lip curled. "That's not because I'm Called. It's because of Kerrec."

She spoke the name as if it had a bitter taste. She had not forgiven the man for abandoning her to the caravan. That too Euan could use.

He put on an expression of wry sympathy. "Your brother?" he asked.

"Not in this life," she said.

Ah, so, he thought. "He's too protective, is he? Or not protective enough?"

"He's too everything," she said. She spun on her heel. "I'm hungry. They always feed me too much. Would you help me with it?"

"Gladly," he said, and he meant it.

Once more her mouth curved in that enchanting half-smile. "I've seen what they've been feeding you," she said. "You shouldn't have to be eating soldier's rations here."

He shrugged. "They don't love us. We've killed too many of them—won too many battles, too, even if we lost the war. We can hardly blame them for taking what revenge they can."

"You have a great deal of forbearance," she said. She sounded a little surprised. "I had always thought—"

He showed her all his teeth. "Oh, we're wild enough. We take heads. We eat the hearts of heroes. That doesn't stop us from understanding how an enemy thinks."

"Of course not," she said. "The better you understand, the easier it is to find ways to defeat him."

Euan's heart stopped. The Called were mages. He

had let himself forget that quite important fact. Many mages could read patterns and predict outcomes. Mages of the Mountain could do more than that. Even one who was completely untrained and untested might be able to see too clearly for comfort.

He shook off his sudden fit of the horrors. It was a lucky shot, that was all. She showed no sign of denouncing him as a traitor to the empire.

Her dinner was certainly better than the one his kinsmen would be getting. He was not fond of the spices these people poured on everything, but the bread was fresh and good. There was meat, which he had not had in days, and it was not too badly overcooked. She left him most of that. He left her all of the greens and the boiled vegetables. "Horse feed," he said.

That half smile of hers was a lethal weapon, if she wanted to use it that way. "I do want to be a horse mage, after all," she said.

He saluted her with a half-gnawed bone. "I hope a cavalryman is allowed to eat like a man, then, instead of a horse."

"You eat like a wolf," she said. "They must be feeding you even worse than I thought."

"It's not what we're used to," he admitted.

She nodded as if in thought. There was a line between her brows. When she spoke again, it was to change the subject. "Tell me about your country."

"In the south and west we have forests like yours," he said. "Beyond that, past the spine of mountains, it's a broad land of heath and crag. Rivers run there, too fast and deep to ford, and cold as snow. The wind cuts like a knife and sings like a woman keening for her lover. The bones of the earth are bare as often as not. It's a hard country, but it raises strong men."

"My father said there are fish in the lakes there that are as big as a man, with flesh so sweet that the gods could dine on it."

"Your father has been there?"

"He fought there," she said. "Does that bother you?"

"No," he said. "War is life. A man is only a man if he's fought well. I suppose your father did if he was in the legions. Which was his? The Valeria?"

She started as if he had stung her. Aha, he thought. So that was her proper name. She recovered quickly. "Yes. Yes, that was his legion."

"We call them the Red Wolves," he said. "Mothers terrify their children with the threat of them. They're the great enemy. It was the Valeria that took us in the last battle and brought us into the empire."

"You don't hate them," she said. "I'd think you would."

"They're a worthy opponent," he said. "War has its balance. Someday we'll defeat them and lead them in halters through our camps."

"You are different than anything I expected," she said slowly.

"Is that a good thing?" he asked.

It took her a moment to answer. "I'm not sure," she said. "I'll think about it."

Euan thought he might be in love. This was not his first imperial woman, by far, but it was certainly the first who had wanted everyone to think she was a man. He would have liked to see her hair before she chopped it off. He would have liked even more to see what she was like under the sexless clothes she wore.

He was sure it was love when he came back to the rest of the hostages and found them lying back, replete after a feast identical to the one he had just finished. Someone had put in a word, it seemed. He could guess who it was.

They were all in her debt, and Euan made sure they knew it. He did not tell them her secret. If they had eyes to see, then they could. Otherwise, he would enjoy the field without a rival.

Chapter Four

The dark man's name was Kerrec. He never actually told Valeria that himself. She heard it from the commander in Mallia.

That was her first grievance. By the time he packed her off with the caravan, she had a dozen more. He seemed determined to keep her from being grateful for her rescue, and equally determined to make her dislike him intensely. He was cold, arrogant, secretive, and intolerably condescending, and he had not a speck of charm.

The worst of it was, she could not hate him. She could never hate anyone who sat a horse like that.

Only one other thing almost persuaded her not to despise him. He had told the commander in Mallia nothing of her sex, only that she had been assaulted by the infamous pack of lordlings that had been preying on travelers and the odd local. The commander, like everyone else who heard the story, had been delighted with its ending, and more than pleased to grant her whatever she needed, horse and clothes and provisions and all.

Kerrec had not betrayed her to the caravan master, either. Both the caravan master and the commander had deduced on their own that she was Called, and treated her accordingly. Whether intentionally or because he simply did not care, Kerrec had done a great deal to help her on her way.

She found his perfect opposite in the barbarian prince who rode with the caravan. She had seen sacks of meal that rode better, but he did try, especially after she offered a suggestion or two. He was the biggest man she had ever seen, though not the broadest. He was still young and a little rangy, with long legs and big square hands. His hair was as red as copper.

There was a great deal of it. He wore it in thick braids to his waist. His cheeks and chin were shaven, but he cultivated thick red mustaches. His eyes were amber and tilted upward above high cheekbones, like a wolf's. They had a wolf's wicked intelligence, and a spark of laughter that never quite went away.

He loved to talk. His command of Aurelian was less than perfect, but he never let that stop him. She learned a fair bit of his language that way, and taught him a fair number of new words in Aurelian.

He had all the warmth and charm that Kerrec lacked. She reminded herself frequently that he was an enemy, but she was not about to let that stop her from enjoying his company.

She decided, by the third day out from Mallia, to forget the man who had rescued her from the hunt. She was unlikely ever to see him again. She made herself useful to the caravan, helping with the horses and lending a hand wherever else seemed appropriate. Her dreams were still as likely as not to have Kerrec in them, but she could turn her back on those.

Five days out from Mallia, while the caravan prepared to cross a bridge over a deep gorge with a river rushing far below, two young men rode up behind them. One was riding a sturdy brown mule, and was a sturdy brown person himself. The other rode bareback on a horse as delicate as a gazelle. His clothes were worn to rags, but they looked as if they had been rich when they were new. Traces of embroidery still lingered at the neck and hem of the long loose robe. His mare's bridle swung with wayworn tassels. Her bit was tarnished silver.

The rider was as slim and fine-boned as the mare. His cheekbones were tattooed with blue swirls. In the center of his forehead was a complicated pattern of circles within circles in red and black and green.

Valeria had felt the two riders behind her since the night before. They were hunting, and their quarry was the same as hers. Even before she saw their faces, she knew that they were Called.

The brown man's name was Dacius. He came from a town south of Aurelia. The other, Iliya, was from much farther away. He was a prince of Gebu in the land of spices. "A year and a day have I journeyed," he said in his lilting Aurelian, "coming to the Mountain's Call."

He was a singer as well as a prince. Dacius was a tenant farmer from a noble's estate. They had nothing in common but the Call, but that was enough.

Iliya was even more in love with the sound of his own voice than Euan was. Dacius was a listener. He had a quiet way about him that horses loved. The mule adored him, which was strikingly out of character for her hybrid species.

The caravan took them in. "Three of you at once," the master said in deep satisfaction. "That's more luck than we've had in a handful of years."

Iliya's smile was wide and white in his dark face. It was Dacius, rather surprisingly, who said, "That's good, sir. We're fair to middling useless otherwise, except as hostlers. It will be a good long time before we have any skills worth conjuring with."

"You carry the luck," the master said, "three times three. The gods are kind to us this season."

Dacius shrugged. Iliya laughed. Valeria said nothing.

Everyone expected them to ride together. Iliya's prattle covered the others' silence. When he broke out in song, he insisted that everyone sing with him.

It was a tuneful road that day, up from the bridge by a steep road with numerous switchbacks to a high plateau. They camped there on the windy level.

As usual, Valeria helped look after the horses. Iliya was busy entertaining the guards with songs and stories. Dacius helped with the earthwork that would protect the camp overnight. Even when she could not see them, she could feel them. They were like parts of her that had gone missing and come wandering back.

Euan had been keeping his distance since the riders came to the caravan. After the horses were settled, she found him tending a spit on which turned the carcass of a deer. One of his fellow hostages had shot it that morning with a bow that he had borrowed from a caravan guard. There had been a great to-do when the emperor's guards realized what he had in his hand, which had taken all of Master Rowan's skill to settle.

Now at evening the hostages were playing some game nearby that involved a set of knucklebones and a fair amount of either guffawing or snarling depending on how the bones fell. "Not in the mood to play tonight?" she asked Euan.

He started and spun. For an instant she saw a wolf at bay, with yellow eyes glittering and teeth bared. Then he was Euan again. "By the One God!" he said. "You scared me half out of my skin."

"I'm sorry," she said without too much repentance. "Why are you sulking? Is it too much for you to share a caravan with another prince?"

"I am not sulking," he said sullenly.

"Then what are you doing?"

"Being jealous," he said. "Those are your own kind. It's like seeing horses in a herd."

"They are my kind," she admitted, "but it doesn't feel like a herd at all. It feels strange. It makes me itch inside my skin."

"Really?" He had brightened considerably. "You don't want to abandon the rest of us?"

"Gods, no," she said.

It was like standing in front of a fire to feel the warmth coming off him. He sighed deeply. "Good," he said. "That's good."

The caravan inched its way through a tumbled landscape of ravine and forest. The towns they passed grew smaller and smaller until they dwindled away altogether. They could not see past the next hilltop. Whenever the trees opened or they reached the summit of a hill, the world was shrouded in mist and rain. Even when it was not raining, the clouds hung so low that they seemed to brush the tops of the trees.

In that perpetual damp and fog, Iliya wilted visibly. His cheerful babble stopped and his singing died away. Valeria had found it annoying while it went on, but once it stopped, she missed it.

There was no cure for his sickness but the sun. In this country, that was a rarity.

Valeria took to riding at the front of the caravan.

Guards rode ahead of her, but they did not block what view there was. She could look her fill at trees, rocks and yet more trees. Dacius saw the virtue in what she was doing and rode just behind her. Iliya trailed after him, limp and green-faced. The Call was strong in all of them. They could not turn back now unless they were bound and dragged.

On the seventh day, or maybe it was the tenth, the clouds actually lifted. Valeria thought for a brief moment that she saw a patch of blue sky.

They were climbing yet another slope. For once it was not so steep that they needed to get off and walk. The pair of guards in front had gone up and over the top. Valeria's horse picked up his pace slightly. Maybe it was the faintest hint of sky, or the minute brightening of the perpetual rain-colored light, but her heart felt lighter somehow. She was so full of the Call that she could hardly think.

As had happened too often before, the road reached the top only to plunge down at once into a deep valley. Just as Valeria paused, the clouds parted. She looked straight across to the country she had dreamed about since she was small.

It was all there. The long green valley with the river running through it. The walled fortress where the valley curved upward again toward the stony slopes. The sharp rise of the Mountain with its crown of snow. Forest surrounded the valley, but it was open and almost treeless, a gift of the gods to their dearest children.

At this distance she could see the walls of the school and the creneled bulk of towers, but little else. She needed no eyes to know what was there. The regular patches of brown and pale green around the feet of the walls were the fields and farmlands that fed the citadel. She could make out the clusters of farmhouses and the lines of hedges. The horse pastures were up behind the fortress, in high valleys protected by the Mountain itself.

The Call broke open inside her and became the whole of her. She had just enough sense left to see that Dacius had come up beside her and Iliya moved ahead of her. The pallor was gone from Iliya's skin. He was as rapt as the rest of them. His eyes were narrowed and his face was shining as if he stared straight into the sun.

The guards had drawn aside. The way was open. They knew, thought Valeria. Those were the last words in her until she sat her hard-breathing horse in front of the gate.

She saw no guards anywhere near it. That did not mean it was unguarded. She looked up at the low round arch. The figures carved on it were so old that they were worn almost smooth. She could just make out a line of horses and riders, and a blurred shape that might be the Sun and Moon intertwined.

The gate was open, with darkness inside. It looked like a gaping mouth.

Her horse snorted softly and shook his mane. She started out of her stupor. Iliya snorted almost exactly like the horse. His mare trotted forward. Her hooves rang on the worn stones of the paving, echoing under the arch. She carried her rider inside.

Dacius' mule was moving much more stolidly but as steadily as she ever had. They were leaving Valeria alone, with the caravan far behind, and nothing ahead but dreams and fear.

Valeria had come too far and with too much confidence to back off now. She took a deep breath and wiped her clammy palms on her breeches. The horse started forward without urging.

The wall was thick, but surely not as thick as this. She was in a tunnel with no end to it that she could see.

It was not totally dark. There were lamps, just bright enough for her to see the way. They seemed to float in the air.

On impulse she called one to her. As she had thought, it was a witch light. She asked it to burn brighter. It flared, blinding her. She damped it hastily. This place was full of magic. It turned the slightest whisper of a working into a shout.

The lamp hung just above her, burning steadily. In its light she saw the fitted stone of the tunnel's walls and the interlocking tiles of its floor. She also saw that the tunnel bent and then divided. One way went up and one way went level.

She slid from the saddle and stood holding the black's reins. There was no sign of the other horses and riders. The horse's calm was not natural, but neither was this place.

She had known that there would be tests. What if this was meant just for her? What if she was barred from the school? She could convince men that she was one of them, simply by cutting her hair and wearing their clothes. Magic was not so easy to mislead.

The Call had come to her. She must be meant for the school. She could pass this test. It was a simple matter of choices.

"Don't think," her mother's voice said. "Feel."

She almost spun around to see if Morag had followed her to the Mountain. Then she caught herself. It was only memory.

It was also excellent advice. She squeezed her eyes shut and made herself breathe in a slow, steady rhythm. Each breath filled more of the world. It drove out thought and fear.

When she was empty of everything but air, she stepped forward. Her eyes were still shut. The horse walked quietly beside her.

She did not turn right or left. She went neither up nor down. She simply walked straight ahead.

Light dazzled her even through her eyelids. She heard voices and hoofbeats, and smelled horses and leather and fresh-baked bread.

She opened her eyes on a sunlit square. The gate was behind her. The clouds had parted, or maybe they had never dulled this place at all. She could feel the magic enclosed within these walls, distinct as the feel of sunlight on her skin.

Iliya was basking in the sun. Dacius looked around him with the same dazed expression she must have been wearing.

Tall grey buildings surrounded the square. People went back and forth inside it, busy with this errand or that. Not all were men. There were a few women in plain gowns like servants. One had a basket of laundry on her hip, and another stood by the fountain in the middle of the square, dipping water into an earthenware jar.

"That's the Well of the World," Iliya said. "It goes down to the source of all waters. It's strong magic."

There was so much magic in this place that Valeria could not tell if the story was true. She was too over-whelmed to argue with it.

Three men walked toward them. One was middle-aged, with the rolling walk and leathery look of the lifelong horseman. The other two were still a little soft around the edges, but they were cultivating the same weather-beaten style.

The older man greeted them in a broad country burr. "Good day to you, young gentlemen. My name is Hanno. I'm head groom in the candidates' stable. We'll take your horses, my boys and I, by your leave."

None of them had the courage to object. Iliya let his beloved mare go with Hanno himself. Valeria said goodbye to the black. He had not been a friend, but he had been a good servant. She would miss him.

While the grooms took charge of the horses, another man approached them. He was dressed no better than the grooms, but his carriage was different. He walked, thought Valeria, the way Kerrec rode.

She met his glance and froze. He seemed a quiet, unassuming person, middle-aged and middle-sized, but the magic in him was so strong and so profoundly disciplined that she could not move or speak for the wonder of it.

He looked them over carefully, one by one. What he thought, Valeria could not have said. He did not seem terribly disappointed. After a while he said, "In the name of the white gods and the master of the school, I welcome you to the Mountain. You will call me Rider Andres."

None of them had anything to say to that. He did not look as if he had expected them to. He turned his back on them and walked off at an angle across the square.

Evidently they were supposed to follow. They exchanged glances. Iliya shrugged. Dacius frowned. Valeria started walking in the man's wake. After a pause, the others did the same.

Rider Andres led them through a narrow wooden door and up a flight of steps. The place to which he brought them was indistinguishable from a legionary barracks. It was a high, wide room with tall windows, open now to let in light and air, and a broad stone hearth at one end. Rows of bunks lined the walls. A hundred men could have slept there.

At the moment, hardly a third of the bunks were occupied. The rest were stripped to the slats.

Rider Andres led them through the barracks and up another, shorter stair to a mess hall and common room. There seemed to be a great crowd in it, but when Valeria stopped to count, there were just shy of thirty people. They were all young, and they were of all tribes and races she had heard of and a few she had not. There were no big redheaded barbarians, but that was the only nation missing.

They all stopped whatever they had been doing and snapped to attention. "Rider Andres," they said in chorus, *"sir!"*

He released them with a nod. "Here are the last of you," he said, "and not before time, either. The testing begins tomorrow."

That seemed to take a few of them by surprise. Valeria would have liked more time to settle in, but she had to thank the gods for the reprieve. The longer she lived in a barracks, the more likely it was that someone would discover that she was not a man.

Her deception only had to survive until she passed the testing. Once she had done that, they had to accept her. She had the magic, just as they did. It would give them no choice.

Chapter Five

Rider Andres left the newcomers to sort themselves out. It seemed a logical thing for him to do. They had all come to the same Call, and they were all gifted with magic in some degree. Those who passed the testing would be part of a brotherhood as close as any that humans knew.

For tonight and until the testing was over, they were all bitter rivals. Some of them had been there for months, since shortly after the Call went out. Those had formed an uneasy alliance. Later comers had fallen into divisions of their own. The last three arrivals, by default, were yet another faction.

"If we're lucky," said a lanky young nobleman in silk and gold, "a quarter of us will pass into the school—and maybe one of those will become a rider.

It's not enough to be Called. That only means you have ears to hear. You have to be a great number of other things besides."

"Such as?" said Iliya. He was his lively and garrulous self again, now he had had his moment in the sun.

"Such as a Beastmaster. A scholar. A reader of signs and omens. A dancer. One of the tests is in dancing, did you know?"

"No one knows what the tests will be," someone said from the edge of the room. "That's what makes them so hard. There's no way to study, and no way to cheat."

"Nonsense," said the nobleman. "There have been riders in my family for generations. We all know what they test for, if not exactly how they test from year to year."

"It's the how that kills you," Iliya said lightly. "I can dance. Will they ask us to sing, too?"

"Sometimes they do," the nobleman said.

"Then I'll be a master," Iliya said. He beamed at them all. "Can you believe it? We're here. We've come to the Mountain!"

His enthusiasm was infectious. Even the nobleman allowed himself a small, tight smile. Valeria could have kissed Iliya. There had been an ugly undercurrent in the conversation, but he had dissipated it.

Not long after the last of the Called came in, servants came with plates and bowls and platters and fed them a simple dinner. The stew was made with roots and beans and vegetables, no meat, but it was good, and filling. It came with loaves of the heavy brown bread that Valeria had smelled baking, and wedges of sharp yellow cheese. To drink with it they had a cask of ale and a tall jar of wine.

They were all encouraged to eat and drink their fill. "There will be no breakfast tomorrow," the chief of the servants said, "and nothing to drink but water until the testing is over. Enjoy yourselves while you can. The next time you see this much food, you'll either be eating it in the candidates' mess or taking potluck on the road."

A collective sigh ran through the room. Someone at the end opposite Valeria dived for the bread. As if that had been a signal, they all fell to it.

In spite of the warning, she refrained from gorging herself. She wanted strength, not a sick stomach. She drank a little wine to steady herself, but she watered it heavily.

Not every one of the Called could hold his liquor. Some did not hold their food so well, either. By the time she left, the mess hall reminded her forcibly of a soldiers' tavern.

She was the first to leave. All the bunks were made up, including three new ones. She recognized her saddlebags at the foot of one, and Iliya's shabby-elegant and heavily embroidered pack on the bunk above it.

She intended to sleep as long and well as she could manage, but for the moment she was still wide awake.

The door to the outside was not barred, which surprised her. She had thought that the Called would be locked in until after the testing.

Something touched her awareness as she opened the door and slipped through it. It felt like a light set of wards, just enough to let a mage know that someone had gone through the door. Without even thinking, she raised her own protections. The wards withdrew, convinced that nothing was there.

She found her way by the same instinct that had disposed of the wards. This place was so full of magic that she could follow the currents of it wherever she wanted to go.

One led her to the stable where guests' horses were kept. Her black and Iliya's bay mare and Dacius' mule were stalled side by side and perfectly content. Of course they would be. Here of all places, people knew how to look after horses.

She fed each of them a bit of bread that she had brought from the mess hall. They were pleased to accept tribute, although none of them was hungry.

Once she had given them their due, she sought out another current, one that led her past the rest of the horses in the stable. None of them was anything but ordinary. She had yet to see any of the white stallions. When she tried to discover where they were, she was gently but firmly turned aside. *All in good time,* said a voice that was not a voice. She knew somehow that it was one of the stallions.

The current she followed was leading toward something much more mortal. The stable door opened on a narrow street. At the end of that she turned left into another square than the one she had seen when she first entered the school. This one was empty in the evening light, although she could sense the presence of people behind the blank walls and narrow windows. Behind one of those walls, she found the people she was looking for.

The hostages reacted variously to her arrival. Donn snarled and went back to his mug of ale. Gavin and Conory grinned and saluted her. The others were asleep in beds much more luxurious than she had been given.

"He's in the jakes," Gavin said before she could ask. He raised his voice in a roar. "Euan! Euan Rohe! Wipe your arse and come out of there. You've got company."

"No need for that," she said. Her ears were still ringing from Gavin's bellow. "I only wanted to see that you were here, and that you were well. And to apologize for—"

"The magic had you," Conory said. "We know." He filled a mug sloppily and held it out. "Here. It's almost decent, for imperial horse-piss."

Valeria drank a sip to be polite, but then she excused herself. This was not a night to spend drinking with the Caletanni. She needed her head in one piece for whatever would happen in the morning.

She took a different and somewhat roundabout

way back. The sun was setting and the shadows were long. The school was much larger than she would have thought, as large as the town of Mallia, where she had joined the caravan. Now and then she saw people intent on errands of their own, but none of them spoke to her. They all seemed to be servants, or else everyone here wore the same plain clothes. She had yet to see anyone but Andres whom she would have recognized as a rider.

Euan caught up with her on the edge of the square with the fountain, directly inside the gate. She felt him before she saw or heard him. It was like a storm coming, a presence so strong that it almost frightened her. He had no magic except the power to lead men, but that was enough.

She could have escaped before he found her. She stopped instead and waited beside the fountain, while the sunset stained the sky with blood and gold.

Her eyes were full of it when she lowered them to meet his. He seemed taken aback. The magic must be running strong in her, for him to see it.

He was too proud to say anything about it. Instead he said, "You didn't stay."

"I didn't mean to be rude," she said. "I'm not supposed to be out."

"Neither am I," he said with a hint of his usual humor. "Our test is to stay put until called for."

"I'm sure they won't cast you out for failing it."

She saw the gleam of teeth under the red mustache.

It was hard sometimes to tell whether he was smiling or snarling. At the moment it seemed to be a bit of both. "No, they're saddled with us until the emperor tells them to let us go."

"I didn't know they answered to him," she said.

"Sometimes they do." He seemed to realize he was looming over her. He sat on the fountain's rim, not too close to her. "Now tell me why you really came to find me."

"That was why. And," she added, "because I couldn't sleep, and it was an excuse to go prowling."

That was certainly a smile. "Now that I can believe. What will you do when you're a rider? The discipline's hard, I hear. It's like being a priest."

"Riders ride," she said. "That's what they are."

"Any time they want?"

"Often enough," she said.

"Well then," said Euan, "when you pass all the tests, promise you'll come once in a while to rescue me. I'm no kind of rider. They'll have me hauling manure to make me useful."

"When I pass the tests," she said. The evening air was chill, but that was not why she shivered. "If you have any luck to offer, I'll take it."

"I make my own luck," said Euan. "I've plenty to spare." He smiled a remarkably sweet smile. "Take it with you, as much as you need. Go and sleep. Dream of victory. Be the bear and the bull and the stallion. Be strong."

If he only knew, she thought. She had a powerful, almost overwhelming urge to kiss him.

That would have been a very unwise thing to do. She hoped her departure did not look too much like flight.

Chapter Six

As the first light of dawn touched the summit of the
Mountain, the Called stood in a line in the inner court
of the school. They were all perfectly silent except for
the chattering of teeth.

They had been awakened in the dark by the ringing
of a bell. Except for the clothes they had worn to sleep
in, everything that each of them owned was gone.

The few who, like Valeria, had slept fully dressed
were lucky. Some of the rest were naked, and most
wore only a shirt. They had to get up and march where
Rider Andres led, just as they were. Then they had to
stand in the courtyard, shuddering in the early-
morning cold. It might be summer in gentler countries,
but winter still lingered in the mountains.

Daylight grew slowly. Valeria watched the Mountain

brighten. It seemed to hang above the wall in front of her, luminously white against a cloudless sky.

The Call had gone silent. She felt strange without it, like an empty cup waiting to be filled.

Somewhat after full light but before the sun climbed over the wall, she heard the measured beat of hooves on stone. A double row of riders on shining white horses came riding in beneath the arch opposite the Mountain, just as she had heard in all the stories.

Her throat closed. Her eyes were stinging with tears. She had waited so long and traveled so far and given up so much, all for this.

The riders halted facing the line of the Called and spread in their own line. There were eight of them, dressed alike in boots and breeches and coats of a familiar style and plainness. She was wearing much the same, in the same drab brown color.

Their horses were smaller than they had been in her dreams. Apart from the white gleam of their coats and the magic of their existence, they were stocky and thickset and rather plain. Anywhere but here, she would have called them sturdy grey cobs with arched noses and—

Oh, no, she thought. No. That could not—

Two of the riders moved ahead of the rest. One was an older man, almost as grey as his horse. The other, in the circumstances, did not surprise her at all.

He did not alarm her, either, but that must be shock. She was looking at the end of her hopes. Of all the people in the world who could have appeared to test her, it would have to be the one man outside her family who knew what she was.

Kerrec looked just as chilly and arrogant in this place as he had in Mallia, but here at least he fit. His grey cob greeted her with a dark ironic glance and a flicker of humor that almost tricked a smile out of her. The stallion had taken a wicked delight in pretending to be a common horse. Even she had fallen for the deception, although that, he confessed with a slant of the ear, had not been easy to accomplish.

She supposed she should feel flattered. This was one of the white gods, and he had let her know that her magic was strong enough to stretch his powers a little.

The older man was speaking. Valeria made herself listen. She was not likely to be here much longer, but until Kerrec saw and recognized her, she could pretend that she was still a candidate for the testing.

"I am Master Nikos," the man said. "This is First Rider Kerrec. Those behind us are riders of the school, with whom you will become familiar as the testing progresses. Our stallions you will come to know when you are ready. This who condescends to carry me is Icarra. Petra carries First Rider Kerrec."

Valeria bowed to the stallions with the feminine names. Those were the names of their mothers, which they kept as a matter of honor. There would be more to each name, the name of a First Sire, but that, too, she supposed, would come to light when she was ready.

As she straightened from her bow, she saw that a few others had done the same. Iliya was one, Dacius another. Most of the Called still stood at attention. The nobleman, whose shirt was silk and whose legs were as white and thin as a bird's, was actually sneering. *He* did not bow to anyone, his attitude said.

Petra had his eye on that one. The nobleman did not seem to care. Did he even know?

He must. He was Called.

Master Nikos went on in his dry precise voice. "I see that some of you understand the proprieties of the school. Let it be your first lesson, then. Men have no rank here and no station but what they earn through the stallions. Whatever you were before you passed our gate, forget. Here you are newborn. Everyone is older and wiser and loftier than you. Loftiest of all are the stallions. If you came here in the delusion that you would master them, wake now. No man is a stallion's master. He may be companion, he may be partner—but master, never."

Valeria saw how they were all, men and stallions, noticing who listened and who did not. She noticed for herself how many of the Called did not seem aware that the stallions were part of the testing. They must be too scared or cocky or confused to see it.

"We will divide you now," Master Nikos said, "eight by eight. Eight is the number of the Dance. In eights you will work and ride and, when time permits, play.

Be assured that when your eight is broken, as others fail the testing or withdraw voluntarily, those who pass will continue. No one of you will suffer for the failure of the others."

"There will be time to play?" someone asked.

"This is only the first testing," the Master answered. "It is the shortest and simplest of all, and the least dangerous. The consequence of failure is dismissal, but no worse. Your whole life here, if you pass the next three days, will be testing, and some of it will be deadly. Even I am still tested." His eyes swept their faces. "You may always choose to leave. If any of you chooses now, you will be escorted back to barracks, your belongings returned to you and a horse given you if you brought none. You are free to go."

There was a silence. No one moved. Valeria thought about it. Every moment that passed brought her closer to betrayal. She could walk out now and no one be the wiser.

She could not do it. The Mountain held her. The stallions watched, studying her. None of them had cried out against her, although they all knew perfectly well that she was female.

Master Nikos nodded as if pleased. "Good," he said. "Good."

He beckoned. Three of the riders came out of the line. Kerrec made the fourth. They rode up and down the rank of the Called.

The stallions did the choosing. It was subtle, almost

imperceptible, how the horse paused an instant before the rider tapped the candidate's shoulder.

Petra halted in front of Valeria. She looked up into Kerrec's expressionless face. There was no sign of recognition in it. His hand fell on her shoulder.

He did not name her female and impostor. He said nothing at all. She jerked forward to stand with the others whom Petra had selected. Iliya and Dacius were there, and to her disgust, the arrogant nobleman. He seemed to think that a First Rider was no less than his rank deserved.

Four more came out of the line to stand with them. When they were all together, Kerrec dismounted with quick grace. "Name yourselves," he said.

The nobleman was first on the left. He opened his mouth for what was clearly a lengthy proceeding, but Kerrec cut him off. "You may lay claim to one name," he said. "Choose it well. If you pass the tests, it will be the one by which you are known forever after."

The nobleman looked as if he had bitten into a lemon. "Only one name? But I am—"

"You are no one," said Kerrec. "Choose."

"Paulus," the nobleman said sullenly. "I'll be Paulus."

"Good," said Kerrec. His eye was already resting on the next.

The four whom Valeria did not know were called Marcus, Embry, Cullen, and Batu. The first three were ordinary enough, black-haired and olive-skinned people of Aurelia. Marcus had a quickness about him that made her think he had a temper, and Cullen had a surprising crop of freckles—a mark of barbarian blood, like his short, upturned nose and square jaw. Batu was something else altogether. He was as black as a ripe olive, with a broad, blunt face and hair in a hundred oiled plaits wound close around his skull. He had come even farther than Iliya to answer the Call, from a country where horses were all but unheard of.

She was the last of the line, and the most reluctant to speak. She could not believe that Kerrec did not recognize her, but when his eye fell on her, it was as blank as before. "Valens," she said. "My name is Valens."

He nodded briskly as he had to everyone else. "Now you know each other," he said. "Come with me."

The other eights had already left the courtyard. So had the remaining riders and their stallions. Kerrec left Petra behind and brought his charges into a dormitory much smaller than the barracks in which they had been staying. With its wood-paneled walls and mullioned windows, it might have been a room in an inn. The beds were hard and plain, but they were beds rather than bunks, four on one side of the room and four on the other. On each lay a saddlebag or a pack, a set of clothes and a pair of boots.

Valeria's saddlebags lay on the bed farthest from the door, as if someone knew that she had been out wandering last night. Its advantage was that it was closest to the hearth. Iliya's was next to it and Batu's across from it.

"Put on these clothes," Kerrec said, "and rest if you can. There's a room yonder for the shy or the incontinent. In an hour I'll come to fetch you for the first test."

Valeria almost thought that his glance had fallen on her when he spoke of the inner room. It was a bathroom, she discovered, with a large wooden tub and something Valeria had heard of but never seen, a water privy.

She could have spent the whole hour playing with the water that ran from pipes, not only cold but, to her lasting delight, hot. But there were others waiting and a test coming. She settled for a quick scrub of face and hands before she stripped off her travel-worn clothes and put on the new ones. The coat and breeches were dark grey instead of brown, but they were otherwise identical to the riders'. The boots were riding boots, and they fit well. There were a belt and a cap, which she put on. The cap was embroidered with a silver horsehead.

She went out to face the rest, feeling awkward and shakily proud. Most of them were already dressed, except for one or two who professed to be as shy as she was. She wondered a little wildly if any of them was protecting the same secret.

It was odd to see them all dressed alike. Nothing could make Batu look less exotic, but Iliya seemed almost ordinary without his ragged robes. Except for the clan marks on his cheeks and forehead, he was enough like the rest of them to be barely noticeable.

None of them had much to say. The reality of the testing was coming down on them all. Some lay down and tried to rest as Kerrec had commanded. Iliya paced like a tiger in a cage until Marcus growled at him, then he sat on the floor and tried visibly not to twitch. Cullen amused himself with plaiting ropes of sunlight and shade. He had so much magic in him that he left a faintly luminous trail when he moved.

Valeria did not dare lie down. If she did, she would fall asleep, and she needed to be wide awake when Kerrec came back. She sat on the bed and tucked up her feet and reached for the quiet place inside her, where her magic was.

It was elusive. When she did find it, it was full of white horses. They were standing in a circle all around her, staring at her.

It was quiet, in its way. It was also deeply disconcerting. Her magic was hers and no one else's. Her mother had taught her that, and she believed it. What business had these horses, even if they were gods, to trespass in it?

The horses did not see fit to answer. They were studying her.

"Still?" she asked them.

They did not answer that, either. She was going to have to live with their silent scrutiny, whether she liked it or not. She could only hope that they came to a decision about her sooner rather than later.

Chapter Seven

When the hour was up, it was not Kerrec who came to fetch them but a young man somewhat older than they. His grey coat was edged with a thin band of lighter grey, and the badge on his cap showed a horse dancing against the rays of the sun. He named himself a cadet captain, and let them know that he was four years past his Calling.

He led them briskly through a confusing variety of halls, corridors, courtyards and alleyways to a square of grass surrounded by the inevitable grey stone walls. Kerrec was waiting there, and grooms with horses.

One of the Called behind Valeria groaned. He had voiced the disappointment they all felt. These were not white stallions but common bays and chestnuts.

To add insult to injury, as Paulus observed in a clearly audible mutter, they were all either mares or geldings.

"These mounts are lent to us by the School of War," Kerrec said after they had formed their line in front of him. "They will administer the simplest of the tests. Each of you will choose a horse, then groom, saddle and bridle him. Stand then and wait on further orders."

Some of the Called were relaxing and smiling. Valeria was much too suspicious for that. She had seen a white shape in the shadow of the portico, and felt Petra's eyes on her and the rest. This test was not what it seemed.

There were twice as many horses as candidates. Paulus went straight to the tallest, whose coat was like a gold coin and whose mane was a fall of white water. He was even showier than the hunters' horses outside of Mallia. He was also sickle-hocked and camped out behind, and that lovely big eye was as dull as dirt.

The others were slower to choose. Embry hesitated between a pretty sorrel and a plainer but steadier-looking bay. He chose the bay, with a glance at Paulus that told Valeria he had seen the point of the test.

Valeria made herself stop watching the others and make a decision for herself. Iliya had taken the ugliest of the horses, a hammerheaded brown mare whose eye was large and kind. She was well built except for the head, with a deep girth and sturdy legs. Valeria might have taken her if Iliya had not got there first.

The rest of the horses varied in size and looks, but for the most part they were alike in quality. As she debated the merits of one and then another, she could not help noticing that Batu stood apart from the others with a look almost of terror on his face.

She slipped from the line and went to stand beside him. "You haven't seen much of horses, have you?" she asked.

He shook his head. "The Call when it came was a terrible shock. I should never have listened to it, but it gave me no choice. Do you think, if I leave now, it will let me go?"

"Don't leave," she said. "It wanted you. It must have felt you were right for it, even if horses are strange to you. Is there any one here that makes you feel righter than the others?"

He started to shake his head again, but then he stood still. His eyes narrowed. "That one," he said, pointing with his chin at a stocky dun. "That feels…" His eyes widened. "She says—she says come here, don't be a fool, don't I know enough to listen when someone is talking to me?"

Valeria laughed. "Then you had better go, hadn't you?"

He hesitated. "But I still don't know—"

"She'll tell you," Valeria said.

The mare shook her head and stamped. Her impatience was obvious. Batu let go of his uncertainty just long enough to obey her.

The mare would look after him. Valeria turned back to her own testing. She was the last to choose. The others were already busy with brushes and curries and hoof picks.

She would do well to take her own advice. One horse on the end, another mare, looked as if she had been waiting patiently for the silly child to notice her. She was a bay with a star, stocky and cobby. If she had been grey, Valeria would have taken her for one of the white gods.

We are not all greys. The voice was as clear as if it had spoken aloud. There was a depth to it, a resonance, that shivered in Valeria's bones.

Horses never stooped to words if they could avoid it. The fact that the mare had done so was significant. Valeria bowed to her in apology and deep respect. She could feel Petra's approval on her back like a ray of sun. This was his mother, and she had chosen to be included with the common horses. It was unheard of for the Ladies to do such a thing, but they did as it best pleased them.

The mares had distinct preferences in grooming and deportment. Valeria knew better than to argue with them. When the mare's coat was gleaming and her mane and tail were brushed to silk, the groom who had held her brought a saddle and a bridle. She was even more particular about those.

If this had not been a test and therefore deadly serious, Valeria would have been enjoying herself.

She even had time while grooming and saddling to watch the drama at the other end of the line, where Paulus was discovering that he really, truly was not an imperial duke here.

He had stood for some time, holding the golden horse's lead, until he realized that none of the grooms would respond to his glances, his lifts of the chin, or even his snaps of the fingers. The one assigned to his horse had brought a grooming box and left it. Eventually it dawned on him that he was expected to groom his horse himself.

He drew himself up in high dudgeon. Before the words could burst out of him, he caught Kerrec's pale cold eye. Something there punctured his bladder to wonderful effect.

Valeria was dangerously close to approving of Kerrec just then. Paulus struggled almost as badly as Batu, but he struggled in silence. Batu, she noticed, was listening to his mare, and while he was awkward and often fumbled, he did not do badly at all. Paulus paid no attention to his horse's commentary, such as it was. The horse truly was not very bright.

At last they were all done. The horses were groomed and saddled, with the would-be riders waiting beside them. Kerrec walked down the line, pausing to tighten a girth here and tuck in a strap there. When he came to Paulus, he arched a brow at the groom. The man came in visible relief and, deftly and with dispatch, untacked and then retacked the horse.

Paulus' face went red and then white. When the groom handed the reins back to him with the bridle now properly adjusted and the saddle placed where it belonged, he held them in fingers that shook with spasms of pure rage.

Batu did not have to suffer a similar ignominy. Apart from a slight adjustment of the girth, Kerrec found nothing to question. The dun mare flicked a noncommittal ear. She was a good teacher and she knew it.

Valeria was the last to be inspected. She held her breath. Her stomach was tight.

Kerrec slid his finger under the girth and along the panel of the saddle. He tugged lightly at the crupper, which won him a warning slide of the ear from the mare. When he reached for the bridle, she showed him a judicious gleam of teeth.

He bowed to her and stepped back. Valeria found that gratifying, though it would have been more so if he had shown any sign of temper.

He seemed already to have forgotten her. "Now of course we will ride," he said. "One by one and on my order, you will do exactly as I say. Is that understood?"

Several had been ready to leap into the saddle and gallop off. They subsided somewhat sheepishly.

"Valens," said Kerrec. "Mount and stand."

Valeria started. She had been expecting to be called last as before. Naturally he had seen how she relaxed for what she expected to be a long wait, and had done what any self-respecting drill sergeant would do.

She scrambled herself together. He was tapping his foot, marking the moments of the delay. Even so, she took another half-dozen foot-taps to take a deep breath, center herself, and get in position to mount properly. The bay mare stood immobile except for the flick of an ear at some sound too faint for Valeria to hear.

Valeria mounted with as little fuss as possible, settled herself in the saddle, and waited. As usual Kerrec gave no sign of what he was thinking. "Walk," he said.

The test was simple to the level of insult. Walk, trot and canter around the grassy square in both directions. Turn and halt, proceed, turn and halt again. Dismount, stand, bow to the First Rider. Return to the line and watch each of the others undergo the same stupefyingly simple test.

Iliya, who was third to ride, was already bored with watching Valeria and Marcus. When he was asked to canter on, he accelerated to a gallop and then, just as his horse would have crashed into the wall, sat her down hard, pivoted her around the corner, and sent her off again in a sedate canter. His grin was wide and full of delighted mischief.

"Halt," said Kerrec. He did not raise his voice, but the small hairs rose on Valeria's neck.

The hammerheaded mare stopped as if she had struck the wall after all. Iliya nearly catapulted over her head.

"Dismount," said that cool, dispassionate voice. Iliya slid down with none of his usual grace. His knees nearly buckled. He caught at the saddle to steady himself.

"Return to your place," Kerrec said.

Iliya's face had gone green. He slunk back to his place in the line.

After that no one tried to brighten up the drab test with a display of horsemanship. Even Paulus followed instructions to the letter.

He was the last. When he had gone back to his place, Kerrec sent them to the stables to unsaddle, stall, and feed their horses. They were all on their guard now, knowing that every move was watched. It made them clumsy, which made them stumble. To add to the confusion, the horses responded to the riders' tension with tension of their own.

Marcus tripped over a handcart full of hay that Cullen had left in the stable aisle, and fell sprawling. Cullen burst out laughing. Marcus went for his throat.

Cullen reeled backwards. His hands flailed.

Almost too late, Valeria recognized the gesture. She flung herself flat.

Embry was not so fortunate. He had paused in forking hay into his horse's stall to watch the fight. The bolt of mage-fire caught him in the chest.

Valeria tried from the floor to turn it aside. So did Iliya from the stall across from Embry. They were both too slow.

Embry burned from the inside out. He was dead before his charred corpse struck the floor.

Marcus rolled away from Cullen. Cullen stood up slowly. His face, which had seemed so open and friendly, was stark white. The freckles stood out in it like flecks of ash.

"Someone fetch the First Rider," Paulus said. His voice was shaking. "Quickly!"

Valeria was ready to go, though she did not know if her legs would hold her up. The backlash of the mage-killing had left her with a blinding headache. When she tried to get up, she promptly doubled over in a fit of the dry heaves.

Someone held her up. She knew it was Batu, although she was too blind and sick to see him.

Kerrec's voice was like a cool cloth on her forehead. That was strange, because his words were peremptory. "All of you. Out."

Batu heaved her over his shoulder and carried her out. She lacked the energy to fight. By the time she came into the open air, she could see again, although the edges of things had an odd, blurred luminescence.

Batu set her down on the grass of the court. Dacius was doing the same for a thoroughly wilted Iliya. Paulus stood somewhat apart from them, as if they carried a contagion.

It was a long while before Kerrec came out of the stable. Two burly grooms followed. One led Cullen, the other Marcus. Their hands were bound, and there were horses' halters around their necks.

Dacius' breath hissed. Iliya and Batu did not know

what the collars meant. Paulus obviously did. So did Valeria.

She watched with the same sick fascination as when Kerrec executed justice on the man who tried to rape her. Just as she had then, she was powerless to move or say a word.

Master Nikos rode into the court through one of the side gates. A pair of riders followed him. Their stallions were snow-white with age and heavy with muscle. They walked like wrestlers into a ring, light and poised but massively powerful.

The Master halted. The riders flanked him.

There was no trial. There were no defenses spoken. Only the Master spoke, and his speech was brief.

"Discipline," he said, "is the first and foremost and only rule of our order. It must be so. There can be no other way."

He raised his hand. The grooms led the two captives to the center of the court and unbound their hands.

They did not move. Valeria saw that they could not. The binding on them was stronger than any rope or chain. It was magic, so powerful it made her head hum.

The riders rode from behind the Master. As they moved off to the right and the left, the stallions began a slow and cadenced dance with their backs to the condemned. The steps of it drew power from the earth. It came slow at first, in a trickle, but gradually it grew stronger.

The two on foot, the one who had killed and the

one whose loss of discipline had caused the other to kill, began to sway. Their faces were blank, but their eyes would haunt Valeria until she died.

The end was blindingly swift and blessedly merciful. The stallions left the ground in a surge of breathless power. For an instant they hovered at head-height. Then, swift as striking snakes, their hind legs lashed out.

Both skulls burst in a spray of blood. Not a drop of it touched those shining white hides. The stallions came lightly to earth again, dancing in place. The bodies fell twitching, but the souls were gone.

The stallions slowed to a halt and wheeled on their haunches to face the stunned and speechless survivors.

"Remember," said Master Nikos.

Chapter Eight

"And they said this test wasn't deadly." Iliya had stopped trying to vomit up his stomach, since there was nothing in it to begin with.

They had been sent back to the stable to finish what they had begun. Embry's body was gone. The only sign of it was a faint scorched mark on the stone paving of the aisle. The horses were still somewhat skittish, all but the bay Lady who had selected Valeria for the testing. It was done, her manner said. There was no undoing it. Hay was here, and grain would come if the human would stop retching and fetch it.

Her hardheaded common sense steadied Valeria. The testing would not end because two fools and an innocent had died.

"This is war," Batu said. "That was justice of the battlefield."

"It was barbaric," Dacius said. He had been even quieter than usual since Embry died, but something in him seemed to have let go. He flung down the cleaning rag with his saddle half-done. "This is supposed to be the School of Peace. What do they do in the School of War? Kill a recruit every morning and drink his blood for breakfast?"

"Take dancing lessons," Iliya said, hanging upside down from the opening to the hayloft. "Learn to play the flute." He dropped, somersaulting, to land somewhat shakily on his feet. "Don't you see? It's all turned around. War is peace. Peace is war. And if you let go and kill something—" He made a noise stomach-wrenchingly like the sound of a hoof shattering bone. "Off with your head!"

"How can you laugh?" Dacius demanded. "Did the mage-bolt addle your brain?"

"That depends on whether I have a brain to addle." Iliya snatched the broom out of Batu's hands and began to sweep the aisle. He swept the scorched spot over and over and—

Batu caught the broom handle above and below his hands, stilling it. Iliya looked up into the broad dark face. "We're all going to fail," he said.

"We are not." The words had burst out of Valeria. As soon as they were spoken, she wished they had not been. Everyone was staring at her.

She gritted her teeth and went on. "Do you know what I think? I think we're the strongest. The best mages, or we could be the best."

"How do you calculate that?" Paulus asked in his mincing courtier's accent.

"Cullen had no self-control," she answered, "but he was strong enough to kill. Marcus was trying to strangle him with more than hands. Embry thought he could stop a mage-bolt."

"It's far more likely we're the idiots' division," Paulus said with a twist of the lip. "Three of us died for nothing before the first day was half over. Does any of you begin to guess how much more difficult the rest of the testing will be? We couldn't even keep the eight together for a day."

His logic was all too convincing, but Valeria could not make herself believe it. "The strongest can be the weakest. It's a paradox of magic."

"I know that," he said. "Which school of mages were you Called from? Beastmasters?"

"Apprentice mages can be Called?" That she had not known. "Were you—"

"I was to go to the Augurs' College," Paulus said as if she should be awed. "So were you a Beastmaster?"

"No," she said.

"Ah," he said. He shrugged, almost a shudder. "It doesn't matter, does it? We'll all leave as Cullen did— in a sack."

She had been thinking of him as older than the

others. He carried himself as if he were a man fully grown, afflicted with the company of children. She realized now that he was terribly scared, and that he was no older than she.

It did not make her like him any better. It did soften her tone slightly as she said, "Stop that. If this magic is discipline, then part of discipline is teaching ourselves to carry on past fear."

"I'm not afraid!"

"Don't lie to yourself," Dacius said. "We're all afraid. We thought we'd learn to ride horses, work a few magics and after a little while we'd be in the Court of the Dance, weaving the threads of time. It wasn't going to be terribly hard. The worst pain we'd suffer would be bruises to our backsides when we fell off a horse."

"That's absurd," Paulus snapped. "*I* never thought it would be easy. You commoners, you hear the pretty stories and think it's as simple as a song. It's the greatest power there is."

"I heard," said Batu, "that no one who wants it can have it. Wanting taints it. Power corrupts."

"You have to want the magic," Valeria said, "and the horses. That's a fire in the belly. A rider can't rule, that's the law. He serves and protects. He's no one's master."

"You recite your lessons well," Paulus said. "The truth is what you saw out there. It's death to lose control. That's what it comes to. Discipline or death."

"Then we had better be disciplined," said Valeria.

* * *

Dinner was as much water as any of them could drink. It was pure and cold, like melted snow.

"Water of the fountain," Paulus said as he tasted it. For the first time he sounded capable of something other than scorn.

Valeria could taste the heart of the Mountain in that water, fire under ice. It satisfied her hunger so well that she did not even think of food.

Sleep struck her abruptly as she got up from the table. She staggered up the short flight of stairs and into the sleeping room. She was just awake enough to kick off her boots before she fell into bed.

The dream was waiting for her. It was full of white horses as always, but for the first time since the Call came, there were riders on their backs.

She recognized the place from a hundred stories. It was a high-ceilinged hall somewhat larger than the open court in which Marcus and Cullen had died. Tall windows let in white light. At the end, framed by a vaulted arch, the Mountain gleamed through the tallest and widest window that Valeria had ever imagined, with glass so pure that not a bubble marred its surface.

The floor of the hall was raked white sand. Pillars of marble and gold rimmed it, holding up a succession of galleries. Three rose on either side. In the lowest gallery opposite the Mountain, in a box by themselves, three Augurs stood in their white robes and conical caps. A secretary sat just behind them with tablets and stylus.

Under the Mountain was a single gallery. Draperies hung from it, crimson and gold. In the back of it was the banner of imperial Aurelia, golden sun and silver moon interlaced under a crown of stars, gleaming against a crimson field. On either side of it hung two others. One was luminous blue, with a silver stallion dancing against the unmistakable conical shape of the Mountain. The other was the golden sunburst on crimson of the imperial house.

This was the Hall of the Dance, where the white gods danced the patterns of fate and time. In her dream they were entering as they had come to the place of the testing, eight of them in a double line, walking in that slow and elevated cadence which was distinct to their kind.

She recognized the riders' faces. Master Nikos led one line, First Rider Kerrec the other. Rider Andres rode behind the Master. She would learn the others' names as the testing went on. They would be her partners and companions when—if—she passed the testing.

Someone was sitting in the royal box under the gleam of the Mountain. She expected to see the emperor as he was depicted on his coins, a stern hawk-faced man with a close-clipped beard. Instead it was a young woman with a face as cleanly carved as an image in ivory. She was dressed very plainly in a rider's coat and breeches, and her hair was in a single plait behind her. The elaborate golden throne on which she sat seemed gaudy and common against that unflawed simplicity.

Only after Valeria had examined her thoroughly did she find the emperor. He stood behind the throne with his hand on the young woman's shoulder, dressed in rider's clothes as well. He was younger than Valeria had imagined, and less stern. His hair was still black, although his beard was iron-grey. His eyes were warm, smiling into hers. Magic sang in him like the notes of a harp.

He reminded Valeria of Kerrec. It was certainly not his warmth or the smile in his eyes—grey eyes, not as pale as Kerrec's, but still unusual in this dark-eyed country. Take off the beard and the smile and thirty years, and there was the First Rider to the life.

Could it be…

The emperor had one living son, and he was half-barbarian, which Kerrec certainly was not. Another, legitimate son, the heir, had died years ago, leaving his sister to take his place. Kerrec must be related in some convoluted degree, like every noble and half the commoners in Aurelia.

In the shadows behind the emperor, a man was standing. Valeria could not quite make out his face. He was taller and wider in the shoulders than the emperor, but somehow he seemed stunted. Something was wrong with him, something that crept out toward the emperor and surrounded him with a flicker of darkness and a flash of sudden scarlet.

In the hall below them, the riders began the Dance. She could almost understand the patterns. They were following the skeins of destiny, tracing them in the raked earth of the floor. The air hummed subtly, and the light began to bend. Time was shifting, flowing. The stallions swam through it like fish through water. The riders both guided and were guided by them. The magic ruled them even as they ruled it.

With no sense of transition, she had become part of the Dance. The stallion she had dreamed before, the young one with the faint dappling, carried her through the movements.

She simply sat on his back. When the time came, she would guide him, but in this dream he was her teacher. There was a deep rightness in it. This, she was made for.

When the bell rang before dawn, she was awake and refreshed. The others woke groaning or cursing and dragged themselves out. There was no breakfast, not even water, but Valeria did not miss it. The water of the fountain was still in her. Batu, she noticed, seemed at ease. The others were pale and hollow-eyed.

They had their orders from the night before. There were horses to feed, stalls to clean. When they were done, they had to find their way to a certain room within the school. It was middling large and middling high, and filled with desks and benches. Each desk held a stack of wax tablets and a cup of sharpened styli.

The rest of the eights were there already. None of them had lost a single member, let alone three. They drew away from the latecomers, whispering among themselves.

Valeria exchanged glances with the others. She lifted her chin. So did Paulus. The other three followed their lead. They marched boldly down to the front of the room and took the seats that had been left for them there, separated somewhat from the rest.

Valeria ran a finger over the tablet in front of her. It was a smooth slab of wood coated with wax, blank and ready to be written on.

She had not expected to find herself in a schoolroom, even though this place was called a school. All the schooling, she had thought, would be in the stable and on the riding field. It was odd to think of book-learning here.

She looked up from the tablet to find Kerrec at the lectern. He had come in so quietly that she had not even heard him. Neither had any of the others, she noticed. The buzz of conversation was rising to a roar.

He cleared his throat. The silence was instant and complete. "Today we test knowledge," he said. "If any of you is unable to read or write, go now with Rider Andres. You will be tested elsewhere."

"And failed?" asked Paulus.

There were a few gasps at his daring. Kerrec

answered as coolly as ever. "No one fails for simple lack of skill."

"Then what do we fail for?"

"Lack of understanding," said Kerrec. He looked away from Paulus, dismissing him.

One by one, a dozen of the Called rose, clattering among the benches, and made their way toward Rider Andres. Batu was not one of them, which surprised Valeria somewhat. Iliya was. He glanced back before he passed through the door. He was openly scared, but he grinned through it and saluted them.

When the last of them was gone, Kerrec scanned the faces of those who were left. Then, like any other schoolmaster, he said crisply, "Tablet. Stylus."

Valeria's schoolmaster had been her mother. Kerrec might be stern, but Morag had been formidable. She would have asked far more difficult questions than his. "What is the school? When and by whom was it founded? Who are the white gods?"

But as with the test of riding the day before, Valeria began to sense that there was something hiding beneath the childlike simplicity. There was a pattern in the questions.

She looked down at the lines of her brief answers. *The School is the academy of horse magic. It was founded in the year that Aurelia was founded, by the first emperor. The white gods are the firstborn children of time and fate.*

The flow of questions went on. She filled one tablet, both sides, and went on to the next. Her hand was writing without troubling her mind overmuch. He was not asking anything that she did not know. As the questions advanced, they needed more time and longer answers. She wrote well and quickly, and was finished, mostly, long before he asked the next question.

While she waited, her stylus began to wander of its own accord. She watched without trying to stop it.

It was tracing the pattern of the Dance that she had seen in her dream. Somehow it seemed to relate to the questions Kerrec was asking, although she could not see exactly how.

It was a maze, she realized as it grew on the tablet. Within an oval boundary, paths crossed and recrossed on their way to an open center.

As she stared at it, she glimpsed flickers of memory or dream. She saw the emperor's face and the face of the woman on the throne, and behind them another man. He had been a shadow in her vision before, but now she saw him clearly.

There was a distinct likeness among them, although the stranger was taller and his face was blunter, and his hair was gold-shot brown rather than glossy black. That must be the bastard son, the half-barbarian. On another path, which crossed theirs repeatedly, she saw Euan Rohe and the hostages of the Caletanni.

Those paths were dark where they crossed. On one she saw the emperor dead, on another a figure that she recognized with a shock as Kerrec lay broken on a stone table. On yet a third, Euan Rohe hung from a gallows, his naked body pierced with a hundred wounds.

She wrenched her mind away from those horrors, back toward the rim of the maze. The young stallion stood there as if he had been waiting for her to notice him. His white calm soothed her.

"What is this?"

Valeria started so violently that the stylus leaped from her hand and fell with a clatter. The sound of it seemed deafening, but none of the Called looked up. They were all scribbling studiously.

Kerrec bent over her. He had the tablet in his hand, the one with the maze. "Come with me," he said.

When she stood up, that did attract attention. Kerrec's glare quelled even the boldest of them. Somehow, while she was lost in her maundering, another rider had come to stand at the lectern. "Explain," he said, "how one fits a saddle properly to a broader back."

Valeria could have answered that if she had not so obviously failed the test by losing interest in the questions. She tried to hold her head up as she followed Kerrec through the door behind the lectern.

The door led to a narrow hallway and then to a small room that must be a study. It had a worktable and a pair of stools and an ancient and visibly comfortable chair. Books and scrolls and tablets lay on every available shelf and surface. Its single window looked out into the court where Cullen and Marcus had died.

Master Nikos was sitting at the worktable, frowning at what looked like a book of accounts. He looked up in some surprise at their arrival.

"Your pardon," Kerrec said, "but this couldn't wait." He set the tablet in front of the Master.

Master Nikos studied it for some time. Kerrec stood at ease like a soldier. Valeria tried to imitate him, but her knees kept wanting to collapse under her.

This was it. This was the end. She would be revealed as a female and sent away in disgrace.

After a terribly long while, Master Nikos looked up. His frown had changed, although Valeria could not have explained exactly how. "Where did you see this?" he asked.

His voice was mild, almost gentle. Valeria answered as steadily as she could. "I dreamed it," she said, and belatedly added, "sir."

His lips twitched very slightly. "Did you? When?"

"Last night, sir," she said.

His brows went up. "Indeed. Tell me. When you drew this, could you see anything other than the lines on the tablet?"

"Faces, you mean?" She nodded. She was not relaxing, but she was less terrified than she had been.

This was not going the way of any punishment she had ever had. "I saw people. And horses—stallions."

"Tell me," he said.

She did the best she could. The Master and the rider listened without comment. Once she had put it in words, it sounded weak and foolish.

"That's all I can remember," she said at the end of it. "It's the water, isn't it? It gives dreams."

"You recognize the water?" Master Nikos asked.

"We all do," she said. "It tastes the way the Mountain feels."

"Feels?" the Master echoed her.

Her cheeks had gone hot. "I know I'm not saying it well. Words don't seem to fit. I can't—"

"No," said the Master. "You can't." He glanced at Kerrec. "This one broke through faster than any I've seen. Even you took somewhat longer."

Kerrec astounded her with a smile that made him look remarkably human. Of course it was not aimed at her. "I was still floundering when Petra kicked me into the wall and knocked some sense into my head."

"Broke your arm, too, as I recall," the Master said.

"Oh, no," said Kerrec. "That was pure stupidity. I tripped over my own feet and snapped my wrist." He rubbed it, flexing the hand as if it still remembered pain, and shook his head. "I was a terrible combination—both clever and arrogant. Petra dealt with me as I deserved."

"They will do that," said Master Nikos. "So, what of this one?"

Kerrec froze into his grim and familiar self again. "This is the one the Lady chose."

Master Nikos' brows went up. "Ah, so. Well then. We won't waste time with any more of the lesser testing. Is any of the others fit to partner him?"

Kerrec frowned in thought. "Not really, no. There is one, but he needs every one of the minor tests. Unless…"

"Yes?" the Master prompted when he did not go on.

"Unless we ask the Lady."

"You know what they think of all our testing."

Kerrec almost broke into another smile. "Humans are idiots. That's a given. Will you ask her or shall I?"

"I'll ask," the Master said. "You go."

Kerrec bowed. He barely glanced at Valeria. "Come," he said.

Chapter Nine

Valeria was glad to be out of the Master's study, but in the hallway she stopped short. Kerrec was nearly to the stair before he realized that she was not trotting obediently behind him. He halted and turned.

"Listen," she said. "Do what he said. Don't waste time. I've failed. Just let me go. I'll slip out quietly and not bother anyone."

Kerrec seemed honestly surprised. "What makes you think you've failed?"

"Haven't I? I was woolgathering when I was supposed to be answering questions. Isn't discipline paramount? Didn't men die yesterday because they had none?"

Kerrec drew in a breath. He was probably praying

for patience. "Come with me," he said. "This isn't a thing to be shouted down hallways."

She could hardly argue with that. He turned again, and she followed him down the stair. The courtyard was occupied by a group of riders on white stallions, but they were absorbed in their exercises.

Kerrec stopped under the colonnade. Over his shoulder she could see the horses transcribing patterns that seemed random but struck her with a deep resonance. Every dance, even the most casual, was keyed to the rhythm of the world.

She had to tear herself away from the pattern and focus on Kerrec. Even he was different. He was brimming with magic. It gleamed along his edges and coiled in his eyes.

He was a master of the art. His discipline was impeccable. His mastery...

"It's beautiful," she said.

She had not meant to say it aloud. She braced for his reprimand, but he barely even frowned. "There is no greater beauty," he said, "and you can see it. Do you really believe you've failed?"

"You pulled me out of the testing," she said.

"Because you were done with it." He fixed her with a steady silver stare. "You passed. You saw through to the pattern. The rest will be plagued with simplicity until they either do the same or fail. You have no need for that. There is one thing we must still determine, and one last test which you'll share with the rest of the Called. Otherwise there's nothing to discover."

She bit her lip. There was another thing, but he knew it already. If he was not going to mention it, then she certainly was not about to.

"What—" she said. She brought her voice under control. "What do you need to determine?"

"One thing," he said. "Come."

Valeria stood under the gallery in the Hall of the Dance. The bay Lady was with her. A groom had brought the mare after Kerrec left Valeria there with a simple order: "Stand and watch."

The Lady was neither saddled nor bridled. She was there as Valeria was, to watch. She was also standing guard, though against what, she did not see fit to tell Valeria.

As endless as that day had seemed, it was still short of noon. The morning exercises went on in the hall as they did in the riding courts. Somewhat to Valeria's surprise, the horses in the hall when she came were not the oldest and most powerful of the stallions but the young ones, still dark or dappled, who were just learning the ways of the Dance.

They worked in fours and eights. Sometimes there were a dozen in the hall, more often eight. While Valeria stood beside the Lady, watching and wondering what she was supposed to see, four left and four came in. Kerrec rode one of them.

Kerrec was even more beautiful on horseback than she remembered. Here in the heart of his magic, he had no need to hide what he was. He could show himself for a master.

On foot he was infuriating. She could not decide whether to hate him or simply despise him. As she stood in the hall, she decided that she was in love.

The others rode well, and it was lovely to watch them. Kerrec was perceptibly better.

Out of nowhere in particular, Valeria remembered one of the questions that Kerrec had asked shortly before she stopped listening. "What are the levels of mastery within the school?"

She could see the tablet in front of her and the stylus digging into the wax, writing the answers.

First, mastery of animals. That was the simplest, and came in childhood. The Called were always masters of beasts, although few of the order of Beastmasters were actually Called. When the Called came to the school, if they passed the testing, they learned the first of the arts, the art of riding horses.

Second, mastery of men. Through the power of the stallions they learned to rule and guide. They could be princes and kings if their law allowed it, but the stallions cared nothing for such things. Men who cared too much were released from the school. Hunger for power had no place on the Mountain.

Third, mastery of the elements. Earth and air, fire and water, yielded to them as beasts and men had. The stallions were like a burning glass, concentrating their power. They were great mages, those riders who rose so high.

Fourth and highest, mastery of time and the Dance. Few riders ever reached this eminence. Master Nikos was one. Kerrec was another. These, in union with the stallions, could walk in the past and foresee the future. Tradition had it that once in a great while, in the cusp of destiny, one of them could shift the tides of time and make them run according to his will.

Valeria watched the young stallions move in their simple patterns. They were not raising great powers. They were students as she was, and only a few of them would come to the great Dance.

They were dancing a pattern that almost made sense. It had the emperor in it, and the young woman who must be the emperor's heir, and the taller, fairer young man who looked both like and unlike them. Valeria glimpsed another face, which at first she thought was Euan Rohe's, but this was older and harsher. It was his father's, maybe.

The landscape of her vision was dark, lit with fire. A stone loomed against the stars, standing alone on a barren hilltop. Robed figures gathered in a circle around it. She smelled blood, strong and cloying, and the sweet stink of death.

A tattered thing flapped in the wind, wound around the top of the stone. It was a banner, a legionary standard with its device of sun and moon. Then she realized that there was something inside it. A man's body was wrapped in the standard. His hands and feet were spiked to the stone. Blood dripped slowly, glistening in starlight.

Sunlight stabbed her skull. The Hall of the Dance was full of it. The bay Lady stood between her and the darkness.

The young stallions were still dancing, but Valeria could not stomach any more of it. Although she had been told to stand and watch, she had done as much of that as she could. She needed the sky, and the unclouded daylight.

The Lady knelt. Valeria dragged her leg over the broad back. The bay mare rose in a smooth motion and carried her out.

Valeria lay on the grass. The sky went on forever. She heard the mare grazing close by, and felt the rhythmic beat of hooves on the earth as in each court, the stallions danced.

That rhythm ruled the world. The stars sang it. It sent the moon through its phases. The sun rose and set within it.

It was as powerful as anything that was, and yet it was unspeakably fragile. In an instant it could shatter, falling into darkness and silence.

"Something wants to destroy you," she said to Kerrec.

She did not particularly care where he was. He could hear her, she knew that.

As it happened, he was sitting on the grass beside her, almost under the bay mare's belly. "We've always had enemies," he said.

"I know. I've heard stories. The Red Magicians. The cult of the Nameless. Half the nobles in the court of any given reign."

He snorted. "More than half in this reign. We're superannuated, they declare. Our powers have eroded, if they ever actually existed. We're a worthless collection of mountebanks on fat white ponies."

She sat up and stared at him. "They actually say that?"

"That and worse," he said. "I don't suppose you were ever tested for the Augurs' College."

"That would be Paulus," she said.

"Of course it would be," said Kerrec. As usual, she could not tell what he was thinking. He masked himself too well.

She could see why he might, if he was seeing and feeling such things as she had since she came here. She was only a child, untrained and hopelessly confused. It must be overwhelming to be a master.

He stood and reached down, pulling her to her feet. The earth was unsteady under her, but his hand was strong. As soon as she could stand on her own, he let her go. "Your testing is done until tomorrow," he said. "Apart from your duties in the stable, your time is yours to do with as you please."

"What if I want to go back with the others?"

"You could do that," he said. "It's not necessary."

"I think it might be," she said.

He lifted a shoulder in a shrug. "As you please," he said.

But she did not leave quite yet. "Did you find what you were looking for?" she asked.

"You know we did."

She hardly knew what she knew, but she nodded. "Is it that overwhelming for you? Or is it worse?"

He offered no answer. She had not expected one. That, like so much else in this place, was for her to discover.

The rest of the Called were still in the schoolroom answering questions of deliberately infuriating simplicity. Valeria slipped in as quietly as she could, found a desk and a set of blank tablets, and let herself drown in words.

They were only words. She made sure of that. She had had enough magic to last her for a while.

Chapter Ten

The School of War occupied the northeastern corner of the fortress. It had its own gates and its own staff of guards and servants, even its own stables. There were no white gods there, only ordinary horses, and precious few stallions.

The hostages had been delighted to discover that once they were admitted to the school, they were no longer treated like battle captives. They were students like all the others. They shared a room in the dormitory, with as much freedom to come and go as any of the offspring of imperial nobles and rich merchants for whom this place was an entry into officers' rank in the emperor's armies.

"Remember," Euan Rohe had told his kinsmen before they came here. "They want to civilize us, which means carve us into puppets. Let them teach us everything that we can learn—the better to use it against them when the Great War comes."

They were good men, his kinsmen. Every one was a member of his own warband, sworn to him by oaths of blood and stone. The arrogant imperials had made no effort to select princes of opposing tribes, or even to discover what enmities there might be among their enemies. That, the One God willing, would be their undoing.

The lessons so far were ghastly enough. It was beneath a prince's dignity to play the slave to a stable full of hairy, farting beasts, but if the war demanded it, then he would do it. The riding was painful but slightly less insulting. As for the handful of hours each morning in a box of a room with tablet and stylus, learning to read and write the imperial language…

"We didn't come here for that," Gavin said in disgust. "These scratchings on wax stain our souls."

"They help our cause," Euan said. "They're not the runes that only priests can touch and live. These will gain us knowledge we might never have had otherwise. They give us power."

"They give us corruption," Gavin muttered, but under Euan's glare he subsided. He submitted to instruction, and learned his letters, although he flatly refused to form them into his name. He knew better than to snare his soul.

Euan did not tell these loyal kinsmen that he

already knew how to read. His father had insisted that he be taught. The old man was wise when he was sober, and he could see farther than most.

Letters, for a while, would be Euan's secret. He pretended to struggle as the others did, and watched and waited.

He did not have to wait long. The message came through one of the grooms, a pallid young creature with a perpetually startled expression. He looked flat astonished now, but he spoke the words he had been given without a slip or a stammer.

"Tomorrow as the sun touches noon," was Euan's answer. "Outside the walls. Follow the trail I set."

The boy bowed. He did not argue, as the recipient of the message almost certainly would.

He would come to the summons. He would not be able to help himself.

Euan Rohe walked openly out of the School of War, testing for once and for all the limits of his position there. No one gave him a second glance. He stood outside the high grey walls and took a long breath. It was not free air, but it was as close as he would come until this game was over.

Hunter's instincts came back quickly in spite of more than a year in cities or under imperial guard. Euan took in the lie of the land, chose his track, and set about leaving a trail that another hunter could follow.

* * *

The place that Euan found was pleasant, a clearing in the forest that robed the Mountain's knees. The great stands of trees were almost bare of undergrowth, but the clearing was carpeted with grass and flowers.

When he first came there, he had thought the flowers much thicker than they were. Then as he walked onto the grass, all the white blossoms took flight. They were butterflies.

He sat in the midst of them and sipped water from the bottle he had brought with him. It was still cold from the stream farther down the Mountain. He had a bit of bread in his bag, and cheese and dried apples, but he was not hungry yet.

The one he waited for arrived just after the sun touched the point of noon. He made no secret of his passage through the trees. That was deliberate, and might be construed as an insult.

Euan stayed where he was, propped on his elbow in the grass, with the water bottle in his hand. The other man rode on horseback. His mount was white, but it was not one of the gods from the school. Euan was interested to discover that he could tell the difference.

The man on the horse was small and dark and sharp-featured for a Caletanni, but he was too tall and fair to be an imperial. He looked like what he was, half-blood, with his brown hair and freckled skin. He wore his hair in a long plait, which was considered quite daring in the imperial city, but he went clean-shaven. He was not daring enough to affect the full fashion.

"Prince," Euan greeted him.

"Prince," he replied, swinging down off the horse with grace that few Caletanni could match. He tied up the reins and left the beast to graze, and came to stand over Euan.

"Good of you to come alone," Euan said. "Or is there an army on the other side of the hill?"

"No army," said the prince from Aurelia. He had a suitably imperial name, but the one he claimed in front of Euan was Gothard. "There is a company of guards not far from here. Do I need to summon them?"

"Not yet," said Euan. He gestured expansively. "Come, sit. Be free of my hall."

Gothard was not amused. "None of this is yours," he said, "even after you've won the war. Remember the bargain. Aurelia's throne belongs to me."

Euan smiled his most exasperating smile. "I won't forget," he said.

Gothard made no secret of his doubts, but he refrained from putting them into words. He said instead, "So. You're in the school. How goes it? Have you found a rider yet?"

"Maybe," said Euan. "It's only the third day since I came here. Do all your caravans march at a snail's pace?"

"Only when time is of the essence," Gothard said sourly. "Gods. You should have been there a month ago. Tomorrow is the Midsummer Dance. It's a bare three months until the Great Dance."

Euan did not comment on the pagan oath. It was a habit, one could suppose, from living with imperials. "I'm well aware of the time," he said. His voice shifted to the half-chant of an imperial schoolboy's recitation. "We have to be in Aurelia on the autumn equinox, when the emperor celebrates his feast of renewal, four eights of years on the throne of this empire. The white gods will leave the Mountain for that, as they have not done in a hundred years, and dance in the court of the palace. That will open the gates of time and allow us—the One God willing—to impose our will on what will be. Then the emperor will die and his heir be disposed of, and a new reign will come to Aurelia."

"If it can be so simple and so tidy," said Gothard, clearly annoyed by the mockery, "we'll thank every god there is, whether he be One or many."

"I'll do my part," Euan said with studied patience. "I'll find the rider who can be persuaded—one way or another—to subvert the Dance. You have enough to do. You've no need to fret over that."

"None of it is worth a clipped farthing if you fail."

"There now," drawled Euan. "I wouldn't say that. If we can't control the Dance once it's away from the Mountain's power, we can certainly corrupt it. We'll have our war, one way or the other."

"There will be war," said Gothard, "but who will

win it? The Dance can determine that—but only a rider can rule the Dance."

"It will be done," Euan said. "And then you will have your part to do, and so will others. In the end, we'll win the war."

"I envy you your surety," Gothard said.

Euan smiled sunnily. "I'm a raving barbarian and you're an effete imperial. Of course I'm a blind optimist. You'll be my voice of reason, my wise philosopher."

Truly Gothard had no humor. He was fast reaching the limits of his temper. Euan waited to see if he would say something ill-advised, but instead he froze.

Euan heard it a moment after he did. A hoof chinked softly against rock. A bit jingled even more softly.

Gothard's grey horse had been standing still, head down and hind foot cocked, asleep. At the sound of another horse's passing, he threw up his head.

Gothard drew a complex symbol in the air. Euan saw the shape of it limned in dark light. His skin prickled.

Two riders rode into the clearing. They were mounted on white gods. Through the veil of Gothard's sorcery, the creatures' coats glowed like clouds over the moon. The men were shadows encasing a core of light.

Euan sat perfectly still. Gothard's horse stood like a marble image. Only Gothard seemed at ease. He was alert but calm. Euan had understood that Gothard was a fair journeyman of one of the innumerable schools of imperial magic, but this was a little more than journeyman's work.

The riders never saw them. One of the horses might have cast a glance in their direction, but if it did, it did not sound the alarm. They rode on through the clearing and away.

The sun had shifted visibly when at last Gothard let go the spell. He sagged briefly and swayed, then thrust himself upright. He had to draw a deep breath before he could speak. "It's safe," he said. "You can move."

Euan stretched until his bones cracked, then rotated his head on his neck. His muscles were locked tight. He released them one by one, a slow dance that Gothard watched with undisguised fascination.

Euan let his dance stretch out somewhat longer than it strictly needed. When he was as supple as he could hope to be, he was on his feet. "You're a better sorcerer than I thought," he said. "I salute you." He followed the word with the action, the salute of a warrior to a champion.

Gothard accepted it with little enough grace. Euan left him there, sitting next to his motionless horse, and slipped away into the shelter of the trees.

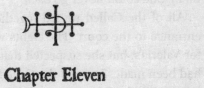

Chapter Eleven

The last test of the Called fell three days before Midsummer. It was the only public test. Those who passed could regard it as an initiation into the life of a rider. Those who failed had the right to vanish into the crowd and be mercifully and formally forgotten.

A great number of people were gathered in the largest of the riding courts, seated in tiers above the floor of raked sand. All the riders were there, and all the candidates who had passed this test in their own day. Students from the School of War, guests and servants filled all the rest of the benches.

Some of the Called had family there. One whole flock of peacocks belonged to Paulus. Valeria saw how pale he was and felt almost sorry for him. She at least did not have to fail in front of a legion of brothers and uncles and cousins.

That gave her an unexpected pang. Her family would never see her here, or know whether she succeeded or failed. Whatever happened, she had left them. She could never go back.

All of the Called waited together in the western entrance to the court. The eights were intact except for Valeria's, but she suspected that certain decisions had been made. Some of the Called had a drawn and haunted look. Others seemed dulled somehow, as if the magic had drained out of them.

Only a few still had a light in them. Some actually shone brighter. Iliya was one. So was Batu. And, she saw with some incredulity, Paulus.

She could not see herself, to know what the others must see. She felt strong. She had slept last night without dreams, and been awake when the bell rang at dawn. Now at full morning she was ready for whatever was to come.

Supper last night had been water from the fountain and nothing else. There had been no breakfast, but she was not hungry at all. She was dizzy and sated with the air she breathed.

She smiled at Batu who stood next to her. He smiled shakily back. "Luck," he said.

"Luck," she replied.

* * *

The hum and buzz of the crowd went suddenly quiet. As before, Valeria felt them before she saw them. The stallions were coming.

This time no one rode them. They were saddled and bridled, walking beside their grooms.

Her heart began to beat hard. There was not a sound in that place except the soft thud of hooves on sand, and now and then a stallion's snort or the jingle of bit or bridle as he shook his head at a fly.

There were eight of them, as always. She had not seen these eight before. They were massive, their coats snow-white. These were old stallions, how old she was almost afraid to imagine. Their eyes were dark and unfathomably wise. The tides of time ran in them. With every step, they trod out the pattern of destiny.

She had an overwhelming desire to fling herself flat at their feet. All that kept her upright was the realization that if she did that, she would not be able to get up again. She stood with the rest of the Called, wobble-kneed but erect, and waited to be told what to do.

Kerrec had appeared while the stallions arranged themselves in a half circle in the center of the court. He called the candidates together in eights, with the broken eight last.

The test was as deceptively simple as all the rest. Each man was to select a horse, mount and ride.

"Ride how?" asked a gangling boy from the second eight.

"That is the test," Kerrec said.

By now they knew better than to ask him to explain. They exchanged glances. Some rolled their eyes. Others were praying, or maybe incanting spells.

Valeria did not envy the first rider in the slightest. He selected himself, shrugged rather desperately and left his fellows and walked out onto the sand.

The crowd's silence deepened. The stallions stood unmoving. They did not fidget as ordinary horses would. Their stillness was monumental, rooted in the earth under their feet.

The young man stood in front of them. His head turned from side to side. He was blind, Valeria thought. He could not see what he was supposed to see.

When he moved, his steps were slow. His fists clenched and unclenched. He wavered between two nearly identical white shapes. They looked like brothers, with the same arched nose and little lean ears.

His choice was visibly random. He seized the rein from the groom and flung himself into the saddle.

The stallion did not move a muscle. At first the rider heaved a sigh of relief, but when he asked the stallion to advance, his answer was the same total stillness as before.

A titter ran through the crowd. The rider flushed. His body tensed. Just as he would have dug heels into the broad white sides, the stallion erupted.

The rider went off in the first leap. He landed well,

rolling out of reach of the battering hooves. The crowd applauded that, but he did not stay for the accolade. He was gone as he was allowed to do, vanished and forgotten.

The second rider could not choose at all. He turned and fled. The third chose reasonably well, mounted gracefully, and plodded a lifeless circle before he conceded defeat.

Valeria had lost count before any of the would-be riders managed a ride worth noticing. The crowd had been by turns amazed and amused, but even devoted followers of the art were glazing over.

Then a candidate mounted and rode—really rode.

He was a wiry little creature with the pinched face of a starveling child, but he was light and quick on his feet. In the saddle he blossomed. The stallion danced for him, a stately pavane that won a murmur of approval from the benches.

Valeria noticed an important thing. It was the stallion, not the rider, who danced. The rider had the sense to sit perfectly still and not interfere. His expression lingered in Valeria's memory. He was half terrified and half exalted.

Three more received the gift of the dance, out of three eights. The winnowing was fast and merciless. No one died, but one broke an arm and another left with a bloodied nose.

Then there were the five of them, the broken eight,

who were either the best or the worst of them all. The entrance that had been so crowded seemed echoing and empty. The four who had passed the testing so far had drawn to one side, watching with a combination of smugness that their ordeal was done and sympathy for those who had still to undergo it.

People were whispering in the crowd, telling one another why this eight was missing three. Their attention had sharpened.

Paulus went first. He had the most to lose and the least patience to spare. He walked straight toward the tallest of the stallions, but halfway there, he veered aside. When he halted, he was face-to-face with the least lovely of them, a comically long-nosed, long-eared creature with a mottled pink muzzle and a spreading pink stain around one eye.

Paulus' lip curled. At the same time his hand crept out and came to rest on the heavy crested neck. A small sigh escaped him, as if something inside him had let go. He mounted as punctiliously as always. The stallion shook his mane and pawed once, then gathered himself and rose in an extravagant and breathtakingly beautiful leap.

Valeria felt the lightness, the sheer joy of that dance. It was perfectly startling and perfectly wonderful. Paulus rode it in terror and delight, until he had to laugh or burst into pieces.

The rest of them rode on that lightness. Batu, then Iliya added their own steps to the dance.

Then there were two. Dacius came forward with

steady steps, but the magic had passed him by. The stallions turned their backs on him.

He did not seem crushed as most of the others had been. He shrugged and sighed, and bowed to the stallions and then to the crowd. They ushered him out with a rhythmic stamping of feet.

Valeria stood alone while the court fell slowly silent. It was even harder to be last than first. Every eye was on her. Every face was expectant. Would she pass? Would she fail? How devastating would it be if she did?

The stallions had turned to face her. They were waiting as the spectators were, but they must know how she would choose. They were the living incarnation of foreknowledge.

She had a brief, wild urge to simply ask them, but that passed. None of them in particular called to her as the Lady had. They were all Great Ones, gods among gods. Any one would be pleased to show her the full force of the magic for which she was born.

She stood in front of them and offered herself. She did not know which to take. Surely if they were willing to carry her, they could decide which of them was most inclined to do it.

Their amusement tingled in her skin. They found her impudence refreshing. She had not meant it to be any such thing, but gods had their own way of looking at human behavior.

After a moment, one of them came forward. He was one of the brothers with whom the first candidate had failed. His eye was kind, in its way. He invited her to take the rein and mount.

She did as she was told. If he pitched her into the crowd, she would let him. It was his right to do with her whatever he pleased.

He danced for her. It was a portion of the Great Dance, the pattern that opened the wall between worlds. He stopped short of that, with great care, but she felt how close he came. He asked nothing of her but that she be still, and that she learn. This was her magic, he was telling her. This was her place and her power.

The end was a dramatic departure from the Dance, an exuberant coda. He rose as his cousin had for Paulus, straight up on his hind legs, and leaped. Eight times he did it, and each time the crowd gasped in awe.

He came down lightly, dancing in place. Valeria had given up any pretense to grace. She clung blindly to his mane and tried to remember how to breathe. He was breathing hard himself. Even for a god, lifting that much flesh and bone through so many leaps was a powerful effort.

It dawned on her slowly that people were screaming and stamping and yelling the name she had taken. She did not see why they were so excited. She had done nothing but cling for dear life while the stallion danced.

She slid from his back and stood on shaking legs. The others who had passed were all around her, slapping her on the back, cuffing her until her ears rang. She was too

weak to fend them off. They swept her clean off her feet
and heaved her onto their shoulders.

The riders were coming down from the benches.
Kerrec was on the sand already, with Master Nikos
close behind him. She wanted to be on her feet, one
of many, not riding on their shoulders like a hero.

She struggled, weakly at first, then more strongly.
Batu and another burly young person whose name she
did not know were carrying her. Hands caught at her.
She began to fight in earnest.

It was as clear as the pattern of the Dance. Her
flailing hand struck Batu's ear and rocked him. At the
same instant, as she lost her balance on his shoulder,
one of the clutching hands tangled in her coat.

She fell headfirst through the crowding bodies.
Her coat wrenched free of its fastenings. Her shirt
caught in it and tore. Her arms were bound in strangling leather and cloth. She could not help herself at
all.

She lay with the wind knocked out of her. The
forest of legs had drawn back in a spreading silence.
Iliya's voice spoke, clear and penetrating. "By the
Mother! That's a—"

Paulus stooped over her. He wrenched at her belt.

No. She did not know whether she said the word
or simply thought it. It filled her from edge to edge
and spilled over in absolute and implacable refusal.

She had more discipline than Cullen had. She did
not kill Paulus. He flew up and away and landed hard,

but he was alive. The wound to his pride would be worse than any of his bruises.

She got her feet under her and stood up. No one reached to help. She was more aware of the stallions than of the human crowd. They were watching dispassionately. Of course they had known this would happen. It was as inevitable as a phase of the moon.

She could not look into every face. She settled for Master Nikos', aware that Kerrec stood close by him, silent and expressionless. "My name is Valeria," she said. "I'm sorry I lied. Everyone said I couldn't be Called—except that I was. I thought if I let you all think I was like the others, then once I passed, you would—"

"That is not the way of things," Master Nikos said. His tone was gentle, which surprised her. "I, too, am sorry. But a woman cannot—"

"She did pass," Kerrec said. "We can't deny that."

Master Nikos' mouth snapped shut.

"Master," said Kerrec, "I think this is not a deliberation for the open court. If you would be pleased to—"

"Yes," said Master Nikos. "Yes, of course." His eye caught two of the riders. "See to her," he said. And to the rest: "The celebration will continue. Andres, look after the candidates. Lords, ladies, honored guests, a feast and entertainment have been prepared. If you will follow my riders, they will show you where to go."

It was admirable, and remarkable, how quickly confusion settled into order. One of the riders who had been set in charge of Valeria brought her coat. All of its buttons were gone, but it covered her enough for modesty. She was glad to have it back again.

A path opened through the crowd. No one wanted to touch her, as if female gender could pass to them like a fever. She resisted the urge to taunt them. Her mood had gone wild.

The stallions were still watching. They were not going to help her. No one was. She was alone as she had been from the moment she was Called. She was the gods' mistake, or maybe their jest. A human could never tell, with gods.

Chapter Twelve

"Absolutely not!"

First Riders Mikel and Gallus and Regan had formed a wall of adamance. Nikos was saying nothing. Kerrec wished he could do the same, but there was the simple truth that all of them refused to see.

"She passed every test," he said doggedly. "The Lady chose her out of all the Called. The Great Ones declared her champion of the testing. She is the most powerful candidate that we have had since the gods know when."

"It doesn't matter," Mikel said. "She's a female. She belongs to the Moon. Our power comes from the Sun."

"She has our power," Kerrec said. "*Ours.* Pure and strong and straight from the source. I've never seen a human like her. She's almost like one of the stallions."

"That's blasphemy," said Mikel. "She's strong, yes. Then let her go to the Beastmasters or the ladies of Astarra. They can handle power of that intensity, and focus it in one of their familiars. She does not belong here."

"The stallions say that she does," said Kerrec. "The Ladies have blessed her. She sees through the world's illusion. She understands the Dance."

"And that makes her dangerous."

It was the first time Nikos had spoken since their council began. His voice was soft, but it would have taken more courage than any of them had to interrupt him.

"She is the Moon's child," he said, "but the Call came to her and the white gods accept her. She's too strong to ignore and too perilous to send away. Maybe Astarra could control her, but I have my doubts of that. Not this one. Not this magic. She's our burden to bear."

"The stallions won't do it," Regan said. "It will be left to us. Gods! I never signed on as an executioner."

"You wouldn't," Kerrec said.

"What else can we do?" Mikel asked. "We can't keep or, gods forbid, train her."

"Why not?"

"Train a woman? Is it even possible?"

"I would do it," Kerrec said.

"Of course you would," said Mikel. "You're too young to know better."

Masters had discipline. They did not come to blows. Kerrec focused on his breathing until it was firmly under control, and unclenched his fists with deliberate care. "I may be young, but I'm not blind. I see that the stallions not only reckon her worthy, they see in her a power that none of the male candidates can match. That power must be controlled—and not by killing the body that houses it. If we do that, we incur the wrath of heaven. That same heaven, I do remind you, which Called her here."

"That could be debated," Mikel said.

"All the more reason to keep her here where we can watch her, and train her as only we know how to do. Because most surely, brothers, if we don't do it, someone else will."

"Who else can—" Mikel stopped short. Good, thought Kerrec. He had remembered how to think. "Oh, no. He wouldn't—"

"She would be a gift of the gods to the one we refuse to name," Kerrec said. "Do you want him to get hold of her, with her power over the stallions?"

"All the more reason to get rid of her," Regan said, echoing Kerrec's words of a moment before. "We'll raise wards against retribution, and do it as quickly and cleanly as may be. We can't risk keeping her alive."

"Wards can avert a thunderbolt," said Kerrec, "but can they keep the stallions from turning on us?"

He watched that prospect sink in. They were all

blind bigots, but they were still masters of the art. They knew the stallions.

Kerrec pressed his advantage. "Without the white gods we are nothing but overwrought Beastmasters. Our art does not exist unless they complete it. If we refuse this one whom they have blessed, we forfeit their goodwill."

"And if they turn against us," Gallus said, "the empire will lose its heart. The barbarians have been waiting for just such a thing. They'll fall on us like a wave breaking."

"If there is anything left to fall on," Kerrec said. "This empire's existence is bound up in the stallions—in the Dance, in the magic that they embody. If the stallions abandon us, we'll break into a confusion of warring states. There will be no empire. There will be nothing but chaos. The emperor will do what he can, but between the warlords within and the barbarians without, he'll be doomed to fail." Kerrec leaned toward them all, as if he could lift each one up and shake sense into him. "You know what's been foreseen. You've seen the number of futures in which the empire falls, and the terribly few in which it endures. Without us, without the Dance, even those few may vanish. We can't afford to refuse this candidate, brothers. Woman or no, she is one of us."

"Never," said Mikel. His voice was clotted with disgust. "I will not have a woman in my court, laying hand on my horses. I will not suffer her hysteria if she falls and breaks a nail. I will not—"

"This woman," Kerrec pointed out through

clenched teeth, "has been living as a man since spring. I believe we can trust her to conduct herself with suitable restraint."

"I won't have it, either," Regan said. "They are different, boy. They can't be handled in the same way. They're weaker, more delicate. Our candidates' trials are hard enough on a man's constitution. A woman would sicken and die."

"Everyone knows," said Gallus, third in the chorus, "that the Moon's children lack the strength of the Sun. Granted that she needs tutelage in the use of her magic, she is still not fit to be taught here. Our methods are not suited to a woman. Astarra is not ideal, but surely, in the circumstances—"

"Listen to yourselves," Kerrec said in amazement. "None of you has a wife—and no wonder. Presumably you had mothers. Did you learn nothing from them? At all?"

"Enough," Nikos said before the others could erupt. "Kerrec, this woman cannot be admitted to the school. Even if the riders would tolerate her, the masters will not."

"She must be trained," Kerrec said.

"So she must," said Nikos, "and you will do it."

Kerrec had expected nothing else. He was simply surprised that he had not had to fight for it. "You will give me complete discretion?"

"Within the bounds of the stallions' approval," Nikos said.

Kerrec bowed to that. "And if she excels? If she proves herself as well as any candidate? Will you reconsider her place here?"

Nikos paused. The other First Riders were rumbling to the boil. Kerrec kept his eyes steady, willing the Master to see this matter clearly and not through a fog of useless prejudice.

"I will think on it," Nikos said at last.

That was the best Kerrec could hope for. He bowed again, lower. "By your leave?"

Nikos waved him away. "Go. Deal with her. The sooner the better."

They had shut Valeria in one of the storerooms. It was better than a prison cell, and she had found a way to make herself useful. She was sitting in a tangle of straps and buckles, rubbing oil into the discrete parts of a bridle.

Kerrec watched her for a while before he alerted her to his presence. He had never thought that she looked particularly masculine, but he supposed that if one had not first seen her naked in the midst of attempted rape, the disguise was convincing enough. Her features were strong for a woman's and cleanly carved. Her body was slender, her limbs long, her breasts small. She moved with a strength and surety that was not common among her sex. Women learned young to shorten their steps and weaken their bodies in the cause of attracting males.

Even so, her skin was too soft to be a man's. Her hands were narrow, with long supple fingers. Her neck was long and smooth, with the black curls falling softly on it as she bent to her work. Her mouth was full, the kind of mouth that in another woman would beg to be kissed.

Kerrec was not a monk or a eunuch priest. He could well appreciate beauty in a woman. But if he was to be her teacher, he must put all such thoughts aside. She needed instruction, not seduction.

He scraped his foot along the floor. She looked up. At sight of him, her face closed. "You could be more imaginative," she said. "My mother locked me in the root cellar."

"I believe we have one," he said. "Would you prefer it?"

"Why not?" she said with forced lightness. "She said a woman could never be Called. Has there never been one? Ever?"

"Not ever," he said.

"I don't believe it," she said.

"It's true," said Kerrec. "The stallions remember. You are the first."

"Why?"

He was not prepared for the directness of that. He should have been. "Gods know," he said.

"It's not false, is it? It's real. I can feel the stallions, and the Ladies behind them. I can see patterns. The Dance—"

"It is real," Kerrec said.

"It doesn't matter, even though I passed the testing. I'll be sent away. Or killed. Have you come to kill me?"

Her sight was brutally clear. It was part of her gift. "You will not be killed or sent away," he said. "You can't be admitted to the school, but you are allowed to stay. You will have instruction. Whatever the gods have in mind for you, you will not face it without knowledge."

She had not been expecting that. He watched the play of emotions across her face, the shuttered mask forgotten. She was angry and disappointed, and no wonder. But this was more than she had any right to expect.

"I'm…to learn?" she said. "How—"

"I will teach you," he said.

She was less than delighted. The best he could say was that she was resigned. It hurt a little. He would have liked her to be happier about it.

"You knew this would happen," she said. "You've known all along what I am. Why didn't you speak?"

"You were Called," he said.

"That didn't make any difference to anyone else."

"It did to me."

"Why?"

She was as persistent as a small child. "Not every family is glad to lose a son to the Mountain," he answered.

"You're the firstborn?"

He nodded.

"I'm the fourth," she said, "but the first daughter. I was going to be a wisewoman in Imbria when Mother got tired of it."

"That would be like keeping an eagle to chase the crows off the corn."

That startled her into laughter. "What, you're a farmer's son, too? And here I was thinking you were at least as high up as Paulus."

Kerrec refrained from responding to that. It did not matter what he had been before he came to the Mountain. He said, "Bring the bridle with you. Once you've finished cleaning it and put it back together, it's yours."

She stood up hastily, but he noticed that she had the whole bridle in her hands, bit and reins and all.

"A First Rider may have a personal servant," he said. "You will occupy that position. It will give you—"

"Won't people talk?" she interrupted him. "They all know what I—"

"You will not interrupt," he said coldly. "A First Rider's servant has a room of his—or her—own. It's small but adequate, and offers you both privacy and modesty. You will perform such duties as I set you, while pursuing the studies of a rider-candidate. I will expect the same of you as of any other candidate. Is that understood?"

"Quite well," she said.

The ease that had been growing between them was

gone. He refused to let himself miss it. She must be perfect in her discipline and impeccable in her pursuit of her studies if she hoped to remain here. No one must be able to accuse either of them of impropriety.

In time he would explain it to her. For now it was enough that she observed his distance and imitated it.

He turned without another word. She was behind him as he left the storeroom.

Chapter Thirteen

While the youngest of the rider-candidates celebrated their success with a revel that ran far into the night, Valeria cleaned saddles and ran errands for her new master. He was ingenious at finding things for her to do. He was also merciless in demanding that she do everything exactly as he wanted.

It was obvious that he had not had a servant in quite some time. His rooms were clean, after a fashion. The First Riders' tower had servants for that purpose. They were not dedicated to any task more complicated than sweeping the floors and making the beds. His clothes were washed regularly, at least. He must insist on that.

Everything else was left to itself. His clothes were piled wherever they happened to fall. His belongings were in a shocking clutter. She found books everywhere, and pots of ink and pens and scraps of parchment and enough tablets to test another year's worth of the Called, tumbled in with bits of harness and stray buckles and, buried in a corner, an ancient and crumbling saddle that must once have been resplendent. The gold plating on it was tarnished or gone, the straps and billets were missing and the seat was worn through.

It was more than a full day's work to make order of that chaos. She did what she could, for a start, while Kerrec went off on some business of his own. She supposed he was attending the feast.

For her there was a loaf of bread and a jar of quite decent wine, which she ate and drank when she remembered. The bread sank like a stone. The wine went straight to her head.

She was shifting books from the floor to a shelf when he came in. Night had fallen. None of the lamps was lit, but she had a witchfire hanging above her, casting a cold blue light on her work.

Kerrec was weighted down with plates and bottles, which he set on the table. "What are you doing?" he asked her.

"Something I shouldn't?" she guessed.

"No," he said. "No, no. It's very diligent. It's also rather late. You should eat and then sleep."

"I ate," she said. "I'll sleep when I can. I'm wide awake now."

"I brought you dinner from the hall," he said. "You did earn it."

"I was the champion of the testing," she said. It was petty, but she could not stop herself. "Who drank the champion's cup? Paulus?"

"No one," he said. He uncovered plates and poured from bottles, as deft as if he had been the servant.

She truly had not been hungry until she saw so many different delicacies arranged in front of her. She recognized bread and roast fowl. The rest she had only heard of.

There was a great variety of everything, but not so much that her stomach revolted. When the edge was off her hunger, she paused. "No one drank the champion's cup?"

"The champion was not present," he said. He had sat across the table from her while she ate.

"Should I have been?"

"No."

She nibbled a bit of stewed fruit. "You must all be in a terrible state."

His lips thinned. "You will do best to keep your head down and your face out of sight for a while. Eventually everyone will grow accustomed to you."

"You think so?"

"The quieter you are, the more likely it is."

She bit her lip. She had no good reason to provoke him. He had taken her when no one else would.

Whatever hope she had of learning the ways of her magic, he was the means to that end.

She bent to the feast that he had brought her. Her appetite was gone, but she made herself eat every bit of it. If she paid for it later, then so be it. Kindness was not a common thing here. She should take advantage of it while she had it.

The day of Midsummer was a great festival in the empire. Here on the Mountain, it was more. The sun's longest day and the moon's longest night tugged at the tides of time. Just at sunrise, when the moon was still above the horizon, the stallions entered the Hall of the Dance.

Valeria had discovered an unexpected advantage in being a servant—she could watch from the stallions' own entrance. It had been her responsibility to see that her rider was properly dressed, his coat and breeches spotless and his boots polished.

The rest of the riders' servants had left, either to find seats in the gallery or to amuse themselves while the Dance went on. Valeria stayed where she was. This was the first true, full and formal Dance that she had seen outside of dreams.

It was better and stronger than dreams. She woke from it to find her face wet with tears, but she could not remember having shed them.

This Dance had not changed the world. It had confirmed the stars in their courses and steadied the sun as it rose toward the summit of heaven. It was a Dance of strength and stability. When it was done, the Augurs raised their staffs in a gesture that, she had learned, meant *It is well*.

She could feel it in herself as the riders left the Hall. She was stronger. Her head was clearer. Her heart was light as she went to her duties. They were few today, and when she had done them, she would be free to do as she pleased.

Everyone was talking of the second great event of the day, the coming of the young stallions to the school. Riders had gone up to the spring pastures days before and brought back those in their fourth year. Today they would see the inside of these walls for the first time. Riders would take them in hand and assess them before beginning their training.

After the ordered perfection of the Dance, this was happy chaos. Riders drove the herd down the processional way from the north gate into the central square of the citadel, which was paved with grass and surrounded by high walls. Some of the riders were already in the square, mounted on older stallions. Spectators watched from windows and balconies.

Valeria had squeezed onto a balcony midway down one of the walls from the entrance. She did not know any of the people crammed in with her, including the pair of riders. They did not seem to know who she was, either, which suited her perfectly.

Long before the horses came in sight, the waiting

crowd heard the thunder of hooves. It grew louder as the herd drew nearer. Valeria could feel the vibration in the stones under her feet.

She could feel the coming of power. These were gods, raw and young. They came like a storm off the Mountain, pouring into the square, a tumbled stream of black and brown and grey, with here and there a flash of white.

They were rough and bony and big-headed and beautiful. They swirled around the square like the herds of Valeria's dreams. There were fragments of the Dance in the patterns, and movements that with time and teaching would transmute into art.

They shied at the confinement of walls, but most settled in time and stopped to crop the grass. A few remained rebellious, and would not stop running.

One was standing perfectly still in the center of the square. Valeria started slightly at the sight of him. He was nearly white, with a hint of dappling like the face of the moon.

She knew him. She had dreamed him over and over, but he was not the calm presence of her dreams at all. His stillness was somehow ominous, like a storm rising.

Her skin prickled. The others were gods, but this was something more. Just as there were levels of mastery, there were levels of godhood. This stallion was born beyond mastery, and almost beyond restraint.

He was angry. He had lived free on the Mountain

and been happy. He knew that he was fated to come here, and that order and discipline were his lot, but he had no intention of submitting to them.

All the young riders and rider-candidates, along with a few of the higher-ranking riders, had come down to the square with ropes slung over their shoulders. Valeria's heart clenched at the sight of Batu and Iliya together not far below her. She should have been there. She should have been with them.

Her anger threatened to match the young stallion's. That could not happen. She must not let it. Discipline was a rider's first virtue. If she ever hoped to be a rider, she had to be more disciplined than any of the men.

The young stallions had drawn in toward the square's center. The circle of riders closed around them. Each young stallion would find a rider, a companion and teacher for his first year. Some riders would take more than one. Others might not be chosen at all. It was the stallions' choice.

The stallions had all gone calm, even the rebels. Only the angry one was still in the center, still seething. He did not want to be calm or focused. Above all, he did not want to submit his will to any pallid slug of a man.

Valeria eyed the distance to the ground. No one else seemed to notice that there was trouble brewing. Men and stallions were finding one another, the patterns drawn like lines of force across the square. The angry one was a smoldering hole in the middle.

Some of his brothers jostled him, crowded even more tightly now that there were humans mixed into the herd. One man, a rider whom she did not know, moved as if to slip a loop of rope over the stallion's head.

The pattern was warping and fraying. Valeria could see the void underneath the world.

The rider was oblivious. When the stallion shook him off, he came on more strongly.

The stallion erupted. His brothers scattered. The rider screamed as he fell under trampling hooves.

All the masters ran from the corners of the square. Valeria was aware of Kerrec, youngest and fastest, aiming straight for the death in the stallion's eyes.

Through the tumult of shouts and cries, she heard a master's strong voice calling. "Kill him! Quickly!"

"No!" Kerrec shouted back. He paused, and his death hesitated. "If we destroy the body, we unleash the power. We have to contain him!"

Someone near Valeria was praying. It was one of the riders on the balcony. His face was the color of wax.

The stallion whirled in the center of a widening circle. No one but Kerrec dared come near him. The other masters had stopped. Kerrec was still running. He was going to die. He would touch the edge of that maelstrom and spin into nothingness.

Valeria vaulted over the edge of the balcony and slid down a pillar. The ground came up an instant sooner than she expected. She staggered but managed to keep her feet.

There were riders in front of her. She darted between them into the full glare of the sun. There was no time to pause or take stock. She ran blindly toward the thing that was no longer exactly a stallion. His mane and tail had turned to streamers of fire.

Something small and dark tried to thrust her aside. She knew dimly that it was Kerrec. As gently as she could, she lifted him with her magic and set him out of harm's way.

She faced the stallion. His rage beat on her. She could feel its power, and yet it did not frighten her. Something in her was resonating with it. She could take it, shape it. She could, with effort, take the edge off it until he could control himself.

He glowered at her. She glowered back. "You are a Great One," she said. "Isn't it time you remembered it?"

His ears went flat. His lip curled.

"What would you do on the Mountain? Be a foal again? Try to crawl back to your mother's teat? Here is where you belong. This is what you were born for."

He shook his head and snapped at her, but his fit of temper lacked force. She slipped past his bared teeth and laid a hand on his neck. It was rigid. She smoothed it in long strokes, digging in until the knots loosened.

The world had settled in its orbit. The earth was solid again. The rest of the stallions were creeping closer, with riders half hiding in their shadows.

The stallion warned them off with teeth and heels.

They backed away. None of them was strong enough to challenge him.

That, thought Valeria, was the trouble. No one had ever been able to control him. "You are dangerous," she said, "unless you learn to rule yourself. Great One or not, they'll kill or cull you. Do you want to waste yourself that badly?"

His head lowered. She would not call him chastened, but the defiance had drained out of him. Her fingers worked under his mane, massaging his crest. He sighed and gave in.

Chapter Fourteen

For the second time in three days, Valeria had aroused consternation among the riders. If she had had any hope of changing their minds by saving them from the Great One's rage, that vanished in front of those stony faces. She had made matters worse, not better. She had reminded them that a woman could outdo them all.

They had brought her from the square to a room in the citadel, the round floor of a tower with high, narrow windows letting in the light. Between the windows hung portraits of old masters and great stallions.

The living masters had the same stern and unreadable faces as their painted counterparts. They sat at a half-moon-shaped table, so that they faced her in a semicircle.

Valeria would rather have faced the stallions. She stood as straight as she could and tried not to look as if she wanted to burst into tears.

After a long while, Master Nikos sighed. The sound echoed around the room. He folded his hands on the table and leaned toward her. "Suppose you tell us what you thought you were doing," he said.

Valeria swallowed. "I was doing what had to be done," she said, "sir. The Great One was out of control. No one was able to stop him."

"And yet you could."

"I do apologize," she said, "if I interfered with the destined destruction of this Mountain and every living thing within a day's journey."

Kerrec made a strangled noise that sounded suspiciously like laughter. She refused to look at him. Her eyes were fixed on Master Nikos. He was not laughing, but he had not risen up and thundered anathema at her, either.

"You are a difficulty," he said. "Even the most resistant of us cannot deny that you did what no one else was able to do. At the same time, you are here on sufferance. Your formal position is that of a servant. Servants do not tame renegade Great Ones."

"So make me a rider," she said.

It had slipped out. She never meant to say it aloud.

"That will not happen," said the Master on the end opposite from Kerrec. "Not while I live, and by the gods, never after I'm dead."

He was an old man, as rigid in the mind as in the spine. He was afraid, she thought, and it made him angry. He did not want the world to change. Above all, he did not want a woman to change it.

She opened her mouth to ask him why he hated women so much. Before the first word came out, Kerrec said, "I am responsible for her. Whatever sentence you pronounce is mine to serve."

"That is absurd!" the old man sputtered. "You cannot—"

Kerrec regarded him blandly. After a while he stopped sputtering.

Another of the masters, younger but no less obstinate, said grimly, "You won't do it. You won't be allowed. This game has gone on long enough. Let us dispose of her and be done with it."

"No." Master Nikos said that, to Valeria's surprise. "She will continue as before. She has our thanks for the service she has done us, but now more than ever she must be taught the proper restraint of her power. If needs must, she will participate in lessons and exercises with the rider-candidates, at her master's discretion."

Valeria stopped breathing. Her glance shifted to Kerrec. The Master had laid the burden of decision on him. She caught herself praying to whatever gods would hear.

Kerrec said nothing. He rose from his chair and came around the table. His shoulder shifted, a gesture as subtle as a stallion's. She was to follow.

She did not look back, although she knew they would erupt when she was gone. She could feel the explosion building.

It was no matter to her. All that mattered was the Master's decree.

Valeria would not have been surprised to be shut in Kerrec's rooms with every bit and bridle and strap of leather in the citadel, and ordered to clean them all. Instead she found herself behind the stallions' stable. There were rows of paddocks there. Most held older stallions, let out to bask in the sun, but one in a corner, set apart from the others, held the Great One.

His brothers were in the stable, learning to live in walls. No one trusted him to do such a thing.

"That's a mistake," she said. "Or am I allowed to say that?"

"What would you do?" Kerrec asked her.

"Treat him like the others," she said. "No singling out."

"And if he kills one of them or one of us?"

"He won't," she said. "You know that. You're a First Rider. I'm only—"

"Stop that," he said. "There's a halter on the gate. Fetch him and take him where you please."

The stallion watched their conversation from the far side of the paddock. His anger was not gone, but it had burned low. He had been pacing, pining for his brothers. When Valeria slipped through the gate, he stopped and flared his nostrils at her and snorted.

"Come," she said.

He was not a tame beast, to come at her bidding. He tossed his head until the ragged mane flew.

She leaned against the gate. Kerrec, outside it, had gone still. He was a horseman. He knew what she was doing.

So did the stallion, but his kind were born curious. He could not resist the opportunity to investigate her. He went back to his pacing, but with each round, he came a little closer. His eye was on her, with no anger left in it. He had found something to focus on, and that was its own kind of joy.

Valeria suppressed a smile. He learned fast, once he put his mind to it. He was not at heart a vicious beast. It was only that the power in him was so strong and the flesh so feeble, and he found it all so frustrating. He had hated to be a foal. He loathed to be small and helpless, unable to move or think as he knew in his heart that he should. To be so great and to be shut in so small a space had been more than he could bear.

Now as a young stallion he was closer to what he felt he should be. He did want the art and the Dance. He had not wanted to pay the price for it, the loss of his freedom to run the mountain pastures.

"It's a different kind of freedom," she said. He was

directly behind her. It was a dangerous place to be with a stallion who was not to be trusted.

She trusted this one. "What is your name?" she asked.

She reeled in a sudden blast of light and sound. A god's name was beyond words, and almost beyond human endurance.

"Here he will be called Sabata." Kerrec's voice was quiet. It stilled the ringing in her ears.

The stallion shook his head and pawed, unrepentant. Valeria slipped the halter over his head.

He stared at her in astonishment. She stayed loose and calm, but she braced for an eruption.

It did not come. He was thinking hard. His ears flicked and his mouth worked. He ground his teeth once, loudly, and gave himself to her.

There would be eruptions later, and plenty of them. For now he was inclined to play at obedience. She led him quietly into the stable in which his brothers were.

They called to him in joy and relief. They had been afraid for him. He called back with a fine edge of arrogance, but when she had brought him to a stall near the middle of the stable, he fell on the manger of hay as if he were starving.

Horses did that when they needed to think. He had a great deal on his mind. Valeria let him eat for a while, then fetched brushes from the box by the feed room. While he ate, she brushed the mud and dust from his coat and the burrs from his mane and tail, and cleaned and trimmed his feet.

Kerrec watched in silence. He did not offer to help, and she did not ask him.

It was surprisingly comfortable to work while he watched. She had already learned that he did not intrude. He knew how to let a servant go about her business. She had stopped minding it, or even being distracted by it.

When she was done with the stallion, Kerrec said, "You'll look after him, since he's agreed to it."

"As if I were a rider?" Valeria asked.

"Don't say the word," Kerrec said, but she could have sworn he almost smiled.

She was learning to read him a little. He was terribly young to be what he was, and his defenses were sometimes excessively strong. Still, once in a great while a crack appeared. Then she could catch a glimpse of the man underneath.

This crack vanished as soon as she caught sight of it. He was his cold outer self again, expecting her to saddle Petra for the afternoon exercises. She had saddles to clean then, and plenty of them, which kept her busy until sundown.

Valeria had always been a solitary creature. Even in the middle of a large and boisterous family, she had managed to keep to herself. Here in the school, where women were all wives, daughters or drudges, she was a complete oddity.

The riders did their best to pretend she was invisible. That hurt more than she had expected. For a few days she had been one of them, and now they would not even look her in the face.

She told herself she did not care. Nothing mattered but the teaching.

Kerrec was true to his word, teaching her as the other rider-candidates were being taught. She did not, in spite of what the Master had said, share their lessons. She was alone in that as in everything else. Sometimes she thought that no one in the world cared for her, and Kerrec least of all.

He was a good teacher. His lessons were clear and to the point, and she never succeeded in trying his patience. She did not succeed, either, in tempting him to act like a human being. Now more than ever, he was the First Rider, the great mage, the master of his art. She looked at him and saw him cased in glass, cool and impenetrable. Nothing she did or said could get a purchase on it, let alone lure him out of it.

Chapter Fifteen

Euan Rohe had not expected to be engrossed by his studies in the School of War. He was here for a particular purpose, but the pursuit of that purpose meant learning to fight on horseback. He was no better rider than he had ever been, but one thing he could do. He could shoot a bow or aim a spear from the back of a rapidly moving horse, and hit his target more often than not. It was a surprising talent, but a useful one.

Then there were the hours that he had expected to be deadly dull, shut in walls away from the air and subjected to the torture of books and words. Those books were books of war. The words were strategy and tactics, great battles and great generals, and defeats as well as victories.

"Victory is a grand thing," said the grizzled warrior

who taught the newcomers, "but defeat teaches a commander to be wise. We learn from our mistakes, if we survive them, and we benefit from the mistakes of others. Study the great losses, gentlemen, as well as the great triumphs. Learn to see where failure begins, the better to avoid that failure in the heat of your own battles."

Gavin sneered at that and was caned for it. Punishment here was swift, and the masters never shrank from it, regardless of the rank or station of the victim.

Euan kept his thoughts to himself, good or bad, and avoided the whip and the cane. He was not here to gain stripes. He was here to defeat the empire.

One day that was as hot as days could be on this mountain, he was on his way from a long morning of mounted exercises and an afternoon of lessons in the art of war. Even at sunset the heat weighed heavy. He was alone, having stayed behind to answer questions from some of the imperial recruits as to how he managed to nock an arrow, aim and shoot while the horse was in motion. The men of his warband had gone ahead in search of a more pleasant dinner than they could find in commons.

His kinsmen had laid claim to a little hole of a tavern near the western gate. It was run by a big fair-haired woman whose mother had been a battle captive from the Caletanni. She knew how to brew ale in the real way, the way of the tribes. It was good ale, brown as an acorn and nearly as bitter, and she served it with gritty bread and hard cheese and butter as sweet as any he had tasted.

Imperials scorned butter. It was rancid cream, they declared, and far inferior to the oils in which they soaked their thin and tasteless bread.

His mouth was watering with anticipation. He paid little attention to the sounds of commotion in the tavern. It was always boisterous—the ale was strong and imperials were weak in the head.

Then he heard Gavin's voice lifted above the rest. There were no intelligible words in it. He sounded like a bull at the slaughter.

Euan lengthened his stride.

There were a few imperials in the tavern, but they were trapped there and visibly unhappy about it. Euan's kinsmen had caught themselves a coney, as they would put it.

Euan had thought that they knew better than to flout imperial law with regard to women. Then he saw the jar on the table. It was not the plain, squat earthenware jug in which Gitta served her ale, but a finer glazed pottery with the seal of one of the imperial vineyards. They had been drinking wine, the idiots. From the strong sweet smell and the high flush of their faces, they had not been watering it, either.

Gitta was nowhere to be seen. Her husband, a little brown mouse of an imperial, was cowering behind the bar. The girl who fetched the beer and fed the customers was struggling in the middle of Euan's warband, and giving a good account of herself, too.

Conory let out a yelp. Gavin cursed. They still had their trousers on. It had not gone too far yet, then. They were trying to force wine into the girl, to soften her up. She was objecting, strongly.

Just as Euan gathered himself to wade in, someone brushed past him, running very fast. A sharp scent prickled in Euan's nostrils, like hot metal.

It was Valeria. Euan would know her in the dark, by the way his skin quivered and his heart beat faster.

She was oblivious to anyone but the hostages and their prisoner. She heaved up Conory and tossed him out of the way. Stools and benches splintered where he fell.

Gavin grinned with drunken delight. "Little rider! Just in time. You want some? There's plenty."

Valeria's fist caught him in the teeth. He roared in pain.

He roared even louder when she broke his jaw.

The captive had broken free. Her face was sticky with wine, and wine stained the front of her gown. She snatched the knife from Conory's belt and stood at bay.

They had all forgotten her. Valeria had Gavin down on the floor, the whole massive bulk of him. She was not going to stop until Gavin was dead.

Euan was no coward, but it took every scrap of courage he had to lay hands on Valeria. Somewhat to his surprise, she neither blasted him nor laid him flat.

She went still in his grip, breathing hard, shaking in spasms.

Gavin lurched to his feet. Valeria jerked toward him, but she had come to her senses somewhat. She made no effort to break away from Euan.

Euan let her go. As he had hoped, she stayed where he put her.

Gavin was too far gone to notice that he was hurt. His eye fell on the tavern girl with her torn shift and her ripe breast showing, then shifted to Valeria in her sexless rider's clothes. He reached for one or both, it little mattered which.

Euan sighed faintly. Blasted fools, all of them. They left him no choice. He moved coolly, with considered judgment, to beat his kinsman to a pulp.

Gavin fought back weakly, but after he went down, he stopped even that. Euan looked up from his bloodied body. The serving girl had finally had the sense to get out of there. So had everyone else who was not one of his own.

His warband stared blankly at him. So did Valeria. He scowled at her. "Get out," he said.

She did not move.

He hissed in exasperation. "The watch will be here any moment. Get out before they see you."

She still did not appear to understand.

He wanted to seize her and shake her, but that would have been a very unwise thing. "If you're caught in one more difficult situation, you can bet the emperor's gold that you'll be tossed out of this place. Now will you leave, or do I have to pick you up and carry you?"

She did not like it, not even slightly, but he had got through to her at last. She stared at her bruised and knuckle-split hands as if she had never seen them before, locked them tight under folded arms, and vanished into the rear of the tavern.

She had escaped none too soon. Just as Euan saw the last of her, a troop of guards tramped and rattled toward the tavern. They found Euan standing over the unconscious and badly battered Gavin, and the rest of his warband forming into a shieldwall between their prince and the world.

Euan called them off. "Go on. Let be. This is my fight."

They would not obey him. The wine was still in them, even if it had gone sour. There was a battle brewing, and for once in his life Euan neither wanted it nor could see a way out of it.

"What is this?"

The voice was clear and cold. It brought the guards to rigid attention. Even Euan's kinsmen yielded to it. Euan felt its power, the power of a strong mage.

First Rider Kerrec surveyed them all. His brows drew together at the sight of Gavin. He knelt on the filthy floor and laid his hand on the bloodied forehead. Euan found he could not move, either to retreat or to resist.

Kerrec looked up beyond Euan at the man in sergeant's stripes. "He's still alive. Fetch Healer Martti. Tell him to bring his kit."

The man ducked his head like a servant and ran.

Kerrec had already forgotten him. He ordered the guards to herd Euan's kinsmen together and escort them back to their quarters. They would hear from him later.

That left Euan stripped of his shieldwall, with half a dozen guards around him and Gavin barely breathing at his feet. "I'm sure you can explain this," Kerrec said.

"You can't tell by looking?"

Kerrec's nostrils flared ever so slightly at the insolence. "I would rather you told me."

"There was a woman," Euan said. "They had got into the wine. They were attempting to force it on her."

"I see no woman," said Kerrec.

"She escaped," Euan said.

"Indeed," said Kerrec. "There was a woman. And you tried and sentenced the one who forced her."

"It is my right," Euan said.

"Not here."

Euan did not answer that.

"You realize that if he lives, he'll be expelled from the School of War. Hostage or no, he broke one of the sterner of our laws."

"I do know that," Euan said. "Our laws are like enough to yours."

Kerrec inclined his head slightly. "You are not the

law here. Whatever you were, that has to be forgotten. For this you could be court-martialed."

"For defending a woman?"

"For stepping above your present station," said Kerrec, "and for violating the peace of this place."

"That was already violated," Euan said, "although the woman was not."

Euan was head and shoulders taller, but Kerrec still managed to look down his nose. "The woman was fortunate. You will stay until we know whether this one lives or dies. You are his servant and his dearest brother. Do you understand?"

"Well enough," Euan said. He kept most of the growl out of it.

Gavin would live. He would be a long while healing, and he might not walk as straight as he had before, but Martti the healer had skill enough to keep his soul in his body. He had the proper fear of the One God in him, too, once he was awake enough that Euan could remind him of the imperial sentence for holding a woman against her will.

As for Euan, there was no court-martial after all. Whatever Kerrec had done or said to the powers in the School of War, no one said anything of that night's doings. Euan was safe—and so, thank the One, was Valeria. The plot could go on.

Chapter Sixteen

Valeria could have killed Euan. How dared he order her about as if he were a rider? But damn him, he was right. She could not afford another moment in the hard glare of the Masters' scrutiny.

She did as he told her. She left him to face the consequences of the whole bloody mess, and took the coward's way, out the back and down an alley reeking of stale beer and worse.

She nursed her bruises and her skinned knuckles and ran through the memory over and over. She should never have gone near the tavern. She had gone looking for Euan, and found a nightmare unfolding itself all over again.

Euan's kin were like any other males in a pack. The wine was in them, they saw a female, they had to have her. The serving girl was fortunate that they had fixated on getting her drunk. What they would have done after that, Valeria knew all too well.

Her mind had gone blank. She was remotely aware that she had got Gavin down and was taking him apart. She was equally conscious that when she finished doing that, he would be dead.

She wanted him dead. She looked into that broad freckled face and saw another not terribly unlike it, bending over her, grinning as he set about raping her. There was no Kerrec this time, no one to stop her from taking her revenge—until Euan came roaring in, twice as big and just as maddening as that other rescuer. Then it all went from bad to worse.

She could not face Kerrec that night. She hid in Sabata's stall. He did not mind, and his straw was deep and clean. When he lay down, she curled against him.

She did not mean to fall asleep. It was dawn when she woke. There was just time to scrub her face and hands in the rain barrel outside the stable before she had to begin the morning's duties.

Her dreams had all been of stallions and the Dance. They usually were, but tonight they had been stronger and clearer. The stallions were speaking to her in their way. She dreamed their dreams, the dreams of gods. They stayed with her after she woke and through the whole of that day.

Kerrec said nothing to her. He did not even notice

her bruises. He would have said something cutting if he had, of order and discipline, and the necessity of keeping her head down and her nose out of trouble.

Men were all the same. She hated them. If it had not been for the stallions, she would have shaken the dust of that place from her feet.

The stallions wanted her to stay. The Call was still in her, had become her. Magic simmered in her veins. Her bones were full of it.

Men had failed her, but stallions would not. She would learn from them and let the men do as they pleased.

Valeria's solitude was complete. No one but Kerrec ever spoke to her, and he did it rarely outside of long days' lessons in riding, in books of magic and horsemanship, and in the daily duties of riders in the school. Among humans she was as close to invisible as she could be.

Among the stallions, at night and in the early mornings when the rest of the humans were either asleep or engaged elsewhere, she learned little by little to be a rider. She learned how to sit on their backs and call in the magic and master the powers that she raised.

One morning toward the middle of summer, she had been practicing a particularly difficult variant of the Dance. Petra was teaching her, with Sabata watching, because he was charged with learning it as well. Just as she finished the third repetition, she felt a ripple on the edge of her concentration.

The stallions were unconcerned, but her hackles had risen. She looked toward the edge of the field in which she was riding, and saw a red wolf watching. His amber eyes were intent, trying to take in what he was seeing. The fur on his neck and back stood straight up, and he growled softly in his throat.

She blinked, and the wolf became a man. Euan Rohe stood beside the field.

She had not seen him since the night in the tavern. He had been hunting her, and she had been eluding him.

Now he had caught her, in more ways than one. She slid from Petra's back and thanked him politely as was proper. He bowed his head, blowing warm breath into her hand. She fed him a handful of sugar and walked with him back to the stable.

Euan followed. The stallions did not try to drive him off. Even Sabata, who could be terribly jealous, was choosing to tolerate him.

Sometimes she could not understand the stallions. When Petra was cooled and brushed and settled in his stall with a manger full of hay, Valeria faced Euan.

He was visibly careful not to seem threatening. It was hard, as big as he was, but he made himself as small as he could. "You ride very well," he said.

She brushed that aside. "What do you want? You know you're not supposed to be in this part of the school."

"Are you supposed to be doing what you're doing?" he shot back. "I'm just an uncouth barbarian, but I don't think a first-year candidate is allowed to creep out with the white gods in the morning."

"They called me," Valeria said. "I'm supposed to cultivate obedience."

"Why then," he said, "I'm cultivating repentance. I'm sorry for what my kinsmen did. Gavin will live, but as soon as he can travel, he'll be sent away. He won't lay a hand on any woman in Aurelia again."

"Good," she said, "though you'd have done better to kill him. There's blood between you now."

"That's as it may be," he said. "I'd rather not be sent down for murder."

"There is that," she admitted.

He looked hard at her. "You," he said. "Are you well? What they did, for a woman it's a hard thing—whether she's the victim or the defender. Even a woman as strong as you."

She realized that her jaw had dropped. He stood there, big and bright and outlandish, and understood more about her than any supposedly civilized man ever had.

He did not seem to know how unusual he was. He frowned. "You're *not* well. That's why you're avoiding everybody. By the One! I'll kill that son of a—"

"I am well," she said as firmly as she could. "I just never—no man ever—you're not like anyone else."

"Why? Because I haven't gone after you like a bull in rut?"

She laughed shakily. "Yes, because of that. And because you understand. How is that? What makes you different?"

He shrugged, rolling his wide shoulders. "I have a mother. Sisters. They talk to me. Sometimes I even listen. My mother swore an oath when I was small that she would never let me grow up thinking I was better than a woman. 'Bigger is not better,' she said. 'Usually it's worse. Remember what the imperials do to a man who rapes a woman, and reflect on the reasons why.'"

"Was she one of us?" Valeria asked.

His gust of laughter was more than half shock. "God, no! Her ancestors were kings when my father's fathers were still grubbing in the mud."

"So your blood is pure," she said. She had to touch him. She could not help herself. He tensed a little as her hand came to rest over his heart, but he did not draw away. "We're distant cousins, I think. My mother comes from Eriu."

"That's why," he said. Was he breathless? "That's why your eyes are different."

"Mongrel eyes," she said. "No pure blood here."

"Purity only matters if you're a priest or a king."

"Are you both?"

He was oddly reluctant to answer. Finally he said, "Not a priest. Priests are…strange."

"So are mages."

"It's not the same." His finger brushed her cheek. She shivered. "You don't know you're beautiful."

She should have struck him for that, but she could not lift her hand to do it. "You're making fun of me."

"Never," he said.

"I'm not—"

"Learn to see yourself," he said. "Beauty is power. Beauty and magic and brilliance all together—those can rule the world."

"I don't want to rule," she said, peevish with discomfort. "I want to be a rider."

"There is a difference?"

You wouldn't understand.

She did not say the words. She said instead, "Beauty gives nothing but grief. Give it a female body and every beast in the woods goes howling after it."

"For most beasts," he said dryly, "female alone is enough." He touched her again, this time to tilt up her chin so that she had to look into his eyes. "Think of what I said. It's a weapon. You can use it."

"What, to conquer armies with the bat of an eyelash?"

"Why not?"

"I can't do that," she said.

"Can't or won't?"

This time she did hit him, or tried. He caught her hand and kissed the inside of her wrist where the blood was running hot and quick. His breath was warm. His mustache tickled. It was almost enough to make her pull away, but not quite.

She did not want to think of Kerrec's smooth-shaven face or his graceful compact body. She knew that body rather well by now, having looked after it for over a month. This one she did not know at all.

She should not try. He was an enemy. He tempted her, charmed her, seemed to understand her. He could be lying through his teeth.

Her magic was useless here. She tried to remember the miller's son whom she had been meant to marry, but even his name escaped her. If he was lucky, he had found another wife, one who was not already married to a strange and difficult magic.

Euan had no magic beyond the fact of being young, male and royally born. He was beautifully clean and simple.

She needed simplicity. She pulled his head down and kissed him. She meant to be fast and hard, but his arms went around her and his lips warmed. He turned her sudden attack into a long, slow, lingering thing.

She was dizzy as if she had drunk the fiery poteen that her mother's family sent from Eriu. Her body tingled. There was a deep warmth in her belly, spreading upward from the meeting of her legs. She ached there, but it was a pleasurable ache.

His hand ran down her back, not too firm, not too light. It came to rest below the curve of her buttocks. She arched toward him. She could feel the hot, hard thing under his trousers.

Her breath came fast and shallow. She had in no

way forgotten her grievance against his sex. The anger in her was hot and strong.

This was different. She wanted it. She needed it. She knew that if she took this, instead of being taken against her will, she would start to heal. It was important that she heal.

The stallions were watching. They would let no harm come to her. This must happen. It was part of the Dance.

Euan started to draw back, but Valeria stopped him. Even though he let himself be held, he said, "Not here. Not now. Tonight—somewhere safer."

She knew of nowhere safer than the stallions' stable, but he would not understand that. "Tonight," she said not altogether willingly. "Meet me here. I'll think of a place where we can go."

He was amenable to that. He took his time in kissing her goodbye, but in the end he had to go. So did she. She was still Kerrec's servant, as little as she wanted to remember it.

❉

Chapter Seventeen

Euan knew better than to betray the slightest hint of his elation. Not only had he caught the school's most troublesome student at lessons he knew the masters would not have approved of, he had found her more than willing to play into his hand.

He had been thinking he would need a long, slow campaign. Women who had been forced, in his experience, wanted nothing to do with any man. This one had transformed her anger into passion. He sensed in her no fear. It had burned away.

The day was unbearably tedious. Only the urgency of his mission kept him from running out on it all. He must continue to play the well-mannered royal hostage. Valeria was part of a much larger plan, and he could not sacrifice the rest of it to his hunger for her.

Evening came none too soon. Some of the imperial nobles in the House of War had taken it into their heads to be hospitable to the barbarians. Euan was hard put to escape from the revel before dark. He had to confide in Conory, who looked enough like Euan by lamplight that if their hosts were too drunk to count, they might not notice that one of the barbarians was missing.

He did not tell Conory who the woman was whom he was meeting. Conory was too polite to ask. It amused him to play at being Euan, while Euan, as he observed, had all the luck.

Luck indeed, Euan thought as he made his way to the white gods' stable. He had bathed before he went out, and put on clean clothes. His hair was still damp in its thick braid.

She was not in the stable. The stallions had been fed, and were eating as stupidly as horses always did. Euan saw nothing godlike in it, or for the moment in the thickset white or greyish beasts who did it. Divinity in such circumstances was entirely a matter of faith.

Euan found a chest to sit on, and perched there rather uncomfortably. The grinding of jaws and the rustling of hooves in straw, combined with the wine he had drunk before he escaped, made his eyelids too heavy to lift. He struggled to stay awake.

Sleep crept up on him in spite of his best efforts. He started out of it to discover that night had fallen. Moonlight filled the stable.

There was no moon tonight, and the stars were hidden in cloud. The light shone from the stallions, a blue-white shimmer, bright enough to cast shadows.

Completely without thinking, Euan made the sign of the One. The stallion nearest, who had come to peer at Euan over the door of his stall, snorted wetly. Euan could have sworn he was laughing.

In this ignominious state, wiping bits of wet hay and less delightful things from his face and coat, Euan looked up to find Valeria looking down. She was flushed and her cropped curls looked windblown. She wore the same nondescript coat and trousers as always. She was beautiful enough that for a moment he was content to simply stare.

"I'm sorry," she said, as close to flustered as he had seen her. "I was kept later than I expected, then he found something else for me to—"

Euan was on his feet. He would not have moved if she had recoiled, but her body swayed toward him.

They did not go elsewhere after all. In the deep clean straw of an empty stall, with a stallion leisurely chewing hay on either side, they went down in a tangle.

His clothes came off first. Hers were more stubborn. He unbound the breastband with the sense of a man unwrapping a gift.

She was not what she would be, not yet. Her curves were scant, her breasts still budding. When she was grown she would be magnificent. Tonight she was as lovely as a young doe in her first season.

That was not simply poetry. He truly was her first. She had courage—her breath hissed at the pain, but she did not cry out. Her legs locked around his waist, and her fingers wound themselves in his hair. He was well and truly bound.

Her thighs were strong. She had endurance, and a rider's sense of rhythm. She rode him like one of her stallions, with a casual assumption of authority that left him breathless.

He could have been outraged, but she had driven all rational thought out of his head. He had come to seduce her, and she had bound him with her spell. It was astonishing—glorious.

He tried, but he could not keep up with her. He was the great bull of the people, high prince of the Caletanni. He fell in defeat before a slip of an imperial girl.

He dropped like a stone. She rose over him. She could kill him now. He had no strength to stop her.

She brushed his lips with a kiss, and stayed there, hovering, with those gold-flecked eyes fixed on his face. Princes were always stared at, and handsome ones even more so. Even at that, he had never been examined quite so thoroughly. He wondered, with a shiver deep inside, just how much she could see.

She neither killed him nor denounced him. She smiled, long, slow and deeply content, and ran her finger down his face from eyebrow to jaw. "Beautiful," she said.

His cheeks flushed hot. Her touch cooled them, then her kisses heated them again.

Before she could drive him quite insane, she released him from her spell. With a long sigh, she slid down to lay her head on his shoulder, and stretched her arm across his chest.

He dozed for a while. When he started awake, she was still there, warm against his side. Her breathing was deep and even, but when he moved, it quickened. She looked up from the hollow of his shoulder.

His smile had no calculation in it. He was glad to see her there, glad to be there.

She did not smile back. Her eyes turned smoky grey when she was thinking. "You were my first," she said.

"I know." He drew her hand up to his lips and kissed it. "It's a great honor."

"You do mean it." She sounded faintly surprised. "I thought men of your nation were—"

"Barbarians?" He grinned at her. "We are. It's an honor to be chosen by a king's daughter."

"I'm nothing royal. You know that."

"I do," he agreed. "You're something more. The white gods dance for you."

"Not that it matters to their riders," she said.

Euan struggled mightily to hide the surge of excitement. She was bitter—how much, he had not suspected until he heard it in her voice. She was much further gone than he had thought.

The One had not done giving gifts, it seemed. Euan had to take this one very carefully, and take even greater care not to drop or break it.

When he could trust his voice to be noncommittal, he said, "Riders are only human, even if they are famous sorcerers. Not like the stallions, who are gods."

"Riders make the laws," she said. "They say I can't be one of them. If I'd been born a man—"

"If you had been born a man," Euan said, "you wouldn't be what you are."

"Yes," she said. "I'd be a rider."

Imperials made a great virtue of logic. Euan did not see the use in it himself. He paused for the duration of a breath, then asked, "Have you ever heard of the School of Olivet?"

Her frown answered him even before she spoke the words. "No. What is that?"

"It's a school of horse mages," Euan said. "Olivet was a master here, but after a while he tired of the laws and limitations and withdrew to found his own school."

"Did he?" She was intrigued, but she was not ready to surrender yet. "Why would he do that?"

"Have you ever thought that you might not be alone? How many others have come this far only to be turned away? You're the strongest, and you won the testing, but even you have been shunted aside. Wouldn't you rather be the chief of riders that you were meant to be?"

She sighed so deeply her body shuddered. Still she clung to her resistance. "If it's such a wonder of a place, why have I never heard of it?"

"It's not spoken of here," he said, "as you might imagine. They won't want you of all people to learn that there's a place where you'll be welcome. You're too strong, and they're afraid of you. They're keeping you where they can see you."

"Yes," she said, "but there was no word of it before, either. I listened to all the travelers' tales. There was never one about Avila."

"Olivet," Euan said. "He was hidden for a long time. For years he was with us. Then he had his own Call to come back to the empire and open a school. That was not so long ago. It's still new, and with this school suppressing anything that's said of him, travelers won't be telling tales yet. In time they will. I don't have any doubt of that. Maybe some of them will be of you."

"Maybe," she said.

He could feel her withdrawing. There was more he could have said, but he stopped before he lost her. He had tempted her. He should let the temptation sleep now, and let her think.

He slipped away while she was deep in thought. She made no effort to stop him. He would come back, and she would want him again, and ask him what more he knew.

He would tell her. Then, the One willing, she would fall into his hand. If the One was especially kind, the stallion would come with her, the young one whose life she had saved.

That was Olivet's great failing. He had been driven off the Mountain before he could secure any of the white gods. Now Euan was close to winning one, and the rider to control him. It was an entirely incidental gift of the One that the rider was female and beautiful, and that Euan could not get her out of his head.

Chapter Eighteen

Summer was passing. Up on the Mountain, the leaves were beginning to turn. Down in the school, tension was rising. On the day when summer turned to autumn, the chosen of the riders must be in the imperial city with their stallions, prepared to dance before the emperor. It was the greatest of the Great Dances, the dance of the empire's fate.

Eight riders would dance the Dance, and eight stallions. Twice that number would ride to Aurelia, attended by servants and guards. Most of those servants would be rider-candidates.

They were fighting over it in their barracks. Valeria saw them in the mornings, bruised and scowling. One was sent away after he trapped another with magic. He was lucky not to be executed for it.

Valeria had her own transgressions to atone for, if she should be caught at them. The nights were so full that she spent most of her days drunk on lack of sleep. The stallions taught her how to dream awake, or she would have had to make a choice. She would have had to give up either their teaching or the hours afterward with Euan.

He came nearly every night to the stallions' stable. When she was done with her lessons, he was waiting. He taught her his own art of resting without sleep, so that her mind could drift away while her body lay warm and sated.

She was happy, although she knew perfectly well that it would not last. Euan could not stay. He would finish his year in the School of War, then go off to whatever else the empire had in mind for him. She knew he hoped to go home.

For now, she could be glad that he was here. He was beautiful and strong, and he devoted himself to pleasing her.

He had reasons for that, of course. She did not care to know what they were. If he hoped to use her as a spy, he would not gain much that he could use. The riders shared no secrets with her. What the stallions shared, he was not born to understand.

A month before the Great Dance, the riders were ready to go. Valeria had packed and repacked Kerrec's belongings and the few that were her own until she could count them off in her sleep. Petra would go, that went without saying. He was the strongest of the trained stallions, and Kerrec was his rider.

The day before they were to leave, a powerful storm came off the Mountain. It lashed the citadel with wind and hail, and drenched it with rain. There was no riding in the outer courts that day, and the riders' training took itself indoors for a day of books and harness cleaning.

Valeria went looking for Kerrec at midmorning. He had promised to test her in certain exercises of magic, and she had been waiting for an hour, reading and rereading the same passage in the book of spells that he had given her to study. It was completely unlike him to be late for anything. He never forgot, either. Something must be wrong.

She called up a small seeker spell and sent it on its way, and followed close behind.

It did not go far, only to the Master's study. Valeria knew better than to eavesdrop. That did not stop her from slipping as close to the door as its wards would allow, and sharpening her hearing with a subtle working.

The prickle in her spine had been right. They were talking about her.

"You know we can't leave her behind," Kerrec was saying. "She's too dangerous on her own, and no one here is willing or able to deal with her."

"One of the riders will look after her if he's commanded," said Master Nikos. "The Dance will take most of your strength, and whatever is left, you know your family will want. You can't let yourself be torn by the need to look after a child."

"That child," Kerrec said, "is the strongest mage of her age and level of training that I have ever seen. Now granted I'm young and haven't seen all that you have, but tell me the truth. Have you seen anything like her?"

"Not in my time," Master Nikos admitted grudgingly. "Even so, this is the most vitally important Dance of your life. It has been a hundred years and more since it was last done. It may not be danced again while you live. It must be done perfectly. The patterns must be flawless. There must be no slip or error, and no wavering. The empire's stability rests on the execution of this Dance."

Kerrec could not have been pleased to be lectured as if he had been a rider-candidate, but his response was quiet. "I do know that. I am ready, and so is my stallion. Nevertheless, my student must come to Aurelia. That is a premonition, Nikos. She must come."

Master Nikos was silent for a while. Then he said, "I have a premonition of my own. No good will come of this."

"Less good will come of leaving her here," Kerrec said. "When we reach the city, I'll take her to my sister. She'll be safe there while I'm occupied with the Dance."

"Are you sure of that?"

"Surer than I am that either she or this school will be safe if we leave her behind."

Master Nikos sighed gustily. "Very well. You know the risks and their cost. There's nothing more that I can say."

"I don't think you'll regret it," Kerrec said, "in the end."

"I would hope not," said Master Nikos.

One thing Valeria had not been letting herself think about. If she went to Aurelia, she would not see Euan again for months if at all. Like Kerrec, she knew she had to go, but it was not as easy as it might have been.

Euan was not in the stable when she went there. She was late, but she had been later on other nights. Tonight, if he had come, he had not waited.

The stallions were unusually quiet. Instead of their usual night's instruction, they had given her a vision. She saw herself on Sabata's back, riding a pattern she almost recognized. There were stars underfoot and darkness over her. Everywhere she turned was impenetrable night.

It was a brief vision. There was nothing overtly frightening in it, and yet she could not get it out of her head. It had something to do with the Dance in Aurelia, but what, the stallions were not telling.

She needed Euan. She needed his warmth and his solid presence, and the forgetfulness he could give her.

She knew where he must be, but she could not make herself go there. She had not set foot near the School of War since the brawl in the tavern. Tonight was not the night to face that memory.

She slipped into Sabata's stall. He cocked an ear at her but did not lift his head from his manger. She slipped her arms over his broad warm back and pressed her face to his neck, drawing in the warm smell of clean horse. It kept her from bursting into tears. Euan knew that she was leaving in the morning. He could at least have come to say goodbye.

She left Sabata to his hay. He went with her into the night, riding soft and quiet in the back of her mind.

Kerrec had been safely asleep when she crept out. He was awake when she came back, sitting in her cupboard of a room with the moon shining through its window, breaking through a wall of cloud. He looked as if he had been there for some time and was ready to stay until morning.

Then she was almost relieved that Euan had abandoned her on this of all nights. The only scents on her were horse and hay and the sudden squall of rain that had drenched her as she crossed the last courtyard.

"We're leaving before dawn," he said. "That's the word from the Master. You won't be sleeping much tonight, if you sleep at all."

If she had slept in the stable, she would have been caught there when the grooms came for the horses.

Euan had been wise. Had he known? Or had he been prevented from coming?

"Why?" she asked Kerrec. "Is something wrong?"

"Probably not," he said. "The guard's been doubled. You'll stay as close to me as my shadow. No wandering off. Do you understand?"

"Tell me what it is," Valeria said.

She held her breath. She was pushing her limits, and she knew it.

This time he let it go. "It's nothing the Master can name. A feeling, that's all."

"Can you name it?"

His brows drew together. He had a surprising beauty by moonlight, like an antique carving.

That was not a sensible thought. She was still missing Euan. This was a man and young, something she did not often remember, and he was sitting on her bed. She hated his arrogance and his cold distance, but she was in love with the way he moved. Even sitting still, he was perfectly upright, perfectly poised, with a dancer's balance.

Her wandering wits had taken her far away from the question she had asked. When he answered it, she almost did not understand what he meant. "I don't know if it has a name. Something's waiting on the road. We'd best be prepared for whatever it is." He paused. "What is it? Do you know something?"

"No," she said. She was telling the truth. The vision the stallions had given her had nothing to do with this. It was about the Dance, and that was in Aurelia.

"Ah," he said as if it did not matter. "Well. Maybe it's nothing. An extra company of guards won't hurt us, and might even be useful. Some of those passes will need every hand we have, to get the mules and horses over."

"You'd think the stallions would fly," Valeria said.

He surprised her with a sudden smile. "Oh, but that would be too easy. They'll make us work. It's our lot in life."

She could not help but smile back. On those rare occasions when he showed the lighter side of himself, he was irresistible.

He stood up. He seemed almost awkward, which was not like him at all. "You'll want to sleep as much as you can. Be sure to wake at the night bell. I've left a thing or two for you in the outer room for the journey."

She did not know what to say except, rather weakly, "Thank you."

"Don't thank me yet," he said. "Go. Rest. Until morning."

He left so quickly she almost thought he was running away. Could it be? Was the great rider afraid of a woman in her bedroom at night?

Sometimes he was almost human. Then he found a way to make her hate him again. He would be his old and unpleasant self in the morning, she was sure.

Meanwhile she was thinking of him in ways that would have made Euan furiously jealous.

"I," she said to the moon, "am an idiot. What would *he* want with me? He's as blind to women as a eunuch priest."

The moon might have begged to differ, but Valeria was not listening. She stripped and lay down in her solitary bed. It was not cold, that much she could say for it. It still kept the warmth of Kerrec's presence.

She would rather have had a living body in her arms, even if it cost her whatever sleep she might have had. As it was, she slept longer than she had in a month, but when the bell roused her, she felt as if she had not slept at all. Her dreams had been dim and strange. They slipped away even as she woke, but the memory of sadness and the shiver of fear stayed with her.

She shook it off. The storm had dissipated in the night. The sky was clear, the stars eerily bright. The moon was setting. It would be a fine late-summer day with a taste of early autumn.

She dressed and hefted her pack and saddlebags. Kerrec's gifts were waiting outside. The bow was a horseman's bow, made light for a woman's hand, but strong. There were two quivers of arrows with it, and a knife almost long enough to be a sword.

That was a measure of his foreboding, that he went so far as to arm a woman. She slung the bow in its case behind her and belted the short sword around her waist. She was loaded down as she made her way to the market square where the caravan was forming.

The stallions were waiting in the middle, four times four of them. A few had riders standing by them, but most dozed by themselves with a groom here and there. The rest of the horses were mortal beasts, and the pack train was a long line of mules.

Petra napped, hipshot, near the end of the line of stallions. Valeria looked around for the sturdy chestnut that she had selected from the common stables yesterday. It would be like the grooms to forget to bring him out, but after a moment she saw him with the rider-candidates' horses. Most of those were still riderless, which suited her perfectly.

She angled across the courtyard toward the red gelding. Before she was halfway there, a white whirlwind roared over her. She staggered and clutched at the first solid object her hands could reach.

Sabata's mane tangled in her fingers. His neck arched, snaky with fury. He hissed like a cat and struck at the chestnut.

The gelding was no fool. He backed away hastily, dragging half the line of remounts with him. Sabata shook his mane at the lot of them and presented himself broadside.

She did not clamber astride as he was ordering her to do. "You can come," she said. "I'm not the one to stop you. But you've never carried a rider. You don't know what you're in for."

He pinned his little curling ears and refused to listen. He was not going to let her ride anyone else. She would ride him or she would walk.

"Very well," she said. "But I did warn you. Come here."

She was not entirely sure he would obey, but now that it seemed she would cooperate, he was glad enough to do as she told him. She had to go all the way to the stallions' stable for a saddle wide enough to fit him, and a bridle made for that short, broad, deep head. He sucked in his breath and fussed at the girth, but he tolerated it. He champed the bit in amazement at the taste of cold metal on his tongue.

He was still contemplating the novelty when she led him back to the caravan. By then most of the riders were there, and all of the servants. They stared. Some scowled, and others whispered to one another.

She kept her chin up. This was Sabata's decision. The riders did not like it in the least, but they were not about to cross a Great One.

Kerrec was one of the last to come out. Only Master Nikos was still missing. He took in the scene with a lift of the brow that was all the comment he chose to make. When she set about mounting, he was there to steady the stirrup and the horse.

Sabata did not buck or panic as a mortal horse would have. He was stronger than a mortal horse, too, and bore her weight easily. But he forgot to breathe.

Kerrec stroked his neck and whispered in his ear. She felt Kerrec's loving amusement, although none of it showed in that mask of a face. Sabata wheezed, sighed hugely and shook himself from ears to tail.

"You," said Kerrec, singling out a rider-candidate. "Make sure her horse is ready. She'll be changing mounts on the road."

Valeria glanced over her shoulder. The rider-candidate he had chosen was Paulus. Valeria would not have done that.

Paulus would not have, either. His glare in her direction was sulfurous, but he obeyed the First Rider. That much discipline he had learned. He took the chestnut's rein and mounted his own nondescript brown mare.

Then at last Master Nikos came out with an escort of riders, guards and servants. He, like Kerrec, took in the sight of Valeria on the Great One's back and said nothing. That surprised her. She had thought a master would argue with a Great One, but apparently not.

It was nearly sunup when they rode out. Valeria had been scanning the faces of the crowd that gathered to see them off, searching over and over. There was no big redheaded man anywhere. No Euan, and no goodbye. It would have had to be secret, but she did not care. She needed it. She found herself hating him for abandoning her.

She turned her mind resolutely to the horse under her and the ride ahead of her. The anger stayed, but she buried it. She would bring it out again when she had time.

Men, she thought. In the end they were all vermin.

Sabata walked very carefully, getting the sense of the weight on his back. His brothers and cousins came to surround him, carrying riders who had given up hope of commanding them. They were a grand procession, riding out of the citadel in the first rays of the sun.

Chapter Nineteen

Sabata lasted until nearly noon. He would have gone longer, but Valeria could feel the tiredness in his unaccustomed muscles. She stood up to him then. When he snapped at the chestnut for daring to carry the one he considered his, she slapped him hard.

The pain was slight and passed quickly, but the shock lasted for a good hour. Sabata had not had such discipline since he left the mare band as a weanling.

"It's about time, then," Valeria said with a notable lack of sympathy.

He sulked along beside her with ears flat and nostrils wrinkled, but he did not threaten the chestnut any further.

No one but Kerrec would speak to Valeria, but that was nothing unusual. Neither were the stares and whispers behind her back. They were closer, that was all. There was no getting away from them.

In camp the first night, she looked after Sabata because he would let no one else do it. When she went to tend Petra and the chestnut, she found Paulus there and most of it done. She moved to do the rest, but he blocked her. "I'll do it," he said. "First Rider's orders."

That was not exactly true. She had heard what Kerrec said. "Get a start on it," he had said. "Valeria will come when she's done with the young one."

The last thing she needed to do tonight was get into a fight, but she was still raw with Euan's absence, and she had had enough of cold shoulders and hostile stares. She planted herself in front of Paulus. He would have to knock her over if he wanted to finish the chestnut's rubdown.

She watched him think about it, but his eye slid toward Sabata, who was quietly eating grain at the end of the line, and he blanched. That left him with nothing to do but stand and glare.

"Listen," she said. "We can play this game forever in the school, but out here we can't afford a war. I'm sorry I lied to you all about what I am. I'm even sorry I won the testing, since it was for nothing. Less than nothing, from what's happened since. Can we at least have a truce? We're in the same caravan, for the same reason. We need each other, however little we might like it."

"Are you sorry for that?" Iliya demanded, pointing

with his chin toward Sabata. She had not seen him come up with Batu.

She looked where he pointed. A faint sigh escaped her. "No, I'm not. Will it help if I'm sorry I'm not sorry?"

Paulus' scowl deepened. Iliya frowned as he tried to make sense of that. Batu laughed suddenly. "I wouldn't be, either. Do you know what I think? I think if you were a man I would hate you because you're so much more than I'll ever be. Because you're a woman, I don't need to bother with hate. I'm angry because we traveled so far and went through so much and I never guessed—but that's not anger at you, not really. I'm mad at myself. We all are."

"Except Paulus," Iliya said. "He hated you to begin with. Now he just hates you more."

"I do not." Paulus drew himself up. "I couldn't possibly hate you more than I did before. I'll never be your friend. Don't even think it."

"Not for a moment," Valeria assured him. "Still, even if we loathe each other, we can be allies, can't we? It happens all the time. Look at the empire and the Caletanni."

"Why would I want to be *your* ally?"

"If you really are a duke's son," she said, "I don't need to answer that."

His teeth clicked together. "Allies have to trust one another. You came here on the back of a lie. How do we know that anything you say is true?"

"You're a mage," she said. "You can tell."

"Oh, I do hate you," he said.

"We know you do," she said. "Truce? *He* wants us to work together. Can you do that much?"

"I have to, don't I?" he said bitterly.

She did not offer a handclasp. That would have been too much. "Allies, then," she said.

"Allies," said Batu and Iliya, a heartbeat before Paulus grudgingly said the word. She had not been asking them to say anything. The fact that they had, made her feel much less alone.

"We were the broken eight," Iliya said. "We had to fail, or we had to succeed beyond anyone else. That binds us, even if we can't call it friendship."

"You have to admit," Batu said, "there was never an eight like us. Three dead, two failed, three passed and one leaped right up over us and found herself on the back of a Great One. They may never make you a rider, but the gods don't care. They've done it in spite of everything."

"They've done it in spite of me," Valeria said. "I didn't mean—"

"Of course you did," Paulus said. "We all do. Just not so fast. Are you going to let me finish with the horses, or will you do it?"

"I'll do it," she said.

"We'll all do it," said Batu. "Then we'll eat. Are you hungry? I'm starving."

Batu's gift, Valeria thought as she worked with them

to settle the horses, was to turn a budding war into an uneasy but reasonably peaceful alliance. He seemed actually relieved to have her back in the circle again. Iliya, too. Paulus was disgusted, but he always had been. Paulus would never be happy as long as someone else was better at anything than he was.

She would have gone off to eat by herself, but Batu would not let her. The hardest part was filling her bowl from the rider-candidates' pot under all their eyes, and sitting down between Batu and Iliya. Once she had done that, the rest was easier. They were working hard to forget what had happened since the testing. They almost succeeded in making it feel natural.

She was grateful to them for that. They let her go finally, because they were as tired as she was, and morning came early. Her bedroll was spread by Kerrec's, with no one else near and the stallions close by. They were a little apart from the rest.

Kerrec was already wrapped in his blanket. She thought he was asleep until he said, "You did well there."

She paused in slithering into her bedroll. "That was Batu. Did you put him up to it?"

"Batu is a born peacemaker." Kerrec raised himself on his elbow. The nearest fire was too far away to illuminate anything here, but there was enough light from a sliver of moon that she could make out the pale outline of his face. "You need allies. You've been too much alone."

Not at night, she thought. Euan and the stallions had seen to that. She bit her tongue before she spoke the words aloud. "I don't mind being alone," she said.

"Most mages are solitary children," he said. "Even the ones with great followings are alone in the crowd. That's why we form alliances, schools, priesthoods, cabals—anything to lessen the loneliness."

"I'm not lonely," she said. "I like being by myself. It's quieter. No one troubles me."

"What, no one at all?"

She was glad it was too dark for him to see her expression. He was provoking her. She could not seem to armor herself against it. "Why are you doing this? What benefit do you get from it? Are you trying to help, or are you simply cruel?"

She heard the hiss of his breath. That had stung. Good, she thought. "Those were your friends," he said, "your comrades in arms. They were ill-advised to turn against you, and you were unwise to let them. Riders who pass the testing together are bound in heart and magic."

"I'm not a rider," she said. "That's been driven home to me far too often."

Kerrec snorted. "I heard what Batu said. He's right. The stallions have made their own judgment. No matter what we may say, you are what you are."

"Would you say that in front of the other riders? Would you even dare?"

"I have," he said. "They can't hear it. It's more than they're ready to face."

"Why? What's so terrible about a woman and this magic? Most schools of mages make no distinction between male and female. The few that do are more likely to exclude men than women. Why is it so unbearable that a female should be given this gift?"

She had not meant to burst out with all of that. She blamed it on the dark and the moon and the way his voice sounded warm in the night, nothing like his cold daylight self.

He was silent for long enough that she knew she had overstepped and he would not answer. Then he said, "I think it's jealousy, and a fair amount of fear. We don't like to admit it, but the stallions don't rule on the Mountain. The Ladies do. The Lady who came to you in the testing is a Great One, as Sabata is. It's unheard of for one of them to come down and pretend to be a mortal horse and examine one of the Called. Sabata is her son, did you know?"

"No," Valeria said. "No, I didn't. Then she was—"

"She was judging you," Kerrec said, "but you knew that. She was deciding whether to send you the one who was meant."

"That is…amazing," Valeria said, "but what does it have to do with the riders refusing to accept me?"

"Everything," he answered. "The Ladies never come down, never trouble themselves with mortals. They bear their sons for us and their daughters for themselves, and of what they think or do, even what they really are, we know next to nothing. Most of us are content with that. It lets us think they're too far beyond us to be bothered, and from that we conclude that only the stallions will concern themselves with the empire and dance the Dance."

"And only men will ride the stallions." Valeria shook her head. "Any decent horseman knows a woman makes a better stallion-handler than a man. A man is a rival. A woman is the queen mare."

"But you see," he said, "a woman has never been Called. Not in a thousand years. We allowed ourselves to conclude that none ever would be. Then you came."

"You knew," she said. "You knew what I was, and you never said a word."

She thought maybe he shrugged. It was in his voice. "I could feel the Call. I asked Petra, and he said to let you be. Then the Lady came."

"You told me that before. It doesn't explain anything. The others are absolutely horrified, but you never were."

"I'm the youngest," he said. "I suppose I'm still flexible."

"That can't be all it is," she said. "Why are you the only rider who can stand the thought of me?"

It seemed that she had finally gone too far. He did not answer that. When she looked, he was lying down with his back to her, and his blanket was pulled up over his ears.

She hissed in frustration, but short of hauling him out and shaking an answer out of him, there was nothing she could do.

She finished crawling into her bedroll. With all she had to think about, she barely even thought of Euan. Only on the very edge of sleep, just before she slipped off, did she know a brief stab of anger and then of sadness. *He's not dead,* she thought halfway into her dream. *Why am I...*

The thought never finished itself. Whatever the dream was, it was gone when she woke.

Chapter Twenty

This caravan traveled more quickly than the one that had brought Valeria to the Mountain. It had much farther to travel, and a much more urgent errand. The riders had to be in Aurelia well before the Dance.

After eight days on the road without sight or sound of a threat, some of the travelers were beginning to wonder why they needed an army of guards. "Maybe it's a diversion," one of the rider-candidates said. "Maybe there's going to be an attack on the Mountain."

The others scoffed at him. Valeria did not believe it, either. If anything had threatened the Mountain, the stallions would have known. They were quiet, keeping their thoughts to themselves. It was easy to think of them as horses and forget what else they were.

The caravan was still deep in the mountains. A day or two before, she had stolen a look at the guides' maps and seen that they were angling through rough and remote country instead of taking the longer but easier way through the northern passes. They were avoiding attention, and keeping the stallions away from unfriendly eyes.

Even with that, they were coming toward the end of the mountains. Then was a green plain in a ring of snow-crowned peaks, rolling down to a broad bay of the sea. On the bay with its sheltered harbor was the city of Aurelia.

There was no indication at the moment that they were coming to gentler country. The road was little better than a goat track, winding up along knife-edged ridges and down into steep and narrow valleys. The mountains rose higher and higher around them.

This way, as steep and difficult as it was, was the only pass through that jagged range. They had not seen so much as a village in two days. In two more days, if all went well, they would come down out of the pass and find themselves on the edge of the plain.

The stallions were unperturbed by the roughness of the road. Valeria had the distinct sensation that they were humoring their riders. They could have walked through veils of time and space and gone wherever they pleased, but humans had to do it the hard way.

That day they stopped early. It was still broad

daylight, but they had come to the last large, level space that they would find until they reached the lowlands. Travelers had obviously camped here before. There was a stone-wall enclosure for the mortal horses, and a circle of stones filled with the ashes of old campfires.

It did not look as if anyone had camped there in some time. The grass in the horses' enclosure was thick and tall. The stallions shared it while the riders made camp, but one by one they leaped the wall and sought out their riders.

Sabata hung over Valeria's shoulder while she baked bread for the servants' dinner. He was a frightful nuisance, but after the third time she tried and failed to push his head out of the way, she sighed and let him be. He was interested in the barley bread, and ate part of her share when it was cool enough to touch.

Batu and Iliya and even Paulus had grown used to him. As Batu remarked, "We'll all be feeding our dinners to white horses when the time comes. Hers came first, that's all."

That was an eminently sensible way to look at it. Sabata approved. He lipped Batu's hair and charmed an apple out of him, then dribbled bits of it over them all.

Valeria was smiling when she went to her bedroll. It was set apart as usual, with Kerrec's between it and the rest, and the stallions just behind it. She wrapped herself in her blankets, for the nights were cold at this height, and closed her eyes.

* * *

A stallion screamed in earsplitting rage. Valeria was moving—bumping, swaying. Her head was full of fog. It ached horribly. She groped for the comfort of her magic and fell headlong into emptiness.

She clawed her way back up. There was no passage of time in this world she had fallen into, but somehow she knew that hours had passed in the place where her body was. She also knew, as her mind cleared slightly, that she was on the back of a horse. She was trussed like a sack and hung face-down over a saddle. Someone was riding behind her, holding her in place.

Her magic was still out of reach. She was dizzy with trying to find it.

The stallion screamed again. It was Sabata. There was the sound of a struggle and a man's sharp curse, then the clatter of hooves and an explosion of breath on the back of her neck.

The rider either dismounted on his own or fell. Valeria started to slip. She tucked her head and tried to roll, but even with that, the landing knocked the wind out of her.

She lay in a heap. Sabata was standing over her. She could feel the heat of his body and the stronger heat of his rage. His magic was trapped, but that was not the reason for his anger.

She rolled and wriggled until she was on her back. Then she could sit up. She was half-blind with the ache in her head, but she could see well enough.

Tall trees loomed overhead. Light filtered through the branches. Two dozen men on horseback had stopped to stare. Half of them were ordinary dark-haired men in hunting clothes. The other half seemed as tall as the trees, and their hair was either gold or copper.

In between them was a man who seemed half of one and half of the other. He was tall, but not as tall as the Caletanni. His hair was light, but not as light as theirs. With a small but powerful shock, she recognized him from her visions of the emperor and the Dance.

Maybe he was the emperor's son. Maybe not. Whatever the truth of that was, one thing was absolutely certain. He was a mage. Even with her magic closed away where she could not touch it, she could recognize the power in him. His spell had trapped her and Sabata and, she saw as she turned her head, Kerrec.

He was bound hand and foot as she was, but he sat upright on the back of a plain bay horse. There was a net of magic over him, so strong she could see it in the daylight. It held him perfectly still. The only living part of him was his eyes. They were open, alert and fully as enraged as Sabata.

"Tell your stallion to stand aside," the mage said. His accent was not Caletanni at all. He sounded like Kerrec. When she gaped at him, he said with even less patience, "Tell him we will unbind your hands and feet and let him carry you, but he must let us near enough to cut the cords."

"No," said Valeria. That made him gape in his turn. "I'm not riding him. He's too young. Give me a horse that's strong enough to carry me. I promise I won't try to bolt."

"You will not in any case," the mage said, "but your promise is reassuring." He gestured toward the dark-haired men, who must be his guards.

They came forward warily, even after Sabata moved off at Valeria's insistence, and cut her bindings and hauled her to her feet. She promptly lost the last of her dinner in the roots of a tree, but once her stomach was empty, she felt better.

There was a horse waiting for her, which she managed to mount without disgracing herself. She stroked the horse's neck in apology and glared at Sabata when he snapped his teeth in the gelding's face.

Sabata followed reasonably tamely as the riders took to the road again. It was a narrow track winding among trees, mostly uphill. The Caletanni rode in the front and rear. The Aurelians were in the middle, surrounding their captives.

The mage was behind her. He was strong. He had snatched a First Rider and a rider-candidate out of an armed camp under the eyes of two quadrilles of stallions, and captured and more or less controlled a Great One.

Valeria had had no inkling. She wondered if the stallions had.

She looked back over her shoulder. The man

seemed mortal enough. His face was shuttered and his lips were tight. He was tiring, maybe, but she could not feel any weakening of the bonds.

Somewhere deep down below her magic, she was afraid. Fear made her angry, and that was good. It kept her headache from overwhelming her. She had to think clearly, to be ready for whatever came, in whatever form.

Kerrec was riding in front of her. Even spellbound and half-conscious, he rode beautifully.

He must be the reason for this. She must be incidental, and Sabata, like an idiot, had followed and been caught along with her.

Those were not comforting thoughts. Neither were her speculations as to what their captors meant to do to them, especially Kerrec. She was not dead yet, which meant she was going to be kept alive for a while. Probably she would live long enough to find out why the three of them had been captured.

The Aurelians did not speak to her or to each other. The Caletanni exchanged a word or two now and then, but they were mostly silent as well. They made as little noise as possible, riding under a shield of magic, up and over a long ascent and down to a big rambling house in a sudden clearing.

It was a hunting lodge, built entirely of wood except for the hearths, which were of stone. Trophies of the hunt were everywhere. The rugs were hides of bear and deer and boar. Antlers and skulls hung on the walls. She noticed gaps where weapons might have hung, but those had all been taken away.

The Caletanni carried Kerrec into the depths of the lodge. The Aurelians left her in a room that did not much resemble a prison cell, or a root cellar, either. It was nearly as big as the house in which she was born, with a bed in it that could have held all her brothers and sisters and a dog or two for good measure. Sabata could have taken a corner of it and barely crowded her out, if she had not seen him safely settled in the stable before she came into the house.

She missed him. The room was enormous, and it was cold. The fire in the hearth barely took the edge off the chill.

There was a copper basin by the fire, full of steaming water, and all the necessities for a bath. After the hot water had warmed Valeria's bones, she found a thick robe to wrap herself in. Servants, whom she had last seen doing guard duty on the road, brought mulled wine and roast venison and fresh-baked bread.

Her first impulse was to refuse it all, violently, and run screaming after Kerrec, but sense prevailed. She needed her strength. She should eat, then she should sleep.

The room was warded within and without. She could not use magic, but neither would the wards let any other magic touch her. She was as safe as she could be in enemy hands.

Chapter Twenty-One

Morning found Valeria awake in the enormous bed. She had been trying for half the night to break the wards or else slip through them, without success. Her headache was notably worse.

She closed her eyes for a few moments. When she opened them, Euan smiled down at her.

She squeezed her eyes shut. That was not the dream she wanted, at all.

When she looked again, he was still there. His smile had died, but it lurked in his eyes. He had abandoned the drab coat and breeches of the School of War for the richly embroidered tunic and vivid plaids of the Caletanni. There was a golden torque around his neck and a heavy gold armlet on each arm. He was as gaudy an object as she could bear to look at this early in the morning.

"I should have known it would be you," she said.

"You're angry," he said. "Will it help if I grovel?"

"Nothing will help," she said, "but letting us go."

He raised his brows. "Don't you want to know who we are and what we want?"

"You're enemies of the empire," she said. "You want to disrupt the Dance. You didn't go about it very well. It won't make any difference just to take one rider, even a First Rider. That's why they went in double strength, in case something happened to one or more of the riders. Now you've taken us, they'll be on guard. You won't get near them again, even with the magic that you've managed to raise. The stallions will stop you."

"You know a great deal," he said, not obviously making fun of her, but she could feel it underneath. "Come with me. We need you."

She stayed where she was, buried in blankets. "Not without clothes, I'm not."

"In the chest," he said, "at the foot of your bed. Would you like me to help?"

"Get out," she said.

He laughed, but he got out. She could feel him on the other side of the door.

She was tempted to take half the day to put on whatever she found in the chest, but something else had crept through the wards, a sense of urgency.

The clothes in the chest were women's clothes. She

tossed them across the room. She would have shredded them, except for the one who was calling her. His anger was much stronger than hers.

She stalked to the opposite wall and snatched up the blouse and short jacket and the divided skirt. The boots were riding boots, at least. The skirt was a little better than useless. She pulled it all on, cursing the excess number of fastenings.

Euan was still outside the door. It was not locked, which surprised her. She glowered at him. "When I get back," she said, "I want proper clothes in that chest."

"I had thought those *were*—" He stopped before she could hit him. "I'll see to it. Will you come now?"

"Didn't I just say I would?"

She knew she was walking a thin line. Euan was not a friend, no matter how many nights they had been lovers.

This morning he needed her. That made him tolerant. She resolved to keep her temper under control, the way she was learning to do in the school. Rider's discipline was to be calm and focused no matter what she might be feeling underneath it.

She needed every scrap of that as she came nearer to the force that called her. It was Sabata, of course. He was locked in a stable with wards on it so strong they made her stomach heave. Even through those she could feel his rage.

She broke the lock with a little rage of her own. It

was wonderfully satisfying to spray the metal in molten droplets across the door. Even more satisfying was the sudden pallor of Euan's face.

He must have forgotten the extent of what she was, or else never believed it. Magic was not common at all where he came from. But the magic she had was not common anywhere.

Sabata had broken down the inner walls of the stable. They were smashed to kindling and flung up against the outer walls, which the wards protected from destruction. He stood in the middle of the empty space, pulsing so brightly that she shaded her eyes. She moved toward him carefully. He was no danger to her, not really, but he was angry enough to forget himself.

She had hardly thought it before he exploded in a whirlwind of hooves and teeth.

Euan was behind her. She struck him with a blast of her own rage. It was focused and controlled as Sabata's was not, and it drove Euan back without harming him, out of the door and into the safety of the stableyard.

Sabata could not touch him there. The stallion did not care. The man was gone, that was all that mattered.

He came quietly to Valeria and breathed into her hands. "Can you get us out of this?" she whispered into his ear.

It flattened. As little as he liked to admit it, he could not. The wards were too strong.

"There must be a way," she said. "You need to eat and drink, to keep up your strength. I'll try to find Kerrec. He'll know what to do."

Sabata snapped lightly at her. He was frustrated even more than angry. He was too young and weak. This body was still growing and changing. He was not master of it yet, or of the power that had been born in it.

She comforted him as best she could. He had not destroyed the hayloft or the grain bin, and the water barrel was full. She fed and watered him, then groomed him with a twist of straw. They were both much calmer when she was done.

Euan was still outside when she came out. "No one will come near him but me," she said. "No one else should try."

"That shouldn't be too difficult to arrange," he said dryly.

"You don't think you can use him against the Dance, do you? He's a Great One, but he's terribly young, which is how you can hold him captive at all. His control is poor. He wants to carry a rider, but he's not really ready. If you had to steal a white god, you should have stolen any one of the others—if you could have held him."

"He was the one that came," said Euan. "He insisted on it, rather strongly."

She could imagine how strongly Sabata had insisted. "What do you want of me?" she asked.

"Really. Tell me the truth. I'd be dead if you didn't want or need something you think I have. What is it?"

He should not have been as surprised as he seemed, if he knew her at all. It was the first time she had ever seen him at a loss for words. "I think," he said, "you had better come with me."

She was not afraid to follow him. Euan, like Sabata, would not hurt her if he could help it. He could still kill her, just as the stallion could, but not unless she pushed him to the limit.

This place was enormous. There were wings opening into wings. A maze of dark, wood-paneled corridors led to blind turns, sudden courtyards and occasionally a hall big enough to ride in. Large parts of it must be underground or built into the hillside, because she did not remember its being nearly so large on the outside. Whoever had built it must have had a mind as twisty as these passageways.

She tried to remember the way, but she was hopelessly turned around by the time Euan halted. This hall was smaller than some, and its windows opened on a long view of hillside and trees and, in the distance, the glimmer of a lake. A man was sitting against the light from the windows, playing chess on an inlaid board. His opponent was visible as a flicker of light and shadow. It was substantial enough to move the pieces, but Valeria could see through it as if it were made of glass.

She hardly needed that to know that the man was the mage who had captured both a First Rider and a Great One. He was little more than a silhouette, except for his hand. There was a ring on his finger, heavy gold, set with a carved black stone. Her eyes would not fix on that stone for anything she could do. The harder she tried, the more they slid away.

His magic was in the stone. She raised her eyes from it to his face, narrowing her eyes against the glare, peering until his features came clear. He looked more like the emperor than she had thought when she first saw him, but mostly he reminded her of Paulus. He had the same mincing accent when he spoke, and the same air of grievance with the world.

"You took your time," he said.

"The stallion is calm," she replied, "for the time being."

He curled his lip. His eye bent to the board and fixed on the king, which was crowned with a golden diadem. It marched unimpeded toward the enemy's camp. "Checkmate," he said.

The shadowy opponent dissipated into sunlight. The man's hand swept over the board. The pieces scurried for cover, diving beneath the squares or springing into the box that lay beside the board.

Only the knight stayed on the board. He was beautifully carved, shaped like a rider on a cobby white horse. The horse tossed its ivory head and sprang into Valeria's hand.

She stared down at the chess piece. Once it touched her skin, it turned into carved ivory, cool and inert in her palm. She laid it down carefully.

"You have strong magic," she said.

"Are you awed?" he asked.

"No."

That stirred him out of his boredom. "You are."

"I'm not." She sat where the shadow-thing had been. It made her shiver, but she was not about to let him see that. "Euan thinks I'm too clever for my own good. Suppose you tell me what you want, and what it has to do with me."

"You are clever," the mage said, "and well above yourself. What are you, a farmer's daughter?"

"And you are an emperor's son," she said. "Does it matter, in your order, what you were before you were called to it?"

"In my order we are all princes," he said.

"In mine," she said, "we are all horsemen."

"But you are not a man," he said.

She smiled her sweetest smile. It made him blink. "Nor do I wish to be. So, sir prince, what do you want with a farmer's daughter?"

"Not what you might be thinking," he said with a glance that dismissed the whole graceless length of her. Even in a skirt, it said, she was no more alluring than a boy.

"Gothard," Euan said in a surprising growl, "get over yourself and answer her question. Or I will."

"Gothard?" said Valeria. "That's not an Aurelian name."

"So it isn't," Euan said. "I believe they call him Marcellus Aurelianus when he's at home."

Valeria nodded slowly. "Yes. Yes, that's the name I remember from my lessons. Not that I care, mind you. Rude is rude, whether you're a slave or a prince. He's not going to answer my question. Do I have to keep guessing?"

Gothard's face had gone stiff. Euan looked as if he was fighting back laughter. "You guess well in light of what you know," he said. "We have in mind to influence the Dance, yes. We work toward a certain future, and the Dance can shape it."

"Then why do you need me? I'm newly Called. I'm years from being able to dance the Dance."

"If you were to stay on the Mountain," Gothard said, "most likely you would never dance it at all. They won't grant that privilege to a woman."

"You don't know that," she said. "No one does, even the riders."

"You know them," he said, "and you can say that?"

Her jaw set. She wanted to keep defying him, but he was too nearly right. "It's not me you need, anyway, is it? It's the First Rider. I'm just an accident."

"Actually," said Gothard, "no. You are an anomaly. A woman has been Called, and a Great One has come to her. These are great things, unheard-of things. I'm not a mage of the Dance, or an Augur, either, but I have a degree of foresight. I see how the tides of time swirl around you."

She shivered, but she said, "It doesn't matter. I'm too young to make a difference."

"We don't think so," Gothard said. "My ally here has told you of a school of horse mages where a woman would be welcome. Have you thought about that?"

"Not much," she said.

His lip curled. Whatever he might think of her importance in the realm of magic, he clearly had a low opinion of her intelligence. "You should think about it," he said. "Think hard. You'll never be more than a servant on the Mountain. Here is a place where you will be welcome, and where your arts and powers will be venerated."

"I don't know anything about it," she said. "I've never heard of it. There are no stallions there, no white gods."

"There will be," he said. "They'll come to you. The Mountain doesn't rule them, whatever the riders there might think. They rule themselves. They'll go where the true power is."

"If that's so," she said, "why aren't they there already?"

"They're waiting for you," Gothard said.

She shook her head, but there was no use in arguing. "It's less than a month until the Dance. I still don't know what you think I can do to it, or why you think I would."

"That will come clear in time," said Gothard. "For now, be content to keep your stallion under control, and to ponder your choices."

"And those are?"

She was trying his patience sorely, but he had more self-control than she might have expected. He kept his temper, just. "To help us willingly or unwillingly. To act under duress, or to act freely as a rider of the School of Olivet. Not a candidate, you will notice. A rider of the first rank, and likely to rise quickly, if your talents are as considerable as I'm told."

"I don't have the choice of leaving?" she asked. "What about Kerrec? Where is he? What are you doing to him? You'll never make him play your game. He's a First Rider. He can't be won away for any—"

"Mestre Olivet was a First Rider," Gothard said.

"Kerrec won't betray the school," she said. "He's not capable of it."

"That remains to be seen," said Gothard. He turned his shoulder to her, dismissing her.

"That went well," Euan said.

Valeria glowered at him. She was in no mood to make light of anything, let alone a case of obvious treason.

Not that he would see it as such. He was a barbarian. He wanted the empire to fall.

"I don't like that man at all," she said. "I don't care how beautiful his magic is. He's an arrogant bastard."

"He is that," Euan agreed, "but he's also my cousin, and he's useful to our cause."

"Not mine," Valeria said.

"It could be," said Euan. "Wouldn't you be glad to have free rein with your powers?"

She decided not to answer that. Her silence seemed to satisfy him, to a point. He left her in the room she was thinking of as her prison, and shut the door on her.

He did not kiss her. Maybe he thought of it, but if so, he did not let her know it.

She flung herself on the bed and buried her face in cushions, and thought about tears. But those would solve nothing. She decided to stay angry. Anger was useful, if she controlled it properly. Anger would keep her from giving in.

Chapter Twenty-Two

Kerrec was drugged. It was an unusual potion, not so much for the herbs that were in it as for the magic that acted on them. He occupied himself for a long while in untangling the different elements. They were complicated, but he liked complicated things. The Dance was the most complicated thing of all. This was mere simplicity beside it.

It was simple but effective. He could think, more or less. He could see, if his eyes happened to fall open. His body was perfectly immobile. He could not even twitch a finger.

"Good morning, brother," a voice said above him.

He could not turn his eyes to see who belonged to the voice, but that did not matter. He only had one brother, and that brother belonged to the voice.

Gothard moved into his range of vision. "You're weaker than I thought. Or am I stronger? How long has it been since we saw one another?"

Kerrec would not have answered even if his lips had obeyed him. Gothard knew as well as he that it had been five years since they were in the same place at the same time. Gothard had been a sullen boy then. Now he was a bitter man.

He did seem a fraction less bitter now that he had Kerrec in his power. "Imagine," he said, "the great mage, the master of gods, captured and held like a common mortal. Are you regretting now what else you could have been?"

The spell had slipped from Kerrec's head and shoulders. He still did not choose to speak.

"You could have been emperor," Gothard said. "You gave it up, with your name and rank and all else, when you went to the Mountain. That doesn't trouble you at all?"

"I know it troubles you that Briana is heir," Kerrec said.

"Of course it does," said Gothard. "She's younger than I am. She's female. Her only qualification for supplanting me—the only one, out of all that we both are—is that her mother was Aurelian and empress, and mine was barbarian and a concubine. Therefore she is legitimate and I am not, and she is heir and I, beyond appeal and beyond recourse, am not. Can she lead armies in war? Can she keep the respect of the legions? Can she—"

Kerrec allowed himself to smile. "You were always an easy mark," he said.

He saw the blow coming. He could turn his head enough to ride with it, but it still half stunned him. His cheekbone might be broken. He could not muster enough power to read his body, let alone heal it.

Pain was illusion. It was not easy to convince his body of that. His eyes persisted in leaking. He blinked at Gothard through the tears.

"Do you know," said Gothard, "your little doxy reminds me of our sister. Is that why you keep her? Gods know, there's not much to her yet. Though I suppose, mewed up on the Mountain, a man will take whatever he can find."

Kerrec had always had one advantage over Gothard. He could control his temper. It was harder now than usual, but that was the drug, he told himself.

"You are going to learn a lesson," Gothard said. "I will peel you away layer by layer, body and spirit. When you are naked to the winds of heaven, then I will have a task for you. It will be well suited to your talents. You may even, by that time, enjoy it."

"Anger may serve you now," Kerrec said steadily, "but a time comes when it betrays even the strongest mage."

"Oh, but it's not anger. It's jealousy and hate. I do hate you, my dear brother. You had the prize in your hand and you scorned it. You walked away. You abandoned it for yourself and for any heirs your so-disciplined body may beget. That was purely selfish, brother. You could refuse the throne, but you refused it for your sons as well. Do you think they'll forgive you?"

"Most men of sense would thank me," said Kerrec. "I set them free."

"Selfish," Gothard said, "and arrogant. Always arrogant. No one is better than you. Are you amazed that I could master you with magic? Are you shocked? Indignant? Horrified?"

"I'm impressed," said Kerrec. "The House of Stones was a wise choice for you, as schools of magic go. The stones can channel your temper as well as your magic—for a while. In the end, you'll either learn to control it, or it will control you."

Gothard sneered. "Always the same condescending cant. You'll never know real joy, real anger, real fear, not on your own. But I'll teach you. You'll be a whole man before I'm done with you. Then I'll break you. That will give *me* joy, brother, and considerable satisfaction."

"You talk a great deal," said Kerrec, turning his face away.

He braced for another blow. Somewhat to his surprise, none came. Gothard said to someone out of his range of vision, "Prepare him."

The spell was gone. So were his clothes. Kerrec could move within the limits of the shackles that bound him hand and foot.

A massive man in a leather mask stood over him.

The mask was blank and featureless. There were not even eyes.

With great difficulty Kerrec kept his face blank. The Brothers of Pain, who wore that mask, were mages as well as torturers. Their magic was subtle and terrible.

This was a journeyman of the art. His mask was brown and not the Master's blank white. It was small comfort. He would still challenge every scrap of discipline Kerrec had left.

Kerrec looked past him at Gothard and said, "Ah, how disappointing. I had thought you would break me yourself."

Gothard refused to answer. He nodded to the torturer. The man nodded back.

At first there was no pain. There was pleasure, which was startling. The hooded man touched him as a lover would. The thick fingers were as delicate as a woman's. They found the places where his body shivered in delight. They saved the obvious for last, bringing him almost to the point of release again and again, but never quite letting him go. They fluttered and teased and eventually tormented. But for the rags of discipline, Kerrec would have begged for mercy.

He built a wall inside. Once that was up, what they did to his body did not matter. His spirit was impregnable.

The drug was like a creeping vine. It worked tendrils between the stones of his wall, and cracked and split them. It wrapped strong, woody branches around the fragments. They crumbled one by one.

At long last the torturer flicked a finger just so. The pain was exquisite. The release burned like molten lead. He screamed. His belly convulsed as if hot metal had spurted over it.

Then his tormentor let him be. It would not be for long, he knew. He could not make himself look ahead to the next refinement.

Horses, his Masters had taught him, *even the white gods, live in the moment. For them it is always and perfectly now. Time for them is all one. Therefore the Dance; therefore their power. There is no past or present or future. Only what is.*

He would think like a horse. He would be in the now. He would think of nothing, not pain, not fear. He would remember nothing and anticipate nothing. He would simply be.

Someone fed him. He did not see a face, only a pair of hands that forced a bland gruel into him. When he refused to take it from spoon or bowl, they shoved a funnel down his throat and poured it in. Water followed it.

After his feeding, his tormentors left him alone. He stank of sweat and sex, with a crust drying on his belly and in the hairs of his groin. It itched. He could not reach to scratch it.

That was a torment. He wriggled and shifted, but

he was bound too tightly. He lay still and tried to build his inner fortress again. He would keep trying. It was all he could do.

The Brother of Pain came back. Kerrec, caught in the perpetual now, did not know or care how long it had been. He had soiled himself, maybe more than once. He could feel the burning of outraged skin where he lay in his own filth.

That almost made him laugh. He was a rider. His backside was as tough as old leather. He was also fastidious, enough to be a joke among the riders. They said he bathed three times a day, which some days was not far off.

The torturer cleaned him with those deceptively gentle hands. The water was warm and scented with herbs. The towels were soft and the salve cool and sweet. Kerrec lay on his face while the Brother of Pain stroked his back and buttocks.

He was not prepared for the sudden, sharp thrust, although he should have been. He clenched against it in pure outrage. That made it much worse. It turned indignity to outright pain.

Then pain became pleasure, and that was worst of all. It was not the rape, not that he was being used like a brothel boy. It was that he could not shut it out.

Lie back, they told women, *and think of something else.* That was the horror of it. He could not. He was absolutely in the moment, and completely in his body.

Without any raising of power on his part, a vision came to him. He saw a field newly plowed in spring. He saw a hunt, and the quarry on the ground. She had skin like cream and hair so black it glinted blue. She was fighting with everything she had.

Valeria. Her name was a handhold. She had never been grateful to him for saving her from violation. Maybe she would have fought her way free, after all. She was much more than he had known then. How much more, he was still discovering.

Her face hung in front of him. He dwelt on each separate feature. The curve of her cheek, the faint dimple in the corner of her mouth, enthralled him.

Voices were whispering. At first he ignored them. All his focus was on Valeria.

The voices crept through the walls of his resistance. All too soon, the words came clear.

"Think of what you gave up. You gained magic and power, very great power, but you forfeited the throne. Is that fair to your heirs? Should you not rule both the stallions and the empire?"

He tried to shut out the voices, but they only grew clearer in the silence of his mind.

"Think," they whispered. "Your brilliance, your power, your discipline. What emperor has ever been as perfectly trained as you in the arts of both magic and empire? What man has ever been more deserving of the throne? Your breeding is flawless. Your mastery is unparalleled. You are the youngest First

Rider that the Mountain has ever known. Your destiny is above all others."

No, he said inside himself. *I will not listen.*

"Look before you—see. What an emperor you will be! What beauty, what power. What mercy and justice. All your people will love you, and your enemies will despair."

His mind filled with visions. He saw himself in a golden diadem, wrapped in a mantle of crimson silk, seated on the throne in Aurelia. He saw the court bowing before him. The massed ranks of the legions roared his name. He was no longer simply Kerrec. He was his old, imperial self.

"Ambrosius! Ambrosius! *Ambrosius!*"

"Ambrosius Aurelianus." The Brother of Pain spoke as softly as a woman. "Great lord, noble prince."

Kerrec gritted his teeth. He was not his imperial highness Ambrosius, crown prince of Aurelia. Not now. Not ever again. That had ended the morning he woke and looked up toward the Mountain and heard it singing. He walked away without a glance. He had not looked back since.

The voices whispered and whispered. They told him he was wonderful, he was glorious, he was irretrievably wronged. "You should rule. You, and none other. The emperor should die. You can be the instrument of his death. His life can lie in your hand."

Kerrec probably should not have spoken. It was a

failure of discipline, but he had to say it. "It is useless to tempt a man with the last thing he could possibly want."

That stopped the voices, at least for a while. He hoped the torturer was taken aback.

"No one with a grain of sense wants to be emperor," Kerrec said. "The hours are endless and the responsibility crippling. Every move is watched. Every breath is counted. Not one thought can be his own, until he determines whether his advisors will allow him to think it."

"How is that different from the life of a rider?" the torturer asked in that soft, cooing voice.

Visions flooded at the sound of it. Every slight, every humiliation, every shameful moment that Kerrec had ever suffered on the Mountain reared up and crashed down on him. Life as a nameless nobody had not come easily to an escaped imperial heir. He had been a monster of arrogance and grandiose ignorance. His peers had hated him. His masters had despised him. The stallions had humbled him in every way they knew.

No. Again, finally, he had the sense not to say it aloud. *It wasn't like that at all. I was a flaming idiot, but no worse than many another. I took my lumps as we all did. I was happy. I loved it, even when my body and pride together were one enormous bruise.*

The visions were relentless. He was a fool and blind. He told himself lies to cover the truth. He had been unspeakably wretched and bitterly homesick.

Then his father found him.

He tried to run from that. Of all the memories hidden inside him, it was the most painful. He had faced it four times, once in each test of rank. By the fourth, the edge was a little blunted.

This was all edges. Memory was agony. Every word, every glance, cut like slivered glass.

The emperor came to the Mountain unannounced on the last day of the testing. Kerrec had expected him sooner, and hoped that he would come much later. Never would have been best, but that was too much to hope for.

Artorius chose the most important day of all to appear with next to no escort. He had traveled as if to battle, armed and mounted on fast horses. The guards at the gate recognized him as a mage of another school, but did not see the emperor in the windblown, mud-stained, and travel-worn rider who came asking to speak to their master.

He had warded himself from his son. The first Kerrec knew of the arrival was in the middle of the final test, when he looked up as his mount began one of the leaps, directly into his father's eyes.

Kerrec stayed in the saddle. The gods loved him that day, or he would have tumbled to the sand. Maybe he would have failed the test, and his father would have reclaimed him and taken him back to Aurelia.

As it happened, he not only stayed on, he completed the test. He passed the last of it in a daze, and accepted the champion's cup with numb surprise. By the time he was carried off to bed, he was so full of wine and beer that he did not care who had come to claim him.

He was called to the Master's study the next morning. The Master was not there. Artorius was sitting in the Master's chair, hands tidily folded, completely alone. There was not even a guard hidden behind the ancient and much faded tapestry.

Kerrec stood stiffly at attention, but he did not bow. He was a rider now. Riders bowed only to the stallions.

His father studied him for a long time before deciding to speak. Kerrec had a cramp in his neck from standing so stiffly, which would torment him for days afterward. He gritted his teeth and withstood the pain.

"So," said the emperor. After so long a silence, his voice was a little too loud for comfort. "The Call came on you quickly. Even the Augurs had no warning."

Kerrec lifted a shoulder in a slight, willfully insolent shrug. "It's too late now," he said. "I've passed the testing. I belong to the Mountain."

"Not necessarily," Artorius said. "You are the first imperial heir to be Called, but there is precedent for sons of lesser rank. The emperor may supersede the Call, if the empire's need requires it."

"At the moment," Kerrec pointed out, "it does not. There is no war in progress. The barbarians are as quiet as they can ever be. Even the nobles are more for you than against you. Has that ever happened before?"

Artorius was keeping his temper with obvious effort. "Once or twice," he said. "Tell me. Why did you leave without a word?"

"If I had said anything, would you have let me go?"

The emperor hesitated just long enough that Kerrec knew the truth, regardless of what he actually said. "I would have tried to understand. The Call is sacred, and the Called must never be hindered. But for it to come to the imperial heir—"

"I'm not your only child," Kerrec said. "If you'll listen to me at all, you'll put Briana in my place. She's young, but she's sensible. Her magic is strong. She—"

"That is no longer yours to decide," the emperor said gently.

Kerrec went perfectly still. He had known what answering the Call would do. When he came to the Mountain, the riders had been relentless in warning the noblemen that once they were accepted, they forfeited everything. They became equal to the slave and the pig-keeper who passed the testing beside them. There was no exception, and no appeal.

He said so. "Even you can't drag me home from this."

The emperor's brow arched. "I may not have to. You're not a rider yet, only the beginning of one." The long hands unfolded. "I give you a year before your breeding betrays you. You can't live the common life. It's not in you."

"Why not? You can. You'll dip your wand in anything that—"

Finally Kerrec had succeeded in breaking that imperial calm. He had brought his father to his feet and won himself a sweeping, solid blow. He dropped to one knee with his ears ringing, but he did not fall. He saw the disappointment in the emperor's eyes, then the flinch of guilt.

"I'll show you," Kerrec said. "I'll be the best rider there ever was."

"Don't strain yourself," said Artorius. Suddenly he sounded very tired. "Stay here and you have no father. You have no family. You have no existence outside of this place."

Those were the words of the rite of binding to the Mountain. The Master had spoken them the night before. They had not seemed so final then, or so empty of hope.

"You know I'll stay," Kerrec said. "I have no choice."

"There is always a choice," the emperor said. "You were all my hope. Now you are nothing. You are not even kin."

Kerrec would never let him know how those words tore at his heart. He bent his head, the most that a rider would allow himself in a gesture of respect to a human creature.

The emperor's face went cold. "My son is dead," he said. "The empire will mourn. The priests will sing the rite over an empty tomb."

"That's absurd," Kerrec said. "You can't—"

"The dead may speak," the emperor said, "but the living have no ears to hear."

He turned his back on Kerrec. He shut him out. He rendered him into nothingness.

The pain of it was almost beyond bearing. But Kerrec was as stubborn as his father. He would not beg or plead. Above all, he would not repudiate the Call. He belonged to the Mountain now. There was no turning back.

That was twelve years ago. He had not seen the emperor since. Sometimes Briana came to the Mountain, or Kerrec went to Aurelia or one of the lesser cities on errands for the school, and she was there. As far as the emperor was concerned, his elder son no longer existed. His name was erased from the great book of the lineage. An effigy lay in the City of Bones, the tombs outside Aurelia's walls.

Kerrec was a dead man. He might walk and talk and ride white stallions, but his heart was as cold as a corpse. He loved nothing. Nothing loved him. He had reached the pinnacle of his order and found nothing there but emptiness.

Chapter Twenty-Three

Valeria's dreams in captivity were fever dreams, dreams of fire. She would wake flushed and trembling, with her body throbbing as if she had been with a lover.

One night she started awake. Euan was sitting on the side of the bed, dressed in plaid breeks and a golden torque. His hair was loose. He smelled of beer.

He was not drunk, but he was not sober, either. She meant to scowl and order him out. Instead she caught herself hungering for his touch.

She watched her hand creep out until it touched his arm. It brushed the soft coppery hairs above his wrist, stroking them smooth.

He smiled. If he had said anything, she would have driven him away, but he had the sense to be quiet.

His mood must be as odd as hers. He let her push him back onto the bed and unfasten his belt. She pulled off his breeks. He was still a little slack, but he was growing hard.

She teased him with fingers and tongue. His breath caught. She smiled to herself. His back had begun to spasm.

She brushed his eyelids with a kiss. The charm she laid on him was one of the simplest of all. Any village witch could have worked it. She gave him dreams. If he chose to dream of her, then so much the better.

His arms clasped air. "Valeria," he breathed. "Valeria!"

Very carefully she rose from the bed and backed away. She had insisted, with force, that she be given clothes fit to ride in. She pulled on the shirt and breeches and the closely fitted boots. She combed her hair with her fingers, yanking out the tangles.

On the bed, Euan was making slow and luxurious love to the bolster. She suppressed a pang of guilt. He was her people's enemy. She was giving him better than most people would have said he deserved. He thought he was spending the night with her, then in the morning he would remember wonders.

She turned her back on him. Kerrec was somewhere in this maze of a place.

Her dream tonight had been of him. She had seen him lying on a stone table, and his body was stippled with bruises. A man in a mask bent over him. The mask was eyeless and featureless. She had never seen one like it before, but she knew what it meant. The Brothers of Pain had been haunting children's nightmares since the empire was young.

It was not an easy hunt. She was shaking with urgency, but she had to be supremely careful. She had to be invisible to magic, while hunting for a man who had been shielded by strong magic.

Sabata could not help her. He was under siege from more directions than she could count. In some ways he was in worse straits than Kerrec.

She roamed the darkened halls until dawn, but she never found the room in which she had dreamed of seeing Kerrec. A different kind of urgency called her back finally to the room she thought of as her prison. The charm was wearing off. She had just enough time to throw off her clothes and slide into bed with Euan before he twitched and snorted and was suddenly awake.

He smiled warmly and brushed her lips with a kiss. She tried hard to answer his smile, but the best she could do was a wary squint.

That made him laugh. "Mornings never were your favorite time of day," he said. "Here, wake up. Kiss me. Then put on your clothes. I have a surprise for you."

Her heart leaped, but she crushed it down. Euan would not give her Kerrec, free or otherwise. Something else had him bubbling over with excitement.

"I wanted to tell you about it last night," he said, "but then I thought, no, let her be innocent for yet a while. It's very good, this surprise. I think it will make you happy."

Nothing but Kerrec, freedom and the road to Aurelia would do that. She bit her tongue to keep from saying it.

She gave him his kiss, a brush of lips across his. Naturally he wanted to turn it into something more. So did she, in spite of herself. It was a while before she could pull herself away and dress again in the clothes she had just got out of.

He had little to do but pull on his breeks and belt them, and braid his hair out of the way. He waited, dancing slightly with impatience, for her to finish bracing herself to face the day.

After two days of fog and rain, it was a beautiful morning. Sunlight sparkled on the wet grass. Wisps of cloud dissolved over the mountains.

The eastward wing of the lodge opened onto a grassy terrace that looked out over the valley and the lake. A table was spread there. Silver and crystal gleamed in the sun. Sprays of autumn flowers wound among the plates and bowls and cups.

Gothard was sitting at the table, looking as if he had been carousing all night. Valeria knew the marks of too much magic sustained too long. They looked remarkably like the aftermath of debauchery.

A stranger sat with Gothard. Her first thought was that Gothard had captured another rider. Her second was that he had only captured half of one.

He was an older man, maybe Master Nikos' age. His hair was abundant and beautifully silvered, sweeping back in waves from an elegant and aristocratic face. He was the very image of a senior rider, with his perfectly upright carriage and his air of quiet mastery. And yet when Valeria looked at him, she thought of an apple with a worm in its core.

"Mestre Olivet," Euan said from just behind her.

"My lord," said the man, inclining his head. His dark eyes came to rest on Valeria. A gleam woke in them. "And this—can it be…?"

"It can," Euan said. He sounded terribly smug. "This is Valeria. Valeria, this is—"

"Olivet," said the man, rising and coming forward. He caught her hand before she could escape, and kissed it. "My lady! It is an honor. A very great honor. To stand in the presence of such power—to know that it might consider—" He sighed deeply. "Ah! The gods are kind."

This was supposed to be a seduction. The elegant breakfast, the beautiful setting, were meant to lull her into complacence. Then she would be ripe for what Mestre Olivet had to say.

She did want to hear it, but not for the reasons he might be expecting. He was a mage, and strong, but the power of a rider, the power of the Mountain, was nowhere in him. When she looked for it, she saw open wounds, and all the stallions' magic bled away.

Only one thing was left of the powers of a master.

He could seduce the gullible. His eyes drew people in, and his voice cast a spell.

He insisted that she eat before he began his speech. He filled a plate with his own hands, choosing dainty bits of things that he must think a lady would find tempting. Left to herself she would have gone for the corn porridge and the hotcakes, but he selected little pastries and delicate slices of smoked fish wrapped around slivers of vegetables or fruit. Everything was either sweet or sweeter, and most of it had more charm than substance.

She choked it down and resolved to find herself a real breakfast later. When she could not eat one more bite, she slid the plate away as politely as she could.

Mestre Olivet seemed as relieved as she. "Good," he said. "That's good. Now come."

She had braced herself to be talked at, at length. Instead he took her to a stable not far from the one in which Sabata was imprisoned. Horses were waiting, saddled. They were mortal horses, and none was either white or grey. They had a look of studied patience.

"If you please, lady," said Mestre Olivet, "I would like to see you ride."

Valeria almost laughed. Euan was grinning. He had known. He also knew that she would rather ride than anything else in the world.

She was not ready to thank him yet. She knew the look of a test by now, and this was one.

She took her time choosing a horse. Of the six that were there, the red mare seemed the least resigned to her fate. Valeria introduced herself courteously, letting the mare sniff her hands, then stroking the mare's head and neck. The saddle was pinching. Valeria requested another, and waited until one was brought that fit less poorly, if still not well.

When the mare was saddled, Valeria mounted. The mare stiffened, expecting pain. It took some few minutes to convince her that there would be none. She was ready then to offer her paces, with evident pride, in the order in which she had been taught them.

Someone who did not know the Dance might think that she danced. She shifted from foot to foot. She sidled neatly across the riding court. She spun and reared. She bowed prettily.

Valeria gave up trying to ride and sat quietly, doing her best not to interfere. It was nothing like the test of the Dance that Petra had given her on the Mountain. That had been great power and strong magic. This was trickery.

None of the people watching appeared to know the difference. Gothard might, but he had not troubled himself to walk as far as the stable. Mestre Olivet was smiling in evident pleasure. "You have great art," he said when Valeria brought the mare back toward him and halted. "Great art. A little rough, a little unpolished, but that will come. You, lady, are a rider."

Valeria bit her tongue. She had been going to ask if the mare was mistrained, and if that had been the test, to know what to do in the face of so many errors.

But Mestre Olivet said, "This that you chose, she is the best of our school. You rode her beautifully. We can teach you, indeed we can."

"There are other women in your school, yes?" said Euan.

"There are several," Mestre Olivet answered. "None as talented as this, but they are among my best pupils. Women, I find, are more supple of mind and more delicate in their responses. Their bodies fit less well into the saddle than men's, but they are less difficult to teach and more willing to take correction. Once they begin to learn, they learn quickly. They love the horses, and the horses return the favor."

"So it's not just a magic for men."

"There is no magic to the riding of horses," said Mestre Olivet. "Experience, perception, observation— all of those, one hones to a high art. The rest is plain hard work and simple attention to detail."

This man had held the rank of First Rider. He had been a mage of great power and discipline. Now he denied it all.

And yet, Valeria thought, for him she could be a rider. Maybe she could teach as well as learn. Maybe he could be persuaded to pass on what he had known, even if he had left it behind.

She was slipping, if she could think such thoughts

after such a ride. He was still talking. "All the years that the men on the Mountain claim are necessary to make a rider—nonsense. They cloak their art in obscurity, whereas the truth is divinely simple. A year, two years, and any talented horse or rider can achieve the heights of art."

"It can't be that easy," Valeria said before she could stop herself.

"So they say on the Mountain," said Mestre Olivet.

Chapter Twenty-Four

Valeria smiled and nodded and listened as best she could. Mestre Olivet seemed not to notice that she was giving him less than her full attention. Her mind kept wandering. She kept remembering what the stallions had taught her. Men could be mistaken, but surely the white gods knew how to dance the Dance.

Mestre Olivet made no move to visit Sabata. He did not speak of the stallion or express interest in him. All his talk was of his school and its noble students and its even more noble patrons, none of whom she had ever heard of. He never talked about the horses.

Finally, late in the day, she could escape. Sabata needed to be fed and looked after. Mestre Olivet did not offer to help.

A real master would have asked to see the stallion,

to be sure he was properly cared for. Valeria found that she was quite out of patience with Mestre Olivet. She attacked the stall cleaning with such force that Sabata backed away and snorted. She apologized to him, but a few moments later she was spreading straw with much more enthusiasm than was strictly necessary. He backed to the door and sneezed explosively.

She flung down the last armful and stamped her feet in frustration. "That *man*," she said to the stallion. "That man! I cannot believe that he ever made rider, let alone First Rider. He is an absolute and empty windbag."

Sabata pawed the door. He wanted out, and no wonder.

She should ask before she acted, but she was in no mood to be sensible. She shot the bolt. In the same moment, she pushed the wards outward as far as her strength would allow. That was surprisingly far. Gothard was not done for yet, but he was a great deal weaker than he had been. As far as she could tell, he did not know what she had done, or if he did, he made no move to stop her.

Sabata stood in the doorway, nostrils flared as wide as they would go. Without warning he launched himself into the free air.

For a heart-stopping moment she knew he would break through the thinned and weakened wards and escape. The temptation was overwhelming. But he resisted it. He threw up his tail and ran around and around the field in front of the stable, but he never offered to go past the subtle shimmer of the wards.

When he had run the wildness out, he trotted up to her and blew into her hand. She slipped arms around his neck. He was barely sweating. She inhaled the warm musky scent of him, burying her face in his mane. "You should have gone," she said.

He snapped his teeth next to her ear, but he knew better than to nip. She was there. He would stay. That was all there was to it.

That night she had to endure an endless dinner with the man whom everyone seemed to be regarding as her new teacher. Afterward, Euan followed her to her room.

She surprised herself with how much she wanted him. Or maybe she should be honest and admit that she wanted what he had to give her. It was a release. It took her mind, however briefly, off her predicament.

He fell asleep almost at once, and she made sure he stayed that way. She got up, dressed, and went hunting with redoubled urgency.

She was almost too urgent. She would not have heard it through the pounding of her heart, but she happened to pause in a hallway not too far from the one that led to her room. The doors on either side were locked. Most of the rooms felt cold and empty.

One at the far end was occupied. The sounds coming from it raised the small hairs on the back of her neck. They were almost too soft to hear, and not particularly strident. They were still sounds of pain.

Instinct screamed at her to run in hurling bolts of magic. She forced herself to go quiet and listen. The sounds continued.

She crept forward as silently as she could. She barely breathed. She approached the door and pressed her ear to it.

She could not be sure whose voice she heard. The small gasps and suppressed whimpers could have come from anyone, man or woman. Still, all things considered, there was no question as to who was in there and what was happening to him.

It went on for what seemed a very long time. Her nails had drawn blood from her palms by the time it stopped. Footsteps sounded, moving away from the door. She stopped on the verge of running for the nearest block of shadow.

She had to think fast. If this was Kerrec, and if she was going to get him out, it had better be tonight. She had no plan, no preparations and no means of escape. Except...

The hardest thing she had ever done was to turn and walk away from that door. Within a few strides she was running.

Euan was still asleep. She cast the spell again, although it was a risk to both of them, to keep him under until morning. While he snored on the bed, she pulled what she needed from the chest of clothes, rolling it together and fastening it with belts. Then she ran for the stables.

No one was standing guard there. She got Sabata out easily. The riding horses were a bit more of a challenge. She had to groom and saddle them in the dark, and lead them out without setting off the rest of the horses. For that she used a variation on the same spell that bound Euan.

She was tiring. Magic drew from the same well as physical strength, but faster and harder. She would have to use it judiciously if she was also going to carry a semiconscious man from a prison cell to the yard in front of Sabata's stable. At least the stallion could keep the horses under control while she ran back to Kerrec.

The door was locked. She had expected that. There was a spell for it, which her mother had taught her. She did not have the herbs to burn, but the words were strong in themselves. She drew the rest out of her own magic, knowing what it would cost, but no longer able to care.

Kerrec was lying on the stone table that she had seen in her dream. He was naked, his body clothed in bruises. None of them had broken the skin. That would come later, if she left him there.

At first she thought he was unconscious, but as she started to dress him in the shirt and breeches she had brought, his eyes opened, peering at her without recognition.

That was not supposed to hurt. She finished dressing him, set her teeth, and heaved him up onto her back. He wheezed with pain, but she could not help that. Staggering slightly under his weight, she carried him out.

She paused only once, to shut and lock the door. That would baffle searchers for a little while.

It was a long, hard way back down to the stables. The gods were with her. She met no one out walking the hallways at night. There was no one in the stables, and the yards were empty and still.

Sabata was still waiting. The mortal horses were asleep, nose to tail. They woke quickly when she slung Kerrec over the bay's saddle.

So did he. He scrambled blindly until he was sitting upright. His head drooped, but his back was almost straight. Even in pain, even semiconscious, he could ride.

She had bet their lives on that. She kept the bay's rein as she mounted the black. Sabata was already moving. There were no gates where he was, and fences came down before he touched them. He passed through Gothard's wards as if they had not been there—and that was a very interesting fact, if she had had time or wits to think about it.

She hesitated as she approached the wards. Sabata glanced over his shoulder. His eye drew her onward.

There was a slight tugging as she passed the wards, a hint of resistance, but nothing more. They had not broken or fallen. No alarm had sounded. She, with Kerrec beside her, had simply flowed through them.

She followed Sabata because she could think of nothing better to do. She knew nothing of the country, and the ways he took seemed as good as any. They were mostly south and east, she noticed. He was taking them out of the mountains.

Just before the sun came up, he stopped. The trees had opened on a grassy clearing. There was a stream, cold and clean, and room for the horses to lie down and roll after she had pulled off the saddles.

Kerrec had dismounted on his own, although his knees collapsed under him after half a dozen steps. She did what she could for him. The box of medicines that she had put together at the school must be in Aurelia by now. She had cold water, a few handfuls of feverfew and a bit of comfrey that she had found growing wild near the lodge. With a little magic and a charm or two, they were the best she could do.

Kerrec was quiet while she worked, except for a hiss now and then when she could not help but hurt him. He kept his eyes on her. She could not meet them except in quick glances. They were too raw. Whatever had been done to him had stripped away years of defenses.

She did not know the person who looked at her out of those eyes. The Kerrec she knew was a cold and haughty man. At vanishingly rare intervals, he showed a spark of humanity. Sometimes she tried to imagine him with a woman, or for that matter a man. The effort made her head hurt. There was passion in him, and plenty of it, but it was all given to the stallions and the art.

He still had his magic. The discipline was there, surrounding it with walls and shields. Torture had not touched that.

The same could not be said of his spirit. When she looked into his face, she did not see a man at all, but a deeply wounded boy. There was no arrogance left.

The Brother of Pain had not broken him, not quite. His soul was like his body, badly bruised but still intact. She had come in time for that much at least.

He was refusing to sleep. She finished making camp, which did not take long. She would not risk a fire so close to the lodge. His eyes followed her as she came back toward him. "You have to sleep," she said, kneeling beside him. "Sleep heals."

"Dreams can kill."

His voice was a raw shadow of itself. She coaxed more water into him, until he grimaced and turned his face away. "I'm here," she said. "So is Sabata. We'll stand guard over your dreams."

He made a rasping sound that after some time she recognized as laughter. "A child and a half-broken colt. What do you think you can do?"

That was more like the old Kerrec. She resisted the urge to slap him. He did not need more bruises, even if he had asked for them.

She settled for silence. He shocked her by saying, "I'm sorry. That wasn't called for. I can't seem to keep my tongue in order."

"It's no matter," she said. "We'll watch over you."

"Yes." It was a sigh.

He still struggled. He had been fighting sleep and dreams too long. He could not stop.

She took his head in her lap. Even with the herbs she had given him, his forehead was burning hot. She cooled it with a cloth dipped in water from the stream.

"Good," he said dreamily. "Cool."

She laid her palm against his cheek. It was rough with stubble. She had never seen him dirty or untidy before. He had always been perfectly clean.

She was losing her grip on herself. When she tried to remember Euan, she could not see his face. Kerrec's kept coming between.

It was not supposed to do that. But here she was, and not with Euan.

She could not stay here long. For now, Sabata was hiding them from discovery, but it would be much better if they increased the distance between themselves and Gothard. Valeria kept an eye on the sun, ready to move when it came halfway to the zenith. Kerrec had fallen asleep, thank the gods. If he could manage even an hour, he would be the better for it.

Valeria started awake. She had closed her eyes for a moment. When she opened them, the sun was gone.

The sky was thick with cloud and a chill wind was blowing. She smelled rain.

She could feel the sun faintly through the clouds. It was past noon. She had slept far too long.

Kerrec was snoring softly. Her legs were numb. She eased herself from beneath him. The horses had their backs to the wind, heads down, waiting for the rain. Sabata stood guard.

He snorted at her. He was not sorry he had let her sleep, but it was time to wake and ride.

She hated to rouse Kerrec, but when she touched him after the horses were saddled, she could feel that he was awake. He would not let her help him up. His face was set and his breath hissed, but he pushed himself to his feet and stood reasonably steadily.

Once in the saddle, he took a moment to simply breathe. Valeria left him to it under cover of mounting her own horse and turning the gelding where Sabata led.

The rain began soon after they left the clearing. Under the trees it was not too wet, yet. Valeria had brought a blanket for each of them, which kept off the rain that penetrated the branches.

They rode without speaking. Valeria watched Kerrec, at first for worry and then because her eyes would not leave him. He seemed unaware of her. His pain was a constant thrum on the underside of her awareness, but she thought it was a little less than it had been. Simply being away from that room, on the back of a horse, with sky overhead, was helping to heal him.

* * *

The day grew darker, the rain heavier. The wind had an edge to it. Kerrec began to shiver. Valeria was none too comfortable herself.

"Sabata," she said to the white blur ahead of her. "Sabata!"

She felt his response. If it had been set in words, it would have been, "Hold on. Just a little farther."

She was not at all sure that Kerrec could hold on. She rode her horse up beside him. His head was bowed. The blanket had slipped from it. His hair was plastered to his skull.

She slid from her saddle to his horse's croup and wrapped her arms around him. His whole body was shaking.

"Sabata!" she said again. "We need to stop *now*."

Soon, he replied inside her.

Chapter Twenty-Five

It would never be soon enough before they got out of the rain. It was coming down in torrents. Kerrec was cold to the bone, even with what warmth Valeria could give him.

She could no longer see where she was going. Her horse was following Sabata, she hoped. For all she knew, they were wandering aimlessly through the wilderness of trees.

They stopped abruptly. The bay's nose was pressed to Sabata's broad dappled rump. Valeria squinted through the rain.

There was an opening in the hillside, with a ledge of rock overhanging it. Brambles hung down like a curtain. Sabata disappeared behind them.

Valeria slid to the ground, slipping in the mud, and

led the mortal horses in Sabata's wake. They hesitated to pass the brambles, but she willed them to move and they obeyed.

The cave was surprisingly large and light. A crack, a sort of chimney, led upward in the back of it. It was angled so that rain did not come in but light did, such as there was on as dim a day as this. It was enough to show a ceiling higher than a mounted man's head, and a not too uneven floor of earth and stone. Most wonderful of all, under the chimney was a ring of stones, charred with fire, and nearby someone had piled enough cut wood to warm the place for a week or two.

There was no sign of whoever had left the wood. It was dry and well seasoned. The fire pit looked as if it had not been used in months or years.

Valeria got Kerrec off the horse, leaving the animals to stand—with a pang of horseman's guilt—while she tended the man. She spread the blankets on the floor next to the fire ring, persuaded Kerrec to sit on them, and set to work making a fire.

That was simple. She stacked the logs, arranged the kindling, and spoke the Word that her mother had taught her when she was a child.

The fire leaped from her hand and dived hungrily into the kindling. While it explored its new home, she pulled the clothes off Kerrec, against his halfhearted protests.

She had never seen him completely naked. While she was his servant, he had bathed and dressed without her help.

There was no time now to be modest. His lips were blue. He was shivering uncontrollably.

The fire was burning well, but it took time to grow to its full strength. She tried to persuade Kerrec to drink a little wine, but he was shivering too violently to swallow.

With a hiss of frustration, she pulled the saddles from the two ridden horses, rubbed them down hastily, then shook out the warm and redolent blankets and dropped them over Kerrec. As the horses nosed along the cave's edge for the grass that grew in mats and patches under the ledge, she pulled off her own clothes and climbed under the blankets.

The smell of horse was overpowering, but she found it more pleasant than not. She pressed her body to Kerrec's. His skin was icy. She rubbed his hands until some little bit of life came into them, and folded them between her belly and his. His teeth chattered in her ear. She ran her hands up and down his back and buttocks, rubbing them as she had his hands, being careful not to cause him pain.

Slowly warmth crept into him. His shivering slowed and then stopped. His teeth no longer chattered. The rigidity left him. He sighed, gusting warm breath past her ear.

His blood was flowing again. She knew how strongly by the thing that hardened between them.

She could have drawn away and left him to his blankets and the heat of the fire. She found she did not want to. He was smaller than Euan, and his skin was smoother. He was only a little taller than she, but she knew well how strong he was.

It was odd to kiss a shaven face. The stubble scratched and pricked, but not too badly. His skin tasted of horses and of rain.

At first he was stiff with shock. Then suddenly he gave way. It was like a rush of fire.

With Euan, gods knew, there was passion enough. She loved him, maybe. She lusted after him for certain. With Kerrec it was more. More everything.

Euan had no magic. Kerrec was overflowing with it. Even after torture, exhaustion, the sick aftermath of the drugs he had been fed, he was a master mage. The sheer beauty of what he was made her want to burst into tears, or go all dizzy with joy.

He wanted her. It was not only that he had been cold and was warm again, and his body knew what to do to finish driving out the chill. He looked into her eyes and saw her—herself, no one else.

This man, cold? No more than the sun was. It had all been walls and shields and defenses.

There were no walls here. She kissed him until her head swam. His arms locked around her. His back arched just as she opened to him.

There was no awkward moment, no half-comic tangle as they struggled to fit. He knew and she knew exactly how and where to move. It was as smooth and inevitable as the Dance.

He had taught her that every rider had his own rhythm, and so did every horse. A rider learned to ride whatever he was given, to find the horse's rhythm and match it. But when horse and man were matched by nature, then everything was infinitely easier.

It was the same with this man. His presence that had been such an endless irritation was as soft as the slide of silk. She could feel what he wanted and where he wanted it. What she wanted, he gave her before she had time to think it. They were like one body and one spirit. What thoughts were hers and what were his, she could no longer tell. They were all one.

He had loved her from the moment he saw her, but he had hidden it because he was her teacher. Distance, discipline—he had tried too hard to cultivate them. He had come all too close to making her hate him.

For a dizzying while, her body overwhelmed her mind. Words vanished. The whole world was the touch of his lips and hands, and the heat of him inside her.

She cried out. An instant later, so did he. Her body throbbed. She clung to the moment of climax for as long as she could. But all mortal things ended, and this was briefer than most. She let go and sank with a sigh.

"Why?" she demanded.

They were still joined in the spirit. His puzzlement stumbled through her.

"Why did you hide it?" she pressed him.

"You know why," he said.

"So what if you were my teacher? I'm not so weak I can't refuse a man I don't want—even if he does outrank me."

"It wasn't fair," he said. "And you disliked me so very much."

"I thought you despised me."

"Gods, no," he said. "I was terrified that you would see how undisciplined I really was. I wanted you desperately, but not by force. Not because I was your master and you were my servant."

"You don't know me very well, do you?"

He bridled at that. The union between them stretched but did not, miraculously, snap. "What if I had told you how I felt? Would you have laughed, or would you have slapped me? Would you have hated me even more than before?"

"I don't know," she said. Honesty was not easy, but there had been too little of it between them. "I didn't know you very well."

He laughed. It was almost a gasp of pain. "I don't think I know myself."

She lifted herself on her elbow. It was nearly dark, but she could see him perfectly clearly. She did not think she would ever be blind to him again. He was inside her, as deep down as the stallions were.

This was more than she had bargained for. She had a sudden urge to leap up and run far away. All that held her was the howling of wind outside and the hiss of the rain—and the sight of him lying there, a mass of bruises and half-healed cuts, smiling crookedly. He looked nothing like First Rider Kerrec.

The only thing she could think of to say was, "We should eat, then try to sleep. As soon as the rain stops, we have to ride."

"Yes," he said. Then: "Have you given any thought to where?"

She had hoped he would not ask that. But since he had, she answered, "I think we're closer to the Mountain than to Aurelia. It will be safer there."

"Nothing is safe if our captors do what they set out to do."

"We can warn the riders through the stallions," she said. "You shouldn't—"

"I have to go to Aurelia."

"You can't," she said. "You aren't strong enough."

His jaw set. "I must. I know what they're going to do. I have to stop it."

"Didn't you hear me? You're as weak as a baby. Your magic is full of holes. You won't even get that far. That mage, that Gothard, will kill you."

"Maybe," he said, "but I have to go."

"You do not."

"I do," he said. He reached up and laid a finger over her lips. "No. No more argument. This needs my training, and such discipline as I have left. It needs me. Gothard is strong, but he's not invincible."

"He's stronger than you," she said stubbornly, shaking off his hand.

He shook his head. "Not in himself he's not. I was always stronger, even before I went to the Mountain."

She opened her mouth, then shut it again. He was coming back to himself, and making her feel like a fool. "I noticed before that he looks like you. What is he? Cousin?"

"Brother," said Kerrec.

"But that makes you—"

He nodded.

"His mother was Caletanni. There's nothing of that blood in you. Which means—"

"Yes."

She was not angry. She was hardly surprised. She had guessed a long while since that he had been born a nobleman, and a duke at least. Paulus was too respectful for him to have been any less. But—

"You're dead," she said.

He threw his head back and laughed until the tears ran. She was ready to slap him silly by the time he stopped. His eyes were still streaming, and he was hiccoughing, but he could talk, more or less. "There! You see? I'm in no danger. I'm already dead."

She did slap him then, and not lightly, either. Deep down was the thought that the penalty for striking a deceased imperial heir must be slightly less than the one for flattening a First Rider.

He was in no condition to blast her, and he did not seem inclined to try. He lay in his nest of horse blankets with a new bruise darkening on top of the old ones, grinning like an idiot. "You're not even in awe of me," he said.

"I want to throttle you," she said. "Can you even go to Aurelia? I heard that you died in tragic circumstances, and your family mourned you for a year. If that's what they really thought, and they see you on one of the stallions, or worse, staggering in looking the way you do now, won't you be ripped to pieces for perpetrating a fraud?"

"They know," he said. His grin was gone. "I'm dead to my family. But the blood is still there. I know how to find the cracks and flaws in my brother's power."

"He's found all of yours. He's damned near broken you, you blazing idiot. Can't you see—"

He caught her shoulders and shook her. The storm of anger had taken her by surprise. She was terrified for him and furious with him, both at once.

She tried to speak sensibly. "Whatever he was when you were children, he's a powerful sorcerer now. He's been torturing you for days. Will you please apply your famous discipline and see that you are no match for him?"

"I have to be," he said. It was like a door shutting.

"You are so easy to hate," she said in frustration. "*Why* can't you—"

She never finished. He had pulled her to him and silenced her in the most maddeningly irresistible way of all, with a kiss. She wanted to beat him off, but the fire was rising under her skin. Her fingers tightened just short of raking nails down his back.

She had taken him first. Now he took her. It was a completely underhanded thing to do, but she had lost her indignation somewhere. Anger was still there, burning strongly. It made her all the more eager for him. Love was like war, with bloodshed and sweet pain.

Chapter Twenty-Six

Kerrec was asleep. Valeria had drowsed for a while, lulled by the rain, but as it lessened, she swam toward wakefulness. The horses had left the cave and gone to graze in the thin drizzle.

Sabata was not within reach. She was too dull with sleep to be alarmed yet, but she wondered at it. Maybe he had gone for help. Maybe the caravan of riders was somewhere nearby.

As soon as she thought it, she knew that was absurd. Even if Master Nikos had sent a party to search for the First Rider and his most annoying servant, the greater part of the caravan, with all the stallions, would have gone on to Aurelia. Nothing, not war, not invasion, not ambush in the mountains, could interfere with the Great Dance. Even for the youngest First Rider in years out of count, who happened to be the emperor's firstborn son, the Master could not turn aside from his journey.

That was reality. So was the man asleep by the banked fire, wrapped in horse blankets. When Valeria looked at him, she felt a rush of fierce protectiveness. She could not let him go to Aurelia and be killed. He would have to go to the Mountain, to the Ladies and the white gods. No matter how he argued, she would make sure he went where he was safe.

She slipped back into a doze. The rain pattered into silence. Slow light grew. Morning was coming. She had to get up, break camp and ride.

She could not make herself move. The blankets reeked, but they were warm. Kerrec was buried in rough wool, with nothing showing but a tousle of black curly hair.

Just as she convinced herself that she could get up, a stone clattered outside. She froze.

It was only the horses grazing. She heard one of them snort. Still, she hunted down her clothes and put them on. They were damp and her boots were stiff. She wished she had a weapon, but she did not even have a knife for cutting meat.

Kerrec was still asleep. She laid his clothes close by him in case he woke while she was outside.

There was nothing there but the horses. She told herself that, but she crept out with hunter's caution.

The rain had stopped but the clouds were still thick. Mist veiled the trees.

The horses were grazing far down the stretch of grass. Sabata was nowhere to be sensed. It was perfectly quiet. No bird sang. No wind whispered in the branches. Even the sound of horses cropping grass was muted.

She fetched her bay's bridle, which was as stiff as her boots. Neither he nor the chestnut looked up as she approached.

That was odd. Horses were alert to everything around them, and a human walking toward them with a bridle was worth at least a glance.

She slowed. That moment of hesitation, of dawning suspicion, kept the blow from falling quite so hard. The bolt of magic did not quite knock her unconscious.

She was aware of falling. She saw people around her, taking shape out of the mist. Most of them were in guards' uniforms, with faces she recognized. She looked from them to Gothard and knew a moment of perfect hate.

She concentrated that hate, aimed and loosed it. Gothard reeled, but he was doubly and triply shielded. The worst of the stroke slid away and blasted the earth around him to ash.

"My lord!" a voice called from behind her. She rolled until she could see. Gothard's guards were coming out of the cave, dragging the naked, stumbling, bruised and half-conscious Kerrec. He was laughing. Even when they flung him on his face at his brother's feet, he did not stop.

Gothard kicked him hard. He grunted. His laughter diminished to giggles but did not die away. Gothard hooked his foot under Kerrec's ribs and heaved him onto his back.

He lay still giggling, with his face bruised and bloody. Gothard's foot poised to crush the silliness out of him, but lowered to the ground with the blow unstruck. "Back," he said to the guards. His voice was thick. "Back to the lodge."

"Why do you laugh?"

Kerrec grinned at the Brother of Pain. He was beyond fear. All that was left was mirth. "Wouldn't you?" he said—with difficulty. His lip was split. So was his cheekbone. And his forehead, which had bled abominably before it stopped.

"I find the world less than amusing," the torturer said.

"Ah," said Kerrec, "but it's all a vast pratfall. Everything that is has slipped in the slime of creation and gone tumbling down and down and down and—"

"Kill him," said Gothard, his voice clotted with hate. "Do it as slowly as you like, but kill him."

The Brother of Pain lifted a hand in a gesture that might have begged to differ, but if so, he reconsidered. He shrugged. "As you will, lord," he said.

* * *

"Isn't that a bit of a waste?" Euan asked.

The torturer was plying his trade in a larger room than before, with a gallery from which to observe his handiwork. Euan was somewhat of a connoisseur of torment, as it was sacred to the One. This imperial torturer was a fair journeyman of the art.

Nevertheless Euan said to Gothard, "Breaking him I can see. If he's a slave to your will, he'll be useful when we come to the Dance. Killing him does nothing but indulge your temper."

Gothard threw back his head until he could glare down his nose at Euan. Euan lounged against the rail of the gallery, conspicuously unimpressed. Gothard spat, not quite at Euan. "Tell me, then. What would you do?"

"I would use him," Euan said. "I don't suppose there's enough left of him for the Dance now, but the girl is obviously attached to him. Can't you see the possibilities?"

Gothard's lip curled. "What, apart from the obvious?"

"Even the obvious has its uses," Euan said equably. "This one broke before he bent. The other is younger, it's said she may be stronger, and she's female besides. She risked her life for him once. What might she give to keep him alive?"

"I want him dead," Gothard said.

Euan could not afford to snap this idiot's neck. Fool or no, without him there was no hope of succeeding. Euan unclenched his fists, drew a deep breath, and said remarkably steadily, "You'll get what you want. But use him first. The girl won't capitulate to save her life, but she'll do it for his."

Gothard scowled. Sometimes, Euan thought, he understood the riders' insistence on discipline. This spoiled prince might be a powerful mage, and he was unfortunately indispensable, but he had precious little control of his temper.

"Listen," said Euan as patiently as he could. "Think. We need the girl. The old man has all the words in place and polished smooth, but he lost the horse magic a long time ago. You may gamble that he can control the Dance without it. I'll wager he can't. She's the one who will do it, and she's already proved that she's anything but tame. We can tame her—if we use this man."

"Use him, then," Gothard said with bad grace. "But watch him—and her—that they don't use you."

"I shall be very watchful," Euan said.

Valeria did not remember the ride back to the lodge. She let go of the world as the guards hauled her up and flung her over a horse's back. When she came to herself again, she was lying in the familiar, hated bed. Her hands and feet were bound. The wards on her were so strong that her stomach heaved.

There was nothing in it, which was fortunate. Bound as she was, she would have choked.

Then again, if she had, she would have been spared the inquisition that she knew was coming.

She had stolen her captors' royal prisoner and escaped. She would pay for that. How dearly, she would certainly learn.

She slid into a restless doze. Her wrists and ankles were softly bound, the cords as gentle as they could be, but after a while she ached with lying in the same position. When she tried to roll onto her side, further bindings stopped her. She was tied to the bedposts.

After what seemed a very long time, a figure loomed over her. She looked up into Euan's face.

Of course it would be Euan. She did not know what she felt when she saw him. She still wanted him. She liked him. Loved him? Maybe. But there was the simple fact, the one that overcame them all. He was not Kerrec.

He was not a mage, which at the moment was a very good thing. He sat beside the bed and looked hard at her, searching her face. She hoped she read nothing there but resistance.

"You led my cousin on a merry chase," he said. He sounded almost amused. "He's terribly annoyed with you."

"Listen," she said. Her tongue felt thick and unwieldy. "Whatever you want, I'm not giving it to you. Just start the torture and get it over with."

"Torture?" He seemed honestly taken aback. "What makes you think we'd do that to you?"

"You need to ask?"

"I'm not Gothard," he said, "and you're not Gothard's brother. I don't need to break you. I want to be your ally."

"That's not true."

"It is," he said. "I won't hide it from you—Gothard wanted you on the rack, if not worse. But you're more use to us whole than maimed."

"Why? I'm worthless as a hostage. The school doesn't want me. More likely they'll thank you for getting rid of me."

"You underestimate yourself," Euan said.

"I know what I am. Sabata is the one you really want."

He spread his hands. "We want him, I grant you that. But not as much as we want you."

"Why?"

He did not answer that. "If I untie you, will you promise not to bolt?"

"Where would I bolt to?"

He acknowledged that with a tilt of the head and bent to unfasten the cords. When they fell away, she flexed her arms and legs carefully. They were stiff, and they ached.

She sat up. Euan braced, maybe not even aware of it, but ready to catch her if she made a run for it.

She was not running anywhere, not yet. "I'm hungry," she said.

He was quick to call for food, but he never took his eyes off her. She sat rubbing the arm that ached the most and listening to her stomach growl. "How long was I out?" she asked.

"It's morning again," he said. "Gothard hit you too hard with his sorcery. For a while we were afraid—"

He shook himself. "We—I—made him mend you as much as he could."

She shuddered. Her stomach heaved. The thought of Gothard's hands on her, his magic in her, made her physically ill.

"Don't worry," Euan said with a grim edge. "He didn't touch anything that mattered."

"How would you know?"

"I had a knife at his throat," Euan said, "and Mestre Olivet watched him to be sure there were no tricks. Olivet likes you. Better than that, he's in awe of you. He says you're stronger than any rider he ever saw."

"Stronger than—"

"Stronger than the one who almost got away." Euan tilted his head. His eyes were steady, narrowed just a little, as if he were a wolf and she were prey. "That was interesting, how easily you stole him. I didn't know they taught such skills to rider-candidates."

There was no thought in her at all. She launched herself at him. "What did you do to him? Where is he? What have you done? By all the gods, if you've touched a hair of his head—"

He fended her off too damnably easily, though his eye would swell and bruise where her fist had caught it. "By the One! *I* never laid a hand on him."

"Then I know who did," she said in stillness as sudden as her eruption. "He's still alive. I'd know if he was dead. How long will he stay that way?"

"That depends on you," Euan said.

She stared at him, empty of words.

"Come with me," he said.

Valeria stood in the gallery and looked down at Kerrec. The torturer was taking apart his mind and magic, piece by piece. She could feel it in the air, a deep, subtly shattering vibration.

"This is killing him," she said. Her voice sounded flat. The gallery was shielded. If she had tried to leap off it, she would have struck wards like a wall.

Euan seemed unaware of the currents that ran through the air, that to her were all but unbearable. "He will die," he said, "if this keeps on. Gothard will make sure of that."

"Gothard is a fool," she said. "If you're going to disrupt the Dance, all you need is a cask of thunder powder and a spark. You want to control it, and for that you need a rider. You won't be abducting another, not after this. He's all you have."

"Oh, but he isn't," Euan said. "We still have you."

"Do you?"

He tilted his head toward the figures below. "I've forced Gothard to agree. If I can make a bargain with you, that one lives."

Her heart slammed into her throat. "And if you can't, he's dead."

"You have a fair grasp of the obvious," he said.

"So? What's the price?"

"I'm sure you know."

"I'm not a rider," she said. "There's no proof I can do what you need."

"Mestre Olivet says you can."

"Mestre Olivet is a bag of empty wind."

Euan did not seem either surprised or dismayed to hear that. "Oh, he's a windbag, sure enough. If he really had the powers he claims, he'd have taken stallions with him when he left the Mountain. Still, there's one thing he has, and that's a school of riders who aren't bound to the Mountain. He's been pondering ways to divert the Called—not with any success, mind, but the seeds are planted. Just think what you could do with them."

"Start another school? A real one?" In spite of herself, Valeria felt the pull of temptation. "The Mountain would never allow that."

"How do you know? The Mountain never Called a woman before, either. Maybe it's making changes, and it's the men who are lagging."

She shook her head, more to clear it than to deny what he was saying. "You want me to break up the Dance, change the future and take the stallions away from the Mountain. Do you want me to do anything else while I'm at it? Bring down the moon? Turn the sea to dry land?"

"All you need to do," said Euan, "is break the pattern. Olivet knows how, even if he no longer has the power to do it. He'll teach you."

"For what? So you can destroy the empire?"

"Don't think of it that way," Euan said. "Think of it as creating a new empire, one where your powers will be acknowledged and respected."

"Under barbarian rule."

"Would that be so bad?" he asked.

"I've heard about your god," she said. "He tolerates no rivals. Above all, he tolerates no magic."

"Now that's not true," said Euan. "Magic is held within strict bounds, yes, but isn't that what the Mountain does?"

She shook her head again, harder. "I can't do it. I can't betray my people, my nation, my whole world. Even—" Her throat closed. She forced it open. "Even for him."

"Very well," Euan said. He leaned over the rail, but his eyes were still on her. "One word," he said, "and your rider is dead."

She stared at him. He was so much at ease, so sure of himself. He was still smiling, even in the face of her horror as she saw him clearly for the first time.

She had thought she knew him. She had never mistaken his loyalties, and she had certainly not taken him for a friend to the empire. But she had been so blinded by his big beautiful body and his wild red hair that she had let herself slide past what it meant that he was a prince of the barbarian horde. Worst of all, she had deluded herself into thinking that because he was her lover, he would not use her to get what he wanted.

He had been using her from the first. She was a weakness, a gap in the pattern. He had used her to widen the gap.

Now he thought he had her. Kerrec was his weapon.

There was no way he could know what they had done in that cave. He was not doing this out of jealousy. He was doing it because—why? Because he thought she was slavishly devoted to her teacher? Because he had eyes and she was an idiot, and he had known long before she did that she was in love with Kerrec?

Kerrec would tell her not to give in. No one man was worth the empire.

She was not a man. The school had made sure she knew that in every way possible. She was a woman, and she did not think as a man thought. She did not see this as a simple sum, a life for an empire. It was more complicated than that.

Kerrec would hate her with a true hate, but he would be alive. He would find a way to stop her, or else to stop the barbarians once the Dance was disrupted. If he was dead because she refused Euan's bargain, none of that could happen. No one would know what Euan was doing.

She bowed her head. Her sullenness was not feigned, but it also concealed the fact that her eyes had fixed on Kerrec's face. Let them think they had her, as long as Kerrec lived to fight them. She was expendable, far more than he was. If she was vilified as a traitor, that would not matter to her. She would be dead and he would not.

"I'll do it," she said. "I'll take your bargain. On one condition. Help me get Kerrec out of here. Let him go, and never betray him, or by all the gods, I will make you wish you had never been born."

"Help you—" Euan laughed in disbelief. "You can have him alive, keep him as a pet, walk him on a leash in the garden—but what makes you think I would possibly let him go?"

"If you really do need me," she said, "you will do this. What does he matter, after all, once you have me? His magic's broken. He's dead to the empire. He'll never muster troops or rally the people. He's no danger to you."

Euan eyed her, then the man below. His doubt was like a pressure on her skin. Still, he was male enough and young enough to be cocky. "His magic is really gone?"

"There's nothing he can use," she said. She did not add, "Now." Magic could mend, if slowly, but Euan had not asked and she was not about to tell him.

"Eh, well," Euan said after a while. "He's barely alive as it is. If we toss him out, he's not likely to live long."

"Give me a day to do what I can for him," she said. "Then help me get him out."

She was pushing her luck and his patience, but not quite to the breaking point. He let out a breath and said, "Well enough. Go with the guard and wait. Tell the servants what you need. He'll be there as soon as I can get him out."

Chapter Twenty-Seven

It seemed unbearably long before a pair of Euan's guards brought Kerrec to Valeria's room. The servants had brought most of what she needed, including a copper tub and half a dozen tall jars of steaming water. They bathed him as if he were an infant, while he lay helpless, drifting in and out of consciousness.

It hurt more than she could have imagined to see him like this. She had to stop and pull herself together before she went to work. He was alive, that was what mattered. She would find what was left of his mind once she had done what she could for his body.

When he was clean, she let the servants lay him in her bed, but she stopped them before they covered him. There were not many new wounds, but they were subtler and more painful. Most were burns in the tender skin of the inner thigh and the webs of the fingers.

She salved them carefully, hoarding her anger. Anger could feed magic. She would need it if she was going to undo what the torturer had done to his mind.

She sat on the edge of the bed. He winced in his dream. Everything was pain, his face said, even unconsciousness.

She had one day. Then she had to send him away.

It would have to be enough.

Her mother had taught Valeria some of what she meant to try. The rest was part of the dreams she had had all her life. His magic was broken—shattered. She had to try to make it whole again.

When she was small she had broken her mother's greatest treasure. It was a bowl from somewhere so far away that no one knew its name. It was shaped like a flower unfolding, and it shimmered in a shade of green that her father said was only seen in the sea. Strange and elegant fish swam on it in relief, around and around.

The children were not supposed to touch it. It lived on a shelf above the hearth, where the light caught it but inquisitive fingers could not reach.

Valeria could not resist it. The more she thought about how she was not supposed to touch it, the more she wanted to hold it in her hands and feel its creamy smoothness.

One day there was no one in the house. They were

all out in the fields or working in the kitchen garden. She was supposed to be pulling weeds in the turnip bed, but her mother had been called away to deliver someone's baby, and her brother Lucius was more interested in pretending to be a legionary in battle than noticing what his sister was doing.

She crept into the house and stood looking up at the bowl. Sunlight came in through the small round window in the eaves, catching its green glory slantwise and making it glow in the dim room. It was the most beautiful thing she knew, and the most alluring.

Valeria had some thought of climbing up the chimney or piling chairs and stools until they were high enough. In the end it was much easier than that. She thought about being up high with her hand on the bowl, and all at once she was. Her stomach was fluttering and her head was dizzy, but she was up in the air, bobbing gently under the rooftree.

The bowl was just as cool and smooth and wonderful as she had imagined. She took it carefully in both hands, meaning to hold it for a few moments and then put it back.

As she hovered there, cradling the bowl as if it had been a sleeping bird, something clattered in the yard. It startled her out of her skin.

She dropped like a stone. The bowl slipped from her hands and shattered on the floor.

She sprawled close by it. Later she would learn that she had broken her arm. Now she only knew that the bowl was in shards, and so was her life when her mother found out about it.

She lay on the floor with her body a distant ache, and looked at the shards through a film of tears. They were still beautiful, but all broken. She could mend them, she told herself. She would find a way.

Her mother had come home and found her still on the floor. She had tried to get up, lifting herself with the arm that was broken. When the bones ground together, she fell down again. Then she vomited.

She was a long time healing. While she did that, she set her own punishment, to mend the bowl as best she could. It took even longer than her arm, and it was never quite the same. When it was as whole as it could be, it went back on its shelf. She never touched it again, and she never looked at it. It was painful to remember what it had been, and to see how much less radiant it was now, because of her disobedience.

All of that was in her mind as she contemplated the shards of Kerrec's mind and magic. She had a day to start the healing that would have to continue on its own until he reached the Mountain. One advantage at least a man's mind had over colored clay. Clay could only be glued and riveted together. Flesh and spirit could heal, if there was enough left of them to do it.

It was a huge task—insurmountable. Step by step, her mother had taught her. First find a beginning, then take that shard and find the one that belonged next to it, and place them side by side. One by one, fragment by fragment.

There was a pattern to it. That was the essence of Valeria's magic, to see patterns. Kerrec's had been a thing of beauty and incomparable complexity. Even broken, it hinted at its original shape.

The first, essential shard was a white stallion gleaming in darkness. Petra was whole and perfect there as he was in the outer world. He had been waiting for all of time for Valeria to find her way to him.

She almost fell out of the working in astonishment and relief. Somehow she had thought that because she had sold herself for a man's life, the stallions would abandon her.

There was no thought of that in Petra. He was the same as he always was. He invited her to mount.

In her distraction and confusion, she did not know what it meant until she had accepted the invitation. The joining of his power to hers was like a stroke of sudden lightning. It knocked her flat.

"Lady." The voice was dim and far away. "Lady! Wake up!"

It was Euan's voice. He was shaking and slapping her, trying to bring her back to life again.

Petra surrounded her with white brilliance. The mortal world retreated out of reach. She no longer saw the pattern of shards. She had become it.

The stallion needed her. He could mend the shards,

given time, but he was not human or mortal. She knew how the patterns should run.

He danced the Dance. She shaped its movements.

It was much broken and interrupted. Connections would not close, or would crumble as soon as they were made. Stray bits of magic sparked into flame, then turned on one another or on the two who tried to heal them.

Without Petra's protection, Valeria would have been far out of her depth. Even shattered, Kerrec was strong, and that strength was no longer constrained by discipline. Here was raw power, rebuilding itself almost faster than Valeria could control it.

It kept wanting to twist, to go dark. She fought harder the stronger he became. She was growing afraid. He was too strong and too broken. She might be raising up a monster.

That might be exactly what Gothard and the barbarians wanted. A First Rider perverted from the white magic was a terrible, an unthinkable thing. His very existence would disrupt the Dance of creation.

"Valeria!" Euan was becoming more insistent, and intruding more strongly.

She clung desperately to Petra. He was struggling even more than Valeria, torn and twisted by the corruption of Kerrec's magic.

The stallion's immortal substance betrayed him. Valeria, bound more securely to earth, had that great bastion to cling to. Petra was too much of the higher realms. The seeds of darkness were drawn to him. If they took root and grew, he would be in worse condition than Kerrec.

She did the only thing she could think of, which might be disastrous, but doing nothing was worse. She called the renegade magic to herself. She took it into her center, where her own magic was, and bound it to her own patterns.

She had seen a healer priest do that once. A child had been badly burned on the arms and hands. The priest had taken skin from her back and thighs and bound it to the ruined limbs, where it had taken root and grown.

It had to be flesh of the same body, the priest had said, or the binding would not hold. The body rejected what did not belong to it, even if in so doing, it destroyed itself.

Magic must be different. Valeria felt Kerrec's inside her, but it was not exactly alien. It was as if he had been made to fill her hollow places.

If he could mend, he would mend there. She swam up from the depths into the plain light of day, and Euan's terrified face.

"What in the name of the One were you doing? I thought you were dead!"

She was not ready for the storm of his anger and worry. She let herself flinch away from it. He softened as much as he ever could, with such a guilty expression that she could hardly even hate him. "I'm sorry," he said. "You scared me."

"Never," she said through gritted teeth, "never hurl a mage out of a working like that. You could have destroyed us both."

He hung his head. She caught herself reaching to stroke his hair. "There now," she said a little more sharply than she meant, "it doesn't matter. I've done as much for him as I can. Have you found men and horses to take him to the Mountain?"

"They'll be ready by morning," Euan said. He peered at her. "Are you really not dead?"

"Do I sound dead?"

He snorted. "No, but you look it. You should eat. They say mages need a great deal of provender when they've been working magic."

"Whoever your 'they' might be, they're not far off the mark," she said. "I could eat a little. And so should he."

Then finally she managed a glance at Kerrec. He did not look dead. He looked exhausted and bruised and deep asleep.

"I don't think even he can ride now," she said. "He'll need a wagon. Can you find one?"

"It's done," Euan said. "You're sure you want him to go to the Mountain?"

"He'll be safe there. They'll look after him. And better for your purposes, he'll be out of the way of the plot in Aurelia."

Euan nodded. "That's sensible enough. When we win, the Mountain will be yours. Then you can do with him what you like."

She stared at him. "I thought I was going to Mestre Olivet's school."

"That's what Olivet wants to think," Euan said. "He's not thinking past himself, any more than Gothard is. I've lived on the Mountain. I've seen what's there, and I've seen you. The Mountain is where the stallions are. You belong there. Think of the things you can do to change it, once the old order is gone."

Valeria looked at Euan with new and half-dismayed respect. Of all the temptations he could have offered, that was the strongest. Olivet was a fool who had long since lost his power over the stallions. She had no intention of becoming his pupil. But this was everything she dreamed of. If Euan could really give it to her, if it could really happen—

She could not let herself think that way, even while she said, "I could rule? I could be the master?"

"You could be whatever you wanted to be."

"That is tempting," she said honestly. "I would need teachers, but—"

"It seems to me," Euan said, "that the stallions have been teaching you a great deal more than any rider has offered to do. I doubt they'll stop because there's been a change of regime among mortals. If they were as bound to imperial laws as the riders would like us all to think, you would never have been Called."

"That's true," she said. "They do have their own reasons for doing things. Maybe this is what they want. The empire has stood for a thousand years. Maybe now is its time to die."

"We do believe so," said Euan. He ventured a liberty, reaching to touch her hand.

Her first instinct was to pull sharply away. A second, wiser impulse held her motionless. She did not want this man, not any longer, or so she insisted to herself.

Her body stood somewhat less on principle. Her hand turned to weave its fingers in his. He leaned toward her. She had no will to recoil. His kiss began as a brush of the lips, but deepened into passion.

It was part of the game she had to play for Kerrec's life. She told herself that. It was terribly easy to give way and melt toward him.

He lifted her with no effort at all. The bed was occupied, but the rug in front of the hearth was not.

Just moments ago she had been pure spirit. Now she was pure flesh. The fierce surge of pleasure grounded her firmly to earth. She was truly in herself again.

Had Euan known what this would do for her? Maybe. Maybe not. In the end it hardly mattered.

Chapter Twenty-Eight

Kerrec's mind was in fragments like a mosaic on a palace wall. Here was gold, here was green, here was blue. There was the red of blood, spreading like a stain over the bright shards.

He was not sane. He knew that, but he could not make it matter. The walls of training and discipline were broken. He could raise them again, if he lived long enough. If the Brother of Pain did not break him first.

In his right mind he would never have touched Valeria. There was a price for that, and he was paying it. He knew he had escaped, but also that he had been captured again. He ached in every muscle and bone. His skin was on fire.

The Brother of Pain had come, but Kerrec could not manage to be afraid. He was too full of longing for

Valeria. He wanted her with a hunger that was no saner than the rest of him.

He was empty of magic. All that was left was his awareness of her, and the brightness far down in the heart of him that had been there since he was Called to the Mountain. That was the mark of the white gods, the sense of their presence that would not leave him until he was dead.

Pain was a place. It was always dark, except when it was shot with bloodred lightning. There were stones, jagged of course, and rivers of fire. The ice on the mountaintops burned, and the sky rained ash. His soul turned inward and began to devour itself.

Light crept slowly into the darkness. The pain and its maker receded. The ash turned to rain, and the rivers flowed cool and clean. She was there, all around him, pouring magic into him.

She was beauty bare. A poet had sung that once when he was still a prince, and a remarkably young and callow one at that. He had thought it absurd at the time. Now he understood.

He gathered the fragments of himself. Consciousness hovered just within reach. There was remarkably little pain. He remembered that he had eyes, and opened them.

He did not recognize the room. The two on the rug by the stone hearth, he did know.

She was naked. So was the man who lay with her,

big and ruddy and wearing a great deal of barbaric gold. Kerrec did not need to see his face to recognize Euan Rohe.

The broad freckled hand closed over Valeria's breast. She arched into it just as she had done with Kerrec, and took Euan as she had taken him, with eagerness that he, fool that he was, had taken for love. If that was what it was, then she had plenty to share.

Kerrec could not have said what he felt. Pain was not only a place, but a color as well. There was no name for that color. Eyes of the body could not see it, and words could not describe it.

He squeezed his eyes shut, but there was no escaping it. He could not stop his ears, either, when her cry of satiation burst out a moment after Euan's.

They did not fall asleep like reasonable beings. They lay together, wrapped in one another, and murmured words that burned themselves into his brain.

"Is this like the Dance?" Euan asked lazily, but with an edge that he could not quite hide.

"A little, I suppose," she said. "Those patterns rule all that is. These only rule us."

"You think so? Only us? Sometimes I feel as if we're all the world."

She laughed as a woman will with her lover, soft and rich. "You're a selfish creature. Are you sure you'll be able to bear the sight of someone else on the throne?"

"It's only a throne," he said.

"Only— You don't mean that!"

"Really," he said. "It's only a chair. A ridiculously elaborate one, with a great deal of gold, but my rump would be just as happy on a bench in a tavern. I'll take the gold and leave the chair for Gothard. *He* wants it."

"What do you want?" she asked. "Tell me the truth. What is this for you?"

"War," he answered. "War is life. War is a man's destiny and a prince's only purpose. War serves the One."

"You don't want to rule nations? Be rich? Have all the women?"

He snorted, then laughed. "Of course I want to be rich! I'll take the nations, too, if they're not too much trouble. As for the women, are you looking for rivals?"

"Should I?"

"Keep smiling at me like that and I'll lay the empire at your feet."

"I don't want the empire," she said. "Only the Mountain."

"You know it's yours."

"After I break the Dance," she said. "After I shift it to the path your people want."

"Are you worried?"

"I'd be a fool not to be."

"I'm not," he said. "I know I should be. But looking at you, feeling and smelling you, I can't be afraid of anything in the world."

"Flatterer," she said, but she was smiling. Kerrec could hear it in her voice. He heard the rest of what they did, too, with remarkable vigor on Euan's part, considering how recently he had finished the first round.

The world was splintering again, falling into shards. Kerrec made no move to stop it. His name and self were slipping away. He let them go. All that was left was a memory of her face, with a gust of grief and the twisting of hate. Enemy, traitor. He would, he must, destroy her.

Kerrec had gone inside himself. He was healing, Valeria told herself with more hope than certainty. He was alive and breathing, and his color was better. She had to hope that the rest would come in time.

It was just as well, considering what she had been doing while he slept in the same room. Guilt was a late bloom but a strong one. She had done it for him. As long as Euan was obsessed with her body, he would not think too hard about why she cared so much for another man's life.

Euan had arranged an escort as he had promised. They were waiting outside the lodge in the morning mist, which fell almost as heavy as rain. The world was bathed in a dim grey light. All but the closest trees were invisible, hidden in fog.

Most of the escort were barbarians, but the guards who drove the cart and who rode closest to it were men from Aurelia. Valeria wondered if they knew what Kerrec had been before he was a rider. She supposed they did. Guards knew everything.

She had to hope they could be trusted. She set a wishing on Kerrec even so, a Word of ward and guard. It was not much, but it might wake him if his guards turned on him, and help him escape.

She could not kiss him. The guards were watching, and so was Euan. She had to settle for tucking the blanket around him and smoothing his hair back from his forehead. The first line of guards was already in motion.

She stepped back as the driver clucked to the mules. Euan's arm settled around her shoulders. She gritted her teeth and let it stay. He was claiming her. For the sake of the game, she had to let him.

He could not keep her from standing on the step long after the last horseman had vanished into the fog. When she finally turned, he claimed his arm back again. "Mestre Olivet said for you to come when you were ready," he said.

"So you're Olivet's errand boy now?"

Valeria bit her tongue, but Euan was too delighted with himself to be annoyed. "It amuses me," he said. "We can amuse ourselves for a while, if you'd rather."

She sighed. "No. Best do my duty."

Was he disappointed? It was hard to say. She did not know him at all, when she came down to it. His body, yes—she knew every fingerbreadth of that. Of his mind she knew only what he chose to show.

* * *

"Patterns can be made," Mestre Olivet said, "but also destroyed. Wherever there is light, there is darkness."

Valeria suppressed a yawn. She had been listening to hours of platitudes interspersed with snippets from this book or that. So far she had seen no pattern in it. Between the drone of his voice and the whisper of rain that had begun to fall, she was half-asleep.

Then he said, "This is the Book of the Unmaking."

She started awake. He was holding a scroll in a leather case, gingerly, as if the thing inside could strike like a snake.

She had heard of the Book of the Unmaking. It was a rumor among riders and rider-candidates, and a half-heard story in the gatherings of wise-women to which her mother had taken her now and then. Most people said it did not exist, or if it had, it had been destroyed long ago.

It negated what the stallions were. It unmade what they made. It broke the patterns and scattered them. Its spells, spoken in sequence by mages of great power, could unravel the fabric of the world.

"Is it true?" she asked. "That it can—"

"It's safe enough," Olivet said, "if one is careful—as with all magic."

"This more than most," she said.

He shrugged. "Its reputation is more myth than fact. There is danger in it, I won't deny it, and certain sequences of spells are best not spoken together, but that can be said of any great grimoire."

"Where did you find it?"

She held her breath, but he was always delighted to talk about himself. He sat back in his chair and folded his hands over his middle, settling in for a long and pleasant reminiscence. "I was often in the Master's library in the citadel, reading the old masters and re-discovering arts that had been put aside or forgotten. Even then I was evolving my own art. One evening as I delved into a deep corner full of books that had not been touched in years out of count—with the dust and cobwebs to prove it—I came across a box that looked as if it had not been opened since the library was built."

He sighed. "I still remember the dust on it, how thick it was. The lock was strong, but the spells of warding on it had worn thin. It was not the simplest task in the world to break the spells or the lock. Still, I prevailed. I found this."

Valeria stared at the scroll on the table between them. It was only a roll of old parchment. Olivet was clearly unperturbed. There was no reason for chills to crawl down her spine.

But then, she thought, he had lost the stallion magic. He was still a mage, but the great magics and the beautiful discipline were gone. His power was strong, but it was hollow.

This thing had done that to him. It had drained away the heart of his power.

He seemed unaware of the loss. He unbound the cords and unrolled the scroll as if it had been an ordinary book. "This is the key," he said, spreading his hands across a closely written page.

The letters swarmed like insects. Valeria almost could have sworn that they crawled up over his fingers before slipping down again to the yellowed page.

Was that page parchment? Or was it human skin?

She made herself listen to him. "This is the key," he said again. "Here I found my true art and native calling. I discovered that every power needs its opposite. For powers of light there must be powers of dark. For magic of the Word, silence. For the stallions' magic, this."

"Unmaking," Valeria said.

He nodded. "What is made must be unmade. Otherwise, everything heaps on itself, higher and higher, deeper and deeper, until it comes crashing down. That's the purpose of death—to make way for the generations that come after. If none of us ever died, the earth would fill with creatures until it could hold no more."

"Then you're more than a simple rival to the Mountain," she said. "You're the antidote. The natural enemy."

Olivet shrugged, spreading his hands. "That is one way of seeing it. I see my place as necessary—as a counterbalance."

"But," she said, "you have nothing to balance the stallions."

"I have this," he said, caressing the page as she had never seen him caress a horse. "There is so much beauty here, so many wonders. None of my riders has the power to perceive them. But you…" His eyes on her were hungry. "You were sent. You are the heir of the Unmaking."

It was all she could do to keep her face expressionless. Her belly was a tight and painful knot. Her throat hurt.

"See," he said, unrolling the scroll to a column that was marked with a crimson ribbon. "A simple spell. It balances patterns, then undoes them so that they can be made again. Do you see the beauty in it? Do you see the elegance? It has no need for a god in the body of a horse. This is pure simplicity, magic stripped of all pretension."

She looked down at the column of words. They were in old Aurelian, very archaic. She could barely read them. Before she could breathe a sigh of relief, they shifted themselves into forms that she knew.

Her eyes were bound, compelled. She had to read the spell. It slithered into her mind and coiled there.

She had time, just, to raise wards around it and wall it in. Even so, in passing it touched the edges of the patterns she had been building in her time on the Mountain. It was all she could do to keep them from unraveling.

Beauty? she thought. Elegance? This was deep and subtle evil.

Mestre Olivet seemed unaware that anything had happened. His power was riddled with gaps. As strong as it still was, it must have been remarkable before he lost the greater part of it.

"They caught you, didn't they?" she said before she could stop herself. "After you'd worked a few of these spells, your magic started to change. You couldn't control the stallions any longer. Yes?"

He stiffened. She braced for a storm of anger, but he had enough discipline left to keep it from bursting out. "I no longer needed the stallions. My art had gone beyond them. As yours will—after you have manipulated the Dance. Then the Dance itself may be unmade."

"If you are going to teach me to control the Dance," she said, "then I can't be near this book again until after. I'm not the master you were when you found it. I don't have your protections. It will take the powers I need before I have a chance to use them."

She held her breath and prayed he could not see how badly that single spell had frightened her. Even to save Kerrec's life, she could not subject herself to more of it.

To her enormous relief, he nodded. "Yes. Yes, I see. Your strength is so great, your talent so overwhelming, I have difficulty remembering how young you still are." He rolled up the scroll and fastened the bindings and slipped it into its case.

Then finally she could breathe. He continued to

stroke the scroll's case while he went on. "When the Dance is unmade, you'll have no more to fear. This power is meant for you as it was for me. Once you let go of the Mountain's spell, you'll see its wonders. But first, yes, continue in the old enfeebled way. Only by making can we unmake."

"And only by unmaking can we make," she said.

He smiled, as pleased with that bit of blatant manipulation as she had hoped he would be. "You are a very wise child," he said. "Now then. First, the laws of making. Your rider never taught them to you? No? Well. In my day we learned them as soon as we were tested. Listen now, and listen well."

She listened, and she held her tongue. She felt the spell of Unmaking inside her, coiled within the wards, waiting for a moment of weakness. Please the gods and the powers of the Mountain, these arts that Mestre Olivet taught her so hastily—if they were true arts and not ruined as the rest of his power was—would not only keep the Unmaking at bay, but would destroy it.

Chapter Twenty-Nine

The sun moved in the sky. The moon rose and set. The sun came back again.

The one without a name lay in fitful darkness, rocking and swaying. His body was pain. His spirit was emptiness. He slid in and out of a formless dream.

The rocking and rattling stopped. Voices babbled, rising to a crescendo and then fading. Hoofbeats receded into the distance. There was a moment of silence.

White light blazed upon him. Two white gods loomed above him. Both of them together were more than his maimed soul could bear. He hid in blankets to escape them.

The young one, shadowed with dapples, plucked the blankets from him and tossed them aside. The elder, pure white and massive in his prime, nudged and coaxed and bullied him out of the wagon and onto stumbling feet. He reeled. Warm solidity held him up. He clung to the heavy white neck.

The elder god breathed on him. The pain retreated. His mind was a little clearer. The splinters of his consciousness began to come together.

He struck them apart with fierce repulsion. He did not want to remember. He did not want to have a name again, to have a memory, to know pain.

He looked into the young one's dark and liquid eye. A face was in it, a woman, young, beautiful—enemy. Traitor. Destroyer. He must find—he must kill— He flung himself toward that hated image.

The elder stallion shouldered him aside. He stumbled and fell, and lay gasping on the stony ground. The surge of rage was gone, leaving him cold and sick.

He could feel the stallions standing above him. He braced for the shattering blows of hooves, but a peremptory nose urged him to his feet again. It was the elder once more, the white one, whose name he could almost recall.

The young one snorted explosively and shook his long moon-colored mane. He spun and showed them both his heels, bolting into the glare of sunlight.

The elder stallion sighed. The man whose name was gone wound fingers in his mane and pulled himself onto the broad white back. Once there, his whole body relaxed. It did not matter where he went or what became of him. This was where he belonged. This was home.

The white stallion turned and walked carefully away from the broken wagon. Once he was sure that the man was secure on his back, he gathered his compact sturdy body and sprang into flight.

He was much faster than he looked, and his paces were smooth. The man clung to his mane and let himself be carried wherever the white god pleased.

The emperor's heir had been uneasy since before the caravan came from the Mountain. No one else, even the Augurs and the soothsayers, seemed to see the vision that refused to let her be. Over and over she saw a pattern disrupted and a Dance turned to confusion.

The riders had gone into seclusion on arrival, and their guards and servants had disappeared with them into a house near the palace that had last been opened a hundred years ago. The imperial retainers who had cleaned and prepared it had returned to their more usual duties. No one from outside the Mountain would approach the riders between the quarter moon and the new, until the Dance was over. Their solitude was sacred, and essential to their magic.

Briana was standing above the gate when they rode in. She looked for her brother, but he was not there. She recognized the rest of the First Riders, and lesser riders behind them, fifteen in all. Of the one whose name now was Kerrec, there was no sign.

Fifteen riders, fifteen white stallions. There should have been sixteen. Kerrec should have been there.

She could hardly blame him if he had refused to come. Still, she was disappointed. She had thought better of him. No matter what was between him and their father, he should have been here for this. He was the strongest of the First Riders, even if he was the youngest. The Dance would not go well without him. If her foresight was true, it would go very badly, and bring disaster to the empire.

If he was that spiteful, then she had no use for him.

She had worked herself into a decent temper by the second day after the caravan had come. Her servants were walking softly, and her chamberlain had diverted all the embassies and petitions that required both tact and patience. She would have his head for that, but not immediately. First she was going to strangle her brother.

She went out riding that second morning, alone except for the inevitable company of guards. Her dreams through the night had been dim and confused. Little of them stayed with her after she woke, but the mood they left was even darker than before.

She had to get out of the palace and the city. The walls were closing in. Everything reeked of imminent disaster.

"Sometimes," she said to her captain, "magic is a curse."

Demetria not only had none of her own, she had been born with wards against it. Magic could get no grip on her. She was immune. Fortunate woman.

She did not trouble Briana with false sympathy. A jut of the chin sent two of the guards ahead. She raked her eye down the line of the rest until it straightened. Briana in the middle, thoroughly protected, wished that she could go whirling off into the sky and be free of it all.

People in the city recognized the imperial heir, but her plain clothes and the small size of her escort warned them not to turn her passage into a procession. Now and then someone called her name. Once a stone flew. It struck a guard's shield and glanced off.

The guards at the northern gate saluted as Briana rode through. She acknowledged them with a nod. Her eye was already on the road, which miraculously was empty of travelers. Somehow all the people flocking to Aurelia for the emperor's jubilee had chosen not to travel in that hour. The road was hers. She took it as a gift of the gods.

The village of Sosia stood on a hill above the northward road. A fold of the land cut off the view of the bay, and a long wooded ridge shielded it from the blasts that blew off the mountains. The lack of a view kept the noble and the wealthy away. The soft winds and gentle rains made the grass grow richer there than anywhere round about. Sheep and goats thrived there, and cattle grew fat on the lush grass.

Briana had stopped there often before after a gallop on the plain. There was a dairy near the center of the village, where a traveler could stop for a jar of milk, fresh and foaming from the goat or the cow, a loaf of bread, and a wedge of pungent cheese. That day there were airy, faintly sweet cakes plump with raisins, that came with a pot of honeyed fruit and another of clotted cream.

Briana sat in the garden in front of the dairy to eat her dinner. Since she was the only one there apart from the guards, she could claim the table under the rose arbor. The trellis was thick with white-and-scarlet blooms, and dizzy with fragrance.

She was calmer, but her mood was no better. She ate as much as she could stomach and left the rest for the guards. They had eaten as well as she had, but they were never averse to another round.

The girl who had served them was discreet and quiet. Briana was somewhat surprised after she had eaten, as she was thinking of getting up and riding on, to look up and find the girl standing in front of her, shifting from foot to foot.

Briana knew that look well. Training kept the scowl from her face and made her ask politely, "Yes?"

"Lady," said the girl, "I'd not trouble you, but Grandmother asks—Grandmother begs your pardon, but—would you come, please?"

Briana glanced at Demetria. The captain rose from the bench by the flower bed, but there was no danger here that Briana could sense.

Briana did not need to ask why the grandmother had not come herself. The old woman was blind and bedridden, but she had a gift, and that gift was foresight. If she asked a favor of Briana, she knew what she did and why. Briana would be wise to do as she asked.

Beyond the dairy barn was a small stone building, very old, that had been the farmhouse before the family grew prosperous enough for the handsome structure of stone and timber that stood on the other side of the garden from the dairy. The old house was gutted and the thatch on its roof had worn thin, and from the look and the smell, goats had been living in it until quite recently.

Now there was a stocky, common-looking grey horse dozing with its head down and its lower lip slack, and, lying in a bed of clean straw, a man.

"We found them here this morning," the girl said. "The horse won't let us near the man. He's sick, we can see that much. He wakes up sometimes and talks, but his words make no sense. The horse kicked the healer priest out the door. Grandmother said tell the lady in the garden, she'll know what to do."

The horse lifted its head. Briana caught her breath. In an instant he had transformed from nondescript cob to living god.

Now that he had put aside his pretense of mortality, she recognized that elegant arch of nose and that calm dark eye. "Petra?" she asked.

He dipped his head. Her eye leaped to the man in the straw, knowing who he was even before she saw his face. She sprang toward him and dropped to her knees. The dairy girl squeaked in alarm, but Petra made no move to stop her.

Her brother drew into a fetal knot under her touch. She felt as much as saw the marks of torture on him, bad enough on his body but harrowing on his spirit. The whole beautiful structure of his magic was charred and broken.

Someone or something had set a protection on him. She could feel it, too deep almost to reach. He was healing, slowly, from the inside out. But there was so much hurt, so much ruin...

She could not give way to either horror or rage, not yet. "Demetria," she said without turning, "find a cart and an animal to pull it."

"We have a cart," the dairy girl said. "Mother has a mule."

"That will do," said Briana. "Go with my captain and show her where they are. Then ask your mother to make a posset with curds and honey and such herbs as she knows of, for strength of spirit. Bring it back as quickly as you can."

They left together, the girl running, Demetria striding long-legged behind her. Briana put them out of her mind and bent over Kerrec.

He was awake. His eyes were blurred, but they struggled to focus on her face. "Briana?" His voice was a raw whisper.

She could have wept with relief that he knew her. "Kerrec? Ambrosius?"

His brows knit. "I don't—who—"

"Never mind," she said. "Rest. You'll be home soon."

"Home? Do I—where—"

"Hush," she said.

He closed his eyes. She stayed by him until the girl came with the posset, then she poured it into him. He was reluctant but obedient.

That was completely unlike him. She had been angry at whoever or whatever had done this to him. Now she was growing afraid.

The cart came none too soon. She had no plan, but Demetria had been thinking while Briana alternately grieved and raged over what had become of her brother. In a little while the captain had arranged it all. Kerrec was on his way to Aurelia, and Briana drove him in the covered cart, while the one of her guards who looked most like her wore her clothes and rode her grey mare back into the city.

Chapter Thirty

The guards and their apparent mistress returned to the palace by the public gate. The mule cart with its hooded and silent driver went in by the servants' entrance. No one remarked on the undistinguished grey cob tied to the tail of the cart, or asked to see what cargo the driver brought in.

That served Briana well, but she would have words with the captain of the palace guard when this was over. She drove the cart into the kitchen court, where Demetria was waiting with half a dozen guards.

Two of them took charge of the cart. They would take it back to Sosia. The rest lifted Kerrec out, wrapped in a rug, and carried him to Briana's rooms. The grey cob followed, flickering in and out of vision. Briana had not known the stallions had the art of invisibility, although it should hardly be surprising. After all, they were gods.

Briana had the guards carry Kerrec to the pavilion in her private garden. It was secluded and easy to defend, and Petra could come and go as he pleased. There was a bed in the airy space, in which Briana slept in the heat of the summer. With shutters up and carpets on the tiled floor, and a fire in the shielded hearth, it was comfortable even in winter.

Just now, at the beginning of autumn, when the days were still summer-warm and the nights were barely hinting at winter's chill, it would serve Kerrec well enough. Briana had a bath brought in, with her most discreet servants to attend it, and saw him bathed and shaved and restored to his usual self.

By the time he was laid in bed, her jaw ached with clenching. Wherever he had been, he had crossed paths with a Brother of Pain. The pattern of weals and scars was unmistakable.

So was the way he swam in and out of consciousness. He had been subjected to the deeper torments. They would seem small when they began, but over time they ate away at the mind and spirit. For a mage of his particular order and power, they were devastating. They took aim at the roots of his discipline and eroded them until the power turned on itself. Then the torturer could simply stand back and watch the structure crumble.

Briana had a healer's gift and a fair grounding in the art, but this was beyond her. She paced the floor in a controlled fury, dimly aware that guards and servants stayed well out of her way. Abruptly she stopped. A white wall had presented itself in front of her.

She met Petra's steady dark stare. "There's no one in the healers' temple that I trust," she said to him. "Not for this. Whoever and whatever did this, to dare such a crime, to capture and torture a rider—he would have to be very brave indeed, or absolutely mad." She lashed out with pure fury. "And you! Where were you? How could you let this happen?"

Petra neither lowered his head nor looked away. His eyes were full of stars.

He was not human, and he was not mortal. The patterns of the Dance, the tides of time and fate, were embodied in him. Her mind was too small to comprehend all of what he knew.

"That's nonsense," she said. He could blast her where she stood, and she did not care. "You let down your guard. You failed. Who was strong enough to snatch your rider from under your nose? *Who?*"

"Gothard."

She spun. Kerrec was awake. His eyes were clear.

"Gothard?" she echoed. "Our brother Gothard? He was never mage enough for this."

"It seems we underestimated him," Kerrec said with something like his old dry wit. "Listen carefully. You have to warn the riders. There's a plot to kill our father and disrupt the Dance. They have a mage, a raw power driven by anger and malice, who can break the pattern. That one is even stronger than Gothard. Master Nikos will know who it is and why. The barbarians are using both Gothard and the other. I'm afraid—they never said, but I'm very much afraid—that even if they fail with the Dance, they'll succeed in the rest. Even if the Dance is safe, the emperor will be dead."

He stopped, breathing hard as if the effort of so much clarity had exhausted him. She gripped his hands. He was slipping already, falling back into a fog of confusion.

"Kerrec," she said, wielding his name like a weapon. "Kerrec!"

His head rolled on his neck. His face had gone slack. She resisted the urge to slap him back to consciousness. He was beyond that. He had gathered every scrap of coherence that he had, and every fragment of memory, and set it all in those few words. Now there was nothing left.

She whirled to face Petra. "Fetch my father," she said.

If the stallion had been human, his brows would have gone up. She went well past presumption in ordering him about as if he were a servant.

"Yes, I do," she said. "I'm desperate. A guard or servant won't bring him, not for this. Even for me he won't do it. For you he'll come."

She hoped he would come. Father and son had not

parted amicably at all. To this day the emperor would not hear his son's name spoken, either the one he had carried as imperial heir or the one he had claimed as a rider. Both Ambrosius and Kerrec were dead and gone.

"Tell His Majesty," she said to Petra, "that there is no one else I can trust, and no one who can help. No one else can break the riders' seclusion. For the empire's salvation, let him come."

Petra lowered his head slightly and turned, trotting out of the pavilion. The sound of his hoofbeats died away. She could only hope he would do as she asked. Otherwise she would have to go to the emperor herself and beg.

Of all the things the Emperor Artorius might have expected to find waiting in his rooms when he came up from dinner, a white god was one of the last. The beast had sent his servants into hysterics and reduced his guards to wide-eyed helplessness. He was standing in the middle of the emperor's private parlor, as incongruous a figure as one might expect, apparently sound asleep.

Artorius was not deceived. He bowed as an emperor should before a god, and said courteously, "My lord."

The stallion's eyes opened and his ears came up. He pawed lightly, with care not to damage the floor, and cocked an ear. The emperor, it was clear, was to follow him.

The emperor was tired. The day had been long and his duties burdensome. He was planning a war as well as a jubilee. Sometimes he could not have told which was which.

Nevertheless, this was a god. He had never had such a visitation, nor had he heard of such a thing. If nothing else, it sparked his curiosity. He sighed for his lost sleep, but he bowed again, lower than before, and waited for the stallion to lead him.

Briana had fetched an armload of books from the palace library and was buried in them when her father followed Petra through the garden. Night had fallen. The stallion glowed like a full moon, lighting the emperor's path. She looked up, blinking, as he mounted the flight of steps into the pavilion.

He was not scowling, which was encouraging. He seemed surprised to see her, which was less so. She resisted the urge to hide Kerrec from him. She waited for him to see that the bed was occupied, then to realize who it was.

His face went cold. He turned on his heel, but Petra blocked his way. Briana thought her father would actually shoulder the stallion aside, but he clearly reconsidered.

"Father," she said to his back, "please. This goes beyond a family quarrel. A First Rider has been taken and tortured. There is a plot against the Dance and against you."

The emperor did not move. "Tortured?" he said. "Come and see."

If he had tried to leave then, she did not think Petra would have stopped him. He took a long while to decide, but in the end he turned back and went to stand over Kerrec.

Kerrec was deep asleep. Briana had laid on him a simple but effective spell, using moonlight and water and earth from the garden.

The emperor bent and drew back the blanket. Mage light was brighter than lamplight and much less forgiving. He cast it across the still but breathing body.

Artorius was in no hurry to speak. Briana went back to her books. She had yet to find what she was looking for, which was a way to restore her brother's memory and rebuild his magic. She refused to accept that there was no such thing.

She had almost forgotten that her father was there when he said, "You had better tell me what you know."

She paused to shift her mind from a treatise on the nature of memory, then told him what Kerrec had told her, word for word. His expression did not change as he listened. When it was done, he asked, "That's all he told you?"

"It was all he could tell," she answered.

"It's very little," he said.

Briana should have expected that. This was yet another skirmish in the old war between father and son, and neither of them had any sense when it came to the other. She would have knocked their heads together if it would have done any good at all.

She settled, this time, for banked heat and fiercely controlled temper. "Isn't it enough that Gothard is plotting to kill you and take the throne, with the barbarians to support him? They're plotting to disrupt the Dance and shift the tides of time in their favor. What more do you need?"

"Surer proof than the word of a dead man," the emperor said coldly.

"What of the word of a First Rider?"

"A First Rider whose mind and magic are broken. Who knows what he actually saw, as opposed to what he was persuaded to see?"

"He saw Gothard," Briana said. "I believe that. He was lucid when he told me. It was the truth."

"I need proof," the emperor said.

"Can't you use your common sense? Do you really know where Gothard is?"

"He has been riding through his estates in the north," the emperor said, "administering them as a prince should do."

"Are you sure of that? Are you absolutely sure?" She did not wait for him to answer, but pressed a little harder. "In what way is his word or the word of his messengers more to be trusted than that of a First Rider?"

Artorius was not to be swayed, even by logic. "No matter what the charges, no matter how black the treason, any court of justice would demand no less. The word of one man is not enough. You know this. You've judged more sternly than I have in matters affecting the empire."

"So I have," she said, "and I believe my brother. This is urgent, Father. It's eleven days until the Dance. That's precious little time."

"Then use it well," he said.

"At least increase your guard," she said, "and call in the mages of the Watch. If the seers have seen anything—if the Augurs have marked the omens—"

"It will all be done," he said.

She eyed him narrowly. If he was indulging her fancies, she would call him to account for it.

He was looking down at Kerrec again. She could not read his expression. He laid his hand on Kerrec's forehead. It was not a caress. Her skin prickled.

There was a hiss and a sharp crack. The emperor recoiled. Blue light arced between his palm and Kerrec's brow.

Without a pause for thought, Briana cast a damping spell. The small hairs on her body no longer stood erect. The scent of ozone dissipated. Kerrec lay as still as before.

The emperor flexed his fingers. A slow breath escaped him. "Something has warded him," he said.

She nodded. "It's the stallions, I think, or some magic of the Mountain. There's no ill-wishing in it."

"None that you can see."

"I trust it," she said, "and him."

He sighed. "I wish that I could do the same. I do see that he believes what he told you. But as he is, with the deep torment—the truth may be altogether different."

Briana did not think so, but she had had enough of arguing. "If there is a plot," she said, "and you can't deny that it's likely, regardless of who is behind it— let us lay a trap to catch its perpetrators. If there are none, we lose nothing but time and a little magic. If they do exist, with luck and the gods' help we'll stop them before they make their move."

He did not dismiss it out of hand, which she had been afraid of. He did not embrace it, either, but she had not expected that. He said, "I suppose that's reasonable. What did you have in mind?"

Very little, she thought, but she could hardly tell him that. "We need the riders," she said. "They have to know of this."

"No," her father said. "If we break their seclusion, we play into the enemy's hands—if he exists. We disrupt the Dance before it even begins."

"But they have to know," she said. "They have to be warned."

"You think they haven't been?" His glance caught Petra, who stood in the doorway, so still and silent that he might have been made of marble. "Believe this, child. They know."

"But—"

"Whatever we do," he said, "we do without them.

If there is a plot, it's more important than ever that the ritual of the Dance be observed in every particular."

She had to accept the logic of that. In any case her thoughts were only half-formed. She had to delve deeper into her books and remember the lessons of her own magic.

The emperor stooped and kissed her forehead. She half thought he flinched, but no fire leaped from her. She was properly restrained and contained within herself.

"Stay here," he said, "and do what you can. I'll see that your duties are taken care of until this is over."

"So you do believe him," she said with a small surge of elation.

"I believe that he believes it," he said. "Good night, daughter. Rest if you can. You'll need your strength if you're to fight a battle."

She bent her head. He smiled, a surprisingly warm smile in so stern a face. He was so like his son, in mind as well as body, that her eyes pricked with tears. *Dear gods*, she prayed. *Protect them both. Guard my father. Heal my brother. Save us all from the storm that is coming.*

Chapter Thirty-One

Euan's tongue circled Valeria's nipple, then flicked with a sudden flutter. She gasped. He laughed, a low rumble. She wound fingers in his thick hair. His erect organ throbbed against her thigh. She gathered herself to slide down and take it in.

She froze. White fire had leaped inside her, searing through the darkness, burning away any thought but one.

She never remembered leaving the bed, let alone leaving Euan. She must have paused for a moment, because when she was truly conscious again, she was outside in the morning chill, and she had her riding clothes on. Euan was there, she supposed, but she had no thought to spare for him.

Sabata had come back, and he had captured himself

a human. Mestre Olivet pressed against the wall of the lodge, as white as the hoarfrost. The stallion snapped wicked teeth in his face.

"Sabata," Valeria said mildly. She did not trouble to raise her voice. Olivet looked ready to drop down in a fit.

Sabata's ears flattened, but he moved back a step. Olivet's shaking did not lessen. Valeria realized in a kind of horror that he could no longer read a horse. That was not even magic, it was simple observation, and any horseman could do it. He could not see that the threat was ended, only that the great white thing was still too close. He was blank with terror.

Gods help her, she would never in this world want to become what this man had become. The spell of Unmaking inside her stirred uneasily but then subsided. She asked Sabata politely to draw away even farther. He obeyed with little grace, but he did it.

She moved in beside him. His ears stayed flat, but he did not offer to bite or kick. She slid her arm over his back and laid her head against his neck and said into that little curling ear, "You fool. You endless fool. Why did you come back?"

The ear flicked. He snorted wetly. He was not going to answer her. Nor was he going to leave, no matter what she might be thinking.

She meant to get rid of him. She could at least try to chase him off with whips and stones. But he curved his neck around her and pressed his soft nose into her palm and blew warm breath on it, and she fell completely under his spell. She could have fought it. She chose not to, and maybe that was cowardly. But when she was as close to him as this, she was that much farther away from the Unmaking.

Sabata would not undo the spell trapped inside Valeria. It was too deep, he said, and too firmly rooted. If he removed it, it would cost her all her magic and much of her self.

"But it's small," she said as she settled him in the stable he had been in before. "There's hardly anything to it. Surely—"

He turned his back on her and buried his face in hay. She struck his broad round rump with her fist, but he did not even flinch. She spun and stalked away.

He was in front of her, barring the door. She had not heard him move.

She wanted to retreat in dignity. The sight of him, so solid and so very much of this earth and yet so incontestably a god, broke her down in tears.

He was more than strong enough to hold her up while she cried out all her fear and worry and guilt. She was clean and empty when she finished. If there had been a wind blowing, it would have passed straight through her.

She washed her face in the rain barrel outside the door, and put herself in as much order as she could. Sabata had gone back to his hay. However dangerous it had been for him to come back and risk Unmaking, she was glad he was there.

Just as she passed out of sight, she had a flicker of vision, as if she had seen around a corner to another place and, maybe, the same time. She saw Kerrec on Petra's back, and a woman so like him that she must be his sister.

Her knees buckled in relief. She nearly fell. Once she found her balance, her step was lighter. She went to find Mestre Olivet.

He was in seclusion, the guards said. She could imagine him lying with a cold cloth over his eyes, convincing himself that he had been afflicted by a terrible evil.

If he was that appalled by the close proximity of a white god, how true or accurate were the patterns he was teaching her? She had thought that she would know if they were false. Could she be sure of that?

It was too late for doubts. She retreated to the library, for lack of a better thought, and hunted in it for something that did not have to do with magic.

She fell asleep over a florid romance of a hundred years ago. Its patterns were silly and hackneyed and harmless. They gave her a gift of simple dreams, common and ordinary, with no foreboding in them.

Euan Rohe did not want to leave Valeria alone that night, as strange a mood as she was in now that the stallion had come back. But he had an obligation he could not refuse. He had to hope that she would still be there when he came back, and that the lodge and its inhabitants would be intact.

He brought himself up short for thinking that. Valeria had made her choice. She wanted the Mountain, and no one else would give it to her. The stallion should reassure her. By coming back, he had proved that his allegiance was to her and not to the Mountain.

In any case Euan could not stay to tell her these things. He was not quite disastrously late, but it was a bruising ride. One of his warband lost his horse to a misstep. The horse went down and came up three-legged.

The man was winded but otherwise unharmed. They left him with the carcass of the horse. Either he could walk back to the lodge or he could wait for them to come back that way, and beg a ride on someone's crupper.

Euan would have started walking, himself. Wolves and mountain cats were not particularly hungry at this time of year, but a dead horse was as much meat as some of them saw in a year.

It did not seem that Tavis thought of that. He was sitting by the horse when Euan glanced back, looking as if he meant to fall asleep as soon as the others were out of sight.

Euan shrugged. Some men had to learn wisdom the hard way. Usually it killed them.

There was no time for idiots tonight or any night between now and the Dance. The priests were waiting in the place that Euan's men had found for them. It was a strange place, a perfect circle in the earth, with sides as sheer as walls except to the west, where part of the wall had come down with time and rain. There was a track of sorts, too steep and slippery for horses, and bad enough for men trying to find their way in the last of the daylight.

Euan's skin crawled as he picked his way down to the floor of that place. It was almost perfectly flat. There must have been grass and trees in it—he could see the remnants along the edges—but the priests had peeled away the earth's skin to reveal a floor of black glass. In the center of it they had raised the sacred stone, by means that Euan did not have the rank or the calling to understand. It was black, and by the law of the rite must be unshaped, as it was taken from the earth. It thrust like a finger toward the darkening sky.

There were three priests. There should have been nine, but it was a long way from the border and a long stretch of empire, with legions and imperial spies, in between. Euan was glad to see as many as there were. Three would be enough, in this place, to raise what must be raised.

All of his men were there except for Tavis. Those who had been living at large in the country, away from Gothard and his suspicions, had come in intact, which was even more of a wonder than the number of priests who had survived their journey.

Euan was the last to come down to the floor of the valley. Full night had fallen. The stars for once were not veiled in mist or rain, but were hard and clear. The air had a snap of frost.

This was a rite of night and stone. There would be no light or fire.

The sacrifice was bound to the stone. They must have brought him from the lands of the Caletanni. He was no imperial, with his hair so fair it glowed in the starlight, and skin as white as milk. There was not a blemish on him, not a mark of the torture that would have already begun.

He was drugged, his head rolling slackly against the stone. He looked as if he had already gone to the white place, the place where men went when they were in perfect pain, or when they were going to die.

The priests let fall their dark robes. They were naked beneath, shaved clean from head to toe. The marks of their clan swirled over their bodies in dizzying patterns, seeming to move independently of the skin, writhing and coiling.

Euan knew better than to look too close. The chant was befuddling enough, almost but not quite over-whelming the soft whimpers and strangled screams of the victim as he was given to the One.

It was a slow sacrifice. The cause was powerful and the need great. The invocations were the strongest and the summonings the most terrible. They called the darkness to veil the stars. They begged the One to favor their undertaking, to give them strength for the great thing that they would do in the imperial city. An emperor dead, the pattern of destiny disrupted, the tides of the world shifted and the false gods destroyed—all before the next phase of the moon.

The priests betrayed no suggestion of doubt, no sign of fear. This would be, because it was the will of the One.

They painted the stone with the victim's blood. He lived a long time, long enough to see his entrails wound nine times around the stone and sealed with iron. At the last they wrought the blood eagle, although by then there was little blood left in him. The pale wings of the lungs and the white arches of ribs glorified the One.

The eldest of the priests intoned the blessing, anointing each warrior with blood gone thick and cold. Euan set his teeth at the touch of it on his forehead. Hot blood had a taste and a smell like none other, bright and strong as life itself, but cold blood stank of death.

Death was the One's beloved creation. He bowed his head to the power of it, and let himself be dismissed with the rest of the warband.

The priests would wait until the fighting men were gone. Then they would dispose of the victim. By sunrise, even the bones would be gone, crushed to powder and scattered on the wind.

So would it be for all the enemies of the One. Every worshipper of false gods. Every mage who was not sworn to the priesthood. Every living thing that walked apart from the truth.

Valeria stared blindly into the dark. Sabata was a white light inside her, but within the light was its Unmaking. From that her dream had come.

She had been Euan Rohe. She had felt what he felt, thought what he thought. She had lived inside his body for the space of an evening and a night.

She knew him now. She knew what he was and what he meant to do. Gothard would live only as long as he served his allies' purposes.

When she looked inside herself, she saw no hatred of Euan. She was not even particularly horrified. By the customs she had learned from childhood, he was a blood-stained savage. In his own world he was a good man, loyal to his people and devoted to his god.

She still wanted him, the warmth of his body, the taste of his lips, the way he knew all her tenderest places. If that meant she was corrupted, then so be it. She could not help what her body felt, even while her mind gave a name to everything she had done since she saved Kerrec's life. That name was treason.

Chapter Thirty-Two

Traitor.

He had a name again. His name was Kerrec. He knew her name, too. Her name was *Traitor.* The name she had used when she pretended to be a man, then the name she claimed when the gods betrayed the truth, were lies. *Traitor* was the truth.

He was healing, but his heart would never be the same. He might never get back his discipline, either—not as it was before.

There was warmth inside him, from which the healing came. It made him think of gentle hands and a soft voice speaking words he could not quite catch. It smoothed his ragged edges and mended his wounds, and helped him to make himself whole again.

At first he thought Briana was doing it. Her spells

did help, but they would have been useless without the deeper, stronger enchantment. He did not know who had worked it. It was not one of the stallions, although there was a strong flavor of them in it. It might almost have been—it almost felt like—

She wanted nothing except to destroy him. Someone else had found him and worked the spell on him. Someday he would discover who it was. For now, the best thanks he could give would be to keep on healing.

On what Briana later told him was the third day since she found him in the village, he remembered where he was and why he had been riding to Aurelia. With that memory came enough of the rest that he nearly broke again.

Petra brought him back from the edge. Briana kept him there. He tried to get up and find the rest of the riders, but neither of his jailers would let him go. "They need me," he insisted. "They have to know— I have to tell them—"

"No," Briana said, and Petra made himself into a wall that Kerrec was still too weak to pass. He sank down simmering, determining to bide his time.

If there was any of it left. "What day is this?" he demanded.

"Eight days until the Dance," his sister answered.

He nodded. He gave it more of a dying fall than he honestly felt. As he had hoped, she left him alone.

Petra did not, but he was not human. He did not

fret as Briana did. After a while he wandered off through the garden toward the manger that had been set under an arbor. It was kept full of sweet hay, and in the evening a servant brought an offering of barley and oats and a little corn.

"You should go," Kerrec said. He was the length of the garden away from the stallion, but that did not matter to a god. "Now more than ever, the Dance needs the best and the strongest. You are both."

Petra ignored him. He was deep in the bliss of good hay.

That was the most dangerous weakness of the union between riders and stallions. Each stallion bound himself to a single rider. If that rider was unable to ride the Dance, the stallion nearly always chose the man over the ritual.

"You can't do that now," Kerrec persisted, although he knew it might do more harm than good. "This Dance means too much, and has too many threats against it. You have to let someone else ride you."

Petra was not listening at all. The quality of his not-listening was distinct. Kerrec was lucky, it said, that Petra did not erupt in outrage at the thought of another rider on his back.

"Other stallions allow it," Kerrec said.

Not I. It was a mark of strong feeling that the stallion replied in words.

That was as far as Kerrec dared to go. He eased himself out of bed, taking his time. Dizziness came and went. There was surprisingly little pain. He was weak, but not as weak as he had expected. He could stand. He could even walk.

Whoever had sown the seed of healing in him, it was a miraculous thing. The harder he used himself, the faster it healed him. He knew of no school of magic that could do such a thing.

At the moment he did not care. He was barefoot, with no shoes or boots to be found, but his clothes were decent enough. They were servant's clothes, the plain brown tunic and trousers of a stablehand or a drudge in the kitchens. They were also near enough to the casual uniform of a rider.

More of his memory came back as he walked through the garden and into the heir's wing of the palace. This had been his once, and Briana had changed little of it. The archery range was still there. So was the stable, with a fair population of horses. Even some of the servants were the same.

None of them seemed to recognize him. If he had had magic he could use, he would have cast a working to make them see whatever they expected to see. As it was, there was no outcry. No one called his name, either the prince's name or the First Rider's.

He was following patterns, the fretwork of a latticed window, the pattern of sunlight on a tiled floor. They led him down passages that after a while he no longer remembered. He must have left the heir's wing and crossed to the greater palace. He could not have gone as far as the queen's palace, which had been empty since his mother died. He must be somewhere in the region of the state chambers or, behind and below them, the warren of cells and passages that was the chancery of the empire.

These were servants' corridors, with walls of plain brick or stone and bare floors. The beauties of the public palace were not in evidence here.

His passage from one to the other was suitably abrupt. He opened a door and found himself in familiar surroundings. The floor was a jeweled mosaic. The walls were painted with frescoes of gardens and forests. Painted marble busts lurked in niches. He recognized a number of his ancestors and at least one blatant usurper, whose bust had been relieved of its nose and ears and hung with the halter of a traitor. It was meant for a warning, and a reminder.

Mutilated old Fomorius told Kerrec where he was. He was just above the Golden Hall, where each evening the court performed the movements of its own, very earthly dance.

Kerrec's will had stopped being his own some time since. He slipped through another door, back into the drabness of the servants' world, and followed the tugging at his weakened magic. It led him down a narrow stair to a room he had never known existed.

The room was not particularly small, but it was full of odd things. A box held soft shoes of all sizes, some new, some very well worn. On a table next to it was a heap of fabric that unfolded into servants' tabards in the emperor's colors, crimson and gold. There were trays and platters piled on shelves and tables, handled jars from which Kerrec had seen servants pour wine, cups and bowls, and on shelves by the door, a softly gleaming row of water pitchers and ewers for washing the hands after eating.

The first pair of shoes he tried fit well enough and were new enough for his fastidiousness. The tabards seemed all of a size. Dressed now as a proper servant, he opened the inner door.

It did not open directly into the hall. There was a passage, better lit than most that he had seen since he left the garden. Others opened into it. The one he noticed in particular bathed him in sounds and scents that spoke vividly of the kitchens. People were running up and down the stair, weighted down with platters and bowls.

He meant to watch for a while, but a florid personage whom he did not recognize laid eyes on him, scowled and deftly caught one of the runners from the kitchen. Kerrec found himself equipped with a pitcher of wine and ordered into the hall.

The pitcher looked like gold but was much too light to be genuine. After a moment Kerrec realized that it was gilded glass. The part of him that he had thought long dead, the royal prince, sneered at such cheap mimicry. The rest of him was glad of the lesser burden.

He had no time to nerve himself for the plunge. The steward was glowering at him. He fell in with the rest of the servants. They swept him with them toward the door and the hall.

Light and warmth and the mingled roar of conversation, laughter, music, struck him like a blow. He reeled, but somehow he steadied himself. There were patterns—he could see patterns.

He followed the one that seemed most apt, transcribing a circle around the hall. There were cups to be filled. Sometimes they rose up in front of him. Mostly they expected him to find and fill them for himself. They were attached to hands and arms, silk, jewels, gold and silver. Countless faces hovered in front of him, blurring together. Memory faltered before so many.

He in tunic and tabard was invisible. When his pitcher was empty, he was halfway across the hall from the servants' door. Common sense would send him back the way he had come, but he was caught in the patterns that wove and twisted through the hall. People moved in eddies and currents. Factions coalesced and dissipated, touched one another, flowed together or sprang sharply apart.

Beneath a descant of gossip and frivolous intrigue ran a deep undercurrent of tension. War was in the wind, and these nobles were not in harmony with themselves or their emperor.

The emperor moved among them in a stately dance

of order and precedence. He could have chosen to sit on the throne that gleamed at the far end of the hall, but today he was taking the measure of his court. Kerrec could see and feel how the patterns shifted, some factions gravitating toward the emperor, but others veering carefully away.

Artorius seemed regally oblivious. The usual flock of sycophants fluttered and cackled around him. They were a blind, Kerrec knew, and a shield. Through their familiar chatter the emperor could listen to the lower voices. He heard the rumbles of discontent and the murmurs of dissension. He could take a count of those who stood against his war, even before he called them into council.

It was dizzyingly complex for a mind as damaged as Kerrec's. He could not listen to the words. The patterns were more than enough to follow.

Little by little he began to recognize faces. Names did not attach to them, not yet, but he knew these people. They had mattered to him once. Now they were bubbles in a pot, and the pot was coming to the boil.

The emperor had come almost within reach. He did not see Kerrec at all, any more than anyone else did. Suddenly, so suddenly that Kerrec would have missed it if he had not been looking directly at it, Artorius slipped free of his entourage and vanished behind a pillar.

There was magic in what he did. The gaggle of courtiers did not even know he was gone. Kerrec followed the magic.

There was a door behind the pillar, hidden in shadow. It led to a passage somewhat too wide to be a servants' corridor, lit by lamps at intervals along it. Kerrec remembered it dimly. There were corridors like it all through the palace, for the emperor and his family to pass from one hall to the next, or to and from their private apartments.

This one led to the emperor's rooms. Artorius relaxed as he left the court behind, and let his shoulders droop, allowing himself a few moments' indulgence in human weakness.

He neither saw nor heard Kerrec. Nor, and that was damning, did the bodyguard who walked in his shadow. The man was too much at ease. Either he had not been warned to be on his guard, or he had disregarded the warning.

There was a great deal of that in this palace. Kerrec surprised himself by caring that it was so. He was dead here. It should not matter.

The passage ended in a wall and a stair. The light there was dim. There should have been lamps burning above the stair, but they were dark, without even the odor of a spent wick to recall when they had last been lit.

The emperor was perfectly capable of kindling a witch light, but he knew this way well. Maybe he found the dimness restful. He began to climb the stair.

His guard pressed in behind him. At the same time another came down from above, with a soft rattle of weapons and a ringing of mail.

Patterns were swirling dizzily, knotting and tangling around the emperor. Kerrec began to run.

As he ran, the rags of his magic began to knit. He was still weak, still maimed, but there was enough. Maybe. Enough to lighten his feet until he was all but flying, and slow the world to a dreamlike crawl. He saw the blades in the guards' hands. He saw their faces, hard and set, and the death in their eyes.

He flew over the emperor's head and flung back the guard above. The man was slow, so slow. The attack spun him around and into the wall. The knife escaped from his hand. Kerrec felt the crushing of bones, the snapping of the neck from the force of the blow.

He balanced himself on the step and turned almost leisurely. The guard below was not so slow, not so easily surprised. Kerrec could taste the magic in him. It was rising, arming.

The emperor was between them. He had roused, but in the dark he did not recognize his son. He saw his guard dead, the man in the servant's tabard attacking, and never knew of the blade that slashed toward him from behind.

He loosed a mage-bolt. Kerrec flashed aside from it, but felt the searing heat. Part of the stair crumbled under his feet. He launched himself without grace but with all the speed he could muster, over the emperor's head, down on the guard below.

They fell all together, rolling and tumbling down the stair. Kerrec twisted wildly, trying to catch his father, to shield him from the fall and the blade. Memory flickered, knowledge, understanding, but the connections were broken. He could not grasp it. There was only the strength of the body, and what speed he had left.

The knife struck a glancing blow. Kerrec felt it as if it had slashed his own skin. He broke the hand that held it and turned it on its wielder. It slid up beneath the ribs and into the heart.

The assassin fell, pulling Kerrec down with him. Kerrec struggled free. His father was lying at the foot of the stair. He was moving, wheezing. The fall had struck the wind out of him, that was all. The blade had only nicked his side.

Kerrec sat on his heels. He was not breathing too well himself. He was light-headed, as if he had gone too long without food or sleep. The well of his magic was nearly dry.

The emperor had got his breath back. He sat up, wincing at the pull of torn muscles and slashed skin. His eyes took in Kerrec, and knew him. Kerrec saw how they went cold. "What in the name of Sun and Moon are you doing here?"

No thanks for saving his life. No pleasure to see his son. Kerrec had expected nothing else. Somehow he got to his feet. He turned, meaning to walk away, but midway he reeled and fell down.

His father caught him, cursing at what it did to the knife-cut. They went down together, not tidily at all.

There was a pause. Kerrec was not sure he dared start laughing, not so much because his father would be offended as because once he started, there was no way in the world he could stop.

"You could have been killed," Artorius said.

"You would have died first," said Kerrec. The floor was almost comfortable. It was a pity he had to get up again, but there were two dead guards to consider, and gods knew what else might be coming. "*Now* do you believe that you're in danger?"

"I'm in danger every moment of my life," the emperor said. "You on the Mountain with your gods and your magic, you forget what life at court is like."

"The dead do forget," Kerrec said. "So do the living, it seems. Your guards are slack or outright traitorous. Your defenses are weak. Is this some plan too subtle for ordinary mortals to understand?"

"Are you trying to make me throttle you?"

"If it will keep you alive until after the Dance," said Kerrec, "then you're welcome to it."

"That's all that matters to you, isn't it? The Dance."

"If you wish," Kerrec said. He heaved himself to his feet and stretched out a hand. For a moment he thought the emperor would refuse it, but Artorius was not quite as stiff-necked as that. He let Kerrec pull him up. His grip was strong, almost painful.

He gasped as he came erect. Kerrec felt the stab of pain in his own side. It was growing worse. There was a burning in it. But even worse than that was the deeper thing, the thing that explained all too much.

"Father!" Kerrec said. "Your magic—"

"Get me to my rooms," Artorius said.

"Physicians—mages—"

"Stop babbling," said the emperor. "Start thinking."

His words were like a slap. Kerrec pulled his father's arm across his shoulders. Stumbling, occasionally staggering, but never quite falling, they made their way up the stair.

</>#<#

Chapter Thirty-Three

"Poison," Briana said.

Kerrec had done his thinking, quite a lot of it in fact, while he struggled with his father up that endless stair. By the time he reached the top, he knew what he had to do.

So did the emperor. They managed because they must. Artorius walked into his rooms past guards who seemed loyal, but who knew? Not Kerrec, just then.

He was blind to the patterns again. The strength that set his father on his feet had come from him. He did well to stay on his own feet, keep his head down and play the servant.

Servants were waiting in the emperor's chambers. Artorius dismissed them. They eyed Kerrec askance. They knew he was not one of them, but they did not recognize either their lost prince or the First Rider from the Mountain.

For the moment it was enough that they withdrew in silence. One had an errand, to fetch Briana. He performed it with dispatch.

She said what Kerrec had already understood. "There was poison on the blade."

"Do you know what it is?" Kerrec asked her. He had had to sit down, but his head was surprisingly clear. Whatever spell had been set in him to mend him, it was growing stronger rather than weaker the longer it went on.

"I would guess *akasha*," Briana said. "It's nasty—it doesn't harm the body, but it eats away the magic. As to who has done it or why...Father?"

Artorius had collapsed into bed as soon as his servants were gone. She had cleaned and bandaged the wound, but it was too late to scour the poison from his blood. He was still conscious, but struggling. "We can't ask mages to help us. We can trust no one. Whoever has done this—"

"You know who it is," Kerrec said.

"Not until I have proof," said Artorius, as stubborn as ever. To Briana he said, "Find an antidote. Be quick about it."

"What if there's none?" she asked.

"Find one," he said.

Briana set Demetria on guard over her father. She dared trust no one else. Demetria, born warded, immune to magic, could protect him as no one else could.

Demetria came in from disposing of the would-be assassins. She asked no questions. When she was in place, Briana could turn her attention to Kerrec.

At first she had thought he was wounded, too, but there was no mark on him that had not been there before. He was in a most peculiar state of mind. Even as a child he had never been one to be rattled, but that was just what he seemed to be now. He could not settle. He would not eat or sleep.

She got him out of their father's chambers. He could walk, which surprised her, although he needed her shoulder to lean on. He seemed dizzy or drunk, but there was no smell of wine on his breath, and no drug in him that she could detect.

"Patterns," he said. "I keep seeing patterns. In and out, round about…"

Petra was not in the garden when they came there. She got the servant's tabard off him and coaxed him into bed. He tossed restlessly. He was feverish, but he shook off cool cloths and would not drink the tonic she prepared for him.

Finally, in a combination of desperation and disgust, she left him to it. She knew as well as he who had ordered the assassins to attack her father. That they could put on the uniforms of imperial guards and establish themselves in the emperor's personal contingent was not only distressing, it was alarming.

Eight more days, and then the Dance. She was the next target, if this went as such things usually did. Her guards were alert, her wards at their strongest. Her father's guard would have to be examined and purged, and quickly, but at the same time secretly. The same went for the palace guard, and probably the city guard as well.

Everyone that she could trust in this matter was either tossing on the bed in front of her or doing much the same in the emperor's rooms, or standing guard over the garden or the emperor. Her mind raced through names and faces in court or council. The few who were honest or honorable were weak or vulnerable, or useless in a battle of magic. The temples had their own concerns, few of which served her purpose. The riders…

In this she was alone. Whatever choices there were, she had to make them.

"Briana," her brother said.

His voice was steady. He sounded sane. His eyes were almost clear.

"The Dance," he said. "The Dance counters the poison."

She was all fuddled. She could not be sure she understood him. "What—"

"There is no potion or counterspell for *akasha*," he said, "except the Dance."

"But how—"

"I don't know," he said. "I don't remember. I just know this. We have to do what we can for him until the Dance."

"What can we do?"

His eyes closed. He was breathing hard. She was trying to lean on him, and he was too frail to support her.

She had to think for herself. That was easy when she was judging the law or making order in the empire. But this was anything but simple, and the stakes were desperately high.

Briana had not meant to fall asleep. The guard who woke her was apologetic, but Demetria needed her.

She had been sleeping with her head on a stack of books, not one of which offered anything useful. There was a crick in her neck and a cramp in her back, and the imprint of a scroll case on her cheek.

She would have gone as she was, but her maid Maariyah was lying in wait for her. Maariyah had a way of conveying volumes with a glance, and this glance declared that she had suffered days of creeping about, keeping secrets and letting guards do what servants could do far better and with less fuss. She said none of it, but herded Briana into the bath and, quickly but thoroughly, made her fit to be seen.

Briana knew better than to twitch. Still, time was running on. Then as Maariyah's deft fingers plaited her hair, her maid said, "Lady, you know I have a sister, who married a man from up by the border."

Briana twisted around in shock. Maariyah had never, in all the years she had been looking after

Briana, indulged in idle chatter. That she would do it now was inconceivable.

There was no spell on her. She arched a brow as Briana gaped at her. "My sister's husband," she went on imperturbably, "serves with the personal guard of your brother—not the one who is dead and who is sleeping in your garden and being waited on by ham-handed soldiers rather than servants who know their business. The other one, the one who is supposed to be out looking after his estates."

Briana closed her mouth carefully.

"To be sure he's been looking after them," said Maariyah, "on both sides of the border. In Aurelia, too, says my brother-in-law. Did you know he's been here since the day before yesterday?"

Briana had not, but it was hardly surprising. "He was to return by tomorrow," she said with studied coolness. "Is it significant that he's early? Rude, of course, not to pay his respects to his family, but I'm sure he meant to do it before the Dance."

"I think you should speak to my brother-in-law," Maariyah said.

Briana suppressed a sigh. "I have to go to my father. That can't wait. Can your kinsman be here before noon?"

"He's been on night duty," Maariyah said. "We can rouse him early."

"Good," Briana said. "Have him here before the noon bells ring."

* * *

Demetria had the emperor barely under control. He was up, bathed and dressed. When Briana came in, he was all too obviously bent on going out to perform the day's duties. "No one must know," he said with an air of having repeated himself a great deal more than once. "I must go on as I always do, or this battle is lost."

"It's perfectly acceptable for an emperor to seclude himself before a rite as vitally important as this," Briana said from the door. "Leave the lesser obligations to your ministers, and put off the greater ones. There's nothing that can't wait."

"On the contrary," he said. "Both of us can't disappear at once. That's even more suspicious than my appearing to be less than my usual self. Which, I promise you, I will do my best to avoid."

"You need to rest," she said, "and recover if you can. You can't do that if you're going yet another round with the war council and the council of ministers. Not to mention—"

"If we're to have any hope of seeing the Dance to its completion, I have to be seen, and I have to appear to be strong."

"Maybe not," she said. "I think it may be better to seem weak. Let them think they succeeded."

"They did," he pointed out with a distinct edge of irony.

"They wanted you dead or worse," she said. "Kerrec told me something, Father. He said, 'The

Dance is the antidote.' He couldn't tell me more, but surely he would know."

"And they would not?"

"Maybe not," she said. "If that particular poison were known to be countered by the Dance, why would they use it? It's all very well to bleed away your magic, but what good is it if the Dance—the thing they want most to disrupt—can bring it back again? They want you weak and out of play. If they think you're well under the *akasha's* influence, they may grow overconfident and betray themselves. Then we can trap them."

"How? With what?"

"I don't know," she said, "but I will. Just give me time."

He frowned and rubbed his forehead as if it ached. He was a little stiffer and more upright than usual. He was in pain, and not altogether successful in hiding it.

"Father," she said, "let me make your excuses to the councils. I'll come back after—maybe even with the proof you were asking for."

Her words alone, even those words, would not have done it, but he had gone pale. Briana and Demetria between them tipped him off his feet and carried him off to bed. It was a mark of his weakness that he did not blast them both for their presumption.

Chapter Thirty-Four

On the morning after Sabata came back to the lodge, its inhabitants prepared to leave it. In thirteen days the Dance would begin. They had to be in Aurelia well before that, to do what must be done.

Gothard had left with his guards two days ago, riding ahead of the rest to Aurelia. The only imperials left apart from Valeria were Mestre Olivet and his attendants. Everyone else was Caletanni.

Something had happened in the night. They all had an air of exaltation, of purpose raised from the mundane to the extraordinary. It radiated from Euan when he came to fetch Valeria. He had two of his men with him, who set about packing what belongings she was presumed to have.

She felt heavy, drugged. She put on the clothes that

were laid out for her, ate what was put in front of her, and went where she was told.

Sabata was with the horses outside the lodge, his silver coat gleaming in the early-morning light. She had half hoped he would not be, but he of all creatures must be a part of this. He tolerated the common animal that waited to carry her, and the remounts in a string behind. They were mares, which maybe was intentional, and maybe softened his resistance.

If someone had been that perceptive, she doubted it was Mestre Olivet. He had lost the gift of understanding horses. It also appeared that he had lost the art of riding them. He was waiting in a litter balanced between two horses, a rather impractical and precarious contraption for some of the roads they would be riding on, but no one remarked on it. The rest of them went on horseback like sensible people.

They rode fast, even with the litter to drag them down. Time was short. Urgency lashed them on. The gods were with them, giving them clear skies and balmy weather, and no rain in the valleys or snow in the passes. The Caletanni sang as they rode, warchants and hymns to their god.

The easygoing men she had known were gone, as if the lightness in them had been burned away. They were like tempered blades. There was a hard gleam on them, and a deadly edge.

When she looked at Euan out of the corner of her eye, she saw the red wolf running lightly through the wood. He was wild and dangerous and completely alien. He made her insides melt.

That first night, when they stopped for a late and hasty camp, Valeria knew better than to leave the tent that was pitched for her. That did not stop her from doing it. She waited until the camp was quiet, when the cookfires were put out and all but the sentries had gone to bed. Only she had a tent, and Mestre Olivet. The rest were asleep under the stars.

She moved as soft as wind and fog, gliding through the sleeping men. Sabata was standing guard on the edge of the camp. She could see him gleaming in the moonlight.

He passed no judgment. The infidelity of riding another horse was unbearable, but he did not care what she did with a man.

Euan had rolled himself in his blanket not far from Sabata. The others avoided the stallion, but Euan was inclined to face down his fear. That meant that he was separated from the rest by a small but significant distance.

It was convenient, although she could not be sure it was intentional. She let him see her as she crossed the empty space. He did not move, but the rhythm of his breathing quickened.

She slipped beneath his blanket. Under the cloak that wrapped her, she was naked. The air was sharp with frost, but she was hardly aware of it. The heat in her was stronger than any earthly chill.

She unfastened his breeks and took him inside her. They made love without a sound. It was fast and fierce, with little tenderness. This was not a tender night.

At the end of it she lifted herself over him. His face was pale in the moonlight, his eyes colorless. She half expected them to gleam like a wolf's, but they drank the darkness as human eyes should.

She kissed them until they closed. He lay as if waiting for her to do what she would. She rose, wrapped herself in her cloak and slipped away.

Valeria had thought she would fall over in her tent and sleep like the dead, but the night was full of dreams. Memory of Euan's body blurred and faded into another body altogether, smooth olive skin and supple limbs and swift, controlled strength. She knew she was dreaming, and yet it was vividly real. She could feel Kerrec beside her, a breathing warmth, with a scent of horses and crushed grass.

Even in her dream she wondered at the serenity of it. Patterns were coming together beneath the surface of things. War was brewing, not only the emperor's war on the barbarians but war within the empire. Death and slaughter were as close as the blanket over her. And yet she dreamed of a lover—and not the one with whom she had lain in the night.

"That one's dangerous," Conory said.

They were riding out of camp the next morning.

Euan and Conory had taken the rear. Valeria rode ahead on the bay mare, with the white god just ahead, flickering in and out of the mist.

Conory was not talking about the stallion. His eyes were on Valeria's back. She rode as they all did on the Mountain, as if she were part of the horse. No one else in this company could come close to that.

Euan shifted in the saddle. Conory's glance saw all too much. "She's a witch," he said. "She's got you under her spell."

"All women are witches," Euan said.

"Not like that one. At home they'd give her to the One."

"Not here," Euan said. "We need her. We've precious little hope of carrying this off without her."

"I don't trust her," Conory said.

"I do," said Euan. "We're the only ones who can give her what she wants. She'll do what it takes—you'll see."

"I do hope so," said Conory.

"Jealous, cousin?"

Conory bared his teeth. "Not hardly, cousin. She's not got her pincers in me."

"Maybe I've got mine in her," Euan said.

"You'd better hope so," said Conory, "because there's no treachery worse than a woman's—and worst of all is the woman in your bed."

Euan refused to be provoked. Later, when this was over, he would thrash Conory, and soundly.

Conory knew it. He laughed at it. "If I'm alive and whole to be thrashed, I'll thank you for it. You watch her, brother. And mind you do it with what you've got above your neck, not below."

Euan cuffed him for that. He swayed aside. The horse veered under the sudden shift of weight, stumbled and shied at a bird that erupted from under its feet.

Conory laughed as he fell, and laughed as he hauled himself back up, too, to the taunts and cheerful jeers of the rest of the warband. Even Valeria let go a smile, though maybe only Euan saw it.

Chapter Thirty-Five

Aurelia was larger than Valeria could ever have imagined. They came to it late the seventh day after they left the lodge, riding in with the last of the day's crowds.

So many people were coming to the city for the emperor's festival that she suspected a Caletanni warband would barely draw a glance, but they were cautious even so. They wore coats and trousers in the imperial style, with horsemen's cloaks and hoods that covered their faces. There were no weapons visible, and their pack train, with the remounts, had stopped in the town that stood at the head of the gorge above the city. They rode the last stage fast and light, taking on the appearance of a noble in a litter with his mounted escort.

Valeria rode in the middle of them. She was trying, not at all successfully, to keep from gaping at the sights. The sight and smell of the sea along the wide curve of the harbor, the immensity of the walls and towers, the gates of all sizes and shapes and degrees of splendor, left her speechless. The patterns that ran through them, the innumerable strains of magic that had been worked in this place for a thousand years, dizzied her with their complexity. She had to fight free of them and force her eyes to see as ordinary people saw, or she would not be able to see at all.

There were so many houses, so many people. She had never conceived of so many in one place, living on top of one another in towers that rose four and five and six stories, looming up against the sunset sky.

Sabata was thrown even more off balance than she was. He had found the school intolerable when he first came to it, with its walls shutting out the free air. This was a hundred, a thousand times worse.

She slipped from the mare's back to his. She needed to be as close as that, to wrap her arms and legs around him. His neck was rigid. Small shocks ran through his body. His back had coiled and his gait slowed and suspended until he was dancing almost in place.

He was perilously close to the trapped rage that had nearly brought down the school. She stroked him long and slow, and crooned in his ear.

The others had drawn in dangerously close. She could not spare any of herself to warn them.

Somewhat late but just in time, she heard Euan's voice. "Back off a bit. One kick from that and you'll go straight over the moon."

It should have been Mestre Olivet who said it, but he rode in his litter well ahead of them, a distance that widened as Sabata minced and fretted his way through the city.

After a while, the stallion quieted enough to walk instead of prancing. He was not calm, not even slightly, but he had brought himself under control.

Valeria slid to the ground but kept her arm over his back, walking beside him. He heaved a sigh and blew out sharply, and let go the tension, although he kept a close eye and ear on the city that closed him in.

From what she overheard, they were taking less traveled ways, trying to be unobtrusive. If those were what passed for deserted, the rest of the city must be one vast crush of people. Past the gate and the first square, they had to go two by two, and then in single file, pushing through crowds and sidestepping shops and taverns that overflowed into the street.

Sabata was not the only one to find this place overwhelming. The Caletanni were slower to lose their composure, but the deeper they penetrated into the city, the more ruffled they became. They were growling in their own language, some of which she could puzzle out, although she could not tell which of the speakers was which.

"Your fault for getting separated from the old blowhard."

"No, his for running away from us. What's his trouble? You'd think he was afraid of the white nag."

"The nag or the witch who commands it."

"Wasn't there supposed to be a guide? I thought his lordship was sending someone to show us the best way in."

"Not that I heard."

"Well, I did. We were supposed to meet a man in his lordship's livery outside the walls, and he was supposed to help us avoid the public streets. So why did we—"

"I was following the old bastard. What were you doing?"

"Sitting on my thumbs." That was Euan. "Damn this place! It's enough to fog any man's wits."

"You do know where we're going, I hope," one of the others said.

"More or less," said Euan. "It should be up the hill and around the corner there, unless they've moved it since the last time I was here."

"This is the old bastard's fault. If he's got us lost or led us into a trap, I swear—"

"Save it until you're sure," Euan said. "Now be quiet. We don't need people taking more notice of us than they already have."

The growling barely subsided, but there were no longer any words in it.

They ascended the hill with dragging, frustrating slowness, pushing against the current of people. A long wall ran along the summit, with another running down on the left hand. There were gates in the left-hand wall but none in the one ahead. They turned right as the road bent, and found themselves looking out across a wide-open square.

The square's center was a garden, a startling outburst of green in the expanse of stone. The high walls of houses looked out on it, some with towers, some without. At the far end was the dome of a temple, sheathed with gold so bright it hurt Valeria's eyes.

Euan let go his breath in a strikingly horselike snort. "By the One! They did move it. But I know where we need to go."

"Where is this?" Valeria asked.

Euan's eyes were cold, but as they rested on her they warmed. "That's the back of the palace yonder," he said, cocking a shoulder at the long row of towers on the right, "and the dome is the temple of Sun and Moon, from the back—there's a much bigger square in front, where all the processions go. And over there, with the low grey tower, that's where the riders are."

"And the Hall of the Dance?" said Valeria.

"You can't see that from here," he answered. "It's on the other side of the palace. There's a tunnel in between, they say, so the stallions don't have to show themselves to unsanctified eyes until they come out for the Dance."

Valeria nodded and lowered her eyes. She did not want them to see how she marked where everything was, or how she kept on doing it as they rode along the edge of the square in the dimming light and turned down another street between two featureless walls. One wall was made of white stone and the other of rose-colored bricks.

There were fewer people here, though still more than she had ever seen in one place. They were all intent on getting themselves home before dark. A good number of them carried lamps or torches, unlit as yet but ready for nightfall.

Euan seemed sure of where he was going, which was well as the light dimmed. Servants came out to light lamps beside the gates and doors, and people in the streets lit their lamps and torches. A soft glow spread over the city, turning it to a tapestry of black and gold.

There were no taverns along this way, no shops to close up for the night. Companies in silk and gold swept grandly past, going to or from the pursuits of princes. Some were mounted, many in litters. Now and then a gilded carriage rattled and clattered on the paving.

Sabata's mood was like a storm building. Each passing carriage sent him closer to the edge. He was glowing like the moon. All too soon, he would throw off sparks.

Valeria caught his mane and swung herself onto his

back again. He twitched under her, but then he sighed faintly. His light dimmed somewhat.

Just as she was about to warn Euan that if he did not find what he was looking for soon, she would not be answerable for the consequences, he slowed his horse and then halted. The door to which he turned was unlit.

The house might have been deserted, but Valeria's skin shivered. Carefully she lowered her wards, just enough to gasp and slam them up again. She would never forget the smell and taste of Gothard's magic. This place was thick with it.

His presence coiled inside the walls like a worm in an oak gall. Euan raised his hand to hammer on the gate, but before he could move, it opened soundlessly. No porter was visible. Witch lights hovered within.

"Braggart," Euan muttered. He braced himself visibly and kicked his horse forward.

Sabata went in with a bare instant's hesitation. The stink of magic did not seem to trouble him. If anything, it relaxed him.

The first courtyard was empty, but the witch lights drifted inward. Euan snarled at them but followed. In the second courtyard, men were waiting to take their horses.

The Caletanni dismounted gratefully, groaning as they worked out the knots and cramps of hours in the saddle. Valeria stayed where she was.

One of the men came forward and bowed to the pavement. His eyes rolled at the stallion, but he said with creditable steadiness, "Lady, a place is prepared for him. If you will come…?"

Sabata snorted with a complete lack of elegance, and shook his mane. He yawned in the man's face and advanced on him.

The man turned rather quickly. He did not exactly run, but his stride was very quick.

This house was even larger and more complicated than the lodge. Its wall enclosed a small city of buildings, with the largest in the middle and the rest clustered around it, and bits of garden running through them all.

There seemed to be several places in which horses were kept. One, close by the central house, looked as if it had been recently vacated and hastily cleaned. Its walls were stone and its doors were thick and bound with iron.

It was a prison for horses. Sabata curled a lip at it but did not object to being led in. There was straw to sleep on, hay to eat and barley in the manger beside the barrel of clean water. He circled the stable three times, inspected the scents that had been imperfectly scrubbed away, and left a ripe and redolent marker directly in front of the door. Then he went to his dinner.

Once he was settled, the guide relaxed perceptibly. He blinked at Valeria, looking somewhat stunned, and said, "Lady, we understand that you look after him, and that is his wish. But if there is anything you need, or that he needs—"

"He's satisfied," Valeria said. "He'll do until morning, if no one troubles him."

"Oh, no, lady," the man said fervently. "No one would dare." He swallowed. It was hard to tell in lamplight, but his cheeks seemed to have gone slightly darker. "Lady, my name is Belus. I'll come if you call me."

Valeria blinked. She reeled in a moment of intense homesickness, tied to a memory. Men had been like this with her sister Caia—blushing and babbling and offering her anything, anything she wanted, she only had to ask.

No one had ever blushed or babbled at Valeria. It must be Sabata, she thought. The awe of him attached to her.

Even so, she caught herself smiling as Caia used to do, and saying sweetly, "Belus. I'll remember. You're very kind."

"Oh, no," he said. "No, lady. The kindness is all yours."

She let her smile linger, let him bow and kiss her hand, and escaped, she hoped, without embarrassing either of them.

The memory of home clung as she made her way through the maze of this place, following a witch light that came to find her outside Sabata's stable. Two rooms to sleep in, one room to gather in, a room for her mother's herbs and potions, a kitchen, a store-room, a privy on the other side of the kitchen garden—what more did a house need? The room she was supposed to rest in was as big as her father's house and his cow barn and half the outbuildings. The bath beside it had a tub big enough to swim a horse in. There was enough gold and silver, silk, mosaic and colored stone to buy the whole village of Imbria and everything in it.

She could imagine her mother standing in that elaborate room, dressed in her plain and practical clothes, with her hair in its tightly disciplined knot and her brow lifted ever so slightly. "Getting a bit above yourself, aren't you, girl?"

"You don't know the half of it," Valeria said to the memory, startling the maid who had come in to bathe and dress her.

The girl did not stay startled long. She was used to oddities, her manner said. She was quick, quiet and impervious to protests. She had been sent to serve, and she would serve. That was that.

Valeria had heard of the tyranny of servants, but this was her first experience of it. It was disconcerting to begin with, but on top of memories she had been suppressing since she ran away to answer the Call, it was close to unbearable. She would far rather, that night, have been back in her mother's root cellar than sitting in this gilded prison, balanced on the sword's edge between betrayal and treason.

Chapter Thirty-Six

It was after noon by the time Briana had finished making her father's excuses. Clerks and servants accepted plain speaking, but lords in council needed endless circles of discussion before they would concede that yes, the emperor should seclude himself before the great rite of his reign. She made sure it was understood beneath the surface that the emperor was ill, although with what, she left it to them to speculate.

She was exhausted as she made her way back to her rooms. Maariyah's brother-in-law had slipped her mind completely.

Maariyah had not forgotten, nor had she let her kinsman escape because Briana was hours late. When Briana came in, Maariyah was waiting for her, and there was a man snoring on one of the couches in the anteroom. He was so obviously in need of sleep that Briana hated to wake him, but Maariyah was not so tenderhearted. She set him brusquely on his feet and said, "Tullus. Pay your respects to the emperor's heir."

He was certainly a soldier. There was no trace of sleep in his face as he snapped to attention and saluted Briana with the full ceremonial. It was somewhat lacking in the usual clash and glitter, since he wore neither armor nor livery, but she took it in the spirit in which it was meant.

"At ease," she said.

She sat in a chair. He would have kept on standing, but she leveled her eyes at him until he dropped stiffly to the couch.

She took the measure of him. He was a big man, though not as big as a barbarian, with a rough-hewn face and deceptively flat dark eyes. There was no magic in him, but when he looked at her, those eyes narrowed slightly.

Her own narrowed to match them. Deliberately she strengthened her wards. He squinted and drew back a barely visible fraction.

He could see magic. It was an uncommon gift, and useful, too, in serving mages.

"You have a message for me?" she asked.

His back stiffened even further. If he was as honest as she suspected, this was not easy for him. He took refuge in soldier's discipline. "Lady," he said, "what I do dishonors my position, but I can't help but—"

"I understand," she said. "The empire's honor is greater than that of any single man in it, even if he be the emperor's son."

"Yes, lady," he said. "I'd never do it otherwise. But this—"

"Your lord is plotting treason," Briana said. "There's been an attempt on the emperor's life."

The stiffness left him all at once. Briana braced to catch him if he fell over, but he kept his feet. "Maariyah said you knew, lady," he said.

"Yes," Briana said.

His shoulders flexed. He would have wriggled like a child, she thought, if he had not had his dignity to consider. The words burst out of him all at once. "Some of us are loyal to the emperor above and beyond the oath we've taken to our lord. We saw what our lord did to his brother, who would have been emperor but for the gods' Call—it's no doing of our lord's that the prince was taken out of captivity and sent back broken to the Mountain. We heard what our lord would do, and who would be his allies. He'll lead barbarian armies into this city, lady, and they'll raise him on their shields and make him emperor. We can't stomach that, lady."

"You have a plan?" she asked. She took care not to mention that Kerrec had not gone to the Mountain. What a man did not know, he could not betray.

"It's dangerous, lady. My lord is a mage, and he's strong. But yes, we do have a plan. I saw him once, lady, when he'd laid his stones aside. I don't know why he did it—maybe he wanted to test himself. He was there without them, lady, and there was magic, but it was dimmer than what I see in you now, with all the wards on you and the protections over you. With his stones he's a blaze of living light. Without them he's a candle burning low."

Briana nodded. "I remember when he was tested, when the order first took him. He had a profoundly ordinary level of power, but the Master told my father that he had a remarkable affinity for the stones."

"We think," Tullus said, "that we can separate him from them. We need help—a mage, someone with power over wards, who knows something of stones. Once they're out of his reach, he can be taken and dealt with as his actions deserve."

"I believe there's a saying for that," Briana said. "Easier said than done."

"We think we can do it, lady," Tullus said. "He's caught up in his barbarians and his plot against the Dance. He's not looking to his guard for trouble—not just now."

"Are you sure of that?"

"As sure as we can be, lady," he said.

Briana pondered that. After a moment she said, "It's a risk. From what we've heard of the plot, he's not the power that's most important to the Dance."

"No, lady," said Tullus, "but that power is only kept in check by his shields and compulsions. Without him there may not be any plot."

"That power," she said. "Do you know what it is? Have you seen it?"

He nodded. "It's a slip of a girl, lady. She was Called to the Mountain, they say, though how that can be, I can't imagine. They wouldn't take her, but somehow she got hold of one of the stallions. She's thrown in her lot with my lord. She's bedmate to one of the barbarians—the one who leads them, the prince from over the border."

"A woman?" Briana said. "A woman was Called? She has a stallion? Are you sure? She's not one of the false mages, the ones who follow Olivet? Is not Olivet himself with my brother?"

"She was Called to the Mountain, lady," said Tullus. "That I'm sure of. Olivet is with my lord, yes, but he's got no power left. Whereas she—lady, what your brother is to the stones, she is to the stallions. I wager she's even more, because she's a strong mage even without the horses. I heard the high ones talking, lady, and they think she can turn the Dance. The stallion she has, they call him a Great One."

Briana sat very still. She had not known any of this. No rumor had come from the Mountain, nor had Kerrec said a word of it. Which meant that the Mountain had suppressed it. Unless her father knew, and had chosen not to tell her. Or—

Tullus was waiting, cultivating patience as guards and soldiers learned to do.

She could not make a decision so quickly. But she

could say, "You'd best go before you're missed. Watch yourself, and wait. I'll send word as soon as I can— no later than the morning, and sooner if possible. Don't do a thing, do you understand? Lie low, and take utmost care that your lord suspects nothing."

"I understand, lady," he said. He rose and bowed and left directly, like the well-trained guardsman he was.

For a long while after he was gone, Briana sat where she was, chin on fist, scowling at the air. The pattern she had been seeing had had Gothard in it, of course, and the barbarians, and the discredited rider Olivet. This young woman, if she existed, was a completely new thing.

Kerrec was awake. He was in the garden, sitting at Briana's worktable, frowning at one of the books in which she had been searching for an answer to her father's trouble.

He looked up as she came toward him. "There are no answers here," he said.

"There are no answers anywhere," Briana said, "and more questions than I can begin to keep track of." She planted her fists on the book, blocking it if he had tried to go back to it, and leaned toward him. "Why didn't you tell me a woman had been Called to the Mountain?"

He went rigid. Whatever she had expected, it was not that absolute, icy rage. His voice made her shiver, because it was so incongruously light and easy. "What, your spies didn't give you an inkling? It's been all over the school."

"The school keeps to itself," she said. "What did you riders do? Swear everyone at the testing to silence? Or simply put a spell on them?"

There was no answer in Kerrec's face. She had not expected one. Nor was she about to take mercy on either his temper or his fragility. "Now I'm told that not only has this prodigy gone renegade, she's our brother's chief weapon. Didn't you think it was of at least minor importance that there was a power of that magnitude, that far out of the ordinary, in the center of the plot against the empire?"

Kerrec's eyes had no color at all. He cultivated discipline for a very good reason—he had a horrible temper. He also, even now, had magic enough to be dangerous. More dangerous than if he had not been broken, because his defenses were in ruins.

She would not let him see her flinch, but met his coldness with a flash of white heat. "Tell me what you know. Now."

His lips were tight, but he got the words out, neat and precise. "Her name is Valeria. She comes from a village north of here. Her father was in the legions. Her mother is a wisewoman. Her Call is real and her power enormous. A Great One came to her, and the Ladies blessed her. She was champion of the testing."

"And the riders rejected her because not only had no female been Called in a thousand years, the very thought of one scared them out of their wits." Briana's knees would no longer hold her up. She dropped to the chair across from him. "Are you all idiots?"

"I didn't think I was," he said, "but I was the worst of us all. The moment she heard of that charlatan Olivet, she ran to him. She sold herself to the enemy."

"Was it that simple? What did you riders do to force that—apart from humiliating her, insulting her and denying the gods' will in sending the Call?"

He thrust himself to his feet, scattering books and pens and inkpots. "You know nothing! How dare you presume to judge?"

She sat back, deliberately calm. "I am the heir to this empire. Judgment is my duty and obligation. I know you, and I know the rest of the riders. It's easy enough to see what happened to a woman who not only passed the tests, she outdid every one of the men who was Called. How did she do it? Cut her hair and keep her coat on? Add a bit of glamour, maybe?"

He was shaking and his face was white, but he had not blasted her yet. "Yes, it's our fault the enemy has a weapon this potent and with this much reason to turn against us. But if she had not been by her very nature dishonorable—if she had not gone running after a rutting bull of a barbarian—"

"You're in love with her."

Kerrec stopped short. "What in the gods' name makes you think—"

"Brother," Briana said, "stop. There's no time for games. Are you absolutely sure she's turned traitor?"

"I am sure," he said.

Briana closed her eyes. She needed a moment's peace, and time to think.

She could feel Kerrec on the other side of the table, smoldering in silence. Had she thought him cold? Yes—so cold he burned.

"Did you ever," she asked him without opening her eyes, "even once, let her know you love her?"

"Yes!" It was a cry of pain.

"How late? Too late?"

"Far too late," he said. "I can't remember. I can't see—I was dying. She had me taken from the Brother of Pain. She took care of me. I woke, and she—and he—were—"

Briana could feel how much he hurt. But she was a hard creature. She had to be, if she was going to rule the empire. "He?"

"The prince," he said, all but spitting it, "of the Caletanni. Euan Rohe."

Her eyes opened. Her brows rose. "Convenient," she said.

"For her? Or for him?"

"He's a magnificent young animal," Briana said, "and by no means a fool. I'm sure he saw the opportunity and seized it—unlike the riders."

"Unlike me." Kerrec sank down. The temper drained out of him, though the anger and pain still ran deep. "I knew she was a woman. I met her on her journey north, and helped to set her on her way. *I* saw the Call, and knew it for the gods' will. When she was unmasked—and not by me—I convinced the Master to let her stay. I taught her. I honed her as a weapon against us."

"I don't think you're the one to be judging that," Briana said. She drew in a long breath and let it out slowly. "This complicates matters considerably. If it had been just Gothard and Olivet and a pack of savages, the plot would be a great deal less likely to succeed. With a horse mage of that strength, and a Great One…as the barbarians would say, that is a worthy opponent."

"She is young," he said, visibly scraping himself together, "and the Great One is barely out of colthood—he came in with the Midsummer herd. For all their strength, they're all but untrained."

"Which, of course," Briana said, "makes matters notably worse. No training, no discipline. Add in a genuine grievance and you have quite a dangerous enemy. Unless…can we win her back again?"

Briana braced against the flash of sudden rage. Kerrec controlled it, but it lingered behind his eyes. "What can we offer that she'll take? They'll give her the Mountain and everything on it."

"They have to win it first," Briana pointed out.

That was empty bravado, and they both knew it. Briana turned her thoughts away from that particular trouble, for a while, and said, "There may be hope even with this. One of our brother's guards has come over to us, and proposed that we separate our brother from the stones that strengthen his magic. He has allies, he says, and a plan."

Kerrec seemed as glad as she to shift the conversation from Valeria. "Do you trust him?" he asked.

"He seems an honest man. He's married to Maariyah's sister."

"A mage?"

"No. Something better for our purposes. He sees magic."

Kerrec frowned. He had a look about him that warned her that he was nearing the edge of his endurance. "They need Gothard to maintain wards and shields, and to break through into the hall. Without the stones, most of his protective magic will be gone. He'll be guarding them with his life. What makes your guardsman think he can take them away?"

"Several things," Briana said. "Our dear brother's arrogance, for one. For another, no one knows you're here. As far as our brother and his men know, you're safe on the Mountain."

"Even if they find out that the stallions rescued me, they won't be looking for me here." Kerrec straightened carefully. What he said next was not easy for him at all, nor did he say it with anything resembling gladness. "We'll have to tell the emperor all of this. We can't keep it from him. We need him."

"He may not be able to help," Briana said.

"He'll have to. I'm not strong enough, and you can't do it alone."

"His magic—"

"His mind is still working, isn't it? We can use that." Kerrec turned, swaying a little. "We can't stand about talking. There's no time. I'll speak to his majesty, if you will—"

"You are going to rest," she said. "Whatever miracle is mending you, you're still a long way from done. Go, sleep for a while. I'll wake you after I've spoken with Father."

He was not at all willing to do as she told him, but he was nearly out on his feet. She half carried him to his bed and lowered him into it. Consciousness let go of him before he touched the coverlet.

Urgency tugged at her, but she paused, looking down at him. Even in sleep his eyes were sunken. The bruises on his face and hands were at their most alarming, and the rest of his body must be even worse, shaded in green and black and purple. His magic had the same patchwork look to it. Memory seemed to have come back in full force, but the effort of it had worn him to exhaustion.

Gothard had a great deal to atone for. She stooped and kissed Kerrec's brow. It was a promise of sorts, that the brother who had come so close to destroying him would pay for what he had done.

Chapter Thirty-Seven

Mestre Olivet had established himself in a room even larger than Valeria's, in a chair remarkably like the imperial throne in the Hall of the Dance at the school. As Valeria came in, she found that Gothard had arrived before her. Mestre Olivet's expression was sour. Whatever had brought Gothard here, Mestre Olivet had had nothing to do with it.

Gothard never smiled. That would have strained his sullenness beyond endurance. But he was perceptibly less sullen than usual. "It's done," he said. "The blow has fallen on the emperor."

"He's dead?" Olivet asked.

"No," said Gothard. "We need him alive, so that the Dance will go on. He's wounded, and the knives were poisoned. The poison eats magic. By the day of the

Dance, he should be as mortal as a man can be. Then, when the Dance is over, we'll dispose of him."

Valeria tried to imagine speaking this coldly, with this much satisfaction, of destroying her father, or even her mother. The thought made her ill.

Mestre Olivet seemed none too pleased by it. Maybe it annoyed him that Gothard had invaded his audience with Valeria. "That's well," he said. "That's well, indeed. But if you will pardon me, while your emperor is unable to protect his Dance, this student of mine must—"

"I should think you would be the student," Gothard said. "You're losing power almost as fast as my father is. Can you stop it, or are you past it? Do you need me to ward what's left?"

Olivet drew himself up sharply. Valeria fully expected to see a mage-bolt fly, but the air barely crackled. Gothard had seen the truth of it. Olivet's magic had unraveled. The spells of Unmaking had undone it.

"I need nothing," Olivet said through clenched teeth, "but your presence elsewhere. There is much to do before the Dance. The less distraction we suffer, the sooner and more thoroughly it will be done."

"You do your work," Gothard said, "and I'll do mine. Be patient with your student. Or should I bid her be patient with you?"

He bowed to Olivet, so low as to be mocking, and saluted Valeria. Olivet kept his eyes fixed on the wall until Gothard was gone. Then he said, "I hope you will pardon me, lady, but tonight I think, after all, you should rest."

Valeria made no secret of her relief. Let him think she was merely tired. So she was, but once freed from the obligation of playing student, she recovered remarkably.

She had half dreaded that either Olivet or Gothard would place her under guard, but it seemed they trusted the wards that lay thick on this house, woven into the stones and anchored to the earth.

She found her riding clothes after a search that, with an effort, managed not to be frantic. They had been cleaned and folded away in the chest at the foot of the bed. Her boots were with them, cleaned likewise. With a prayer of thanks for the kindness of servants, she dressed and glided silently toward the door.

Wards stung her fingers as she touched it, but she had expected that. Hissing a little at the small but effective pain, she looked inside her, peering down deep. Sabata stared back. She washed herself in his white brilliance, letting it fill her until it overflowed.

As she had hoped, the wards no longer saw her as human, but perceived her as a shimmer of light. She ran swiftly down the hallway, alert for guards or servants. Twice she darted into a doorway or the landing of a stair, as someone she did not recognize strode past. One seemed to be a servant. The other was richly dressed and followed by a pair of guards and

second pair of persons in stiff livery. One of Gothard's
allies, she supposed. He looked as haughty as Paulus.
Probably he was a relative.

She escaped the house undetected by men or
magic, and turned in the direction she hoped she remembered. The night was very dark, the waning
moon not yet up. She could see no stars. The air
smelled of damp and the sea.

It was different on foot and in the dark, the dis-
tances longer, the turns less certain. So much magic
and so many human souls overlapped and interwove
that she could make no sense of them. But for Sabata's
presence inside her and her own determination that
she must do what she had set out to do, she would have
turned and run back to the safety of Gothard's house.

She made her way as best she could, keeping panic
at bay and counting turns under her breath. The
streets were nearly empty. All the crowds had retreated
within doors for the night, or been herded out of the
city before the last of the light.

There were no beggars here where the nobles lived,
and no footpads, either, as far as she could tell. Sabata's
power protected her, shielding her from spying eyes
as well as wards and magic.

Just as she was sure that she had lost the way
irretrievably, the long dark street opened into emptiness. On the other side of it, gold glimmered in the
air. That was the dome of the temple, and there were
the walls and towers she remembered, shadowy in the

gloom. Lamps were lit around the square, the light of each forming its own circle, as if each lamp on its pole were enclosed in wards.

The house that Euan had named to her as belonging to the riders was dark. The protections on it were more powerful than Gothard's by far. A fortress of magic overlaid the walls of stone.

Sabata's power rose inside her and unfolded like a cloak, wrapping itself around her. Hidden in it and protected by it, she passed the gate as if it were made of mist.

There was light inside, ordinary lamps burning perfectly mortal oil. The scent of magic pervaded the place. A deep stillness lay on it, a supernal calm. This was not a temple and the riders were not priests, and yet the best word Valeria could find for the quality of that stillness was *holy*.

She walked softly through halls and courtyards, guided by Sabata's presence. She emerged after some time into a grassy court with a low building at the end of it, up against the house wall. There were the stallions, fifteen of them. The peace of this place came from them and flowed through them.

They were waiting for her. She was not to trouble the riders, who were deep in meditation, preparing for the Dance. She had heard that often enough to be completely out of patience with it, but the stallions seemed almost amused. Poor simple mortals, who needed such effort to perceive the most obvious of patterns.

Valeria had been thinking much the same. She drew herself up short. It was all very well for gods to look on mortals as beloved but rather foolish. She was not a god, or anything like one.

Nevertheless she could not help what she felt. She had spent too much time with the stallions and too little with their riders. She had learned to think like a stallion.

She eased open the door of their stable. They were asleep or eating lazily, as if they were common horses in their stalls at night. Their light was muted, but so many together equaled the light of a full moon.

As glad as she was to see them, they were not the ones who needed to hear her message. She meant to pay her respects and then go hunting riders, but when she tried to retreat, the door would not open behind her.

She turned to face the stallions. "I have to tell them," she said.

None of them responded.

Even knowing it was futile, she raised her voice. "I have to! There are plots against them. The Dance—"

"What? What is this?"

The voice floated down from the hayloft. Even blurred with sleep, it sounded haughty. That was the accent of an Aurelian noble, followed soon enough by Paulus as he swung himself down from the loft. He had a knife in his hand and a wild look in his eye, which moderated not at all when he recognized Valeria. "*You!* What are you doing here?"

One of the stallions snorted and pawed his stall door. The sound of hoof striking oak was deafening. It brought Paulus up short.

"Paulus," Valeria said with a kind of resignation. Of course it could not be Batu or Iliya who had been set on watch over the stallions tonight. "I have to speak to Master Nikos. Can you get me in?"

He drew himself to his full height, which for an imperial was rather impressive. "All the riders are secluded. No one is to intrude on them for any reason."

"Not even to stop the disruption of the Dance?"

He was not listening. "Where have you been? Where is the First Rider? Why did you leave us? The Master sent some of the men to look for you, but they couldn't find anything. What have you done? What—"

"I have to speak to the Master," Valeria said.

"You can't," said Paulus.

"I have to."

"*No one* can get in," Paulus said. "Do you understand? They're completely warded. The Dance can't be disrupted. There's no way to get near the riders."

"Yes, there is," said Valeria. "When they come to the Hall, the protections will be gone."

"But who would dare—"

Valeria decided quickly. If she could not get to the Master—and it was all too clear that there was no hope of it—then she had to trust this boy, somehow, to do what he could. She answered him as clearly as she knew how. "An alliance of barbarians, a renegade First Rider named Olivet and the emperor's half-bred son."

"Marcellus? But——"

"They call him Gothard. He has a dire grievance, and altogether too much magic with which to pursue it."

"Marcellus," Paulus said. He seemed less stunned now, and more willing to consider the possibility. "He was completely out of temper when the emperor passed him over and named Sophia Briana his heir. Still, this——"

"He'll kill the emperor," Valeria said, "and wrest the Dance away from the riders, and try to shape the patterns in his allies' favor."

"He can't do that. No matter how powerful he is, he's a mage of stones. He can't influence the Dance. No one can, except the stallions."

Valeria drew a deep breath. This was difficult. "They have a stallion. They have Sabata."

"And a renegade First Rider." Paulus looked as if he wanted to faint.

"Listen," Valeria said. "This prince, this Gothard, is ruthless. He captured and tortured First Rider Kerrec. He's safe now—he was rescued and sent to the Mountain—but Gothard and his allies truly will stop at nothing. The riders must be prepared. I think—I think there will be a spell of Unmaking."

"How do you know this?" Paulus demanded. "Where have you been? If they had Kerrec and they have Sabata, that means——"

"It doesn't matter," Valeria said. "Just get word to Master Nikos. Promise you'll do that."

"Not until you tell me where you've been and what you've been doing. You lied to us all once. How do I know you're not doing it again?"

"It is the truth," Valeria said. "I swear by the Call, it is." She began to draw away. "I have to go. Promise—"

He seized her arm in a painful grip. "What have you been doing? You said they have Olivet. Did he get at you? Have you gone over to him?"

"If I had, would I be here? Would I be trying to warn you?"

"To throw us off the scent, yes. You would."

"Maybe I'm trying to throw *them* off the scent," she said. She wrenched free. "Tell the Master. Let him be the one to judge. If nothing happens to the Dance, you've lost no more than the effort of raising defenses."

He did not respond to that. His face was set in lines of resistance.

She flung her last weapon. "There's been an attempt on the emperor's life. Gothard is preening himself over it. He's tortured his brother nearly to death, and now he's poisoned his father. Gods know what he'll do to his sister, whom he must hate above all, but do be sure he has something in mind."

"You *are* with him," said Paulus.

"I traded myself for Kerrec's life," she flung at him.

"I know what that makes me. If you can stop this, then by the gods, do it."

Paulus lunged. She ran.

This time the door opened for her. She darted out into the night, with Paulus hard on her heels.

He stumbled. She heard his curse, and the thud of his body striking the ground. There was a quiver in her, a ripple of satisfaction. The stallions had aided her escape.

Their will was like a hand between her shoulders, thrusting her out and away from the riders' house, through the square and down the street that led to Gothard's palace. Only then was she allowed to pause. She collapsed against a wall, sobbing for breath. "Why?" she cried to them with what little voice she had to spare. *"Why?"*

She did not expect an answer, nor did she get one. The best they granted her was a sense of inevitability. This was the pattern. She would dance it, as would they all. It would end as it was meant to end.

A mortal could not comprehend the gods. They might let her see a fraction of their purposes, and know a glimmer of the thoughts that moved them, but her mind was too small and her understanding too limited.

Sabata was waiting for her in the confinement he had, however late and unwillingly, chosen. For once he was as serene as the rest of them. She wished that she could share that serenity, but she was human. She could only see the web of deception and dishonor, and herself caught in it, bound too tightly to escape.

Chapter Thirty-Eight

Euan caught Valeria before she reached her rooms. She thought she was being stealthy, but she was crushed by an exhaustion as much of the soul as of the body. She did not even see him until he loomed in front of her. "You've been out," he said. "I've been waiting. Where—"

"Sabata," she said without thinking. "Sabata called me."

He laid his arm over her shoulders and turned. She leaned against him, too tired to resist, and let him support her down the rest of the passage and through the door.

He undressed her gently, without passion, though there was plenty of that inside him if she wanted it. Evidently he believed her. He did not badger her with questions, only said, "Sabata doesn't like the city."

"Not at all," she said.

He had left her shirt, which she found interesting. He lay beside her, fully dressed except for his boots, but did not try to kiss or touch her. "He wouldn't stay if he didn't want to, would he? He's a god. Mortal magic means nothing to him."

Valeria struggled to clear her mind. Maybe he did not suspect that she had been betraying her own betrayal, but he was dismayingly close to other and equally dangerous truths. "He says that it is meant," she said.

That was true. It appeared to satisfy Euan. He stretched and yawned and smiled. "Your gods are with us," he said.

She closed her eyes. As much as she hated to admit it, it seemed he was right.

When she opened her eyes again, wan daylight washed the room. The clouds were thick and grey. She could hear the wind wuthering in the eaves. Faint and distant but still perceptible, she heard a soft roar and sigh that must be the voice of the sea. It seemed restless, like some vast beast disturbed in its sleep.

Euan was gone. Breakfast waited on the table beside the bed. It was simple, bread and fruit and a cup of something hot and bitter but laced with sweetness. At first she grimaced, but after the second sip she rather liked it. It had the feel of a tonic about it. There was no magic in it, and nothing harmful.

The messenger was waiting when she finished. It hovered like an insect in a shaft of sunlight, wings a blur, jeweled body gleaming. When she looked directly at it, it darted away toward the door.

Mestre Olivet had sent it, although it was not his magic that animated it. She found him in a small and cluttered room, with books heaped around him and a shard of crystal in his hand. The messenger hovered above it, poised, then darted down into it. The stone swallowed it.

"You are not a mage of stones," Valeria said.

He smiled. It was not a pleasant expression. "Our noble host is not the master of all magics," he said, "nor does he understand the Unmaking. It may avail itself of other magics as it chooses, if the master has sufficient strength of will."

"Does it swallow them? Destroy them?"

"In time," he answered, "it swallows all that is." He beckoned to her. "Come, sit down. There is much to learn, and very little time."

Valeria sat gingerly across from him, although he had pointed to the stool beside him. The book he drew out of the clutter was all too familiar. She hoped he did not see how she shuddered. She was beginning to regret eating as much breakfast as she had.

She had to carry on. Now more than ever, Olivet could not suspect that she was not his ally but his enemy. She let him turn the book toward her and take up a pointer and point to a passage written in letters that burned themselves inside her eyelids.

"This is the second spell of Unmaking," he said. "There are six, but there is no time to learn them all. Even I have only come to the sixth through years of study. But you with your great magic will need no more. The Dance is in you, set in your bones."

Her hands were cold. She fought to keep them from shaking. Her protections, even doubled and trebled, strained before the power of the spell. The first spell had laired in her mind. This took aim at her heart.

Sabata, she prayed. *Oh, gods, Sabata.*

He was there as always with the rest, the circle of the white gods. Behind them she saw others, powers as much greater than they as they were greater than mortal horses. At first she thought they were Great Ones, but she saw Sabata and Petra in the more familiar circle. Then she met a pair of dark eyes in a lone dark head, and realized that these were the Ladies.

She could not move in the body. Mestre Olivet was watching. In spirit she bowed low in respect and deepening awe.

The Lady whom she had known touched her with a sting of impatience. Awe was for lesser powers, fools who needed the worship of mortals to feed their pride. The Ladies were beyond such things.

Valeria could not help it. She was mortal, as she had been reminded all too often of late. Awe was the price the Ladies paid for revealing themselves.

The dark Lady found that amusing. She had no wisdom to offer, and no advice. She was beyond that, too. But she was there, and her sisters and aunts and grandmothers with her, a white wall against the spells of Unmaking.

They were not going to tell Valeria what to do, still less how to do it. That was for her to discover.

"And if I fail?" she asked them.

They did not answer.

This could drive a person mad, Valeria thought. Small wonder the Ladies never revealed themselves to the riders. Men wanted everything set in words, the simpler the better.

There were no words for what the Ladies were. Valeria bathed for a while in their brilliance. It was almost painful to draw away from it, open her eyes to the mortal world, and listen to Mestre Olivet's spew of words. How like a man to drown even the Unmaking in them, although it was almost as far beyond words as the Ladies themselves.

Valeria was further than ever from understanding why the gods were allowing this thing. She could think of nothing better to do than pretend to listen, try not to let the words from the book crawl into her brain, and hope this day would end soon.

* * *

When Mestre Olivet finally let her go, Valeria was surprised to discover that it was still daylight. As far as she could tell through the thick clouds, it was barely past noon. She felt as if she had been shut in with the Unmaking from dawn to dark.

Olivet had given her no orders, which left her free to go back to her room and sleep. Instead she went to find Sabata.

He was still locked in his stable, pacing the floor and occasionally biting at the walls. She opened the door so that he could come and go as he pleased.

She had expected him to run until he could not run any more, but he was in an oddly quiet mood now his prison walls were open. He walked a little distance from the door, lowered his head and set to work cropping grass as if he had not stood in front of a manger full of excellent hay since he arrived the night before. She folded her feet under her and sat against the wall, watching him. There was a distinct, damp chill in the air, which made her shiver lightly, but she would rather be here than shut in a room that reeked of stone magic.

Gothard found her there. She regarded him in unconcealed surprise. It was far below his dignity to run his own errands, let alone seek out her thoroughly unaristocratic company.

He was none too pleased with it, either, from the way he glared down his nose at her. It was an expression she had seen on Kerrec's face often enough. Odd, she thought, that he had never directed it at her. However arrogant Kerrec was by nature, not once, no matter how infuriating he was, had he made her feel that she was beneath him.

She missed him suddenly, with a sensation as sharp as pain. Gods be thanked he was not here—he must be safe on the Mountain by now. But she could not stop herself from wishing it were Kerrec standing over her and not his brother.

Gothard squinted at her. "Gods," he said. "You're beautiful." He said it as if it were her fault that he had never noticed it before. "I suppose the riders hold that against you, too."

"I think it's quite sufficient that I'm female," she said.

"They say too many hours in the saddle can make a man like a eunuch," said Gothard. "Their actions toward you do seem to bear it out."

Valeria held her tongue. She could testify that in one rider's case at least, it was certainly not so. But she was not about to say that to this man.

He took no notice of her silence. He turned to stare at Sabata, who was doing nothing of interest. Abruptly he said, "If you're going to ride him in the Dance, you had better do something to prepare him."

"Who said I'm riding him in the Dance?"

"How can you not? To change the Dance, we need a stallion, and the stallion has to have a rider. This is the stallion we have. I don't expect Olivet to do it. The old man's past it."

"Sabata is too young," she said. "I can't—"

"He's broken to ride—I've seen you on him. You'll ride him every day between now and the Dance. He only has to carry you for a short time, but he'd better be fit to do it."

"Six days aren't going to—" Valeria began.

"They'll have to," said Gothard. "He needs a saddle, I suppose. There must be a bridle in this place somewhere."

"I'm not going to ride him," Valeria said.

"I think you are," he said. "I'll send one of the grooms. He'll help you to get what you need."

"I don't need anything," she said.

Gothard flung up his hands. "Don't tell me you've gone so far on Olivet's road that you can't ride, either."

"I'm not that far gone," Valeria said grimly.

"Good. I'll send the groom. Do it for the horse if not for me."

"I don't need a groom," she said. "I don't need a saddle. I'll ride him without."

Gothard eyed her narrowly. She glowered back. "Humor me," he said.

"I already am."

He hissed, but he could not fail to see that he had won. She pushed herself to her feet and approached Sabata. She was aware of Gothard's eyes on her back, but he no longer mattered.

Sabata raised his head as she laid her hand on his shoulder. He was calm, with the sweet taste of grass in his mouth and the wind ruffling his mane. "I hate to admit it," she said to him, "but he is right."

Sabata sighed and shook himself from nose to tail. Of course the man was right, his manner said. Was she going to dally another three months or was she going to do something about it?

There was only one answer to that. She took her time as Kerrec had taught her, sending Sabata out on a circle and putting him through his paces around her.

His muscles warmed. His heart beat more strongly, and his breath came deep and steady. He danced a little for the joy of wearing this body in this age of the world.

He was beautiful and he knew it, and he had no fear of what was coming. It would be as it would be.

He paused in his exercises, then turned and looked over his shoulder, inviting her to mount.

She did not ride long, nor did she ask him for the movements of the Dance. It was enough that he carried her.

Gothard by then had grown bored and wandered off. He was not a horseman. His only care for Sabata was that he be fit to turn the Dance in Gothard's favor.

Valeria did not honestly know what Sabata would do. That the stallions would submit themselves to the will of their riders, she knew. She had seen it. But Sabata did not practice submission.

She slid from his back and buried her face in his mane. He swiveled his neck about and blew on her hair. He was not afraid, nor should she be. Even if she died, she would be with him. He would keep her spirit safe, whatever became of her body.

That was not as comforting as he meant it to be. She hugged him until he shook his head in protest. "I'd prefer to stay in the body," she said.

In some ways he was remarkably like his mother. He did not answer that, but wandered off in search of the sweetest patch of grass.

Chapter Thirty-Nine

Briana had a great deal of thinking to do before she
went to her father. She had hoped to do it in solitude,
but two petitioners had got as far as her anteroom.

If Demetria had been at her usual post, even the
Chief of the College of Augurs and the First Lord of
the Imperial Council would not have passed that door.
But Demetria was guarding the emperor. Her third in
command, loyal guardsman though he was, had not
been able to withstand the power of the two men's
titles.

They rose and bowed when she came in. She
inclined her head in return, suppressing the inward
sigh. They were both her cousins in her mother's line,
but very different in personality and looks. The Chief
Augur was a tall and slender man, very elegant, with

a gentle manner and an ivory mask of a face. Duke Gallio had been a legionary commander in his youth, and he had the leathery look of the lifelong soldier, with scars enough to mark his valor.

He was one of the strongest supporters of her father's war. What the Chief Augur thought about it, no one knew. If she had asked, he would have answered as he always did, that it was not his place to offer opinions of that nature. He was a reader of signs and omens, a voice for the wind of heaven.

There were preliminaries, a dance as graceful in its way as the Dance of the stallions, and with its own peculiar power. It smoothed raw edges and softened tension.

She let it go on as long as her uninvited guests were willing to continue. It was part of the game. At last Duke Gallio conceded surrender and came to the point. "Lady, we know the emperor is in seclusion, but maybe you know his mind. It's been a hundred years since the last Great Dance—since anyone raised the power that changes the future. How do we know that future will be anything we can live in?"

"The emperor's will binds the Dance," said the Chief Augur. "It unfolds through him."

"And if the emperor is ill? What then? What happens to the Dance?"

Briana heard this in deep alarm. She swallowed the first words that came into her head and made herself pause, calm down and then say, "The Dance will be safe. The riders will assure it if, gods forbid, the emperor is unable."

The Augur nodded. "The master of the riders is given the emperor's mandate. If the emperor is unable to fulfill it, then he undertakes to do so."

That seemed to reassure Duke Gallio, at least for the moment. It did not comfort Briana as much as it might have. The Chief Augur could have put the First Lord's fears to rest without forcing Briana to serve as a witness. "Reverend father," she said, "is everything well?"

"We are ready for the Dance," he said, "all but the final preparations."

He had not answered her question. "That's well," she said. "But the rest?"

He was unusually reluctant to answer. Finally, with a glance at Gallio, he drew a small scroll from his sleeve. She recognized the crimson cord that bound it and the seals that hung from it. This was the scroll of the omens, which was given to the emperor at each new moon. "This is somewhat irregular," he said, "but in the circumstances, I think it best that you see what is written here."

Briana took the scroll with an odd shiver. That seal was for the emperor to break. She thought briefly of taking it to him, but the Augur himself could have done that. There must be a reason why he had brought it to her instead.

She murmured a Word over the seal, to remove any curse that might attend her breaking it and to ward the contents of the scroll. The seal fell whole into her hand. The scroll unrolled itself.

She could read an omen as clear as that. She bent to the scroll. It was closely written, much more so than others she had seen.

Soon enough she saw what the Augur had wanted her to see. Here in Aurelia she had noticed few enough portents, unless the worsening weather after so long a spell of calm could be counted as such. But there was a widening pattern of signs and prodigies which, if she had drawn them on a map, formed a great circle all around the heart of the empire.

Leviathans in the deep, storms that blew without warning and wrought utter destruction, darkness at noon and storms of fire at midnight, those were the most obvious. But to her eye, the numerous lesser oddities were more disturbing. A swarm of bees had overwhelmed a village near the eastern frontier, killed or driven out its inhabitants and transformed its headman's house into a vast hive. In a town to the north, all the cats had departed, leaving the rats to rule unchallenged. Not too terribly far to the south, cows were calving out of season, giving birth to bizarre deformities—a startling number of which lived until the herdsmen put them out of their misery.

There were dozens of such strange occurrences, and more of them every day. Only one place had none, and that was the Mountain. Everywhere else was plagued with portents.

She did not have to be a horse mage to see the pattern. Ripples from the Dance could spread into the past as well as the future. The empire was in grave danger, and it all hinged on the day of the emperor's festival.

She rolled the scroll carefully and fastened its cords, using the time to find words that would not be misunderstood. Finally, when the omens were hidden again though not forgotten, she said, "Tell me why you brought this to me and not my father."

"The last portent," the Augur said.

She frowned. She had read so many. The last—she had barely skimmed it.

"The lioness in the duke's menagerie at Roviga," the Augur said, "who gave birth to a black filly foal with a crescent moon on its brow. The pattern in the portents, the shape of things around it, points to you, highness. You are, somehow, a key."

Briana shuddered under her skin. This man's gift was to read whole worlds in the passage of a shadow or the turn of a stallion's hoof. Her face, even with all the training she had had, could not be terribly difficult for him to decipher.

The opposite, unfortunately, was not true. Like all master mages, he was warded completely. She could read nothing but what he chose to show. She had known him since she was a child, but whether she could trust him with what she knew—she did not know.

She decided to tell a part of the truth. Not the part

that made her shiver, the part in which she was sure that the omen referred not to her but to the woman who had been Called. That, she found she wanted to keep to herself. If the Augur had not seen or foreseen it, then surely it was not meant for him to know.

She told him the thing that was more immediate and probably lesser, although it was great enough in itself. "There has been an attack on the emperor," she said. "The wound is minor, but the blade was poisoned with *akasha*. He will be alive and aware for the Dance, but he may be unable to influence it to the extent that he had hoped."

Duke Gallio's breath hissed between his teeth. Briana made herself ignore him.

The Chief Augur betrayed no more expression than before. "The emperor is not required to be a mage," he said. "The Dance is a power outside of his, even as he expresses the will of the gods and of the empire. If the riders ride well and the white gods are well disposed, it will matter little whether he brings magic to the rite."

"But it will matter."

He shrugged slightly, a minute lift of one shoulder. "Are you asking whether your magic can turn the tide?"

"Can it?"

"That," he said, "we do not know. As the heir you have great power in your own right. You are bound to the empire as your father is, although in lesser degree. Then of course there is the fact that you, like him, are a mage of rare potency. Whether your power will suffice for this, I cannot see."

"But it might? It's possible?"

"All things are possible," Duke Gallio said in a burst of rare impatience. "A lioness can give birth to a horse foal, and Augurs can wax grave as to the meaning of it. The rest of us have less lofty and more practical concerns. Do you know who attacked your father?"

She had been prepared for that. Again, she answered honestly. "We have reason to suspect that they were agents of the prince Marcellus."

She held her breath. This could be a very bad decision, or it could have gained a pair of allies. She might not know which until the Dance was over.

"I see," the Augur said with no more expression than before. Maybe he had known, or maybe she had made clear a pattern that he had already half understood. "The Dance will require Great Wards, then, and mages of stones to secure them. Guards as well, I think. My lord?"

"I can put the emperor's own on alert," the First Lord said. He was not surprised at all, she noticed, and he had none of her father's insistence that she prove her accusation. If anything, he seemed relieved. "It's only sensible in any case."

"Please," Briana said, although she risked insulting them both, "be circumspect. The fewer people who know the truth, the better."

"By all means," the First Lord said. "Set your mind at ease, Highness. No one will know why we're doing this, unless he can be bound to silence."

"I thank you for that," she said.

The Chief Augur bowed to her in respect that seemed genuine. "Highness," he said, "never forget that we are your servants. Never hesitate to ask of us whatever you must. After we are your father's, we are yours—and before either of you, we belong to the empire."

Briana's throat was tight. She had been bred to receive homage, but there was a depth to this that she had not felt before.

Her father was not going to die and leave her to rule a crumbling empire. The Dance was not going to shatter. If she had to hold it together with her own life and soul, she would.

Maybe the last portent applied to her after all. She found, contemplating it, that she was not afraid. Whatever she was meant to do, she would do it. That was what she was for.

Demetria's sword flicked out, quick as a snake. Artorius' blade flashed to the riposte. Demetria struck again, again, again. At each stroke he beat her back.

Briana held her breath. She would have Demetria's neck—but not until that ell of polished steel was safely sheathed. Her father was remarkably fast on his feet for a man with a wound in the side that even yet was bleeding magic. He began to fall back before Demetria's determined attack.

Just as Briana was about to call a halt, he came alive. His blade was a blur.

He seemed almost cool, but sweat ran down Demetria's face. She retreated a step, two, three, four. The sword flew out of her hand.

She stood grinning. He grinned back.

Briana could not decide which of them to throttle first. Even while she glared at them, she had to admit that her father looked well—if she ignored the fact that his magic had shrunk from a roaring flame to a barely visible ember.

"Father—" she began.

"Briana," he said. He saluted her with his blade and sheathed it with a flourish. "Before you kill your servant, do consider that she was only following orders."

"Orders to do what? Put you out of your misery?"

"Precisely," he said. "Did you notice? The poison is fading. The stronger my blood flows, the weaker the *akasha* becomes."

"You can't spend the next six days playing at soldiers," she said.

"No?" He was in an odd mood, as if he had drunk a little too much wine. Loss of blood made one light-headed. Maybe loss of magic could do the same.

She had been going to tell him about everything— the rash of omens, the plan to trap Gothard—but what could he do, after all? He was entertaining himself perfectly well. He seemed safe. After she was done, if the gods favored her, he would be safer still. She might even stop the attack on the Dance. She was a key, the Augur had said. He had not said anything of the emperor.

"If you won't rest," Briana said, "at least stop grinning and eat something. Maybe even call in a healer, if—"

"No healers," he said. "What are they saying in court? Are the whiners as loud as usual?"

Her breath came a bit short. She made herself answer lightly, and not as if she were trying to hide anything. "Louder. But the rumors are more harmless than you might expect. No one is talking about knives and poison. We're safe for a while."

That pleased him, and had the virtue of being true. His servants brought food, which he insisted that she share. She choked down as much as she could, and escaped before he could grow suspicious. Demetria was eyeing her oddly, but her father seemed content to believe that she had only come to assure herself that he was well.

Maariyah had seen that Briana's messages were delivered. The burden was on Tullus the guardsman to lay the trap and set it to be sprung.

Briana was the bait. She had debated between summoning her brother into her presence, which would be in accord with protocol but might make him suspicious, and calling on him in his own house, which would take the fight to his territory.

In the end she decided to go to him. It had the advantage of surprise, and she could claim precedent. She had been in his house often as a child, though more seldom as she grew older, after Ambrosius became Kerrec and went to the Mountain. Gothard never had forgiven either her or their father for taking away the heirship—as if he had ever had a right to it.

Now she knew just how badly he had wanted it, and just how much he was willing to pay to get it. It saddened her above and beyond the anger. He was her brother, and he had turned against his own blood.

She put the sadness aside until she could afford to indulge in it. With Maariyah and a pair of guards, both of whom were mages with a gift for raising wards, she set off on foot toward Gothard's house.

The guard at the gate was one of Tullus' men. He greeted Briana with the signal they had agreed on, a flick of the fingers at his belt. She arched her brow and tilted her chin. He bowed her through the gate.

Gothard was at home, as Tullus had assured her that he would be. Briana was not admitted at once to his presence, but she had expected that. She settled as comfortably as she could in the anteroom to which his servants directed her, smoothing the skirts she had put on for the occasion.

She ran her hand surreptitiously down her leg to her ankle. One of her daggers was strapped securely, within fast reach. The other, under her voluminous sleeve, slipped into her hand at a flex of the wrist, and then back smoothly into its sheath.

She had no stone in which to focus her magic, but that could be a strength rather than a weakness. Her power was woven through her flesh and bone. It could not be separated from her unless she died.

She slowed her breathing and drew her power into herself. Fear was far away. So was the earth of this empire from which she drew most of her strength. In this place of stone, Gothard had focused the bulk of his magic.

She held herself steady by force of will. The house lay on the earth. She only had to find it through cracks in the stones. Then she could ground herself.

A shock ran through her. There was a white god inside these walls. Once she was aware of him, she could feel him as strongly as the heat of sunlight on her skin. At first she thought him trapped, but there was nothing either caged or desperate about him. He hated walls, that came through very strongly, but he chose to enclose himself in them.

He was the anchor she needed. All of her family were bound to the stallions, although Kerrec was the first imperial heir to be Called as a rider. She rested briefly in the comfort of the god's presence, not thinking too hard about what it meant or what he must mean by it.

Someone was standing in the door of the anteroom. With difficulty she forced her awareness back to the mortal world. The person in the doorway was so powerful that she was surprised and somewhat disappointed to realize that it was a human creature and not the stallion.

It was a woman, quite young, and dressed like a rider. Her hair was cut short, curling on her neck. Her face was a narrow oval, too strong for prettiness, but rather striking in its beauty. If a man was not looking too closely or expecting too much, he might take it for a boy's.

So this was the traitor, Briana thought. Of course she would be that young, if she had only been Called that spring, but it was a little surprising even so. Her magic was so strong and so sure of itself, so much like a stallion's, that Briana felt a little dizzy seeing it in this young girl's body.

She could sense no corruption in it. That interested her. She opened her mouth to speak, but the girl had started and half spun. Before Briana could blink, she was gone. In her place stood one of Gothard's servants. "My lord will see you now," he said.

Briana steadied herself with a deep breath, and wrenched her mind away from the puzzle of the girl who had been Called. Every part of her must be clear and focused. She stood, shook out her skirts and followed the servant.

><|+|><

Chapter Forty

Gothard was praying at the shrine of the ancestors in the central court of his house. The images there all wore imperial faces and the imperial diadem. Briana had a similar shrine in her wing of the palace, but she paid tribute to her mother's family as well, a scattering of ducal coronets and a legionary standard or two.

Barbarians did not offer respect to their ancestors. They had one god and only one, and he was a powerfully jealous divinity.

She waited while Gothard finished his devotions. Her head was bowed and her eyes lowered in apparent respect. Under her lashes she confirmed what her magical senses told her, that there were guards all around the courtyard. Two were visible, over on the eastern side. The rest were hidden in shadows and behind pillars of the colonnade.

All of those pillars were warded, as was the paving underfoot, but the sky was open overhead. There was no better place in this house for the trap the guards had laid.

Briana's heart was beating hard. She made herself breathe slowly. Gothard was taking his time, which was a not particularly subtle insult. He knew perfectly well that because it was a sacred ritual—dedicated to her own ancestors as well as his—she could not object to his conduct.

The guards had begun to move, slipping down along the colonnade. Briana willed the tension out of her body. Gothard seemed oblivious. His wards and protections were quiet.

Even with the warning she had had, the attack caught her by surprise. They came in from all sides, fast and silent. A thrown spear clipped Gothard's shoulder and sent him sprawling. In almost the same instant, a heavy weight struck Briana from behind.

Her brother's body broke her fall. She lay dazed, struggling to clear her head. The stone was close—she could feel it. She scrambled as if in panic. He twisted under her. He was wheezing, gasping for breath.

Her fingers brushed the stone. It burned like fire. By instinct she recoiled.

Hard hands gripped her, hauling her away. She could not see Gothard. The stones underfoot had begun to hum. The man who gripped her heaved her up off them. "Sorry, Highness," he muttered in her ear.

There was a melee in front of the shrine, with Gothard at the bottom of it. If the spear had wounded or stunned him, he seemed to have recovered damnably quickly.

Briana struggled against the too-helpful fool who held her. She could hardly breathe. Her magic was floundering. The sky fed it, but the stones swallowed it. Gothard was growing stronger.

She wrenched free. The hum all around her rose to a shriek. One of the guards had Gothard's ring. His shout of triumph was barely audible.

This was all falling to pieces. Briana scraped her strength together as best she could. The structure of wards that should have risen around her was a ramshackle thing, full of gaps and threadbare patches.

The guard with the ring lurched toward her. He was charring as he walked, from the hand inward. His teeth were set, his face a mask that reminded her incongruously of the Chief Augur.

She had a pouch of warded silk in a pocket of her skirts. He had burned to bone and then to ash before she could draw it out. She dropped painfully to her knees. The ring lay, gleaming darkly, in the heap of nothingness that had been a man.

The wards were not falling. They should have broken as soon as the ring left her brother's hand. Which meant—

Briana flung herself flat. The blast roared over her. Men's bodies fell broken.

The ring gleamed just out of reach. It had been far better bait than she had been.

Gothard stood above her. She braced for the killing stroke, but he stretched out a hand and pulled her up. She could find no wrath in his face, not at her. She could have sworn that what she saw there was genuine concern. "Sister," he said. "By the gods. Are you hurt?"

She gaped like an idiot. Of all things she could have expected from this lethally clever man, this was the most improbable. He had laid a trap for the trap— but it seemed he had no inkling of her part in it.

Her silence made him frown, and not—again amazingly—in anger. He swung her up in his arms, grunting only slightly, and carried her away from all the dead and dying.

She tried to escape. Maariyah was there. Tullus. Two of her own guards. She could not—

He was too strong. Now that the deception of the ring was gone, she felt the greater power it had hidden. It hung on a chain under his shirt, and it was nearly as wide as her palm. It was a master stone, a Great One of its kind, that ruled gods knew how many lesser stones. If she had known, if any of them had known, the actual source of his magic, they would never have tried anything so foolhardy as an ambush in his own house.

"My maid," she said. "My guards. I have to—"

"They'll be seen to," Gothard said. That was more his usual tone, sharp and a little impatient. He carried her out of the light and into stifling dimness.

Gothard's servants looked after Briana, soothing her aching head with cool cloths and plying her with cups and bowls of this concoction or that. She trusted none of them, and turned them all away.

Gothard had gone out to deal with the carnage. He came back just before she could make her escape, wearing a scowl that he barely wiped from his face before he greeted her.

She had been holding her breath, but it seemed he still did not guess what she had been to the conspiracy. "They're all dead," he said. "Your maid, your guards—all of them. I'm sorry."

Briana made no effort to stop the cry that welled up in her. Her fault, her fault. Because she had planned too poorly. Because she had underestimated her brother's intelligence. Because—

Gothard never had been much use around weeping women. Discomfort made him snappish. "Stop it! Stop that. I'll do my best to find out who is behind this. Did anyone suggest you come here at this particular time?"

She stared at him, unable to shake her head, let alone speak a word.

He looked ready to slap her. "Never mind. I'll make sure you're delivered safely home. We'll see each other at the Dance, yes?"

At that she could nod, numbly.

He softened a little, enough to pat her awkwardly on the shoulder. "I don't think this was aimed at you," he said. "You'll be safe once you're home again."

"My maid—" she began.

"I'll have the bodies of your people sent back with due honor. But you should go now. I can't promise there won't be another attack. If that was a feint—"

She could hardly say it had not been.

"Go now," he said. "Go quickly. My guards will escort you. If you're wise, you'll stay in the palace until after the Dance. Keep your wits about you and be watchful. If I've been attacked, you yourself may be in danger."

Her jaw was locked too tight for an answer. In any case he had not expected one. His opinion of her had never been very high, but he would be sure now that she was an idiot.

Maariyah's body lay with those of Briana's two guards in one of the anterooms of the heir's palace. There had been no way to ask for Tullus' body as well. Briana would have to honor him as best she could through the spirits of the others who had died with him.

The embalmers had been summoned. Briana sat with the dead and waited. This was her penance, and her failure.

The tears were burned out of her. *When you fail*, her

father had taught her, *learn from it*. It was a hard lesson tonight.

She heard both her father and her brother behind her. They had not come in together and were not perceptibly pleased to find that they had had the same thought, but for once they laid aside their private war. Kerrec came up beside her and knelt as she was kneeling. Artorius remained standing behind her.

"Our brother has a master stone," Briana said.

"I know," said Kerrec. "You should have suspected. He's been keeping a Great One imprisoned in wards."

"The Great One chooses to be imprisoned," Briana said.

"Even so," her brother said.

Her fists had clenched. They were aching, but she could not unclench them. "There is nothing that either of you can say that I have not said to myself. I did everything badly. I acted too quickly, studied too poorly, cost the lives of loyal people through my errors of judgment."

"You did," said her father. "You also came out alive and unsuspected."

"That was luck," she said bitterly. "I should have—"

"Whatever you should have done," Artorius said, "we now know more precisely what we face. Were you able to see the stone?"

"No," she said, still bitter. "He kept it hidden."

"No matter," Kerrec said. "It's clear enough what its powers are."

He would have said more, but the embalmers had come. One moment he was there. The next, she was staring at empty space.

The embalmers were a sect of healer priests, devotees of the moon's dark. They were all women, and all masked, with soft slow movements and supple gestures. Their order was sworn to silence.

They bowed low to her and lower to her father, and indicated in their subtle way that there were rites they should perform here before the dead were taken away.

Briana paused, looking down into faces that she would never see again in this life. She laid runes of blessing on the guards' foreheads, but on Maariyah's she laid a kiss. Her eyes had filled with tears.

Her father's arm circled her shoulders, drawing her away. He drew her all the way to the garden, where Kerrec was sitting on Petra's back, looking as if he had been carved in stone.

"I didn't know horse mages worked the spells of mist and shadow," Briana said.

"We don't," said Kerrec. "I have no idea how I did that. I needed to be invisible, and to be gone. Therefore I was."

He was scowling. His fingers were knotted in Petra's mane, and his back was stiff. "I don't—like—not knowing what I did. Or how. Or where the knowledge came from. I am—I was—disciplined. I knew all the ranks and divisions of my power. My mind was a thing of order and beauty. Now—"

Petra shook his head and snorted wetly, then turned and nipped his rider's leg. Kerrec's look of pure affront startled Briana into laughter that was half tears. When affront turned to outrage, she lost any power to stop laughing.

She had to sit down rather abruptly. Petra nuzzled her hair. She wrapped her arms around his big solid head and let him pull her back to her feet.

Kerrec had recovered somewhat from his fit of the wallows. Their father was scrupulously avoiding comment. When both of his offspring were more or less composed, he said, "We have a trap to lay—one that, we can hope, will succeed where the other failed. I propose we lay it soon, and as solidly as we can. A master stone will challenge us severely—the more so for that the only intact power among the three of us, daughter, is yours."

"And his," Kerrec said, rubbing Petra's neck.

Briana's brows rose. The stallion appeared to offer no objection.

That was an ally to reckon with—if he would help them. If he could be trusted.

It was preposterous to think of mistrusting one of the white gods, and yet Briana dared not avoid the thought. There was a Great One in Gothard's house, apparently by choice, and a Great One here who had permitted his rider to be tortured into ruin. Only the gods knew the truth of any of it.

Chapter Forty-One

"Have we all wallowed enough?" the emperor inquired acidly. "Shall we talk our way through the Dance, or shall we do what we can to keep it from being destroyed?"

Kerrec could not hear that voice without his hackles rising. It was an old and visceral thing, and he could not help it. He was rather pleased that he kept his mouth shut, and that he swung his leg over Petra's neck and slid to the ground without either falling on his face or strangling his father.

Artorius would never look directly at him, as if he subscribed to the superstition that it was bad luck to meet a dead man's eyes. It was Kerrec's misfortune to feel all too much like a living one, bruised to the bone and half torn apart, measuring his life in numerous small pains.

That was wallowing, as the emperor had said. "Think," said Artorius. "Focus. We know what's coming. Here is what we will do to stop it."

Kerrec refrained from pointing out that it was rather unlikely they would do any such thing. Briana held her tongue as well. Artorius told them succinctly what they would do and when and how.

That, first of all, was to rest and gather what strength they had. Kerrec had rested more than enough since he came back to Aurelia, but his body and mind were both weaker than he liked. If he was going to be in any state to face the Dance, he had to be strong.

Artorius left them to it. Kerrec hoped the emperor would take his own advice. They were a poor army for such a war, but they were all there was.

Kerrec dreamed of stones. He saw them cut and set in rings, or built into towers, or carved into images that shifted and blurred and changed in the way of dreams. He saw a finger of rock standing in a barren circle, and blood running down it. He saw a wheel of fire hung on an iron chain, cradled in Gothard's hands.

The memory of the master stone followed Kerrec into waking. What it meant, or whether it meant anything at all, he did not know. It hovered in the back of his mind while he gathered himself to face the day.

Every morning now he took the count of the scattered fragments of his self, and pulled them together as best he could. Every day there were fewer fragments, and he was closer to whole. But he was a long way from healed.

While he collected himself, the usual servant brought his breakfast. The boy was a mute, and painfully shy. He loved to look at Petra but never dared touch him, even when Kerrec invited him to do as he pleased.

Today he seemed almost brave enough to lay a hand on the broad white shoulder while Petra nibbled the hay that the boy had brought before he fed Kerrec. He might have gone further, but Kerrec was not there to see. He was suddenly, oddly restless. Danger was coming, or the prospect of danger.

He considered the servant's tabard that had served him so well before, but chose instead to be a shadow and a breath of air. It was wonderfully easy to do, but it was completely impossible to explain how he did it. How did he breathe? Or sit a horse?

Everything was quiet in Briana's rooms. She was having her morning bath, attended by other, lesser maids than Maariyah.

Kerrec made his way to the outermost of her rooms. There were voices outside. One must be the guard. The other was young, haughty and hauntingly familiar. It was arguing heatedly, insisting that its owner be admitted, because he was the heir's kinsman and his message was urgent.

"She has many kinsmen," the guard said.

"How many of those are riders?" the young man demanded.

Kerrec had opened the door before his mind knew what his body was doing. "Let him in," he said.

The guard saluted with a clashing of metal. The boy looked as if he had seen a ghost.

That was all too common these days. Kerrec leveled a glare at him. "Get in," he said.

His name quivered through the mists in Kerrec's brain. Paulus, that was it. Paulus went as mute as the servant in the garden, which was not at all a common condition for him, and did as he was told.

Once they were inside with the door safely shut and the guard back at his post, Paulus found his voice. "First Rider! You're supposed to be—"

"Dead? Gone?"

"On the Mountain," Paulus said. "She said—"

"She?"

Kerrec did not know what he would have done then—probably throttled the boy. But Briana was there, and she had taken stock swiftly and thoroughly. "Put him down," she said to Kerrec.

Kerrec let go Paulus' throat. He had hardly been aware of laying hold of it, let alone heaving the boy up until his long legs dangled helplessly.

Once Paulus was back on his feet again, he stood staring at Kerrec, eyeing him as if he were a stallion of uncertain temper and unpredictable habits. Since that was rather an accurate assessment, Kerrec could hardly blame him.

"Come with me," Briana said to them both. The snap of command brought both of them sharply erect.

She led them to the garden, since it was the most easily secured and least public place in her wing of the palace. Petra was finishing his breakfast while the mute servant brushed out his tail. The boy started and would have fled, but Briana said much more gently than she had to either of her kinsmen, "Stay."

He went back to his brushing, darting wary glances at the men, especially Kerrec. Petra ignored them all.

"Cousin," Briana said to Paulus once he was settled with a cup of chilled fruit nectar and honey to soothe his throat. What he was was obvious, even if she had not known that Duke Gallio's eldest grandson was Called. He wore the grey coat and breeches of a rider-candidate, and his boots were made for riding. "Your new station becomes you."

He started to bow, clearly remembered that riders did not do such a thing to any human creature, and settled for a stiff dip of the chin instead. "Thank you, cousin," he said. His voice was a fraction rougher than it had been before Kerrec interfered with it.

Kerrec had had enough of courtly niceties. "What brings you here? When did you see her? Have you gone over to the enemy as well?"

Paulus opened his mouth, but Briana said, "Tell it in

order. And no interruptions," she said with a sharp glance at Kerrec.

That was bloody difficult, but it was a form of discipline. Kerrec had sore need of discipline these days. He bit his tongue until he tasted blood, and fought down the murderous rage that rose in him at the thought of her—the enemy, the traitor.

Paulus obeyed Briana, but he kept darting glances at Kerrec. If that was pity, Kerrec would kill him. It seemed more like shock, which was marginally more bearable.

"I take it you know about the woman who was Called in the spring," he said. Briana nodded. He took a deep breath and went on. "You must know the rest of it, too, if the First Rider is here. He was supposed to have gone to the Mountain. He was also supposed to have been nearly dead."

"I am dead," Kerrec said.

Briana quelled him with a glare. Paulus concealed his expression behind his cup. When he had composed himself enough to go on, he said, "She came to warn us. The Dance is in danger. The prince Marcellus, who is calling himself Gothard, is behind it."

"She warned you?" Briana asked him. "She was admitted to the Master?"

Paulus wriggled like a much younger child than he was. "No," he said. "She never got that far."

"You've spoken to the Master yourself?"

That made him even more uncomfortable. "I can't

get near him, either. No one can. She found me looking after the stallions. She's with the enemy, I'm sure of that. 'I traded myself for Kerrec's life,' she said. But she did try to warn us."

"She never traded anything for me," Kerrec said.

Briana ignored him. "That was dangerous for her," she said to Paulus, "to come to you with what she had to say."

"Not if it was another trap," Kerrec said. "She's in bed with a barbarian. Who knows what the two of them have plotted against us?"

Briana turned her back on him. "Do you think she can be trusted?" she asked Paulus.

"I don't know," Paulus said, and that was not easy for him at all. "She let us all think she was a man, to go through the testing, but she was always straightforward except for that. Mind you I can't abide her—that power of hers is against nature, damn it—but I can't hate her, either. I think she's as honorable as a woman can be. How honorable that is, I don't know."

Briana's expression was wry. "That's a fine, diplomatic answer," she said. "If she made a bargain to save her teacher's life—"

"She swore herself to the enemy," Kerrec said fiercely. "Isn't that enough?"

"No," said Briana bluntly, acknowledging him at last. "It's not. If she's their weapon against the Dance, and her heart isn't with them, that gives us hope."

"Plots within plots," Kerrec muttered. "Wheels

within wheels. When I went to the Mountain, I escaped from that. Now I'm trapped in a nightmare of it."

"No more than the rest of us," Briana said. "Get over yourself, brother. Even if she is in bed with the enemy, that doesn't mean she's sold her soul, too. A woman does what she must—like anyone else, male or female. You're alive because of her. She may still save us all."

"She'll save herself," Kerrec said, spitting the words, "and to the darkness with anyone else."

"With all due respect," said Paulus, "I don't think she's our enemy. I think she's honestly trapped, and she wants us to win, even if it destroys her."

Kerrec's lip curled. "She's seduced even you, hasn't she?"

"That's enough," Briana said, sharp as the cut of a whip. "Stop flailing and think. Is there any way we can get to her, to see what she can do from inside the plot?"

"Not after yesterday," Kerrec said with dark satisfaction. It struck him with a slight pang to see how her face went stiff, but not enough to stop him. "If our brother's house was warded before, it will be sealed up solid now. He may not know you were part of the attack, but he knows that someone wants him disposed of."

"Even so," said Briana, "maybe Petra—"

"Petra is not talking to me," Kerrec said sullenly. "He's besotted with her. They all are. And that should trouble you, little sister. She can corrupt even the gods."

"I think you need a dose of your famous discipline," she said. "When you're capable of thinking rationally, tell us. Meanwhile, we'll carry on without you."

Kerrec did not want to be rational. Whenever he thought of Valeria, he saw her lying in the barbarian's arms, plotting against the empire. "My memory may be in ruins," he said, "but one thing I remember. In the Book of Changes it says, 'One shall come who will both save and destroy the world.' It binds that mortal spirit to a Great One and foretells the end of everything. Even if she saves the Dance, there's still the world to shatter."

"If that's the truth," Briana said, "we'll deal with her as she deserves. Until then, I intend to reserve judgment."

"You do that," Kerrec said nastily. "Then we'll all go down together, all properly reserved and suitably judged."

Paulus cleared his throat. Not many would dare interfere with a royal squabble, but Duke Gallio's grandson had his fair share of crazy courage. "Highness," he said, again with that odd dip of the chin. "First Rider. I shouldn't be here, and now I've delivered my message, I'd best go back where I belong. The Master and the riders, when they come out, will be very glad to hear that you've been found alive and—more or less—well."

Mostly less, Kerrec thought, but he kept it to himself. He was done with wallowing, if not with hating the woman who—the traitor who—

Enough. He stayed with Petra while Briana saw Paulus to the door. Petra was as opaque as he always was when it came to Valeria.

No one, Kerrec noticed, had said anything of his riding in the Dance. He had not dared to think of it himself. But with all that he had heard, his mind persisted in turning toward it.

That, like the rest of his thoughts, he refrained from expressing aloud. He was maimed in mind and magic. He had had none of the days of seclusion and gathering of power that were ordained by ritual. And yet, in four days, maybe…

For today he would let it go. Tomorrow or the next day, he would think of it again. Then on the day of the Dance, who knew? Something might come of it.

Chapter Forty-Two

"Enough," said Valeria, "and enough."

Gothard had made sure that she rode Sabata each morning, by bullying Olivet into standing by while she did it. That had worked well enough for the first three days, but by the fourth, Valeria was not the only one in revolt. Sabata had come out of his stable in one of his choicer moods.

He was not rebellious, exactly, but neither was he inclined to do as any human told him, even Valeria. The weather was no help. The sun had not shone in days, and the air was cold, with a blustery wind blowing, smelling strongly of salt and the sea. It was a wind to get any horse's back up, and Sabata needed precious little excuse.

"God or no," she said to Olivet, who was sitting in

the shelter of the stable door, making strong inroads on a jar of wine, "he is still a horse, and that horse is not in the mood to work."

Olivet rolled a bloodshot eye at her. He had been drinking deeper each day, and beginning earlier. "Gothard says ride," he said. "Gothard is the master of us all. Or should I say, Gothard's stone is our master. Did you know that stone can master stallion? Nor did I. I had rather thought it would be the reverse."

"I don't suppose you can unmake it," Valeria said. It was meant to be flippant, but it did not come out lightly at all.

Olivet blinked. "Unmake stone? Cause stone not to be?"

"Well? Can you?"

He swayed on the stool. "Ride," he said. "His Royal Highness, who hopes to be His Imperial Majesty, says ride. Therefore, ride."

Valeria eyed Sabata. He eyed her in return. His back hunched and his forefoot pawed restlessly. "Run," she said, struck by wild impulse. "Run!"

He ran, but not where she wanted him to go. He circled the grassy court, head and tail high, bucking and blowing. Walls and wards only held him because he let them. He refused to escape.

Olivet snored against the stable wall. The empty jar was loose in his hand. Valeria worked it gently free and laid it beside his foot.

She eyed the walls, up and past the flying form of

the stallion. "I'm sorry," she said, maybe to Olivet, maybe to Sabata, maybe even to Gothard. "I can't do it. I gave my word, but I can't. Even if you hunt down Kerrec and kill him, I can't be what you need me to be."

Sabata finished his run, roared to a halt, spun and set his nose lightly in her hand. He was hungry. He had nothing to say about the rest.

While she fed him, she did her best to think clearly. It might be more reasonable to wait until night, but Gothard or his guards would expect an escape then. If she walked out in broad daylight, she might actually get away with it.

She left Sabata with his head in the manger and no higher ambition than to keep it there until the last of the hay was gone. "So stay," she said with a snap of frustration. "Stuff your face. I don't care."

He never turned an ear. She restrained herself, barely, from slamming the door behind her. By the time she reached the outer gate of the palace, she was at least outwardly calm. She had nothing with her but the clothes on her back and the magic inside her.

The guards looked her over as she walked past, but although she braced for the slam of a spear across her path, neither of them moved. She walked out into the street, just as spits of rain began to fall.

A figure detached itself from the wall. Euan Rohe smiled brightly at her. "Going exploring?" he asked.

As she looked up at that too-familiar face, she knew the meaning of despair. She was not going to get out of this as she had got out of her mother's root cellar. Her path was set. It led to the Dance, no matter what she did or how she struggled.

Her body did not want to acknowledge that. It leaped toward him, darted sideways and bolted down the street.

Euan caught her with humiliating ease. The force of her speed spun him half-around, but his grip was too strong to break.

That did not stop her from trying. He grunted when she caught him in the ribs, and eluded the knee in the groin. With a dizzying heave, he slung her over his shoulder and carried her back inside.

He dropped her onto her bed. She lay breathing hard, with tears of frustrated rage streaming down her face.

"Dear heart," he said, "I can't blame you for trying. But there's only one way out of this."

"Two," she said.

"Well, yes. We can all die. I prefer to think we'll all be kings."

"Aren't you going to ask me why I did it?"

"I know why you did it." He sat beside her and smoothed her hair out of her face. His touch was a caress. "It's hard to change a world. There's yourself to change first, and all your old fears to burn away."

"You could change," she said. "You'd still be a king."

"Ah," he said, "but I want to be more than a king."

"I don't."

"Of course not. You want to be a god."

"No."

"Don't lie to yourself. If you could give it all up, abandon your magic and go back where you came from, would you? Would you marry the man they chose for you and bear his sons and be a woman like any other in this empire? You were born to walk with gods. Look me in the face now and tell me you refuse it."

She looked him in the face, oh yes. "I hate you."

He never even flinched. "Of course you do. You were made for glory and splendor. You may hate that, and me, but you can't deny it."

She hit him hard. He rode with the blow, then as her hand began to draw back, he caught it and kissed the palm. Her fingers clawed. He laughed as he eluded them, caught her other hand, pinned them both and rose up over her. His eyes were full of laughter, and something else.

She would not call it tenderness. It was nothing as soft as that. He stooped and kissed her. She bit him. He licked the blood from his lip and grinned, and kissed her harder. Her back arched. She meant to twist away, truly she did. Not to wind herself so tightly with him that she could not tell where she ended and he began.

Euan Rohe left her pretending to sleep. It was very convincing, but he knew better. The guards were posted, the wards at their strongest. She would not be leaving this house again until she went to the Dance.

He kissed her softly. Her face did not change. He shook his head and smiled. She was a wild creature. He did not know that she would ever be precisely tame.

He could easily become obsessed with her. She was in the back of his mind always, even when, as tonight, he greeted the guests who had come in under cover of darkness.

The priests of the One brought with them a faint reek of carrion and a sense of cold stone. They were fresh from a sacrifice and full of power. When he looked into their shrouded faces, he saw Valeria lying naked in tumbled coverlets, ivory skin and blue-black hair and gold-flecked eyes growing warm as they rested on him. She smiled a slow, rich smile and held out her arms.

He brought himself sternly to order. Priests forswore the pleasure of the flesh. These would hardly be amused to discover that he had heard no word of what they said to him, because he was dreaming of an imperial female.

Euan was all too glad to leave them in the rooms that had been prepared for them. Every comfort had been removed, leaving only bare walls and bare floors, and no luxury to tempt them away from the path of holiness. Even before he shut the door behind him, they were in their circle, beginning the long chant that would not stop until the Dance was done.

That chant hummed in his bones. He had forces to gather and men of the warband to instruct, and Gothard to face sooner or later, to be sure all was in order. He put all that aside for another hour or two or three, and went back to Valeria.

She was still pretending to sleep, but he could feel the tension in her. He lay beside her and ran his hand down her back in long slow strokes. At first she was as stiff as one of Gothard's stones, but little by little the stiffness melted away. He drew her to him, cradling her.

She sighed. He wanted her suddenly, fiercely, but he held himself perfectly still. If he took her now, it would be rape. He did not want to rape her—not now, not ever. He wanted her of her free will, wanting him as powerfully as he wanted her.

He breathed deep, inhaling her scent. She always smelled faintly of horses, which he found pungent on its own and not particularly pleasant, but in her it was deliciously arousing.

When the empire was his and she ruled on the Mountain, they would be a force to reckon with. These doubts now, these small fears and weak compunctions, would fade away. She was young, that was all, and about to change the world profoundly. That would terrify a veteran warrior, let alone a slip of a girl.

Euan would help her to be strong. She might not let him at first, but she would learn. They were meant to be, he and she. The One had brought them together. Even the white gods acknowledged it.

He kept his thoughts to himself, because it would drive her away if he voiced them. The time would come when he could tell her, but not while she was still bound by her old oaths and loyalties. The Dance would scour those away. Then she would have room in her heart for a new world and a familiar lover, and maybe for more. Maybe—

Tonight he dared not even shape the thought for fear he would ruin it. In his arms, finally, she had fallen asleep. It was a light sleep, full of twitches and murmured words, but it was better than nothing at all.

Chapter Forty-Three

One day until the Dance. One brief turn of the sun before it was all ended, one way or another.

The Hall of the Dance was deserted. Tomorrow it would be full of people. Admittance to the rite was a currency more precious than gold, and those who by rank or office were entitled to places in the galleries were besieged. Anyone in want of funds could buy or trade his place and go home a rich man. But in this hour there was no one there at all, except Briana.

She stood in the center of the arena. The sand was smoothed but not yet raked for the Dance. Servants would do that later today. Now, in the dim morning, she was alone but for the wail of wind and the lash of rain against the walls and roof. Those walls seemed to breathe, deep and slow, as the storm battered from without.

She turned slowly. The galleries rose on all sides. On the eastward wall, below a mosaic of the Mountain under the light of sun and moon, the royal box looked down on the pale grey sand. It was sand of the seashore, brought in from the harbor, perfectly ordinary and inexplicably divine.

The boundaries of her magic expanded to fill the hall. She looked up. Her father was standing in the royal box. He had not been there a moment before. He looked like a lamp that had burned low.

There was almost no power left in him, but he was still the emperor. The strands of the empire ran through his hands. The strength of the earth was in him. Even *akasha* could not touch that.

She began to slow and deepen her breathing. The power pulsed with it, focused by the power of this place. Even a hundred years after the last Great Dance, every stone was steeped in magic.

Into the surging rhythm came a new force. She had left Kerrec sleeping in the garden, as he had done almost without interruption since the failed attack on Gothard. He was awake now, and mounted on Petra.

The stallion entered in that slow, cadenced pace which was so distinctive of his kind. They brought with them a wave of strength that nearly flung Briana flat.

Hastily she opened herself to it. It was weak in places, and sometimes it wavered, or else it was too strong. It could never quite find its balance. Kerrec's face was white and set.

It would have to be enough. Briana wove a net of wards and bindings surrounding the Hall and working its way into the earth below. She wrought it of air and water and fire, and sealed it with the power of earth. There was stone magic in it, and fire magic. Horse magic pulsed white in front of her, with more behind it—a power she could not quite grasp, but she was keenly aware of its existence.

It was a long labor, and intricate. Her head began to ache some time before she was done. She clung to Petra's neck. His hooves were sunk in the sand as if rooted in it. Kerrec on his back was trembling so hard his teeth chattered.

Kerrec's control was slipping, shredding. She could not afford to lose it. Petra's raw power was too strong. Unrestrained, it would destroy the structure she was building.

She gritted her teeth and held on. Her father was perfectly motionless above her. He could not anchor her. He had too little magic left. She needed—she had to—

The power beyond Petra was like a firm hand enclosing hers. She thought she saw eyes, not quite green, not quite brown, flecked with gold. They were a little puzzled and a little blurred as if with sleep or dream, but there was no fear in them. They fed her strength with effortless ease.

There was something—she had seen—

It was like the deep healing inside of Kerrec, which was still there, still working its subtle magic. Briana had never known anything like it.

If it was treacherous—

She had to trust it. She had no choice. She was not strong enough alone, and Kerrec was weakening fast. Without this new power, she would fail.

She used it ruthlessly. It offered no resistance.

She dropped out of the working with an abrupt and stomach-wrenching swoop. The web of magic was not as perfect as she could have wished, but it was the best she could do. The traps were laid and the snares set. The rest was in the hands of the gods.

Kerrec was still conscious. That surprised her. Even more surprising was the fact that he seemed to be drawing strength from a deep well.

She almost hated to take him out of the Hall, but Petra had the same thought she did. People would be coming soon. They all had to be out of sight before anyone saw either Kerrec or the stallion.

Their father was gone from the royal box. Briana decided not to go after him. He had more sense at the moment, she hoped, than Kerrec, and she wanted her brother to be safely hidden.

Whatever Kerrec thought of her plans, Petra carried him where Briana needed him to go. The way they took was known only to the emperor's family and a select few members of the imperial guard—a passage under the earth from the Hall to the palace, which happened to emerge not far from Briana's garden. Its doors were sealed to the imperial blood. No one not of that lineage could unlock them.

That, unfortunately, would not keep them safe from Gothard. Briana hazarded the last of her strength and laid a spell on both doors, a variation on the original working. This one fixed itself on barbarian blood, and barred the doors to it. Gothard could pass the first spell but not the second. However he intended to come into the Hall, it would not be that way.

Then she had to rest. It was the last thing she wanted to do, but she had no choice. Although she meant to retreat to her own rooms, she never managed to get so far. She sat on Kerrec's bed for a moment, and woke with the wan daylight fading and stars flickering through the ragged scud of cloud.

She leaped up in a near-panic. There was a banquet in court, there were final preparations to oversee, there was—

Kerrec was sitting at the worktable with his feet up on it, ankles crossed. "His Majesty sent a message," he said. "He's officiating at dinner tonight. You're to put in an appearance, but not until the wine and the dancing. 'Wear your gaudiest finery,' he said. 'If this is the end of the house of Aurelius, let them remember that we were glorious.'"

"Are those your words or his?" Briana demanded.

"His," Kerrec said. "I'm the one without the sense of humor, remember?"

"So is he." Briana stretched the knots out of her muscles. She was hungry enough to sink her teeth into Petra, if he had been there. She had to settle for the platter that was waiting, with enough food on it to feed a small army.

The hot dishes were still steaming and the cold ones still chilly on the tongue. She slanted a glance at Kerrec. "Did you—"

"Who knew how useful a servant's tabard could be?" he answered obliquely.

"You should be in worse state than I am," she said, reaching for a warm loaf of bread stuffed with cheese and olives and savory sausage.

Kerrec shrugged. "It was the Hall," he said, "and Petra. I think—in fact I know—I can ride tomorrow. I can be in the Dance."

Briana went absolutely still. "You what?"

"I can ride the Dance," he said with deliberate patience.

"No," she said. "You can't."

"I can." He uncrossed his ankles and lowered his feet, leaning toward her. His eyes were unnaturally bright. "Don't you see? The Hall healed me. I remember the patterns." He tapped his forehead with a finger that shook ever so slightly. "It's all in here. It's all come back. I *can* ride the Dance."

"Surely you can," she said, "if you seclude yourself for the next eight days, fast, meditate and muster your powers."

"I don't need any of that," he said.

"You're drunk," she said. "Your magic's coming back. It's made you giddy."

"I am perfectly sober," he said with dignity, "and I can ride the Dance."

"Look at yourself," she said. "Listen. And think. We need you most outside of the Dance. You know what we planned. We have to do it. Otherwise—"

"This may be the only Great Dance I ever ride."

She looked into his eyes. The pain there made her throat catch. "Kerrec," she said, "brother, you know what we have to do. We need you badly. We can't do it without you."

"Can't you?"

"No. Especially now, with your strength coming back. We need that. We need what you are, and what you know. And," she said, "what you'll do to those who thought you were thoroughly maimed and as good as dead, when they see you alive and well and sitting beside your father."

He did not smile at the thought. That was beyond him. But his face softened ever so slightly.

She pressed her advantage. "Without you we'd never have known that our brother is plotting against us. You may have already saved the Dance, even without what you may be able to do from outside it, to protect it."

He scowled straight through her. He was thinking. Good. Some of his old self was finally coming back, however brittle and shaky it was. His whole heart and soul must be yearning toward the Dance, but he had to know that she was right.

"Everything happens for a reason," she said. "Nothing is random. We have to believe that you are here because you are meant to be here. Whatever the gods will, this is part of it."

"Now you're talking like a priest," he said.

"Oh, no," she said, "though I remind myself a little too vividly of the Chief Augur."

He almost smiled at that. "You should go," he said. "You have a banquet to attend."

"I will go," she said, "but you will stay, and I will make sure of it. There will be no creeping out to do as you please. Am I understood?"

He sighed. "Completely," he said.

She still did not trust him, but her guards were on the alert. They were mages, and while they might not be stronger than Kerrec, they were well trained in looking after obstreperous charges.

She embraced him suddenly, startling him, and said, "Don't do anything stupid."

"Is sleeping permitted?"

"If you do it here," she said, "you may do it all you like."

He was not happy, but she thought he would be sensible. In any case the sun had set. She had to hurry or she would be late for her father's banquet.

Chapter Forty-Four

The earth held its breath. Dawn came late and slow, thick with fog, but the storm of wind and rain had blown away. Sailors and weathermasters said that the sun would burn through as the morning went on. Maybe that was too much to hope for, but any respite from days of storm was welcome.

Even before the sun rose, every niche and gallery of the Hall was full. People were standing along the walls and perching on the balconies. They overflowed through the gates and out into the great square, hundreds, thousands of them.

Pillars or small towers stood at intervals all around the square, with heralds mounted on them. They would pass word from the Hall of what went on there, and relay the Augurs' interpretations for the empire to hear.

Inside the Hall, the sense of anticipation was rising. An hour before noon, the riders would emerge from their long seclusion. Most of the people had brought food, drink and cushions or stools to sit on. Hawkers of bread and beer, wine and cakes and sausages, were relegated to the square outside, but a good quantity of their wares had found their way into the Hall.

The royal box was empty until midmorning. The emperor himself would make an entrance just before the riders, but Briana, attended by Demetria and one other, took her place somewhat early.

She took her time settling in the chair to the right of the throne, arranging her tiers of skirts and waiting for the assembly to realize that her second companion was not a guard. The uniform was somewhat similar, but his coat was a deeper shade of crimson, and it was edged with gold. Each button was a golden sun, the belt clasped with the golden image of a stallion in the Dance. It was the full dress regalia of a First Rider, identical to what the crowd would see when the riders entered.

There was a chair for Kerrec on the other side of the throne, but he chose to stand just behind Briana. His hand was steady on her shoulder. He seemed perfectly calm, as if he had come to terms with the fact that he would not be riding the Dance.

She mistrusted that calm, but there was nothing she could say to challenge it. She watched and waited as the stir began to run through the crowd, faces staring and voices rising in astonishment. People who were close enough could see the cuts and bruises still healing on his face, and notice that he held himself just a little too stiffly.

Briana kept her smile to herself. The court knew that the prince Ambrosius had been Called to the Mountain, but his presence here and now, at her back, was completely unexpected. No one knew what to make of it.

She could neither see nor sense Gothard anywhere in the Hall. He was entitled to a place in the imperial box, but she did not expect that he would take it. For what he planned to do, he would want to be free in the Hall, not isolated above it all. He would reckon that with the emperor powerless and his sister happily ignorant, there would be no trouble from that quarter.

She hoped that wherever he was, he would see Kerrec in time to be thoroughly thrown off balance. Meanwhile the court was startled enough. The speculation had begun. Alliances were already shifting and consciences being examined, while the lords of the empire absorbed this new and enigmatic development.

Briana smiled up at her brother and laid her hand over his. That caused an even greater flurry. Kerrec's eyes on her had a distinct tinge of irony. He was enjoying this, although he would never admit it.

The crowd was still in full flutter when the emperor made his entrance. He had deliberately chosen simplicity in his attire today, putting on the uniform of a commander of legions, without the helmet or breast-plate and with an empty scabbard in honor of this sacred rite. His head was bare of even the diadem. He was a plain soldier, his appearance said, preparing for a long-awaited war. He honored the festival with his presence, but he did not attempt to dominate it. That was for the riders and the gods whom they served.

At his coming, the Hall fell silent. Everyone who had been sitting was on his feet. They all saluted him, and hailed him with drums and trumpets, roaring out his name. "Artorius! Artorius Imperator!"

He let the shout rise to a crescendo, then raised his arms. Once again silence fell. He lowered his arms slowly and bowed to them all.

He made no speech. That would come later. This was the hour of gods and magic.

He remained standing as the first movement of the rite began. The chiefs and masters of the eight great orders of mages came forward at the eight points of the hall, taking stations in the first gallery.

One by one they invoked their powers. Stone master, sea master, masters of air and fire consecrated the elements here and in the empire without. Mages of sun and moon called on their separate powers, he of the sun in his golden robes, she of the moon all in white and silver. The master of the seers blessed the eyes of every human creature in the Hall. Then last of all the Chief Augur took his place in the Augurs' gallery, raising his staff and intoning, "In the name of

Earth and Sea, Air and Fire, Sun and Moon, vision and foresight and all the senses of the body, may this rite be blessed before the gods. May our eyes be clear and our spirits unsullied. May the gods look on us with favor."

As he spoke, all the strands of magic in the Hall wound themselves around his staff. Briana, who knew what other workings bound that place, saw them as well, hidden beneath the rest. Together they built a structure of wards so strong that she wondered how anyone, even a mage with a master stone, could breach them.

She kept her eye on the master of stones. Her snare was set to trap anyone who wished to harm the Dance, but it had not caught him. He was a quiet man, sturdy and foursquare, with no nonsense about him. He seemed at ease now, waiting as they all did for the ritual of warding to end and the Dance to begin.

The Chief Augur grounded his staff in the center of the Augurs' gallery. Seven of his colleagues arranged themselves around him. Their clerks, anonymous men in black, took places in the corners with their stacks of tablets and sharpened reed pens.

It was a little over an hour before noon. The fog had burned away. The sun was shining through the high windows, dazzling after days of clouds and rain.

Kerrec's hand was still on Briana's shoulder. It tightened to the point of pain.

She could feel them. They were coming. The wards began ever so softly to sing.

* * *

Valeria had been ordered to go to the stable at sunrise and wait with Sabata until it was time. Then Gothard would open a way to the Hall, and Mestre Olivet would guide her.

She went to the stable, true enough. She brushed and curried Sabata until he gleamed, and combed out his mane and the heavy silk of his tail. She did not put on the clothes that were waiting in the feed room, the crimson coat and doeskin breeches of a rider.

Mestre Olivet was still in the house. As far as she knew he was still asleep. Apparently he was supposed to guard her, because the wards that had been so strong were barely there. Gothard had diverted all of his energies into the assault on the Dance.

Patterns were shifting, changing, falling into place around her. One last time, she gambled on her chances of escape. This time there was no Euan to stop her. He had gone with Gothard and the rest.

It felt as if she were being led by the hand. She saw the people flocking toward the square, but her own path led her down nearly empty streets and through gates that opened to her touch. She suspected that she should be afraid, because she had no will in this, but when she looked into her heart she saw the stallions in their circle, white and calm.

The last gate she passed opened on a brief interlude of green, then brought her to a door. It opened as the rest had, and led her down a dim stair to a passage underground. She could feel the weight of earth over her.

There was magic here. The stallions protected her from it, but it was strong. It reminded her somehow of Kerrec. He had passed this way, or would pass. It was hours yet until the Dance, but the fabric of time was already growing thin.

The passage ended below the Hall. She found herself in the colonnade near the riders' entrance. It was not too crowded there, and most of the people seemed to be commoners dressed in their best, very plain compared to the glittering nobles in the rest of the Hall. She fit in well enough in her ordinary riding clothes.

Gothard and his allies were outside. The Hall was woven with wards, which they were not quite ready to challenge. She must be the only person inside who knew what was coming.

The murmur of conversation shifted and focused. She looked up with the rest of the people around her, toward the royal box under the mosaic of the Mountain. The sight of that image transfixed her. It was a long moment before she could lower her eyes to the box.

The golden throne was empty, but a woman had come to sit in the chair beside it. Valeria knew her face, having seen it in more than one vision. She was younger than Valeria had expected, but there was no mistaking that air of quiet power. This was the imperial heir.

There were two people behind her. One was unmistakably a guard. The other…

Valeria's heart went still. It must be some royal cousin who just happened, by a freak of fate, to look exactly like Kerrec—who had the same bruises, going green as they healed, and the same cuts and scars that she had seen on Kerrec's face and hands when she sent him to the Mountain. It could not be Kerrec, here, in the place of greatest danger.

All too clearly it was. He was on his feet and apparently sane. With so many people in between, and so much magic, she could not read him at all.

All too slowly she understood what it meant that he was there with his hand on his sister's shoulder. The heir knew of the plot. That meant the emperor too must know.

Valeria's knees started to give way. Luckily there was a pillar to lean on. Everything she had thought and feared was shifting, because Kerrec was here. Was his mind healed? She dared not send a probe through all the tangled workings in this place. All she could do was stand in the crowd and look up, and fill her eyes with his face.

When the emperor came, she had to tear her mind away from Kerrec. Just as he had been in her visions, the emperor was a handsome man, rather less stern in the face than Kerrec was, but otherwise she could see what his son would look like in thirty years.

Something was wrong with him. Something was missing. Something—

When the rite of consecration began, Valeria was still

struggling to understand what she had seen. The Hall was bound eightfold with magic. Its wards should have been impregnable, but there was a worm in their heart.

Gothard, or someone in his service, had cast a working on the stones of the Hall. It was so subtle as to be almost undetectable. She only found it because she was leaning against a stone, and because she knew that Gothard must have done something to prepare the Hall for his attack.

She looked up again to the royal box. The people in it seemed too calm. She would wager that they did not know of Gothard's spell. Their wards were too coarse-grained—they had not caught this minute wisp of a working.

There was no way to reach or warn them. The riders were nearly here. The sense of imminence was so powerful that she could barely see.

She was in this place because she was meant to be. Whatever she did, she would do because it was inevitable, because the patterns came together just so. And, above all, because she wished to be here. This was where she had to be.

She was almost at peace. What would come would come. She was ready for it, or she was not. Either way, it no longer mattered.

Chapter Forty-Five

The air was singing. The sky beyond the Hall was crystalline, as if clouds and fog had never dimmed it at all. Faint but distinct, Valeria heard the sigh of the sea.

She stood in the eye of the storm. Chaos swirled around her. Beyond the wards of the Hall, she felt a shudder of wrongness, a tear in the fabric of the world. It tasted of stone, old and cold, but this had nothing to do with Gothard. It was different.

Barbarian. As soon as she thought the word, she knew that priests of the One God were there, raising a power that reeked of Unmaking. They were all around the palace, defended by warbands of barbarians, all of whom had come in under cover of darkness, protected by Gothard's magic. There must have been a thousand warriors, and a score or more of priests.

She recoiled from the knowledge of them. The spell inside her was trying to wake, rattling her badly, just when she needed to be most calm. With every scrap of will that she had, she focused away from the terrors outside and toward the ordered beauty of the Dance.

Even that could not help her to escape. While she was lost in the world's confusion, she had gained an escort. Gothard stood on one side of her, and Euan Rohe, barely disguised in a hooded cloak, on the other. There was no sign of Mestre Olivet.

Gothard took her arm with feigned solicitude. His words, hissed in her ear, had nothing gentle in them. "We all owe you a debt, rider, for penetrating the wards without springing the alarm. When this is over, you'll tell me how you did it."

She bit her tongue until she tasted blood, but he knew what she had been about to say. His smile was a predator's display of armament. "When this is over," he said, "I'll tell you how *I* did it."

His grip on her arm was painfully tight. Euan's, on the other side, was gentler, but it was no more likely to let her go.

She stood still between them. Gothard's eyes had gone to the royal box and fixed on Kerrec. His lips were a thin line.

"Did you know?" Euan asked her, quite calmly in the circumstances.

"Not until now," she said.

"I hope you're telling the truth," he said, "because if you aren't, once this is over, he'll die an ugly death."

"That will happen no matter what I do," she said bleakly.

"The bargain stands," Euan said. "You ride the Dance, he lives."

"Whole? Sane?"

Gothard's hand was so tight that Valeria's arm had gone numb. She ignored him. So did Euan. "Whole, sane and in your power."

"You have no right—" Gothard began.

"Without her, there is no Dance," Euan said.

Gothard snarled soundlessly. There was nothing else he could do or say, not with people all around them and a stir beginning, a deep shift in the balance of the Hall.

The stallions were coming. Anyone with any glimmer of magic must have been able to feel it. Gothard had gone white. Even Euan was perfectly still, as if he had heard something faint and far away but impossible to ignore.

Valeria forgot her body's discomfort and the trap she had placed herself in. The play of light in the hall had ceased to be random. There were patterns in the shafts of sunlight and shadow, and in the dance of motes in the light. The people crowded in the galleries were no longer separate beings. They were all one, all part of the pattern.

The stallions came through the one gate that was

not crowded with bodies. They were brighter than the sun, almost unbearable to look at, until suddenly they fell into mortal solidity. Then they were the sturdy white horses she knew so well, ridden by men with familiar faces.

All fear was gone. Even guilt had fallen away. The Dance unfolded in her, pure and whole, as the first steps began. She knew what the second would be, and the fourth and the eighth and the fortieth. She knew where the pattern could vary, and how it could shift. She knew it all, deep inside her, as the stallions knew it.

Gothard's magic was a shackle, and the bargain she had made was a net of chains. She was bound and bound again.

Even that had stopped troubling her. She had become the Dance. It would go as it must go. None of them had any choice, no matter what mortals might think.

She looked up above the riders' heads to the royal box. The emperor was a fading ember. His daughter was a rioting fire, as wonderful in her way as one of the Ladies. And the son, the one who had been maimed and whom she had in part healed, was—was—

She could not describe what he was, except that he was everything. Only the white gods mattered more.

Sabata was waiting. In this hour, mortal distance meant nothing. He was there beside her, although their bodies were half a city apart. When the moment came, he would know. Then she would do what she must do.

Step by step the patterns came together. Moment by moment she prepared herself. Dimly she was aware that Gothard had let her go. Euan had not, but he was part of her somehow. He did not trouble her, not just then.

The Unmaking was still hovering. The priests were controlling it, with difficulty. She bent an edge of the pattern toward it to surround it and hold it back.

The Dance approached its climax. Eight stallions wove and rewove in a skein of flashing legs and shimmering tails. The words for what they did were like incantations. Four-tempis, two-tempis, one-tempis. Travers, renvers. Passage, piaffe, pirouette. As they wound together in a circle, four more emerged into the light.

These were the strong ones, the great dancers, the lords of the powers of air. Their strength was tightly leashed. First Riders rode them—and the Master himself, because Kerrec could not be there.

Until now there had been no music but the air's own singing and the soft thudding of hooves in the sand. As the Great Ones came out, a drum began to beat in a slow, pulsing rhythm.

That rhythm was the beat of a stallion's heart. Valeria found herself breathing in time with it. The circle of stallions opened to admit the great dancers, then closed again, cantering in slow cadence around and around. Inside the circle, the Great Ones came to a halt, each at a quarter of the circle, north and south and east and west, earth and water and fire and air.

For a long moment they stood still. Then they began to dance.

Great haunches lowered. Heavy necks arched and raised. One of them snorted softly. As if that had been a signal, they each began the piaffe, which the untutored would call a trot in place, but it was much more potent than that.

Each deliberate step called up power. The earth below, the air above, came together in those gleaming bodies. They were living fire, supple as water. With each step, their haunches sank deeper and their necks rose higher, and they came closer to taking flight.

At the moment when the great dancers left the ground, the Dance would poise at the crux. Then it could be altered. Then the tides of time would turn, and a mortal hand could shift them toward a new course.

The first stallion quickened his pace. The muscles of his back and haunches rippled, gathering for the leap.

In the instant before he went airborne, the blow fell. The Unmaking roared in from without. Inside the Hall, Gothard unveiled the master stone and raised it above his head. Its core was darkness visible.

The wards of the Hall screamed. The earth shook. Darkness swirled around the sun. The walls of time shivered and cracked. The stallions went mad.

The Hall itself fought against chaos. A net of wards held the stones together and shielded the people against the raw chaos that had erupted around them.

In those wards were traps. They snapped shut around Gothard, Euan and a circle of men scattered around the Hall, mages all, either of stones or of the Unmaking. At the same instant, mages of the imperial orders rose up, calling together what power they had and feeding it into the wards.

Gothard laughed. He had made no move to escape. The master stone began to hum.

The more strongly the wards focused on it, the more the stone absorbed their power. Already their edges were fraying, the outer reaches weakening. The Unmaking waited beyond. When the wards were gone and the makers of the wards consumed, it would rule.

The emperor sagged on his throne. His daughter's face was white. She looked as if she could not move at all. All the strands of the wards came into her hands, and all her power was focused on them.

Valeria could not see Kerrec. The emperor and his heir were caught in sunlight, but everything around them was dark.

The Dance was broken. White shapes whirled out of control. Riders had fallen or clung helplessly to their maddened stallions.

And yet they still, however wild, kept to the shape of a circle. The four great dancers were still in their places, riderless, rearing and clawing air, but their hind feet had not left the ground.

In the center of the circle, darkness gathered. Its heart was a point of light.

That light was all the hope there was. People were stampeding, screaming, dying—falling down stairs and crushed against barred doors. Mage fought mage across the galleries. Bolts of power fell on the innocent or the hapless, and wounded or destroyed them.

Valeria turned her body and mind away from chaos and focused on the pinpoint of light. Suddenly it bloomed.

Sabata stood in the center of the circle. As he raised his head, his eye caught and held her. His nostrils fluttered, calling to her as a mare calls to her foal.

Even if Valeria had wanted to resist, she could not. She left Gothard gleefully destroying his family's magic, and Euan laying himself wide open to the Unmaking, which he called the One God.

There was a low wall between the colonnade and the arena. The wall was warded. Neither stone nor magic resisted her. She set foot on the sand.

She had expected to stagger with the power coming up from below, but it was no worse here than in the colonnade. The circle of stallions spun, a deadly whirl of hooves and teeth. She saw a pattern in it, and a gap. It was narrow and closing fast.

She darted between two heavy, maddened bodies. There was a body on the sand, human, crumpled and still.

Sabata was calling. Valeria moved past the fallen rider, unable to pause or discover who it was. The four great dancers loomed in front of her. She met a wild dark eye, and found nothing there that would yield to mortal persuasion.

The stallion reared up over her like a white wave, battering with hooves. She ducked just a little too slow. The blow caught her arm below the shoulder and sent her sprawling.

The pain was dim and far away. Much nearer was the massive weight crashing down on her, and the madness of chaos in it.

Sabata screamed. The sound ripped the darkness into shreds.

The lesser stallion was gone. Valeria rolled onto her back. Her right arm would not do what she told it to. Delicately Sabata took her left sleeve in his teeth and tugged.

She got up. Sabata was not giving her a choice. He dropped to one knee. She slid her leg over his back, and he stood upright.

The pain in her arm nearly turned her inside out. It was broken—the same one, in almost the same place, that she had broken when she tried to touch her mother's green bowl. She could appreciate the irony of that, here at the end of everything, with the world whirling away like a handful of leaves.

She still had one arm that worked. She wound her fingers in Sabata's mane and sat as straight as she could. He pawed the sand lightly.

Nothing in the Hall had changed. No one even seemed to have noticed that a trespasser had walked on the sacred sand, or that there were thirteen stallions instead of twelve.

Valeria drew a deep breath. An instant later, Sabata did the same. He was waiting for her to come out of her daze and do what she had been born to do.

"Blasted gods," she muttered. Naturally he would not explain. She was supposed to know.

The stallions were turning on one another. Valeria did the one thing she could think of, which was to reach out with her magic and take hold of each one.

She never reflected that it was not possible, because obviously it was. Each stallion was like a different thread on a loom. It was an odd image for a rider, but she was a woman. She knew how to thread a loom, and how to weave a pattern of many colors.

There were thirteen colors here. Sabata's was the brightest, but they were all beautiful, once she had coaxed them free of the darkness that was trying to swallow them. One by one she wove them into a net, a barrier against the Unmaking.

One by one they renewed the Dance. They were all riderless now, all looking to her, finding the pattern in her, the steps of the Dance as it must be danced in this age of the world. Eight of them cantered their circle, perfectly in unison. Four took places again at the corners of the turning world. Sabata in the center began the cadenced gait, beat and beat and beat, that drew up power from the heart of all that was.

With only the slightest breath of warning, he sat on

his haunches and leaped. Four times he leaped, then four again, while Valeria clung blindly, too shocked even to pray.

That was only the beginning. He came down lightly, snorting and tossing his mane. Then, having drawn all power to himself, he danced.

Chapter Forty-Six

Kerrec wanted to die. It was a rational decision, made with deliberate care. He could not be a rider. He could not join in the Dance. Therefore, he preferred to be dead.

There was a minute amount of satisfaction in appearing before the court and the enemies who had wanted him dead, in the one place where none of them had expected to see him, but that satisfaction faded fast.

He felt Gothard slip through gaps in the net of wards and establish himself in the Hall, smooth and subtly vicious as a knife slipping through ribs. There was nothing Kerrec could do about it, but some remnant of inborn idiocy compelled him to try. Even as the stallions came into the Hall, he slipped out of the royal box.

Although he could not see the Dance begin, as he made his way along passages and down stairs he could feel it. It was as close as the blood in his veins, and as distinct as the ache of old bruises and half-healed wounds.

The pattern was there inside him, close and clear as the whorls of his fingertips. It had not left him when he yielded to his sister's persuasion. He knew every step as the stallions danced it, and he knew when Gothard's allies unleashed the Unmaking. They were just a moment too quick, their control just a fraction too weak.

By then he was down on the lowest level, working his way through the mass of bodies in the colonnade. When the attack came, he had just enough time to flatten himself against a pillar.

He rode out the heaving of the earth. When time frayed, he held on—even coming face-to-face with his younger self, a remarkably callow and haughty child rocked by the force of the Call and pulled inexorably toward the Mountain. Somehow, in those wide and startled eyes, he found the will to continue.

People were trampling one another, screaming wordlessly. They were all mad, even the stallions in the arena.

Madness was a gift of the One, the barbarians said. Kerrec, who was already mad, felt no change in his sanity or lack thereof. His mind was perfectly clear. He saw the mages battling around the hall. He also saw the one place where no battle was.

Gothard was in it, side by side with Euan Rohe. The master stone was still drawing in power, binding itself to the Unmaking.

The Dance was in ruins. The stallions had forgotten themselves. The pattern was lost to them, but Kerrec still had it. It was whole in him, perfect and pure.

Just as he moved away from the pillar, the heart of the Dance gave birth to a Great One. Sabata stood in the center of chaos, with his young dappled coat and his wild eye.

And *she* came.

Kerrec never remembered what he did just after that. When he was conscious again, he had gone the length of the colonnade, somehow passed Gothard without killing or being killed, and come to a halt under the Augurs' gallery. The Dance was restoring itself. *She* was controlling it. All the stallions were in her power.

All of them. Every one. The pattern was taking shape again. She spun it out of herself and took it into herself with such beauty and effortless ease that even through the fire of his hatred, he stood in awe.

The Unmaking was as strong as ever. The barbarian priests had sung it into the world, and Gothard's stone was keeping it there. Now, as Kerrec watched, the stone turned that force of not-being against the new-formed Dance, and against the lone power that ruled it.

Twelve horse mages had not been strong enough

to stand against the master stone. One more-than-mage almost was, but only almost. She was still mortal, and the god to whom she was bound was young to this world. One of the stallions in the outer circle faltered, losing the exactness of the rhythm. His misstep fouled the stallion behind him. The circle began to crumble.

No single magic was strong enough to overcome the stone, and no weapon could destroy it. Kerrec did the only thing he could think of, which was to slip the buckle from his belt and weigh it in his hand. It was a heavy thing, a disk of bronze plated with gold, almost exactly the size and weight of the master stone.

He had skipped stones across water in the harbor when he was a child. So had Gothard. Even then the younger brother had had a gift for making stones do what he told them, but Kerrec had won the game as often as not. He never resorted to magic, but he had a knack, a quickness of hand and eye.

Maybe he still had it. The buckle fit comfortably in his palm. The air, roiled by the currents of magic that filled the Hall, had grown thick and almost as fluid as water.

The buckle skimmed those currents, skipping two, three, four, six, eight times. On the eighth leap, it struck the master stone full on and sent it flying out of Gothard's hand.

Kerrec dived after it. Gothard, stunned and empty-handed, could not move at all—but not so Euan Rohe. He lunged toward Kerrec.

Kerrec had just enough warning to throw himself to the side. Euan skidded and went down. Kerrec hurdled him, ducked and rolled, and fell on the stone.

What wards he had were in tatters. The stone's magic burned like acid. He set his teeth against it, ripped off his coat in a spray of golden buttons, and flung it over the stone. He scrambled it up in a bundle, lurching to his feet as both Euan and Gothard sprang at him.

He leaped for the only safety he could see, which was the floor of the Dance. It was beyond foolish, but at the moment he knew only one thing. Neither the mage nor the barbarian could penetrate the last and strongest wall of wards, the one that protected the arena.

Kerrec barely felt them. He was a rider—he belonged there. The stone, which did not, had gone quiescent in its wrappings.

The Dance had found its beauty again, with a purity that he had never seen before. One mind ruled it, and one power shaped it.

He did not want to find beauty there. Not coming out of her. And yet he was too honest to deny it. There was a crystalline perfection to it, a shimmering symmetry.

The gates of time were opening. There were eight times eight, and eight again, each a facet of what was now and what could be.

Whiteness gleamed in front of Kerrec. Where Petra had come from and how he had got there, Kerrec might never know.

He pulled himself gratefully onto that familiar back. When he looked up, he realized that Petra was standing directly below the royal box. Briana was still in it, still struggling to hold together what was left of the wards. He could not sense his father at all.

The gates of the Hall groaned. People were battering on them from without as well as within. They would not hold much longer.

The stone stirred in its wrappings. Kerrec was desperate, or he would never have done what he did. He seized on its power and made of it a healing spell, a spell of calm and of spreading peace. The Unmaking sucked at it, but the stone could turn even that to its use.

Slowly the Hall quieted. The tumult at the doors had muted. There was a battle beyond, but either the emperor's guards were driving back the barbarians, or Kerrec's borrowed spell was stronger than he had reckoned.

The circle of stallions slowed to a halt. The four great dancers stood motionless. Only Sabata still danced. He wound around and through the great dancers, transcribing an interlacing of circles like the intricate knots of Eriu. Where each circle met, a gate glimmered into existence.

There were the futures, one by one. In some, the empire continued as it did now. The emperor went to war, and won as he had before. But those were all too few. In most, either the barbarians broke down the Hall's gate and overwhelmed the Dance, or the Dance escaped but the emperor died, or the emperor survived this day but died later—of the *akasha,* of an assassin's knife, of an enemy's weapon in battle.

And yet it was not as simple as choosing one of the futures in which he lived. Maybe the emperor should not live at all. Maybe the empire only survived if he died.

Kerrec could see all the gates with bitter clarity, but he could not act. Petra stood rooted. All the power was in the hands of one solitary girl. The Mountain had rejected her. The empire's enemies had offered her great rewards to choose the path that most favored them.

Her face was serene. She might have been practicing figures in the riding court in the school, transcribing each exactly, with no expression except a small frown of concentration. Sabata, untrained colt though he was, carried her with ease and grace. He was a god, and in this place he did not suffer the constraints of earthly flesh.

Gradually the pattern of circles carried her closer to Kerrec. At the outermost of them, she looked up into his face and smiled. It was a devastatingly sweet smile. Her eyes were clear, as if her heart were at ease.

Hatred was a simple thing when Kerrec was apart from her. In her presence, he could barely cling to it. She was still Valeria, still her inimitable self.

All the gates were open. The tide of Unmaking was

rising. Once again the void gaped to swallow the sun. Barbarians beat on the gates. Every sign, every portent gathered, poised to fall in a cloud of ill omen.

The sun still shone on Valeria. The ring of stallions around her glowed like the moon. She turned her face to the flood of light. Her eyes were open wide. Kerrec saw the effort it cost her to fill herself with so much power, but she never faltered.

Sabata wheeled, and the gates wheeled with him. One by one they fell away, sinking like stones in a turbulent sea.

Valeria was losing her grip. Her face lost its deep calm. Tears ran down her cheeks.

As the Unmaking loomed closer, Kerrec made a choice. Once more he uncovered the master stone. Once again he focused his power through it, aiming it toward Valeria, pouring it into her.

Two gates remained, two possible destinies out of all that there had been. In one, hordes of barbarians swarmed over the empire. In the other, the empire stood, beleaguered but intact, and for a while— however brief a time that might be—held back the onslaught.

Kerrec could not choose. No one could, except Valeria. She hovered exactly in the middle. Even the Unmaking held back, as if the priests behind it understood that any move, any breath of compulsion, might sway her against them.

She lowered her eyes from the sun to a lesser light,

one that shone from the gallery above Kerrec's head. He felt the power that woke there. It was not Briana's. It flared like embers in a banked fire, then roared into flame.

The emperor's power had come back in full force, bound to the Dance, awakened and healed by it. Kerrec saw him reflected in Valeria's eyes, upright and still as an icon in a temple.

It was still her choice. She was still stronger. She could choose—to destroy the emperor, or surrender the Dance to him.

Once more she met Kerrec's stare. What he saw there made him reel.

Chapter Forty-Seven

Everything had stopped. Even the gates of time were still. Valeria was full of sunlight, overflowing with it, but it had not blinded her. She could still see.

She looked up into the emperor's face, which was more than ever like his son's. His hair was tousled, and there was a bruise on his cheekbone where he must have fallen during the attack on the Hall's wards.

He stared gravely down. He was brimming over with magic, humming and singing with it, but he was perfectly in control of himself. She would have given her good arm to be as calm as he was.

The Unmaking pressed on her, twisting her, sucking away at the power she had gathered. Time mattered nothing to it. Magic was the fuel that fed it. It willed her to turn toward the empire's destruction, and open that gate and let the tides of time run toward the end of everything.

The emperor's face kept her in the world. She would not call him a kindly man, any more than Kerrec was, but he had the gift of understanding. He could see what was in her and what it was doing to her. He laid no compulsion on her, but even more than that, he did not burden her with guilt. Just like the stallions, he set her free to do what she must.

She tried to raise her hands to him. One would not move. The other shook abominably. She folded it to her breast in a sort of salute, and bowed her head in respect.

Sabata turned under her. She had not asked, but it was not against her will. The gates had come alive again. The gate of the Unmaking pulled at her. The other did nothing. It simply was.

She chose simplicity. The Unmaking roared, reaching to suck her down. She clung to Sabata's neck. Even he was buffeted in that fury, but step by step he walked toward the gate she had chosen.

The Unmaking swirled toward it, gaping to swallow it. Valeria had very little magic left to wield. What there was, she scraped together as best she could. She could feel the emperor's will behind her, firm as a hand on her back, and two others coming almost in the same instant.

Kerrec she would always know. The other was his sister. With them, she was strong enough—just. She guided Sabata into the conjunction of circles that was the gate. The Unmaking screamed. She could feel her edges fraying, and the bonds of her body and soul letting go.

It would not matter if she died. Sabata was immortal. He had only to reach the center of the gate and secure it with the power of his presence.

She held on as tightly as she could. Four more steps. Three. Two. She could no longer see. Everything was lost in a storm of darkness. Only Sabata was still real. She buried her face in the coarse silk of his mane and left it to him to make that last step. He advanced steadily, then stepped into infinity.

The Hall was absolutely silent. The sun was shining, clear and bright and blissfully ordinary. Sabata stood in the trampled sand, surrounded by riderless stallions.

Valeria's arm hurt like fury. It had not taken kindly to all the riding and leaping and struggling.

The pain was as beautifully mortal as the sunlight. It told her that she was alive, and that the Dance was over. The Unmaking was still inside her, but it had sunk deep.

The empire would go on for a while longer. The emperor was alive, and his magic was whole. The Dance had restored it. As she lifted her eyes to him once more, she saw the power in him, not just his own, sole and mortal strength, but the strength of the empire. She had done that when she opened the gate that gave him his life and his war and, if not an assured victory, at least no assurance of defeat.

People were stirring, coming to themselves. Some of the fallen riders had begun to regain consciousness. The battle outside seemed to have moved away from the doors.

She was not going to indulge in a fainting fit. Not this time. Sabata was still carrying her easily, which was a good thing. She did not think she could walk.

The rest of the stallions had drawn in close. They were still inside her, still part of her. Whatever was going to happen next, it would come through them before it touched her.

Petra had joined them, but Kerrec was gone. The imperial gallery was empty. People were running out on the sand toward the fallen riders. She recognized Batu and Iliya and Paulus. They veered wide around the circle of stallions, eyes averted as if they were afraid.

Valeria exchanged glances with Petra. He brushed his shoulder lightly past that of the stallion beside him. They unwound in a skein, with Sabata in the middle, pacing out of the Hall as they had come in. The warded passage opened for them but for no one else who might have tried to follow.

Kerrec had left his father and sister to make order in the Hall, and gone hunting Gothard. He still had the master stone, but it proved worthless for leading him to its recent wielder. Where Gothard had been, Kerrec found no trace, not even the scent of magic fading fast.

Outside of the palace square, the city was surprisingly quiet. The battle was still raging in front of the Hall when he slipped through, but the streets beyond had emptied of crowds. The people of Aurelia, wise to the ways of magic, had shut themselves in their houses. Pilgrims and travelers had either fled or found sanctuary. He could hear them in the temples, raising chants of supplication to the various gods, and in the taverns, worshipping an earthier divinity.

Gothard's house was deserted. Even the wards were gone. The walls had a worn look, as if the stones had begun to crumble. All the magic was drained out of them.

Kerrec halted in the inner court. He had been building a beautiful fire of rage, to be quenched by his brother's blood. This empty place left him feeling cold and strange.

If there was a trail to follow, he lacked the power to find it. Gothard, clever to the last, had left himself a bolt hole, but he had been extremely careful to cover his tracks.

Kerrec searched the house from roof to dungeon and found nothing. He came up into the light again and stood for a long while, struggling for control.

Somehow, deep inside himself, he found it. He gathered all of it together and blasted the wall of the inner court.

The stones puffed into dust. The wall slid down like water. The inner rooms of the house lay bare, empty and forsaken.

He turned on his heel. This was conduct unbecoming a First Rider, but he could not make himself care. He left that place behind, with all its memories and its empty spaces.

Valeria supposed she was forgotten. There were riders down, people trampled, a battle in the square and still some sort of festival to salvage if possible. How much any of them had seen of what she did, or if any but Kerrec and his family had understood, she could not guess.

She was feeling rather ill. The stallions had taken her to their stable, where she had drunk from the water barrel with the rest of them, then unsaddled each one and rubbed him as clean as she could. It was not easy, one-handed, but she did it.

If she had been truly dutiful, she would have cleaned the saddles and bridles, but by the time she had made sure each stallion had a manger full of hay and a full water barrel, she had to sit down. Her sight kept narrowing and trying to go dark. Without any particular reason, only the desire to be somewhere safe, she made her way to Sabata's stall and propped herself against his manger. He sidled toward her until her good arm was over his back.

She should find a healer priest to do something about her other arm. She could no longer feel it. Pain had meaning, her mother had taught her. If it stopped before a wound was treated, that was not a good thing.

She would go out soon and go in search of a healer. There must be one nearby. She would go out in a moment. Yes.

Euan Rohe knew in his gut what would happen, once he saw the First Rider sitting in the royal box. When the Dance came to the crucial point, he had only half a hope that Valeria would choose the One over the emperor. He was not at all surprised that she preferred to stay an imperial. She was a legionary's daughter, after all. It was in her blood.

He was already moving, making for an exit that he hoped no one else would remember. It led not outward to the square but inward to the palace.

The hours he had spent in the library at the House of War were bearing fruit. He had in his memory a fair-to-middling accurate map of the palace, with certain passages marked that were not on the usual maps. If he could get out fast enough, he reckoned that he should be able to round up his warband and escape before the emperor's troops moved in.

* * *

He was doing well until he ducked down a corridor to avoid a rattling, clashing company of imperial guards, then found himself trapped between the sound of the guards' coming and a pair of servants idling in a doorway. His only choice then was to go down instead of up. There was another passage that way, marked on the old map with an odd symbol that he had not been able to decipher. He could not remember exactly where it led, but he thought—hoped—that it would get him out of the palace.

Not long after that, he knew he was lost. The passage had branched, then branched again. He had to guess which way to go. One grey stone tunnel was very like another. Some were well lit, others less so. Sometimes there were doors, but none of them seemed to be locked. The one that was, the lock fell apart when he touched it.

That was too strange for comfort, but by then he had gone too far and become too confused to turn back. He had to go on. If he was being led into a trap, so be it.

Rather abruptly, the passage narrowed. The lamps that had been lit all along it were gone. By the light of the last one, he could just see a ladder of metal rungs going up a blank wall.

He went up the ladder. The distance was hard to judge in the dark, but he counted rungs and reckoned them against his body, and it came to six times his own height before his head struck the ceiling.

He clung to the ladder, dizzy with the shock of the blow. Gradually it dawned on him that the ceiling above him had rung hollow. He groped along it, cursing as a splinter stabbed his finger, and found the metal studs that bound the wooden door. After two passes, then a third, he got a grip on a ring. He breathed a prayer to the One and thrust against it.

The trapdoor crashed to the floor in a room that was dazzlingly bright after the pitch darkness below. Its purpose was obvious. Racks of saddles lined one of the walls, with bridles hanging from pegs above them. Along the wall opposite the saddles was a row of wooden bins. There were stools and benches and one ancient, badly sprung chair.

The smell of horses pervaded the place, along with the smell of dust and age. Light streamed in through high windows. He saw sky, clear and blue and impossibly far away.

Euan coughed and swallowed a sneeze. His head was still aching where it had struck the trapdoor. There was a knot on his skull, but the skin had held. There was no blood.

Only one door led out of the room, a heavy wooden panel between the rows of saddles. He gathered his mantle around him and trod softly toward it. He could hear horses breathing outside, and their heavy bodies moving about. There were no human voices.

He opened the door carefully, with his senses at full alert. The stable was dimmer than the room he had left, but still bright enough for comfort. Horses stared at him over stall doors.

They were all greys. He took in those arched noses and those excessively intelligent dark eyes, and began to laugh.

Once he had started, he could not stop. The One had no sense of humor, but the gods of the empire rather too obviously did. They had brought him straight into their own stable, where no doubt he would be judged as he deserved. "I hope," he said to them, "that you don't mutilate me too badly. Make sure my father can recognize my head when your servants send it to him."

The stallions regarded him blandly, as if they were no more than mortal horses. Only one of them moved, a young one, still dappled. He tossed his head and pawed the door of his stall.

The sound was deafening. Euan tensed to bolt, but no troop of legionaries came charging down the aisle.

Slowly his heart stopped hammering. None of the stallions offered a threat, even the noisy one. He made his way carefully down the aisle toward the door at the far end.

As he passed the young stallion, a human head appeared beside the horse's. Valeria seemed even more startled to see him than he was to see her. "What in the world—" she began.

"By the One!" Euan said at the same moment. "What are you doing *here*?"

"I should ask you that," she said. "How did you get in here? What—"

While she spoke, his mind was racing. Here might be his key to escape. At the very least, she was a hostage. The imperials might not know what to do with her when she was Called to the Mountain, but the mage who had saved the Dance was a valuable commodity.

There was, however, the matter of her bodyguards, of whom he counted seventeen. Every one had a bright eye fixed on her, and none more intently than the stallion beside her.

He decided to tell her the truth, or part of it. "I found a way out of the Hall," he said, "and followed it until it led me here."

"You can't stay," she said. "They'll be scouring the city for you—and if they catch you, they'll kill you."

"Or worse," he said. He edged toward her. The stallion flattened his ears and showed him a double row of strong white teeth. Euan stopped. "What will you do? Set your stallions on me?"

Her eyes narrowed. "I should, shouldn't I?" she said.

Euan began to move again, cautiously. This time the stallion merely watched. Euan could see Valeria's hand on his neck, fingers woven in his mane. She looked tired, he thought.

If he stopped to fuss over her, he was dead. As long as he stayed moving, he had a chance. Each step brought him closer to the door. Then there was the riders' house to get through, then the city, then a vast swath of the empire, but he would worry about that when he came to it. First he had to get out of this place.

One move, one word from her and it would be all over. She stood without moving, watching and saying nothing.

The closer he came to her, the more powerful was the temptation to stop. At last, directly in front of her, he gave in. "Come with me," he said.

Did she hesitate for the slightest fraction of an instant? Maybe. Or maybe he was deluding himself. Her face was never easy to read, but at the moment it was an ivory mask. She shook her head. "I can't come with you," she said.

He sighed faintly. "I didn't think so," he said. "Too bad. Here you are, all alone. No one even remembers what you did."

"What I did," she said, "was break my word to you and take away your victory."

"I'll forgive you someday," he said. "Are you sure you want to stay? I might not be able to offer you much but a long run and a slow death, but I'll never leave you to fend for yourself. We'll run and die together."

Her fingers tightened in the stallion's mane. Euan almost smiled. It was not as easy for her to refuse as it might have been. He could almost have sworn that he saw regret in her eyes. "We both know where I belong," she said. Then after a pause, "You'd better go.

They've started killing anyone with a barbarian face. You'd do well to cover yours until you're a long way out of the city."

He hardly needed to ask her how she knew. She was a mage, and she was surrounded by gods. She was also right. The longer he delayed, the less likely he was to get out alive.

He dared one last, mad thing before he dived for the door. He ducked in past the stallion's head and stole as long a kiss as he dared. It was never long enough. She was barely beginning to respond when he darted back, just ahead of the stallion's lunge.

There was no more time to lose. He covered his face as best he could and ran.

Chapter Forty-Eight

Valeria sagged against Sabata's shoulder. She had just done a terrible thing. Even while she let Euan Rohe go, she knew what it would mean. It was a long way from Aurelia to the hunting runs of the Caletanni. He could still die. But if he did not, if he did escape, she had released an enemy who would never rest until the empire was gone.

This time she did not even have an excuse. No one but Euan would die if she stopped him now. She made no move to do that. The memory of his kiss burned and would not go away.

Because of her, the Dance was saved. Because of her, the empire might still be destroyed.

One word and the stallions would go after him. He would be dead, and Aurelia would be safe.

She never said that word. She felt the tides of time shifting as he went, patterns falling into place that would shape the years ahead. She saw where they could lead and what they could do, and she did nothing. The only thought in her, at the last, was that if he died, the grief would be too much to bear.

Kerrec found her sitting among the neatly stowed, if less than perfectly clean, saddles. Her eyes were open, and they seemed to recognize him. Her face was the color of cheese.

He reached to haul her to her feet and shake Gothard's whereabouts out of her, but even before he touched her, he could feel the wrongness in her body. Her right arm hung at an angle that knotted his stomach. Her fingers were swollen and the tips were blue. When he took them in his hands they were cold.

Through the levels of his rage, he understood a number of things. She was alone here. The stallions had been groomed, fed and shut in stalls. Their saddles and bridles were put away. She must have done all of that after salvaging the Dance and, perhaps incidentally, the empire.

It was impossible to hate her. With a sound that was half a groan and half a sigh, he lifted her in his arms.

She tried to fight him off. "You're always doing that," she said. "You need to stop."

"Yes," he said brusquely. "I do."

He firmed his grip on her. She had stopped struggling. Her breath was coming hard. If she had been anyone else she would have been in tears, but she was Valeria. Her eyes were dry.

He carried her to his sister's rooms. It was not very far to go through the riders' passage, and there was no crush of people to face, which mattered a great deal just then.

Briana's servants asked no questions. They brought food, drink, a bath, and a healer, in that order and without comment. If they recognized Valeria, they said nothing.

She had no appetite for the meal they brought, but Kerrec coaxed half a cupful of honeyed milk into her. He was ravenous himself, amazingly so. While the healer priest clucked over her, Kerrec worked his way steadily through the tray that the servants had brought.

Well before the priest was done, Valeria had fallen asleep. He splinted and set the arm and did this and that with the rest of her, finishing with a blessing that made her stir and murmur in her sleep.

The priest frowned at that, but when he spoke, it was to say, "She'll sleep until morning. Be sure she's kept quiet for a day or two. I'll leave certain preparations with the servants, who can see that she takes them. As for you, my lord—"

"There's nothing wrong with me," Kerrec said a little too quickly.

The priest arched a brow. "Certainly there is not,

my lord, but the healing spell she's set in you is draining her more than she can easily manage just now. You can't give it back, she's woven it too well, but you can weave one in return. It's simple enough. You have only to—"

Kerrec's wits had grown horribly slow. The priest had gone on at some length before Kerrec understood what he had said. "Healing spell? *She* set a healing spell?"

"She did indeed," the priest said, "and a very nicely crafted one it is, too. Someone taught her well."

Kerrec scowled. "Are you sure? She's not—this isn't—"

"Oh," said the priest, "I can see it's not the greatest of her gifts. Am I seeing clearly? Is she a horse mage?" He did not wait for Kerrec to answer. "Remarkable. Most remarkable. I've never seen anything like it."

"No one has," Kerrec said.

"I can imagine," said the priest. He bowed to Kerrec, then bowed lower to the sleeping Valeria. "It's been an honor, my lord. I'll come back tomorrow and see that she's mending as she should. She's a great treasure, a great treasure for the empire."

He left none too soon, having said a great deal more than enough. Kerrec had much to ponder, little of which was welcome and less of which was comforting. He had been living with sureties, building his world on them, and now they were all shaken to bits.

He could not stay there, staring at Valeria, not knowing whether to worship her or strangle her. He prowled restlessly out of Briana's rooms and back toward the riders' house, where he should have been long since. He was still First Rider, until or unless he was removed from that office.

Of the four First Riders, only Kerrec survived. Three of the eight riders of the Dance were dead, and the rest were unconscious under the care of healer priests.

Master Nikos was both alive and conscious. When Kerrec came into the room in which he had been laid, he tried to rise. The healer attending him held him down, but he was not to be subdued until Kerrec stood beside him. "Kerrec! Thank the gods. Without you, we'd not only be dead, we'd be food for barbarian dogs."

"It wasn't I who saved the Dance," Kerrec said. It was less difficult to say than he had expected.

Nikos frowned. He was haggard and his power was running at a low ebb, but his mind seemed clear. "I saw you," he said.

"You should have looked behind you," said Kerrec.

Nikos' stare was blank.

"Sabata," Kerrec said, "and Valeria."

There. He had said her name, and it had not choked him.

Nikos' frown darkened. He must be searching his memory, making sense of fragments. There was a pattern there, and he of all mages had the gift to see it.

It seemed he found it. It did not lighten his mood at all. "She saved the Dance. She—did I dream it? All the stallions—did she—"

"She mastered them all," Kerrec said with a kind of bitter pride.

"That is theoretically possible," said Nikos, "but in practice—" He broke off. At first Kerrec thought that he was coughing, but it was laughter.

That was alarming. "Master," Kerrec began.

The healer was not reassured, either. Nikos waved them both off. "Stop it. Stop fussing. I was taught, and I have taught, that the gods have no patience with human pretensions, but until now I never honestly knew what that meant. They Called her. Of course they had their reasons—which beyond a doubt included this."

"Beyond a doubt," Kerrec said.

"Was it as glorious as I remember? Was she—"

He did not finish. Kerrec could have waited, and so avoided answering, but he could not help himself. "She was," he said.

Nikos sighed and closed his eyes. The healer leaped to his rescue, but he was in no worse state than he had been before. Still with his eyes shut, he said, "We should worship her. Or kill her."

"My thoughts exactly."

Nikos fixed Kerrec with a keen stare. As haggard and worn as he was, he still had his strength of will. "Where is she? Is she alive?"

"She's in my sister's rooms," Kerrec answered, "under the servants' care."

"Ah," Nikos said, a long sigh. "Good. She'll stay there until we can deal with her. We will have to. You understand that."

"I understand," said Kerrec.

"We owe her a great debt," Nikos said. "Whether she can be one of us…I don't know."

Kerrec opened his mouth, but shut it again. Now was not the time to argue about it, even without the healer priest about to fall down in a fit. He wanted—needed desperately—to finish his work. Kerrec left him to it.

Valeria was still asleep. There were other places Kerrec could and probably should be, but he had not been able to stop himself from going back to her.

He slept for a while himself in a chair beside the bed, lightly, starting awake when the servants came in at evening to light the lamps, then dozing again as the darkness deepened. His sleep was full of dim dreams and formless confusion. He could feel the city in his skin as he had while he was still the emperor's heir.

People were fighting, rioting, looting and burning. His father's troops fought hard to restore order. They had no time for either subtlety or mercy. Any barbarian they caught, they killed. By midnight the palace walls hung thick with grisly fruit, bodies hung from hooks and heads on pikes. Some of the bodies still moved. Blood soaked the paving below.

Sometime between daylight and deep night, mages hunted down the priests of the One. In his dream Kerrec watched as, one by one, they were captured and flayed alive and hung to die.

None of the mages was Gothard, and none of the barbarians was Euan Rohe. Those two had vanished from the city.

He started awake. Valeria had not moved since he last looked, but her eyes were open. "My arm doesn't hurt," she said.

"That's good," he said. It was not the most graceful thing to say, but he was not graceful when it came to her. He had been hating her so thoroughly, then she had proved him so completely wrong, that he hardly knew what to think.

"You brought me here," she said. "It's your sister's room, isn't it?"

"One of them," he said. "It has the advantage of being quiet, well defended and safe from the clamor of crowds."

"No one's crowding to see me," she said.

He heard no bitterness in her tone. "You don't think so?" he asked.

"I know so," she said. "They're all busy keeping the empire from falling apart. Most of them don't even know how the Dance ended the way it did. The white gods did it, they think, and that's true. I was only a part of the working."

"The most important part," he said.

She shrugged, which made her wince. "You're not out there. Why?"

His shrug was considerably less painful. "I owe you an apology," he said.

That widened her eyes. "What for?"

"For doubting you. For believing you were going to betray us all."

"How—"

"I heard," he said, "before you tried to send me to the Mountain."

"You heard—"

He watched her remember. Her face went stiff. "Gods. You saw—"

"Yes."

"You must hate me."

"I did," he said.

She sat up. Her lips were white.

Kerrec found himself beside her with no memory of how he had got there. His arm was around her, and he was taking away what pain he could, with what magic he had. He had a surprising amount.

"I think I understand," he said, as much to convince himself as Valeria. "You were taken captive, he was there, you did and said what you had to in order to survive. I didn't do even as well."

"You did better," she said with sudden fierceness. "You never betrayed what you believed in."

"Didn't I?" Somehow he had drawn her into his arms. She made no effort to fight him off.

He should not be doing this. He was the only First Rider left. It was not fitting that he should be here, cradling her as a man cradles his lover.

At the moment he could not seem to make it matter. The memory of Valeria in Euan Rohe's arms was still sharp, but that did not matter, either.

The tension was draining out of her. He thought she might be sliding back into sleep. Her voice came up from the hollow of his shoulder, soft and a little slurred. "I did it for you."

He could find nothing to say to that.

"They were going to kill you," she said. "I made them think I was theirs, to keep you alive. I did it, didn't I? You didn't die."

"I didn't die," he said. "Valeria, I'm not worth—"

She pushed away from him. "You are worth everything! Everything. Damn you for it, too."

"I was damned," he said, "and you made me whole again."

"I didn't do it to put you in debt to me."

"I know," he said.

"I didn't do it to ingratiate myself with the Mountain, either."

"I know," he said again. "Valeria, look at me."

She was reluctant, but he waited until she lifted her eyes and fixed them on his face. "I don't know what will become of us, but one thing I am sure of. I'm going to make you forget that barbarian."

She bit her lip. Gods, was she laughing at him?

"I have no grace with women," he said a little testily, "or with precious little else, either."

"Except horses," she said. "When you're on a horse, you're as beautiful a thing as I've seen."

He glared at her. "Will you let me finish my speech?"

She set her lips together and waited in conspicuous silence.

"I have no grace," he said, "and not much gift with words. I have no talent for making people love me. I'd have made a poor enough emperor, and I'm not much of a lover, either—no pretty words, no sense of what to say or when to say it. All I can give you is the truth. I don't want to live my life without you. I don't know if I can."

"I know I can't," she said, "and you severely underestimate yourself. Which doesn't surprise me, all things considered. Do you think your father is a good emperor?"

"A very good one," Kerrec said, "but what does that have to do with—"

"You're exactly like him."

He bristled. "I am not!"

"Exactly," she said. She stopped his mouth with her hand before he could deny it again, and then she kissed him. It was a soft kiss, and slow, not at all what he might have expected.

She was like that. Just when he thought he could predict what she would do, she did something completely out of his reckoning.

He had been a master of patterns, and maybe would be again, but hers were irresistibly complex. Even if he had it all back, he might never understand her.

Then he stopped thinking. He thought too much, that was his trouble. The taste of her, the touch of her skin, the scent of her hair, filled all the places where words had been.

$$\rtimes\!\!\mid\!\!\circ\!\!\mid\!\!\ltimes$$

Chapter Forty-Nine

Valeria lay with her eyes closed. Somehow, while she paused for a brief rest, the night had passed and the sun had risen. She was warm with the memory of Kerrec's presence, her body still singing faintly. She yawned and stretched and smiled.

He was nowhere in the room, but someone was watching her. Although it was not Kerrec, it felt a great deal like him. She opened her eyes.

The imperial heir was sitting beside the bed. She had a book in her lap, marked with a bit of crimson ribbon, but it was rolled shut. Her eyes were on Valeria. Her brows were drawn together, not exactly in a frown, but more as if she were studying this new thing that she had found in her rooms.

Valeria would not have interrupted her thoughts,

but there was a certain urgent matter that she could not ignore. "Lady," she said.

Briana started out of her reverie.

"Lady," said Valeria, "I suppose it's indelicate, but I have to—"

Briana's brows rose sharply. "Of course you do," she said.

She had the same accent as Kerrec and Paulus, but she sounded more sensible somehow. This was a practical person, who saw the obvious as soon as Valeria drew her attention to it, and offered the logical solution. The chamber pot was not gold as Valeria might have expected, but good earthenware, with a well-fitted lid.

Valeria sat up carefully. Except for a deep ache, her splinted arm was surprisingly comfortable.

Briana politely directed her attention elsewhere while Valeria used the pot. When Valeria was done, Briana took the lidded pot with a complete absence of squeamishness and set it tidily by the door. Almost at once, a hand appeared and the pot vanished.

Valeria found that she was gaping. She shut her mouth. "Now I know I'm in high places," she said.

Briana laughed. "I've heard this called the best inn in Aurelia," she said. "We do take pride in our servants."

"It's better than a posting station," Valeria said. She sat on the bed again, for her knees were not as strong as they might be, and wrapped herself in one of the blankets. "Have you seen your brother this morning?"

Her breath came a little quickly as she waited for the answer. Briana seemed not to notice Valeria's tension. She lifted her hands in a graceful shrug. "Not this morning," she said, "but the servants told me he took breakfast in the kitchens, then went off toward the riders' house."

Of course that was where he had gone. Valeria suppressed a stab of pique that he had done it without her. He must have had his reasons—such as that he wanted to let her sleep, and he needed to speak to Master Nikos alone.

She smiled a little shakily at Briana. "He brought me here. I hope you don't mind."

"Not in the slightest," Briana said. "I'd have been annoyed with him if he hadn't. Not that the riders wouldn't have taken decent care of you, if they happened to notice that you needed it, but I do think you'll be more comfortable here."

"That's what he said," Valeria said.

Briana smiled, a broad, bright smile that transformed her face. It was probably presumptuous, but Valeria found herself liking this person very much. She had no pretensions, and no arrogance, either. She was simply herself.

"You must be ravenous," Briana said, "and you must be wishing you had something to wear as well. I'll send the servants to take care of you. I have to ask your pardon that I can't stay."

Valeria could feel confusion rumbling in the earth

and crackling on her skin. Although the Dance had ended and the tides of time subsided, the aftereffects were strong. The Unmaking had left scars.

"I can help," she said. "Just let me eat and dress, then tell me where to find you."

That was presumptuous, too, she knew as soon as she had said it, but she did not try to take it back.

Briana took no offense, nor did she fly into a fit of protest. "If you're strong enough," she said, "we can use you. If you need more rest or more time to heal—"

"I'm as rested as I can stand to be," Valeria said. "You go. I can feel you're needed. I'll follow as soon as I can."

Briana nodded. With a last, quick smile, she strode swiftly out.

Valeria had just summarily dismissed the heir to the empire. She groaned and fell back on the bed. As a courtier she was a disaster. Gods knew what kind of rider she would make, if the school would even take her back.

At the moment at least she had something to do. Breakfast came before the bath or the clothes. It was all extremely welcome, especially the breakfast. Briana had sent riding clothes, new and beautifully made. They fit well, even the boots. The servant helped Valeria to ease the shirt over her splinted arm, tied up the arm neatly in a sling, and arranged the coat so that the empty sleeve hung straight and tidy.

Clean, fed and moderately resplendent, Valeria approached the door just as a woman in a guard's uniform opened it and bowed. "Her Highness has asked me to escort you to her," the woman said.

Perfect service must be a kind of mage craft, Valeria thought. She nodded to the guard. The woman saluted crisply and turned on her heel.

Valeria had been expecting a room with the princess sitting in it, and people running in and out. She found Briana on her feet with no throne in sight, on a wide porch in front of the palace. The square beyond was not too crowded, thanks to the armed men stationed around the edges.

The same was not true of the portico. Sunlight streamed through columns of veined white marble onto a floor of jeweled tiles in black and white and gold. People thronged there in such a whirl of sound and color that Valeria had to stop and steady herself before she could come out into the light.

It was dizzying, but there were patterns in it. Valeria saw the captain of the city guard and a handful of legionary commanders, each in his glittering panoply, charged with making order in the city and the empire. She saw the mayor and council of the city dressed in silk and gold, lords of this council and that court dressed even more splendidly, mages of the various orders in their different colors and liveries, and priests of every temple in Aurelia, along with a flock of lesser luminaries, secretaries, clerks and chamberlains and gods knew what else.

Their movements were not random. They revolved around Briana and around a man standing near her, whom Valeria recognized as the emperor. He was much less elaborately dressed than the lords who surrounded him—in fact looked ready to take horse and ride. He looked well, which she was glad to see. His magic had all come back, and he was strong. If any of the poison lingered, she could see no sign of it.

People were coming in toward him and his heir, and people were streaming away. There were knots and clusters standing apart, carrying on discussions with varying degrees of heat, but their eyes tended to stray toward the emperor and Briana.

All of them were trying to do two things. First, calm the city and find any lingering traces of the enemy. Second, understand what had happened in the Dance. That it had ended with the emperor's reign confirmed, everyone agreed. But how that had happened, and how it had come about, had them arguing bitterly.

Valeria had meant to keep to the background and use what power she had to make order of chaos, but that was not what this crowd needed. Briana was doing that well enough. So was her father. Just as in the Dance, Valeria saw how they all fit with and against one another. It made a kind of tangled sense, like skeins of wool tossed together in a basket.

She left the sanctuary of the door and started to move through the crowd. At first she thought the clamor was quieting down as such things did, rising and falling in waves. Then, keyed to the patterns as she was, she realized that the wave of silence was riding with her. People were staring, and nudging one another.

Mages did it first, then priests. The rest took it up soon enough. By the time she reached Briana, there was not a sound along the length of the portico, and every eye was on her.

Either she could be miserably uncomfortable or she could pretend that she was riding quadrilles in a court of the school. No one was looking at her, not really. They were all remembering the Dance and the white stallions and a work of magic that none of them, even the mages, understood.

Only Briana saw her for herself. The emperor's heir smiled and held out her hand. "Valeria! Welcome. Have you met my father? Father, this is Valeria."

The emperor bowed over Valeria's hand with a smile as warm as his daughter's. "Welcome, indeed," he said, "and well done. I owe you thanks."

Valeria hardly knew where to look. She mumbled something that she hoped was polite enough.

He tucked her hand under his arm and drew her in between him and his daughter. "Now," he said to the rest of them, "are we going to argue until the year turns back around again, or shall we band together to destroy the barbarians?"

Valeria could feel the forces of dissension. No two of them agreed on what to do or how to do it, but they looked at her, and something made them stop to think.

She spoke into that quiet. "You're all wiser than I— I can't tell you what to do. But I can tell you what I see. You've driven back the attack this time, and it was a bad one, but there's worse coming. Your enemies will go to ground now and wait out the winter, then in the spring they'll be strong again. They'll reckon that they lost a skirmish, but there's still a war to win. The more united you are, the better your chances of weathering the storm."

"We'll win the war," one of the lords said, "won't we? You Danced us a victory."

"The stallions Danced you hope. It's not a promise."

A rumble rose at that. Maybe Valeria should not have told the truth, but she could hardly lie. She looked as many of them in the face as she could. "You are the promise," she said. "It's yours to win or lose. If you fight among yourselves, they'll overwhelm you. If you come together, you have everything in your favor—numbers, weapons, strength of armies. They fight in hordes, you in legions. Man for man and on the field, you can take them." She turned to the knot of priests and mages, who were eyeing her narrowly, measuring her against some standard she knew nothing about. "And you. They used one of your own against the empire—because they have no magic to match what you have. They have something else, something worse, but it's a dangerous weapon, as likely to turn on them as on their enemies. You can undo it, if you will. You can unmake the Unmaking."

"What do you know of the Unmaking?"

The man who asked that question was not hostile. He was an old man, and after a moment she realized that he was an Augur. He was not wearing the formal robes she had seen in the Dance, but a plain gown like a priest's. It was white, and priests always wore brown or black or grey or, if they were high priests, red. White was for Augurs.

The Augur waited patiently for her to answer his question. She thought she might trust him, but in front of so many people, all she dared to say was, "I know more than I want to know."

He nodded. It was almost a bow. "Lady," he said.

"No," she said. "Not a lady. I'm a rider, that's all."

His lips twitched. He bowed lower than before. "Rider," he said.

It was only a word, but it had an odd effect on the people who were watching. There was still a great deal of fear and confusion, but the resistance had gone out of them. It was as if a spell had broken.

One by one, then in twos and fours, they came together again, but this time they were not arguing. They were making decisions and settling on strategies. The city would settle, then the empire—for a while. They all knew what the spring would bring.

Now Valeria could fade into the background. Or so

she would have done, if the emperor and his daughter had not kept her between them, and if a new arrival had not focused attention on her once again.

Master Nikos was haggard and hollow-eyed, but he was steady on his feet. Kerrec walked close enough to offer him an arm if necessary. Paulus and Iliya and Batu followed.

They brought with them the same kind of silence that Valeria had. There was a tinge of awe in it, reverence for the keepers of a mystery.

People only stared at them for a few moments before turning back to Valeria with even more avid curiosity than before. Male riders were almost common. She was unique.

She would have hidden if she could, but there was no hope of that. Briana's arm slipped through Valeria's. It was not a subtle gesture, and it was not meant to be. Whether Valeria liked it or not, she had fallen into high places.

The Master halted in front of Valeria. She knew what it cost him to offer her that inclination of the head. It was all she expected, and all he gave her. He was not there to honor her, or, it seemed, to dishonor her, either.

Kerrec's face was expressionless. She had expected that, too. She was past the time when it would have made her angry. She knew what was behind that mask, and why he wore it. Someday she would teach him that he did not need a mask, that his own face was good enough and strong enough to wear in front of the world.

Briana had no such compunction. "Good day, riders," she said, "and welcome. I'm glad to see you up and about. Have you come to claim this rider of yours? Because, sirs, if you don't mind, we'd like to keep her for a while. It seems she has a talent for making order out of chaos."

"So I have noticed," Master Nikos said. His tone was dry.

"But then," said Briana, "that's part of a rider's power, isn't it? To see patterns. To make sense of them. To shape them if he can. Or, in this case, she."

That was a challenge. She smiled, all sweet innocence, but Valeria could sense the steel beneath.

So, evidently, could Master Nikos. "That is a rider's power," he said coolly. "Ours is at your disposal, if you have need of it."

"We do welcome it," Briana said. This was not over, her manner said, but it seemed she was not about to start a battle in this overly public place.

Valeria went limp with relief. The mood here was too brittle to tolerate any further conflict. People were stirring, twitching like nervous horses. They needed to be soothed and comforted.

She slipped free of her royal allies. Whether it was intentional or not, there was a place for her with the riders, beside Paulus at the end. His glance as she took it was sour, but he made no effort to push her out of it. Neither, and that was more important, did Master Nikos.

A sigh ran across the portico. Tension eased. People saw what they needed to see. The riders were together as they should be. Those who could see patterns were reassured. The rest were less inclined to be at odds with one another.

Chapter Fifty

By tradition, after the Great Dance the empire kept festival for eight days, and the riders stayed for all of it. Then on the ninth day they went back to the Mountain.

The emperor's festival had turned into the aftermath of a battle, but by the second day after the Dance, the city had settled enough to allow a somewhat muted celebration. The emperor proclaimed it from the porch of the palace, with characteristic brevity. "Our enemies have done their best to take our joy away from us. I refuse to give them the pleasure. We'll mourn our dead as they deserve, but for now let us celebrate the living."

Valeria was still Briana's guest. That was the heir's decision, and neither Valeria nor the riders contested it. It put off a little longer the need to confront the inevitable.

The first night after she had stood with the riders on the porch of the palace, Valeria fully expected to sleep alone. She went to bed feeling a little cold and bereft, but telling herself that she was being foolish. The riders needed Kerrec far more than she did.

Just as she sank into a restless doze, she felt a weight on the side of the bed, and heard the slight catch of his breathing as Kerrec stretched out beside her. Without opening her eyes, she slid into the shelter of his arms.

Then she could sleep. As before, he was gone when she woke, but this time she knew why. It was enough for her that he had come at all.

That went on for four nights. She never saw or spoke to him, only felt him beside her shortly before she fell asleep. The days were full. She spent them with Briana, going from council to festival and back to council again, and spending part of each day riding or walking through the city.

It was Sabata who brought matters to a head. On the seventh morning after the Dance, Valeria had just come back from an early walk through the city with Briana. There was a formal breakfast to attend, then a ceremony in the temple of the Moon, and after that a round of councils.

Sabata cared nothing for any such human foolishness. He broke down the gate to Briana's wing of the palace, blew past her guards, and terrorized the servants who were trying to bathe and dress their lady and her guest.

Briana seemed not at all dismayed to find a highly and somewhat dangerously annoyed stallion in her bath. She rose dripping from the basin, wrapped a towel around herself, and bowed to him with deep respect. "My lord," she said.

Valeria had finished bathing and was standing in a shift, waiting for the servants to put on the morning dress that, after days of resistance, she had let herself be bullied into. She was in no way sorry to be rescued, although she glared at Sabata. "That was not necessary," she said.

He tossed his head and stamped. She had been away from him long enough. Her arm was healing and her spirit was healed. It was time to stop this nonsense and go where she was meant to go.

He had never been so clear about what he wanted, or so close to human words. "Where am I meant to go?" she asked him. "The riders don't want me, whereas here I'm welcome. I'm useful—they need me."

The riders need you.

It cost his pride dearly to stoop to words. He swung around, scattering servants and sponges and bowls of soap and herbs and ointment, and presented himself for her to mount.

She opened her mouth to protest, but his eye rolled

at her, glaring a warning. She hiked up her shift and pulled herself one-handed onto his back.

With her weight to carry, he had to move cautiously on the tiled floors. That gave Briana time to throw on the clothes she had taken off to bathe, and run up beside Valeria.

"He's taking me to the riders," Valeria said. "You don't need to—"

"I think I do," said Briana. She was perfectly cheerful and perfectly immovable. As she went, she sent a servant with her regrets to the host, another to put off the rest of her obligations, and yet a third to tell her father where she had gone.

By the time they left her wing of the palace, Sabata was moving more quickly and Briana was trotting doggedly alongside. He kept that pace, Valeria noticed, although he could have gone much faster.

They went down through the riders' passage, avoiding the public ways. Briana said nothing—all her breath was devoted to keeping up with the stallion. Valeria would have dismounted and walked with her, but whenever she tried, Sabata warned her against it with a curve of the neck and a snap of teeth. He was carrying her and that was that.

Between two such manifestly stubborn creatures, all Valeria could do was keep quiet and let herself be taken wherever Sabata had in mind. Matters were coming to a head. Sabata was forcing an issue that the riders as well as Valeria had been avoiding.

Although it was two days yet until their departure, the riders' house already looked half deserted. Boxes and bags waited in the outermost court, piled in the shelter of the colonnade.

Valeria began to wonder if the riders were leaving early. It certainly looked that way.

The innermost court had a most peculiar scent to it. Sabata curled his lip and shook his head as if in disgust. Valeria realized what it was when she saw a shrouded figure gliding across the court.

The riders who had died had not been taken to the embalmers' house as she had thought. They had come here. The smell that pervaded the air was the smell of death, thick and sickly sweet, heavily overlaid with the pungency of spices and the sharp dry scent of natron.

There were six stone vats in the hall beyond the colonnade, and a pair of embalmers attending each. Their faces were shrouded and their tongues mute. Master Nikos knelt beside the rearmost of the vats, which was carved with images of death and rebirth.

Sabata clattered to a halt behind him and pawed imperiously. The dead were gone. The living needed him.

Master Nikos finished his prayer, then rose slowly and turned. His grief was immediate and personal. These had been his students, his masters, his friends. Even the oldest of them should have had years yet to live. This kind of death, like death in battle, was not something a rider would have expected.

It shook Valeria to see so clearly into his heart. He was making no effort to conceal himself from her. For the first time she saw him as a man and not the Master. She saw his sorrow and confusion, and his core of stubborn strength.

"You're leaving early," she said.

"I think it's best," Nikos said.

She nodded. "And these?" she asked, tilting her chin toward the dead. "Are they going, too?"

"They'll be sent to the gods here," Nikos said, "tonight."

"Were you going to invite me?"

"Would you have wanted to be?"

"If I'm a rider," she said, "I should be here. If I'm not, then not."

"That is the question," he said. "Are you a rider?"

"I would like to think so," she said, "but the answer lies with you."

Sabata shook his head and stamped. Even through the deep lines of grief on his face, Master Nikos mustered a smile. "It doesn't, does it?" he said to the stallion. "You've done your best to make that clear."

"The school belongs to the riders," Valeria said. "If the riders can't tolerate me, I have no place there, no matter what the stallions may say."

While she spoke, she felt in her skin that others had come into the court of the dead. Sabata had called all the riders who were still alive, from rider-candidate to First Rider. They stood in a half circle behind her.

In Master Nikos' eyes she saw how it looked. Whether they knew it or not, they had taken the stance of guards protecting a royal charge.

She turned to face them. Even Paulus seemed to have resigned himself to the inevitable. Kerrec was almost smiling. She could feel the warmth in him beneath the stern mask of his face. Batu grinned openly.

Briana had stood quietly apart, but now she came into the circle. Sabata graciously allowed her to rest a hand on his neck. "It seems to me," she said, "that the decision has been made. The riders will learn to tolerate one of their own, even if she wears a somewhat different suit of flesh than the rest of them."

"But I don't want—" Valeria began.

Briana turned that sweetly implacable smile on her. "Do you think Sabata cares for that?"

Valeria shut her mouth with a snap. Sabata was laughing.

So were the rest of the stallions. They had not been there a moment before, but now they all were, standing erect and still. She had a doubled guard of gods and mages, who could be either jailers or protectors.

And there it was. She had what she had wanted so badly, just when she had decided she could live without it. That was always the way of things.

She looked from face to face around the half circle of riders, and saw none of the hostility that she had expected. Like the people on the portico, they saw what she had done rather than what she was, but these mages understood it. She was not a woman to them now, or an interloper, but the mage who had commanded all the stallions.

Master Nikos spoke with care, as if he had thought hard and long about what he would say and how he would say it. "We owe you thanks. But for you, all that we have made would be undone."

There were any number of things that Valeria could have said in reply. She thought about justice, and about modesty. She thought about what she had nearly done, and how close she had come to the Unmaking.

In the end she said, "I only did what I had to do."

"We were guilty of poor judgment," Nikos said. "By clinging to tradition and ignoring the gods' manifest will, we nearly lost everything."

"You've lost enough," she said, "and will be a long time recovering. I'll help with that as I can, if you want my help."

"It may not be a question of wanting," he said. "We need it. We need you—if you really are willing to come back to us. Our enemies offered you far more power than we can give you. You'll be back among the Called of this year, subject to the same teaching and the same tests as they. The fact that you can command all the stallions is a matter for legend, I suppose, but there is more to our magic than that."

"Much more," Valeria agreed. "I know there's much

I don't know. Are you willing to teach it? Is that what you want? Because if you only do this because you feel obligated, and not because you believe that I have a right to it, then I'll walk away."

"Indeed?" said Kerrec. "What would you walk to?"

Master Nikos shot him a quelling glance, but neither he nor Valeria paid attention. "I'll find a place," she said. "Somewhere where I'm welcome."

Briana stirred beside her but kept quiet. Kerrec's brows went up. "What makes you think you won't be welcome on the Mountain?"

"What makes you think I will be?"

"I will welcome you," Master Nikos said. "You are a rider. You were Called. There's no one alive now to deny it."

Valeria surprised herself with a surge of grief. The riders who had died had not been her friends at all. But they had been great mages and masters of the art. Their loss was a bitter blow. "The Mountain needs us all," she said.

As she said it, she knew that she had made a choice. She was a rider, too, as the Master had said. There never had been another alternative.

That feeling inside her, that sense of bubbling over, she realized was joy. There was plenty of grief to temper it, but just for a moment she let herself be happy.

The sun had set, but the sky was still full of light. In the court of the dead, the fallen riders had been lifted from the vats of natron and the vats taken away by the silent priesthood. Six bodies, shrouded in white linen, lay on biers of fragrant cedar.

There was no panoply of a noble funeral. There were no mourners paid to wail and tear their hair, no priests circling the biers with chants and incense. No crowds of family and friends filled the court. There were only the riders, the stallions and Briana, who had gone away early in the day but come back as the sun touched the horizon.

Valeria was glad to see her. She was a friend, as well as a rider's kin. She made no effort to put herself forward, but stayed on the edge of the courtyard, watching in silence.

Just as the rite was beginning, someone else joined her. The emperor had come also to bid farewell to the riders who had died for his Dance.

Valeria, in the stiff new uniform of a rider-candidate, was standing between Batu and Paulus. Her place was to keep quiet, manifest reverence and, when the time came, join her magic to the rest. Rather oddly, there was no sense of sorrow in the gathering. Grief remained and would linger long past this night, but the riders were beyond any earthly pain.

As the light began to fade from the sky, Master Nikos came forward into the circle. He was plainly dressed as always, but there was a shimmer of power on him. He raised his hands.

"Regan," he said. "Gallus. Mikel. Andres. Carinius. Petros."

As he spoke each name, a stallion paced toward one of the biers and stood motionless, head bowed over the shrouded dead. Deep silence surrounded them. No wind blew, no night bird cried. The living riders barely seemed to breathe.

This was a Dance—a Dance of stillness. The patterns that crowded everywhere had gone motionless. The tides of time were at the ebb.

And yet the Unmaking was nowhere near this place. Even the spell that still laired in Valeria was quiescent.

"Death is a rite of passage," Master Nikos said softly, so much a part of Valeria's reflections that at first she did not realize he had spoken, "the opening of one door and the closing of another. Our brothers have passed out of earth and into the realm of the gods. They are the blessed dead, who died in battle. Their names shall be remembered." And he spoke them again. "Regan. Gallus. Mikel. Andres. Carinius. Petros."

This time, at the sound of his rider's name, each stallion raised his head and trumpeted. The sound was deafening, multiplied in that space, echoing and re-echoing as voice joined voice in a long, shrilling peal.

In the moment that the blast of sound reached its peak, Valeria felt a drawing at the roots of her power. The stallions had seized it and made it a part of them. Then the fire came down.

Fire was divine, the priests said. This was the fire of the gods, and it seared the dead to ash, even as it restored and renewed the spark of life in the living.

All of it poured through Valeria. In a dim and distant way she knew that she needed to learn control. The power was using her. She should learn to use it.

Time would take care of that—if she had enough. If the war that was coming did not unmake them all.

Tonight she would be a rider among the riders. She would remember those who had died in the working of the Dance, and honor those who lived. In the morning they would ride, all of them together, the living bearing the ashes of the dead in urns that would be set in the houses of silence on the Mountain's knees.

The Mountain was calling. It was a deeper, softer call than the one that had brought her from her mother's house, but it was no less strong. This time there was no one to stop her. She would go where she belonged, where she had always belonged, even before she knew what or who she was.

Sabata had come up beside her, quiet as a cat, with Kerrec close behind. She laid her arm over the stallion's broad back and rested against his shoulder. Kerrec, on the other side, did the same. Their arms linked, with the stallion warm and solid between them.

There was a deep rightness in it, a profound contentment. Sabata sighed. A moment later, Valeria echoed him, then Kerrec. It had been a long battle and a hard one, with a longer and harder one ahead. But for the moment, they all could rest.

* * * * *

From Award-Winning Author

P.C. CAST

The most excitement teacher Shannon Parker expects on
her summer vacation is a little shopping. But when her
latest purchase—a vase with the Celtic goddess Epona on
it—somehow switches her into the world of Partholon, where
she's treated like a queen, let's just say…she's a little concerned.

DIVINE BY MISTAKE

LUNA™

On sale August 29.
Visit your
local bookseller.

www.LUNA-Books.com

LPC80247

Imagine not knowing if your next meal may be your last.

This is the fate of Yelenda, the food taster for a leader who is the target of every assassin in the land. As Yelenda struggles to save her own mortality, she learns she has undiscovered powers that may hold the fate of the world.

LUNA™

*Visit your
local bookseller.*

www.LUNA-Books.com

LMVS80257

LUNA™

On wings of fire she rises...

Born without caste or position in Arukan, a country that
prizes both, Kevla Bai-sha's life is about to change. Her
feverish dreams reveal looming threats to her homeland
and visions of the dragons that once watched over her
people—and held the promise of truth. Now, Kevla,
together with the rebel prince of the ruling household,
must sacrifice everything and defy all law and tradition,
to embark on a daring quest to save the world.

On sale July 25.
Visit your local bookseller.

www.LUNA-Books.com   LCG80255

Introducing…

nocturne™

a dark and sexy new paranormal romance line from Silhouette Books.

USA TODAY bestselling author

LINDSAY McKENNA
UNFORGIVEN

KATHLEEN KORBEL
DANGEROUS TEMPTATION

*Launching October 2006,
wherever books are sold.*

ROGUE Angel™

a priceless artifact sparks a quest to keep untold power from the wrong hands…

AleX Archer
SOLOMON'S JAR

Rumors of the discovery of Solomon's Jar—in which the biblical King Solomon bound the world's demons after using them to build his temple in Jerusalem—are followed with interest by Annja Creed. Her search leads her to a confrontation with a London cult driven by visions of new world order; and a religious zealot fueled by insatiable glory. Across the sands of the Middle East to the jungles of Brazil, Annja embarks on a relentless chase to stop humanity's most unfathomable secrets from reshaping the modern world.

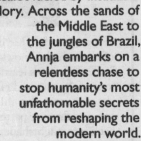

Available September 2006 wherever you buy books.

GOLD EAGLE®

GRA2TR

Something is stirring again...

Seven years ago Kaylin fled the crime-riddled streets
of Nightshade, knowing that something was after her.
Since then, she's learned to read, fight and has become
one of the vaunted Hawks who patrol and police the
City of Elantra. But children are once again dying, and a
dark and familiar pattern is emerging. Kaylin is ordered
back into Nightshade and tasked to find the killer and
stop the murders. But can she survive the attentions
of those who claim to be her allies along the way?

On sale now.

**Visit your
local bookseller.**

LUNA™

www.LUNA-Books.com   LMS80254

If you enjoyed what you just read,
then we've got an offer you can't resist!

Take 1 bestselling
love story FREE!
Plus get a FREE surprise gift!

Clip this page and mail it to the Reader Service®

IN U.S.A.
3010 Walden Ave.
P.O. Box 1867
Buffalo, N.Y. 14240-1867

IN CANADA
P.O. Box 609
Fort Erie, Ontario
L2A 5X3

YES! Please send me one free LUNA™ novel and my free surprise gift. After receiving it, if I don't wish to receive any more, I can return the shipping statement marked cancel. If I don't cancel, I will receive one brand-new novel every month, before they're available in stores! In the U.S.A., bill me at the bargain price of $10.99 plus 50¢ shipping & handling per book and applicable sales tax, if any*. In Canada, bill me at the bargain price of $12.99 plus 50¢ shipping & handling per book and applicable taxes**. That's the complete price and a savings of 10% off the cover prices—what a great deal! I understand that accepting the free book and gift places me under no obligation ever to buy any books. I can always return a shipment and cancel at any time. Even if I never buy another book from LUNA, the free book and gift are mine to keep forever.

175 HDN D34K
375 HDN D34L

Name	(PLEASE PRINT)	
Address	Apt.#	
City	State/Prov.	Zip/Postal Code

Not valid to current LUNA™ subscribers.

Want to try another series?
Call 1-800-873-8635 or visit www.morefreebooks.com.

* Terms and prices subject to change without notice. Sales tax applicable in N.Y.
** Canadian residents will be charged applicable provincial taxes and GST.
All orders subject to approval. Offer limited to one per household.
® and ™ are registered trademarks owned and used by the trademark owner and
or its licensee.

LUNA04   ©2004 Harlequin Enterprises Limited

MIRABooks.com

We've got the lowdown on
your favorite author!

☆ Read an excerpt of your favorite author's
newest book

☆ Check out her bio

☆ Talk to her in our Discussion Forums

☆ Read interviews, diaries, and more

☆ Find her current bestseller, and even her
backlist titles

All this and more available at

www.MiraBooks.com

MEAUT1R3